'I don't want a
woman to mar
child. We will t
divorce and my life will return to
normal again.'

'And what about the child?' Pixie asked with a frown of dismay towards Apollo. 'What will happen to the child in all this?'

'The child will remain with its mother and I will attempt to be an occasional father to the best of my ability. My goal is to negotiate a civilised and workable arrangement with the woman of my choice.'

'You do indeed have a problem,' she commented, with a certain amount of amusement at Apollo's predicament. 'But I really don't understand why you're confiding in *me* of all people!'

'Are you always this slow on the uptake?'

Her smooth brow indented as she sipped her wine and looked up at him enquiringly from below her spidery lashes. 'What do you mean?'

She had beautiful eyes, Apollo acknowledged in surprise, eyes of a luminous clear grey that shone like polished silver in certain lights.

'What do you think I'm doing here with you?' he prompted huskily.

Christmas with a Tycoon

Mediterranean billionaires under the mistletoe

Christmas might be a time for giving, but these billionaires are thinking only of what they can take!

Vito Zaffari might have a ruthless reputation, but when Holly crashes his festive hideaway she leaves with an unexpected Christmas gift…

Apollo Metraxis has made a career of bachelorhood, but the conditions of his father's will force him to choose a bride. Pixie might be the last wife he'd ever choose, but she's soon the only one he wants!

Don't miss either of these fabulous festive stories!

The Italian's Christmas Child
November 2016

The Greek's Christmas Bride
December 2016

Available now!

THE GREEK'S CHRISTMAS BRIDE

BY

LYNNE GRAHAM

MILLS & BOON®

First Published in Great Britain 2016
By Mills & Boon, an imprint of HarperCollins*Publishers*
1 London Bridge Street, London, SE1 9GF

ISBN: 978-0-263-92140-3

Our policy is to use papers that are natural, renewable and recyclable products and made from wood grown in sustainable forests. The logging and manufacturing processes conform to the legal environmental regulations of the country of origin.

Printed and bound in Spain
by CPI, Barcelona

Lynne Graham was born in Northern Ireland and has been a keen romance reader since her teens. She is very happily married to an understanding husband who has learned to cook since she started to write! Her five children keep her on her toes. She has a very large dog who knocks everything over, a very small terrier who barks a lot, and two cats. When time allows, Lynne is a keen gardener.

Books by Lynne Graham

Mills & Boon Modern Romance

Bought for the Greek's Revenge
The Sicilian's Stolen Son
Leonetti's Housekeeper Bride
The Secret His Mistress Carried
The Dimitrakos Proposition
A Ring to Secure His Heir
Unlocking Her Innocence

Christmas with a Tycoon

The Italian's Christmas Child

The Notorious Greeks

The Greek Demands His Heir
The Greek Commands His Mistress

Bound by Gold

The Sheikh's Secret Babies
The Billionaire's Bridal Bargain

The Legacies of Powerful Men

Ravelli's Defiant Bride
Christakis's Rebellious Wife
Zarif's Convenient Queen

Visit the Author Profile page at millsandboon.co.uk for more titles.

I do enjoy an alpha male,
but none of them is a match for my husband.
This one is for you.

PROLOGUE

THE MALE VOICES drifted in from the balcony while Holly hovered, waiting uneasily for the right moment to join the conversation. That was a challenge when she knew she was never particularly welcome in Apollo's radius.

But there wasn't much she could do about that when she was married to Vito, Apollo's best friend. Only recently had she come to appreciate just how close the two men were and how often they talked no matter where they were in the world. Friends from a childhood spent at boarding school, they were as close as brothers and Apollo had distrusted Holly from the outset because she was a poor woman marrying a very rich man. Aware of that fact, she had offered to stay home instead of attending the funeral of Apollo's father but Vito had been shocked at that suggestion.

So far, their visit to the privately owned island of Nexos and the Metraxis compound had been anything but pleasant. The funeral had been massive. Every one of Apollo's former stepmothers and their children had attended. Earlier today the reading of the will had taken place and Apollo had stormed out in a passion, having learned that he needed a wife to inherit the vast empire he had been running for several years on his ailing father's behalf. Vito had shared only that bare detail with his wife, clearly uncomfortable at divulging even that much. But as virtually anybody who knew Apollo also knew of his aversion to matrimony, it was obvious that his father's last will and testament had put him between a rock and a hard place.

'So, you pick one of your women and marry her,' Vito breathed, sounding not at all like the loving husband Holly knew and adored. '*Dio mio*, there's a long enough list. You marry her, stay married as long as you can bear it, and—'

'And how am I going to get rid of her again?' Apollo growled. 'Women cling to me like superglue. How am I going to trust her to keep her mouth shut? If word escapes that it's a fake marriage, the stepfamilies will go to court and try and take my inheritance off me. If you tell a woman you don't want her, she's insulted and she wants revenge.'

'That's why you need to *hire* a wife as if you're interviewing one for a job. You need a woman with no personal axe to grind. Considering your popularity with the opposite sex and your bad reputation, finding her could be a challenge.'

Reckoning that it was now or never, Holly stepped out onto the terrace. 'Hiring a wife sounds like the best idea,' she opined nervously.

Even sheathed in an elegant dark suit, Apollo Metraxis looked every inch the bad boy he was. With shoulder-length black hair, startling green eyes and an elaborate dragon tattoo peeping out of a white shirt cuff, Apollo was volatile, unconventional and arrogant, the direct opposite of Holly's conservative husband.

'I don't believe you were invited to join this conversation,' Apollo countered very drily.

'Three heads are better than two,' Holly parried, forcing herself down stiffly into a seat.

Apollo elevated a sardonic brow. 'You think so?'

Holly refused to be excluded. 'Stop dramatising yourself—'

'Holly!' Vito interrupted sharply.

'Well, Apollo can't help himself. He's always doing it,' Holly argued. 'Not every woman is going to cling to you like superglue!'

'Name me one who won't,' Apollo invited.

Holly blinked and thought very hard because Apollo was universally acknowledged to be a gorgeous, super-wealthy stud and nine out of ten women followed him round a room with hungry eyes. 'Well, my friend Pixie for a start,' she pronounced with satisfaction. 'She can't stand you and if she can't, there's got to be others.'

A very faint flush accentuated Apollo's supermodel cheekbones.

'Pixie wouldn't quite meet the parameters of what is required,' Vito interposed hastily, meeting his friend's appalled gaze in a look of mutual understanding because he had not told his wife the exact terms of the will. Ignorant as Holly was of those terms, she could not know how impossible her suggestion was.

Apollo was outraged by the reference to Holly's friend, Pixie, who was a hairdresser and poor as a peasant. Apollo already knew everything there was to know about Holly and Pixie because he had had the two women thoroughly investigated as soon as Holly appeared out of nowhere to announce that she had given birth to Vito's son, Angelo. Apollo had been appalled by Pixie's grubby criminal background and the debts her unsavoury brother had accrued and which she for some strange reason had chosen to take on as her own. Those debts had resulted in her brother's punishment beating and her attempt to interfere with that had put Pixie in a wheelchair with two broken legs.

Was it any wonder that when her friend had such a bad background he had instinctively distrusted Holly and marvelled at his friend's eagerness to marry the mother of his child? Indeed Apollo had been waiting on the sidelines ever since for Pixie to try and take advantage of her friendship with Holly by approaching her friend for financial help. To date, however, she had not done so and Apollo had been relieved for he had no desire to interfere again, knowing how much that would be resented. And thanks to his ungenerous attitude at their wedding, Holly already resented Apollo quite enough.

Pixie Robinson, Apollo thought again in wonderment as Vito and Holly retreated indoors to change for dinner. He was unlikely to forget the tiny doll-like blonde in the wheelchair at Vito's wedding. She had given Apollo nothing but dirty looks throughout the day and had really irritated him. Holly was insane. Of course she was biased, Pixie being her best friend and all that, but even so, could she really imagine Apollo marrying Pixie and them producing an heir together? Apollo almost shuddered before he reminded himself that Holly didn't know about that most outrageous demand in his father's will.

He had seriously underestimated the older man, Apollo conceded angrily. Vassilis Metraxis had always had a bee in his bonnet about the continuation of the family name, hence his six marriages and unsuccessful attempts to have another child. At thirty, Apollo was an only child. His father had urged his son to marry many times and Apollo had been blunt and honest about his resolve to remain single and childless. In spite of the depredations of the manipulative, grasping stepmothers and the greedy stepchildren that had come with those marriages, Apollo had always enjoyed a relatively close and loving relationship with his father. For that reason, the terms of Vassilis's will had come as a very nasty shock.

According to the will, Apollo was to continue running his father's empire and enjoying his possessions but that state of affairs was guaranteed to continue only for the next five years. Within that period Apollo had to legally marry and produce a child if he wanted to retain his inheritance. If he failed on either count, the Metraxis wealth would be shared out amongst his father's ex-wives and former stepchildren even though they had all been richly rewarded while his father was still alive.

Apollo could not credit that his father had been so foolish as to try and blackmail his son from beyond the grave. And yet wasn't it proving most effective? Rigid with tension as he made that sudden leap in understanding, Apollo stood on the terrace looking out to sea and watching the stormy waves batter the cliffs. His grandfather had bought the island of Nexos and built the villa for family use. Every Metraxis since then had been buried in the little graveyard down by the village church, including Apollo's mother, who had died in childbirth.

The island was Apollo's home, the only real home he had ever known, and he was disconcerted to realise that he literally could not *bear* the idea of his home being sold off, which would mean that he could never visit it or his memories again. He was discovering way too late to change anything that he was far more attached to the family name and the family property than he had ever dreamt. He had fought the prospect of marriage, habitually mocking the institution and rubbishing his father's unsuccessful attempts to recreate a normal family circle. He had sworn that he would never father a child, for as a child Apollo had suffered a great deal and he had genuinely believed that it would be wrong to subject any child to what he had endured. Yet from beyond the grave his father had contrived to call his bluff…

For when it came down to it, Apollo could not contemplate losing the world he took for granted even though he knew that fighting to retain it would be a hellish struggle. A struggle against his own volatile inclinations and his innate love of freedom, a struggle against being *forced* to live with a woman, *forced* to have sex with her, *forced* to have a child he didn't want.

And how best could he achieve that? Unfortunately, Vito was right: Apollo needed to hire a woman, one who was willing to marry him solely for money. But how could he trust such a woman not to go to the media to spill all or to confide his secrets in the wrong person? He would need a *hold* on the woman he married, some sort of a hold that meant she needed him as much as he needed her and would have good reason to follow any rules he laid down.

Although he would never consider her as a possibility, he *needed* a woman like Pixie Robinson. In her case he could have bought up her brother's debt and used it to put pressure on her, thereby ensuring that it was in her best interests to keep her mouth shut and give him exactly what he needed to retain his family empire. How was he supposed to find another woman in that kind of situation?

Of course, had he trusted women generally, he might have been less cautious. But Apollo, his cynical distrust honed over no fewer than six stepmothers and countless lovers, had never trusted a woman in his life. In fact trust was a real issue for him.

His first stepmother had sent him off to boarding school at the age of four. His second stepmother had beaten him bloody. His third had seduced him. His fourth stepmother had had his beloved dog put down. His fifth stepmother had tried to foist another man's child on his father.

Add in the innumerable women whom Apollo had bedded over the years. Beautiful, sexually adventurous women and gold-diggers, who had endeavoured to enrich themselves as much as possible during their brief affairs with him. He had never known any other kind of woman, couldn't quite believe that any other type existed. Holly was different though, he acknowledged grudgingly. He could see that she adored Vito and their child. So, there was another category out there: women who *loved*. Not that he would be looking for one of those. Love would trap him, inhibit him and suffocate him with the dos and don'ts he despised. He suppressed a shudder. Life was too short to make such a mistake.

But in the short term he still needed a wife. A wife he could *control* was the only sort of wife he would be able to tolerate. He thought about Pixie again. Pixie and her weak, feckless brother's financial problems. She had to be pretty stupid, he reflected helplessly, to mess up her life by taking on her sibling's problems. Why would you do that? Never having had a brother or a sister, Apollo was mystified by the concept of such thankless sacrifice. But just how far would Pixie Robinson go to save her brother's skin?

It amused Apollo to know so much more than Holly did about her best friend's problems. It amused him even more that Holly had cheerfully assured him that Pixie couldn't stand him. Holly had to be blind. Obviously Holly hadn't noticed that, in spite of the dirty looks, Pixie had covertly watched Apollo's every move at her friend's wedding.

The beginnings of a smile softened the hard line of

Apollo's wide sensual mouth. Maybe he should take a closer look at the miniature blonde and work out whether or not she could be of use to him…what did he have to lose?

CHAPTER ONE

'MORNING, HECTOR,' PIXIE mumbled as she woke up with a tousled bundle of terrier plastered to her ribs.

Smothering a yawn, she steeled herself to get up and out. She got out of bed to head to the bathroom she shared with the other tenants on the same floor before returning washed and dressed to snap a leash on Hector's faded red collar and take her pet out for his morning walk.

Hector trotted along the road, little round eyes reflecting anxiety. He flinched when he noticed another dog across the street. Hector was scared of just about everything life threw at him. People, other animals, traffic and loud noises all made the whites of his eyes gleam with an edge of panic. Calm and untroubled the rest of the time, he was very quiet and had never been known to bark.

'Probably learned not to as a puppy,' the vet next door to the hair salon had opined when Pixie had asked. 'He's scared of attracting attention to himself in any way. Abuse does that to an animal. But in spite of his injuries he's young and healthy and should have a long life ahead of him.'

Pixie still marvelled at the fact that regardless of her own problems she had chosen to adopt Hector. But then, Pixie had triumphed over adversity many times in life and so had the little terrier. Hector had repaid her generosity a thousand times over. He comforted her and warmed her heart with his shy little ways and eccentricities. He had filled some of the giant hole that had opened up in Pixie's world when Holly and Angelo had moved to Italy.

She had lost her best friend to marriage and motherhood but their friendship had been more damaged by the secrets Pixie had been forced to keep. There was no way she could tell Holly about her brother Patrick's gambling debts without Holly offering to settle those debts for them. Holly was very generous but Patrick was not Holly or Vito's responsibility, he was Pixie's and had been since the day of their mother's death.

'Promise me you'll look after your little brother,' Margery Robinson had pleaded. 'Always do your best for Patrick, Pixie. He's a gentle soul and he's the only family you have left.'

But looking after Patrick had been near impossible when the siblings had invariably ended up living in different foster homes. During the important teenaged years, Pixie had only met up with her brother a handful of times and until she'd finished training and achieved independence her bond with her kid brother had been limited by time, distance and a shortage of money. Once she was working she had tried to change all that by regularly visiting Patrick in London.

Initially Patrick had done well. He was an electrician working for a big construction firm. He had found a girlfriend and settled down. But he had also got involved in high-stake card games and had lost a lot of money to a very dangerous man. Pixie had duly cut down her own expenses, moving out of the comfortable terraced house she had once shared with Holly into a much cheaper bedsit. Every week she sent as much money as she could afford to Patrick to help him pay off his debts but as interest was added that debt just seemed to be getting bigger and if he missed a payment he would be beaten up… or worse. Pixie genuinely feared that her brother's debts would get him killed.

Pixie still came out in a cold sweat remembering the night the debt collectors had arrived when she had been visiting her brother. Two big brutish men had come to the door of Patrick's flat to demand money. Threatening to kill him, they had beaten him up when he was unable to pay his dues. Attempting to intervene in the ensuing struggle, Pixie had fallen down the stairs and broken both her legs. The consequences of that accident had been horrendous because Pixie had been unable to work and had been forced to claim benefits during her recovery. Now, six months on, she was just beginning to get back to normal but unhappily there seemed to be no light gleaming at the end of the tunnel because Patrick's debt situation seemed insurmountable and his life was still definitely at risk. The man he owed wasn't the type to wait indefinitely for settlement. He would want his pound of flesh or he would want to make an example of her brother to intimidate his other debtors.

Settling Hector into his basket, Pixie set off down the street to the hair salon. She missed her car but selling Clementine had been her first sacrifice because she had no real need for personal transport in the small Devon town where she could walk most places. She would return home to take Hector out for a walk during her lunch break and grab a sandwich at the same time.

Entering the salon, she exchanged greetings with her co-workers and her boss, Sally. After hurriedly stowing her bag in her staff locker she caught a glimpse of herself in a mirror and winced. It had been a while since she had looked her best. When had she got so boring? She was only twenty-three years old. Unfortunately cutting costs had entailed wearing her clothes for longer and her jeans and black top had seen better days. She had good skin and didn't wear much make-up but she always wore loads of grey eyeliner because black liner was too stark against the blonde hair that fell simply to just below her shoulders. She had left behind her more adventurous days of playing with different styles and colours because she had soon come to appreciate that most of her clients had conservative tastes and were nervous of a hairdresser who had done anything eye-catching to her own hair.

She cleaned up after her third client had departed. She regretted the reality that yet another junior had walked out, leaving the stylists to deal with answering the phone, washing hair and sweeping up. She checked the appointment book for her next booking and, unusually, she didn't recognise the name. It was a guy though and she was surprised he hadn't asked for the only male stylist in the salon. And then, without the smallest warning, Apollo Metraxis walked in and as every female jaw literally dropped in wonderment and silence spread like the plague he strode up to Pixie and announced, 'I'm your twelve o'clock appointment.'

Pixie gaped at him, not quite sure it could actually be him in the flesh. 'What the heck are you doing here? Has something happened to Holly or Vito?' she demanded apprehensively.

'I need a trim,' Apollo announced levelly, perfectly comfortable with the fact that he was the cynosure of every eye in the place. Clad in a black biker jacket, tight jeans and boots, he seemed impossibly tall as he towered over her, bright green eyes strikingly noticeable in his lean bronzed face.

'Holly? Vito? Angelo?' Pixie pressed with staccato effect, her attention glued to his broad chest and the tee shirt plastered to his six-pack abs.

'As far as I know they're all well,' Apollo retorted impatiently.

But that still didn't explain what a Greek billionaire was doing walking into a high-street hair salon in a small country town where as far as she was aware he knew nobody. And she couldn't be counted because he had never spoken to her, never even so much as glanced at her on the day of Holly's wedding. The memory rankled because she was only human, whether she liked it or not. After trying to ruin Holly's wedding for her by making an embarrassing speech in his role of best man, he had royally ignored Pixie as if she was beneath his lofty notice.

'I'm afraid I have another appointment.'

'That's me. *John Smith?* Didn't you smell a rat?' he mocked.

In actuality the only thing Pixie could smell that close to Apollo was Apollo and the alluring scent of some no doubt very expensive citrusy designer cologne.

'Let me take your jacket,' she said jerkily, struggling to regain her composure and behave normally.

He shrugged it off, more powerful muscles bunching and flexing with his every movement. He exposed the bare arm with the intricate dragon tattoo that had made her stare at her friend's wedding. Then she hurriedly turned away and hung the heavy leather jacket on the coat stand beside the reception desk.

'Come over to the sinks,' Pixie urged, alarmingly short of breath at the prospect of laying actual hands on him.

Apollo stared down at her. She was even smaller than he had expected, barely reaching his chest and very delicate in build. He had seen boards with more curves. But she had amazing eyes, a light grey that glittered like stolen starlight in her expressive face. She had an undistinguished button nose and a full rosebud mouth while her flawless skin had the translucent glow of the finest porcelain. She was much more natural than the women he was accustomed to. Definitely no breast enhancements, no fake tan and even her mouth appeared to be all her own.

As he sat down Pixie whisked a cape round him and then a towel, determined not to be intimidated by him. 'So, what on earth are you doing here?'

'You'll never guess,' Apollo intoned, tilting his head back for her.

Pixie ran the water while noting that he had the most magnificent head of hair. Layers and layers of luxuriant blue-black glossy strands. His mocking response tightened her mouth and frustration gripped her. 'When did you last see our mutual friends?' she asked instead.

'At my father's funeral last week,' Apollo advanced.

Pixie stiffened. 'I'm sorry for your loss,' she said immediately.

'Why should you be sorry?' Apollo asked with unsettling derision. 'You didn't know him and you don't know me.'

Her teeth gritted at that scornful dismissal as she shampooed his hair. 'It's just what people say to show sympathy.'

'*Are* you sympathetic?'

Pixie was tempted to drench him with the shower head she was using. Her teeth ground together even tighter. 'I'm sympathetic to anyone who's lost a family member.'

'He was dying for a long time,' Apollo admitted flatly. 'It wasn't unexpected.'

His outrageously long fringe of black lashes flicked down over his striking eyes and she got on with her job on automatic pilot while her mind seethed with questions. What did he want with her? Was it foolish of her to think that his descent on the place where she worked had to relate to her personally? Yet how could it relate to her? Outside her ties to Holly and Vito, there was no possible connection.

'Tell me about you,' Apollo invited, disconcerting her.

'Why would I?'

'Because I asked…because it's polite?' he prompted, his posh British upper-class accent smooth as glass.

'Let's talk about you instead,' she suggested. 'What are you doing in England?'

'A little business, a little socialising. Visiting friends,' he responded carelessly.

She applied conditioner and embarked on a head massage with tautly nervous fingers. A second after she began she realised she had not asked him if he wanted one but she kept going all the same, desperate to take charge of the encounter and keep busy.

Apollo relaxed while lazily wondering if she did any other kind of massage. The file hadn't shed much light on her sex life or her habits but then two broken legs had kept her close to home for months. As her slender fingers moved rhythmically across his skull he pictured her administering to him buck naked and the sudden tightening at his groin warned him to give it a rest.

Irritated by the effect she was having on his highly tense body, Apollo thought about how much he needed sex to wind down. His last liaison had ended before his father's funeral and he had not been with anyone since then. Unlike Vito, Apollo never went without sex. A couple of weeks was a very long time for him. Had he found Pixie unattractive, he would've backed off straight away; however that wasn't the case. But—*Diavole!*—she was teeny, tiny as a doll and he was a big guy in every way. She rinsed his hair and towelled him dry while he thought about her hands on his body and that ripe bee-stung mouth taking him to climax. It was a relief to move and settle down in another chair.

'What do you want done?' she asked him after she had combed his hair.

He almost told her because he was all revved up and ready to go and he had never before reacted to a woman with such unsophisticated schoolboyish enthusiasm. 'A trim…but leave it long,' he warned her while he wondered what the secret of her attraction was.

Novelty value? He was tall and he generally went for tall, curvy blondes. But possibly he had got bored with a steady diet of women so similar they had become almost interchangeable. Vito had raved about how down-to-earth and unspoilt Holly was but Apollo was a great deal less high flown in his expectations. If Pixie pleased him in bed, he would count her a prize. If she got pregnant quickly he would treat her like a princess. If she gave him a child, she would live like a lottery winner. Apollo believed in only rewarding results.

Of course, she might turn him down. A woman had never turned him down before but he knew there had to be a first time and it was not as though he were in the habit of asking women to have a child with him. And if he spilled all to Pixie then he would be vulnerable because she might choose to share his secrets with the media for a handsome price and that would scupper his plans. So, however she reacted, he would be stuck having to pay her to keep quiet and that reality and the risk involved annoyed him.

Momentarily, Pixie stepped away to right the swaying coat stand, knocked off balance by an elderly woman. In the mirror, Apollo watched as Pixie bent down to pick up and hang the coats that had fallen and he was riveted by a glimpse of her curvy little rump before she straightened and returned to his side.

Her scissors went snip-snip. She was confident with what she did and every so often her fingers would smooth through his hair in a gesture almost like a caress. He glanced at her from below his lashes, wondering if it was a come-on, but her heart-shaped face was intent on her task, her eyes veiled, her mouth a tense line. It didn't stop Apollo imagining those touchy-feely hands roaming freely over him. In fact the more he thought about that, the hotter he got.

When she wielded the drier over him, Apollo tried to take it off her. He usually dried his own hair and then damped it down again to make it presentable but Pixie swore she would do nothing fancy and withheld the drier, determined to personally tame his messy mane.

Until she had had the experience of cutting Apollo's hair it had never crossed Pixie's mind that her job could be an unsettlingly intimate one. But touching Apollo's surprisingly silky hair disturbed her, making her aware of him on a level she was very uncomfortable with. He smelled so damned good she wanted to sniff him in like an intoxicating draught of sunshine. Wide shoulders flexed as he settled back in the chair and she sucked in a slow steadying breath. She had never been so on edge with a customer in her life. Her nipples were tight inside her bra and she felt embarrassingly damp between her thighs.

No, she absolutely was *not* attracted to Apollo. It was simply that he made her very nervous. The guy was a literal celebrity, an international playboy adored by the media for his jet-set womanising lifestyle. Any normal woman would feel overwhelmed by his sudden appearance. It was like having a lion walk into the room, she reflected wildly. You couldn't stop staring, you couldn't do less than admire his animal beauty and magnificence but not far underneath lurked a ferocious fear of what he might do next.

Apollo sprang upright and Pixie hastened to retrieve his jacket and hand it to him. He stilled at the reception desk and dug inside it while she waited for him to pay. He frowned, black brows pleating, and stared at her. 'My wallet's gone,' he told her.

'Oh, dear…' Pixie muttered blankly.

His green eyes narrowed to shards of emerald cutting glass ready to draw blood. 'Did you take it?'

'Did I take your wallet?' In the wake of that echo of an answer, Pixie's mouth dropped open in shock because her brain was telling her that he could not possibly have accused her of stealing from him.

'You're the only person who touched my jacket,' Apollo condemned loud enough to turn heads nearby. 'Give it back and I'll take no action.'

'You've got to be out of your mind to think that I would *steal* from you!' Pixie exclaimed, stricken, as her boss, Sally, came rushing across the salon.

'I want the police called,' he informed the older woman grimly.

The dizziness of shock engulfed Pixie and she turned pale as death. She couldn't credit that Apollo was accusing her of theft in public. In fact her first thought was insane because she found herself wondering if he had come to the salon deliberately to set her up for such an accusation. All he had to do would be to leave his wallet behind and then accuse her of stealing from him. And who would believe her word against the word of someone of his wealth and importance?

Her stomach heaved and with a muffled groan she fled to the cloakroom to lose her breakfast. Apollo was subjecting her to her worst possible nightmare. Pixie had always had a pronounced horror of theft and dishonesty. Her father had been a serial burglar, in and out of prison all his life. Her mother had been a professional shoplifter, who stole to order. If Pixie had stumbled across a purse lying on the ground she would have walked past it, too terrified to pick it up and hand it in in case someone accused her of trying to steal it. It was a hangover from her shame-filled childhood and she had never yet contrived to overcome her greatest fear.

CHAPTER TWO

THE POLICEMAN WHO arrived was familiar—a middle-aged man who patrolled the streets of the small town. Pixie had seen him around but had never spoken to him because she gave the police a wide berth. Acquainted with most of the local traders, however, he was on comfortable terms with her boss, Sally.

By the time Apollo had been asked to give his name and details he was beginning to wonder if it had been a mistake to call in officialdom. He didn't want to be identified. He didn't want to risk the media getting involved. And if she *had* taken his wallet wasn't it really only the sort of behaviour he had expected from Pixie Robinson? She was desperate for money and he was well aware of the fact that his wallet would offer a bigger haul than most. The constable viewed him in astonishment when he admitted how much cash he had been carrying.

Pixie gave her name and address in a voice that trembled in spite of her attempt to keep it level. Sick with nerves, she shifted from one foot onto the other and then back again, unable to stay still, unable to meet anyone's eyes lest they recognise the panic consuming her. Perspiration beaded her short upper lip as the police officer asked her what had happened from the moment of Apollo's arrival. While she spoke she couldn't help noticing Apollo lounging back in an attitude of extravagant relaxation against the edge of the desk and occasionally glancing at his gold watch as though he had somewhere more important to be.

She had never been violent but Apollo filled her with vicious and aggressive reactions. How could he be so hateful and Vito still be friends with him? She had known Apollo wasn't a nice person on the day of Holly's wedding when his speech had made it obvious that Holly and Vito's son had been conceived from a one-night stand. Since then she had read more about him online. He was a womaniser who essentially didn't like women. She had recognised that reality straight off. His affairs never lasted longer than a couple of weeks. He got bored very quickly, never committed, indeed never got involved beyond the most superficial level.

'Don't forget to mention that you went back to the coat stand when the old lady knocked some of the coats to the floor,' Apollo reminded her in a languorous drawl.

'And you're suggesting that that's when I took your wallet?' Pixie snapped, studying him with eyes bright silver with loathing.

'Could it have fallen out of the jacket?' the police officer asked hopefully, tugging a couple of chairs out from the wall to glance behind them. 'Have you looked under the desk?'

'Not very likely,' Apollo traded levelly. 'Is no one going to search this woman? Her bag even?'

'Let's not jump to conclusions, Mr Metraxis,' the policeman countered quellingly as he lifted the rubbish bin.

Apollo raised an unimpressed brow. He was so judgemental and so confident that he was right, Pixie thought in consternation. He was absolutely convinced that she had stolen his wallet and it would take an earthquake to shift him. Her stomach lurched again and she crossed her arms defensively, the sick dizziness of fear assailing her once more. She didn't have his wallet but mud would stick. By tea time everyone local would know that the blonde stylist at Sally's had been accused of theft. At the very least she could lose her job. She wasn't so senior or talented that Sally would risk losing clients to her nearest competitor.

The policeman lifted the newspaper lying in the bin and, with an exclamation, he reached beneath it and lifted out a brown hide wallet. 'Is this it?'

Visibly surprised, Apollo extended his hand. 'Yes...'

'When the coat stand tipped, your wallet must've fallen out into the bin,' Sally suggested with a bright smile of relief at that sensible explanation.

'Or Pixie *hid* it in the bin to retrieve at a more convenient time,' Apollo murmured.

'This situation need not have arisen had a proper search been conducted before I was called in,' the policeman remarked. 'You were very quick to make an accusation, Mr Metraxis.'

Impervious to the hint of censure, Apollo angled his arrogant dark head back. 'I'm still not convinced my wallet ended up in the bin by accident,' he admitted. 'Pixie has a criminal background.'

Pixie froze in shocked mortification. How did Apollo Metraxis know that about her? That was private, that was her past and she had left it behind her a long time ago. 'But *not* a criminal record!' she flung back curtly, watching Apollo settle a bank note down on the desk and Sally hastily passing him his change.

'We shouldn't be discussing such things in public,' the policeman said drily and took his leave.

'Take the rest of the day off, Pixie,' Sally urged uncomfortably. 'I'm sorry I was so quick to call the police… but—'

'It's OK,' Pixie said chokily, well aware that her employer's business mantra was that the customer was always right and such an accusation had required immediate serious attention.

It was over. A faint shudder racked Pixie's slender frame. The nightmare was truly *over.* Apollo had his wallet back even though he still couldn't quite bring himself to accept that she hadn't stolen it and hidden it in the rubbish bin. But it *was* over and the policeman had departed satisfied. The fierce tension that had held Pixie still left her in a sudden rush and she could feel herself crumpling like rice paper inside and out as a belated surge of tears washed the backs of her eyelids.

'Excuse me,' she mumbled and fled to the back room to pull herself together and collect her bag.

She sniffed and wiped her eyes, knowing she was messing up her eyeliner and not even caring. She wanted to go home and hug Hector. Pulling on her jacket, she walked back through the salon, trying not to be self-conscious about the fact that the customers who had witnessed the little drama were all staring at her. A couple who knew her called out encouraging things but Pixie's entire attention was welded to the very tall male she could see waiting outside on the pavement. Why was Apollo still hanging around?

Of course, he wanted to apologise, she assumed. Why else would he be waiting? She stalked out of the door.

'Pixie?'

'You bastard!' she hissed at him in a raw undertone. 'Leave me alone!'

'I came here to speak to you—'

'Well, you've spoken to me and now you can…' Pixie swore at him, colliding with his scorching green eyes and almost reeling back from the anger she saw there.

'Get in the car. I'll take you home,' he said curtly.

Pixie swore at him again and, with a spluttering Greek curse and before she could even guess his intention, Apollo stooped and snatched her off her feet to carry her across the street.

Pixie thumped him so hard with her clenched fist, she hurt her knuckles.

'You're a violent little thing, aren't you?' Apollo framed rawly as he stuffed her in the back seat of the waiting limo.

'Let me out of this car!' Pixie gasped, flinging herself at the door on the opposite side as he slid in beside her.

'I'm taking you home,' Apollo countered, rubbing his cheekbone where it was turning slightly pink from her punch.

'I hope you get a black eye!' Pixie spat. 'Stop the car… let me out! This is kidnapping!'

'Do you really want to walk down the street with your make-up smeared all over your face?'

'Yes, if the alternative is getting a lift from you!'

But the limousine was already turning a corner to draw up outside the shabby building where she lived, so the argument was academic. As the doors unlocked, Pixie leapt out onto the pavement.

She might be petite in appearance but she was wiry and strong, Apollo acknowledged, and, not only did she know how to land a good punch, she also moved like greased lightning. He climbed out of the car at a more relaxed pace.

Breathing rapidly, Pixie paused in the hall with the door she had unlocked ajar. 'How did you know that about my background?'

'I'll tell you if you invite me in.'

'Why would I invite you in? I don't like you.'

'You know I can only be here to see you and you have to be curious,' Apollo responded with confidence.

'I can live with being curious,' Pixie told him, stepping into her room and starting to snap the door shut.

'But evidently you don't think you can live without your foolish little brother…do you?' Apollo drawled and the door stopped an inch off closing and slowing opened up again.

'What do you know about Patrick?' Pixie asked angrily.

Apollo strode in. 'I know everything there is to know about you, your brother, your background and your friend Holly. I had you both privately investigated when Holly first appeared out of nowhere with baby Angelo.'

Pixie studied him in shock and backed away several feet, which took her to the side of her bed. Even with the bed pushed up against one wall it was a small room. She had sold off much of the surplus stuff she had gathered up over the years before moving in. 'Why would you have us both investigated?' she exclaimed.

'I'm more cautious than Vito. I wanted to know who he was dealing with so that if necessary I could advise and protect him,' Apollo retorted with a slight shrug of a broad shoulder as he peered into a dark corner where something pale with glimmering eyes was trying to shrink into the wall.

'Just ignore Hector. Visitors, particularly male ones, freak him out,' Pixie told him thinly. 'I should think that Vito is old enough to protect himself.'

'Vito doesn't know much about the dark side of life.'

It was no surprise that Apollo considered himself superior in that regard, Pixie conceded. From childhood, scandal had illuminated Apollo's life to the outside world: his family's wealth, his father's many marriages to beautiful women half his age, the break-ups, the divorces and the court battles that had followed. Apollo's whole life had been lived in a histrionic headline-grabbing storm of publicity.

And there he stood in her little room, the perfect figurehead for a Greek billionaire, a living legend of a playboy with a yacht known to attract an exceptional number of gorgeous half-naked women. It seemed unfair that a male with such wealth and possessed of such undoubted intelligence should also have been blessed with such intense good looks. Apollo, like his namesake the sun god, was breathtakingly handsome. And he had undeniably taken Pixie's breath away the first time she'd seen him at Holly's wedding.

Apollo might be a toxic personality but when he was around he would always be the centre of attention. He had sleek dark brows, glorious green eyes, a classic nose and a stubborn, wilful mouth that could only be described as sensual. His sex appeal was electrifying and it was a sex appeal that Pixie would very much have liked to be impervious to. Sadly, however, she was a normal living, breathing woman with the usual healthy dose of hormones. And that was all it was…the breathlessness, the crazy race of her heartbeat, the tight fullness of her breasts and that strange squirmy, sensitive feeling low in her pelvis. It was all hormonal and as reflexive and trivial in Apollo's radius as her liking for chocolate, not something she needed to beat herself up about.

A faint little pleading whine emanated from the shadows and recalled Pixie to rationality. As she realised she had been standing dumbly gaping at Apollo while she thought about him an angry flush crept up her face. In a sudden move, she reached for Hector's leash. 'Look, I don't know what you're doing here but right now I have to take my dog out for a walk.'

Apollo watched her drag…literally *drag*…a tattered-looking and clearly terrified little dog out of the corner to clip it onto a leash and lift it into her arms, where she rubbed her chin over the crown of its head and muttered soothingly to it as if it were a baby.

'I have to talk to you. I'll come with you.'

'I don't want you with me and if you have to talk to me about anything I have to say that accusing me of theft and utterly humiliating me where I work wasn't a good opening.'

'I know how desperate you must be for money. That's why I assumed—'

Pixie spun angrily, her little pearly teeth gripped tightly together. 'That's why it doesn't pay to *assume* anything about someone you don't know!'

'Are you always this argumentative? This ready to take offence?'

'Only around you,' Pixie told him truthfully. 'Look, you can wait here while I'm out. I'll be about fifteen minutes,' she said briskly and walked out of the door.

Two steps along the pavement she couldn't quite believe she had had the nerve. After all, the way he talked he knew about Patrick's gambling debts and the threat against his continuing health. She broke out in a cold sweat just thinking about that reality because she really did love her little brother. Patrick didn't have a bad bone in his body. He had made a mistake. He had tried too hard to be one of the boys when he took up playing cards and instead of stopping the habit when he lost money he had gone on gambling in the foolish belief that he could not continue on a losing streak for ever. By the time he had realised his mistake, he had built up a huge debt. But Patrick was working very hard to try and stay on top of that debt. He was an electrician during the day and a bartender at night.

Apollo had dangled a carrot and that she could have walked away even temporarily from the vaguest possibility of help for Patrick shook Pixie. But *was* Apollo offering to help them? No, that was highly unlikely. Why would he help them? He wasn't the benevolent, sympathetic type. Yet why had he come to the salon in the first place and sought her out personally? And then accused her of theft? Her head aching with pointless conjecture, she sighed. Apollo was very complicated. He was also unreadable and impulsive. There was no way she could guess what he had in mind before he chose to tell her.

Apollo examined the grim little room and vented a curse. Women did not as a rule walk out on him, no, not even briefly. But Pixie was headstrong and defiant. Not exactly submissive wife material, a little voice pointed out in his head but he ignored it. He trailed a finger along the worn paperback books on the shelf above the bed and pulled out one to see what she liked to read. It was informative: a pirate in top boots wielding a sword. A reluctant grin of amusement slashed Apollo's lean, darkly handsome features. Just as a book should never be judged by its cover, neither apparently should Pixie be. She was a closet romantic with a taste for the colourful.

Registering that he was hungry, he dug out his cell phone to order lunch for the two of them.

Walking back into her room, Pixie unclipped Hector's leash and watched her pet race under the bed to hide.

Apollo was sprawled in the room's single armchair, long, muscular, jeans-clad legs spread apart, his black hair feathering round his lean strong face, accentuating the brilliance of eyes that burned like emerald fire. 'Does your dog always behave like that?' he demanded, frowning.

'Yes. He's scared of everything but he's most afraid of men. He was ill-treated,' she murmured wryly. 'So, tell me why you're here.'

'You're in a bind and I am as well. I think it's possible that we could work out something that settles both our problems,' Apollo advanced guardedly.

Her smooth brow indented. 'I don't know what you're talking about.'

'For starters, I will *pay* you if necessary to keep quiet about what I am about to tell you because it's highly confidential information,' Apollo volunteered.

Faint colour rose over Pixie's cheekbones. 'I don't need to be paid to keep your secrets. In spite of what you appear to think, I'm not that malicious or grasping.'

'No, but you are in need of money and the press put a high value on stories about me,' Apollo pointed out, compressing his lips. 'You *could* sell the story.'

'Has that happened to you before? Someone selling a story about you?' she shot at him with sudden curiosity.

'At least half a dozen times. Employees, exes…' Apollo leant back into the chair, his strong jaw line taut, dark stubble highlighting his full sculptured mouth. 'That's the world I live in. That's why I have a carload of bodyguards follow me everywhere I go.'

Pixie had noticed the sleek and expensive car parked across the street and a man in a suit leaning against the bonnet while he talked into an earpiece and her grey eyes widened in wonderment. 'You don't trust anybody, do you?'

'I trust Vito. I trusted my father as well but he let me

down many times over the years and not least with the terms of his will.'

Belatedly, Pixie recalled the recent death of his parent and the reference to the older man's will made her suspect that they were finally approaching the crux of the matter that had put Apollo 'in a bind'. It was, however, hard for her to credit that anything could trap Apollo Metraxis in a tight corner. He was a force of nature and very rich. He had choices most people never even got to dream of having and he had always had them.

'I have no idea where you're going with this,' she muttered uncomfortably. 'I can't even begin to imagine any set of circumstances where you and I could somehow settle our…er…problems. Are you asking me for some sort of favour or something?'

'I don't ask people for favours. I *pay* them to do things for me.'

'So there's something that you *think* I could do for you that you'd be willing to pay for…is that right?' Pixie pressed in frustration as a knock sounded on the door.

Apollo sprang upright, all leaping energy and strength, startling her into backing away several steps. He didn't want to get to the point, she registered in wonderment. He was skating along the edge of what he wanted to ask her, reluctant to give her that much information.

And Pixie understood that feeling very well. Trust had never come easily to her either. She loved Holly and her brother and Holly's baby and would have done anything for them. Once won, her loyalty was unshakeable and it had caused her a great deal of pain in recent months that she had had to step back from her friendship with Holly because it was simply impossible to be honest about the reasons why she had been more distant and why she had yet to visit Holly and Vito in Italy. Holly would be determined to help and there was no way Pixie could allow herself to take advantage of Holly's newfound wealth and still look herself in the face. Instead she was dealing with her problems as she always did...*alone*.

She stared in disbelief as a procession of covered dishes were brought in by suited men and piled up on her battered coffee table along with cutlery and napkins and even wine and glasses. 'For goodness' sake, what on earth is all this?' she framed, wide-eyed.

'Lunch,' Apollo explained, whipping off covers as his men trooped back out again. 'I'm starving. Help yourself.'

He whipped off the final cover. 'That's for the dog.'

'The *dog*?' Pixie gasped.

'I like animals, probably more than I like people,' Apollo admitted truthfully.

Pixie lifted the plate of meat and biscuit and sniffed it. It smelled a great deal better than Hector's usual food did and she slid it under the side of the bed. Hector was no slowcoach when it came to tucking in and he began chomping on the offering almost immediately.

'Where did you get the food from?' she asked.

'I think it's from the hotel round the corner. There's not much choice round here.'

Pixie nodded slowly and reached for a plate. Apollo did not live like an ordinary person. He got hungry, he phoned his bodyguards and they fetched a choice of foods at an undoubtedly very stiff price. She helped herself to the fish dish.

'Are you going to tell me what's put you in a bind yet?' she enquired ruefully.

'I can't inherit my father's estate without first getting married,' Apollo breathed in a driven undertone. 'He knew how I felt about marriage. After all, it didn't make him very happy. He was married six times in total. My mother died in childbirth but he had to divorce the five wives that followed her.'

Pixie listened with huge eyes. 'A bit like Henry VIII with his six wives,' she mumbled helplessly.

'My father didn't execute any of his, although had he had the power I suspect he would have exercised the right with at least two of them,' Apollo derided.

'And you're *still* an only child? Why would he try to *force* you to marry?'

'He didn't want the family name to die out.'

'But to prevent that from happening...you'd have to have a child,' Pixie pointed out with a frown.

'Yes. He stitched me up every way there is. My legal team say the will is valid as he was in sound mind when he had it drawn up. I also have a five-year window of opportunity to carry out his wishes and inherit, which is deemed reasonable,' Apollo ground out between gritted white teeth. '*Thee mou*...how can anyone call any of it *reasonable*? It's insane!'

'It's...it's...er...unusual,' Pixie selected uncertainly. 'But I suppose a rich, powerful man like your father thought he had the right to do whatever he liked with his own estate.'

'*Ne*...yes,' Apollo conceded gruffly in Greek. 'But I have been running my father's business empire for many years now and his will feels like a *betrayal*.'

'I can understand that,' Pixie said thoughtfully. 'You trusted him. I used to believe my father when he told me he'd never go back into prison but he didn't even try to go straight and keep his promise. My mother was the same. She said she would stop stealing and she didn't. The only thing that finally stopped her was ill health.'

Apollo studied her in astonishment, not knowing whether or not to be offended that she had compared his much-respected and law-abiding father to a couple of career criminals.

Enjoying her delicious fish, Pixie was deep in thought and surprised that she could relax to that extent in Apollo's volatile radius. 'I get your predicament,' she confided. 'But the terms of the will must be public property, and they aren't confidential, so what—?'

'I have decided that I must meet the terms,' Apollo incised grimly. 'I am not prepared to lose the home and the business empire that three generations of my family built up from nothing.'

'Attachment meets practicality,' Pixie quipped. 'I still don't understand what any of this has to do with me.'

Apollo set down his plate and lifted his wine glass. 'I intend to meet the demands of the will on my *own* terms,' he told her with emphasis, his remarkable green eyes glittering below black curling lashes. 'I don't want a wife. I will hire a woman to marry me and have my child. We will then separate and divorce and my life will return to normal again.'

'And what about the child?' Pixie prompted with a frown of dismay. 'What will happen to the child in all this?'

'The child will remain with its mother and I will attempt to be an occasional father to the best of my ability. My goal is to negotiate a civilised and workable arrangement with the woman of my choice.'

'Well, good luck with that ambition,' Pixie muttered, tucking into her meal with appetite while sitting cross-legged on the floor beside the coffee table because there was only one chair and predictably Apollo had not offered it to her. 'It sounds like a very tall order to me… and anything but practical. What woman wants to marry and have a child and then be divorced?'

'A woman I have paid well to marry and divorce me,' Apollo said drily. 'I don't want to end up with one who will cling.'

Pixie rolled her eyes and laughed. 'When a woman knows she's not wanted, she's rarely clingy.'

'Then you'd be surprised to learn how hard I find it to prise myself free of even the shortest liaison. Women who become accustomed to my lifestyle don't want to give it up.'

Pixie set down her plate and lifted the wine glass he had filled. 'You do indeed have a problem,' she commented with a certain amount of amusement at his predicament. 'But I really don't understand why you're confiding in me of all people!'

'Are you always this slow on the uptake?'

Her smooth brow indented as she sipped her wine and looked up at him enquiringly from below her spidery lashes. 'What do you mean?'

She had beautiful eyes, Apollo acknowledged in surprise, eyes of a luminous clear grey that shone like polished silver in certain lights. 'What do you think I'm doing here with you?' he prompted huskily.

Green eyes met bemused grey and an arrow of forbidden heat shot to the heart of Pixie. She froze into uneasy stillness, her heart banging inside her chest like a panic button that had been stabbed because all of a sudden she felt vulnerable...vulnerable and...*needy*, the very worst word in her vocabulary when it related to a man.

'I believe that for the right price *you* could be the woman I marry and divorce,' Apollo spelt out smoothly. 'I would get a wife, who knows and accepts that the marriage is a temporary arrangement, and you would get your brother off the hook and a much more comfortable and secure life afterwards.'

As Pixie's throat convulsed, her wine went down the wrong way and she set the glass down on the low table with a jarring snap as she went off into a coughing, choking fit. He was thinking of her? *Her?* Her and him, the ultimate mismatch? The woman he had accused of being a thief? Was he certifiably insane? Or simply madly eccentric?

CHAPTER THREE

SPLUTTERING AND GASPING for breath, Pixie waved a silencing hand and rushed out of her room to the bathroom. There she got control of the coughing and rinsed her mouth with water taken from her cupped hand. In the mirror over the sink she saw her sad, watering panda eyes and groaned out loud. She looked dreadful. Her eyeliner was rubbed all round her eyes and there was even a smear across one cheek. She did her best with what little there was in the bathroom to tidy herself up.

Apollo Metraxis was offering to rescue Patrick from the debts he was drowning in if she married him in a pretend marriage. *And* had a child with him. *Don't forget the child,* she told herself while she clutched the sink to keep herself upright. She was blown away entirely by the crazy prospect of having a child with Apollo, having sex with Apollo… Swallowing hard, she breathed in deep. It was the most insane idea she had ever heard and she couldn't work out how or why he had decided to approach her with it.

Was he nuts? Temporarily off his rocker after the death of his father? Grounded again, she returned to her room and stared at him.

'That has to be the most ridiculous idea I've ever heard and I can't believe you're serious. I mean…' Pixie paused '…you don't even know me.'

'I'm not suggesting a normal marriage. I know what I need to know about you.'

'Little more than an hour ago you accused me of stealing your wallet!' Pixie fired back at him unimpressed.

'Because I know how desperate you have to be for money. You know that if your brother fails to make a payment or doesn't pay what he's supposed to pay his life could be on the line. He owes that money to a thug, who rules with fear and intimidation,' Apollo countered levelly. 'He could choose to make an example of your brother to deter others from making the same mistake.'

Apollo did indeed know exactly how precarious her brother's position was. Her tummy churned sickly at his confirmation that Patrick's creditor was a violent man because regardless of the beating Patrick had received she had hoped that that was the worst that would be done to him. She paled. 'But that still doesn't explain why you would approach someone like me!' she gasped.

'I told you that I prefer to choose a woman I can pay to marry me. I also want to be in control of the whole arrangement and the way I would set this up would mean that you *had* to follow the rules until our arrangement ends. That feels safer to me. It wouldn't be in your interests or your brother's to cross me or to admit to anyone that our marriage was phony,' he pointed out with assurance. 'Were you to admit that to the wrong person I could be challenged in a courtroom and I could lose my father's estate for ever. If you did betray me, you would be breaking the terms of our agreement and you would land you and your brother straight back into the same trouble that you're in right now.'

It was quite a speech, a sobering and intimidating speech that told her a lot she would rather not have known about exactly how Apollo's mind worked. He wanted a woman over whom he had total control, a woman who had to strictly adhere to his conditions or lose all benefits from the arrangement.

'I hear what you're saying,' Pixie breathed tautly, 'but I think it's twisted. You want a wife you can blackmail into doing what you want her to do, someone powerless. I could not be that woman.'

'Oh, don't underestimate yourself. I think you're gutsy enough to take me on,' Apollo told her with grudging amusement in his gaze. 'Did you or did you not grasp the fact that I am offering to save you and your brother from the consequences of his stupidity?'

Pixie reddened. Silence fell. In the interim, Apollo made use of his cell phone and spoke in what she assumed was rapid Greek.

'You're serious about this…?' she almost whispered in sheer bewilderment. 'But you said you need to have a child as well, and—'

'If you fail to conceive the marriage would end in divorce within eighteen months. I can't afford to waste more time than that,' Apollo imparted without hesitation. 'However, you would still get the same financial payoff. In that way, whether you have a child or not, you would still benefit from a debt-free future. '

A knock came on the door again. This time it was Pixie who rushed to answer it because she desperately needed a breathing space to get her thoughts in order and was thinking of diving for the bathroom again. Two men entered and deftly cleared away the dishes, leaving behind only the wine and the glasses.

'There's no way on earth I could go to bed with you!' Pixie spluttered out bluntly without meaning to as soon as the door had shut on the men's exit.

Apollo studied her in open astonishment and then he

flung his handsome dark head back and roared with unfettered amusement. In fact he laughed so hard he almost tipped the chair back while she stared at him in disbelief.

'I really don't understand how you can find that so funny,' Pixie snapped when he had regained control of himself. 'You're talking about me having sex with a stranger and that may be something you do on a fairly regular basis but it's not something I would do! You're also talking about having an awful lot of sex,' she told him half an octave higher, her voice thinning with extreme stress and embarrassment. 'Because it could take *months and months* to conceive a child. I couldn't do it. There's absolutely no way I could do that with you!'

'You sound a little hysterical and I'm surprised,' Apollo admitted. 'Holly's the starry-eyed type but you struck me as more sensible. Marry me and try to have a child and you won't be struggling in a dump like this to save your brother and make a decent life. All the bad things will go away… I can make that happen. You won't get a better offer.'

Mortification had claimed Pixie because she knew she had sounded panic-stricken. Face hot, she retreated to the bed and sank down on the edge of the mattress. In truth the thought of having sex with Apollo drove every sensible thought from her mind and only provoked a giant 'no' from every corner of her being. A long, *long* time ago she had promised herself that sex would only ever be combined with love in her life. She hadn't saved her virginity simply to throw it away in some immoral arrangement with Apollo Metraxis intended to conceive a child and moreover a child he didn't *really* want.

Apollo studied her in frustration. He didn't understand what was wrong. A woman had never found him unattractive before. He knew she didn't like him but he didn't consider liking necessary to a successful sexual liaison. Sex was like food in Apollo's life, something he enjoyed on a frequent basis and wasted little time thinking about. He was amazed that she had concentrated her objections on the need for a sexual relationship. Head down bent, she sat on the side of the bed in a rigid position with one arm stretched down in an unavailing attempt to lure the terrified dog out from underneath the bed. But the dog was too wary of Apollo's presence to emerge. He could see its beady little eyes gleaming watchfully from deep under the mattress.

'Tell me what the problem is…' he invited impatiently.

'I don't want to have a baby with someone who doesn't love me or my child,' Pixie muttered in a rush. 'That's way too like what I had growing up with the parents from hell!'

Apollo was taken aback. 'I don't want a woman who loves me because she might well want to stay married to me and I will want my freedom back as soon as I have fulfilled the terms of the will. Rejecting a wife who loved me could well lead to her breaking our agreement and telling someone that the marriage was a fake created to circumvent the will and allow me to inherit. And speaking for myself, I can't put love on the table for *any* woman. But, I *would* hope and expect to love my child.'

That admission soothed only one of Pixie's concerns because her brain could not surmount the unimaginable challenge of going to bed with Apollo again and again and *again*. A trickle of heat sidled through her slender frame as she lifted her head a few inches higher and focussed on her tormentor. He was gorgeous and he knew it but that did not mean he would be kind or considerate in bed. What did she feel like? A medieval maiden being auctioned off for a good price? That was nonsense because the choice, the decision was hers alone. And women had been marrying men for reasons far removed from love for centuries. Some women married to have children, some for money, some for security and some to please their families. She was making too much of a fuss over the sexual component. Sex was a physical pastime, not a mental one.

So, did that mean that she was actually considering Apollo's ridiculous proposition? She took a mental look at her life as it was. She was drowning in her brother's debt. She didn't have a life. She couldn't *afford* to have a life. She went to work, she came home, ate as cheaply as she could and saved every possible penny. Aside from Hector, whom she adored, it was a pretty miserable life for a young woman but sixth sense warned her that Apollo, if displeased, probably had the power to make even the life of a rich wife a great deal *more* miserable. Even so, when Holly visited the UK, Pixie went to meet her and they would have a meal and a couple of drinks and for a few sunny hours Pixie would forget her worries and enjoy being with her friend again. If she married Apollo, she would surely see much more of Holly, wouldn't she?

But then nothing could make marrying Apollo for money the right or decent thing to do, she reasoned unhappily. It would be akin to renting out her womb. And although she loved children and very much missed her friend Holly's adorable son, Angelo, from when they had both lived with her, she had never planned to have a child so young or to raise one alone. To plan to do that would be wrong, she thought with a shudder of distaste. And Apollo had also reminded her that circumventing his father's will would be breaking the law and she refused to be involved in anything of that nature.

'I can't believe you are willing to go to such lengths

just for money…but then I've never had enough money to miss,' Pixie admitted wryly. 'I guess it's different for you.'

'I'm already a very rich man in my own right,' Apollo contradicted drily. 'But there is more to this than money. There is my family home on the island where all my relatives are buried. There are the businesses originally founded by my grandfather and my great-grandfather, the very roots of my family. It took my father's death for me to appreciate that I'm much more attached to those roots than I was ever willing to admit even to myself.'

His obvious sincerity disconcerted Pixie. She understood that he had taken those things for granted until he was forced to confront the threat of losing them.

'Lying and pretending wouldn't come naturally to me,' she told him flatly. 'And faking the marriage would also be breaking the law, which I couldn't do. I don't even have a traffic violation on my record,' she told him truthfully. 'Because of my experiences growing up I won't do anything that breaks the law.'

'But we would be faithfully following the terms of the will, which specifies that I must marry and produce a child—boy or girl—within the space of five years. My intent to eventually go for a divorce is not barred by the will. If the marriage is consummated and we have a child it will be, to all intents and purposes, a *normal* legal marriage,' Apollo told her forcefully.

Pixie hovered, her small heart-shaped face pale and stiff. 'I don't want to be involved. I realise that you think I'm an easy mark but I couldn't do it. I won't discuss this with anyone either. I should think anyone I told would threaten to lock me up and throw away the key because they'd think I was crazy!'

Apollo rose slowly to his feet, dominating the room

with his height and breadth. 'You're not thinking this through.' Reaching into his pocket, he withdrew a card and set it down on the table. 'My private number if you change your mind.'

'I'm not going to change my mind,' Pixie told him stonily.

Apollo said nothing. He paused at the door, looking at that soft ripe mouth of hers, his body hardening in response to the imagery flashing through his inventive mind. 'It would've been good in bed. I find you surprisingly attractive.'

'Can't say the same,' Pixie retorted as she yanked open the door with a shaking hand. 'I don't like you. You're arrogant and insensitive and completely ruthless when it comes to getting what you want.'

'But I still make you hot, which infuriates you,' Apollo murmured huskily. 'You're not very good at faking disinterest.'

Her grey eyes sparkled with anger. 'You're not irresistible, Apollo!'

He lifted a lean-fingered hand and tilted up her chin. 'Are you sure of that?' he asked thickly, a Greek accent he rarely revealed roughening and lowering his dark drawl to a pitch that vibrated like a storm warning down her stiff spine.

'One hundred per cent certain,' she was mumbling as his breath fanned her cheek and the scent of him flared her nostrils and her mouth ran dry while her heartbeat raced into the danger zone.

'I bet I could get you to break the law,' Apollo murmured soft and low, all untamed masculinity and dominance. 'I bet I could get you to do just about anything I wanted you to. I even bet that I could make you *enjoy* breaking the rules…'

Her knees were trembling, her feet welded to the floor by the mesmeric effect of those stunning green eyes firing down into her own. 'You'd like to think so.'

Her pupils were fully dilated, her breathing was audible. Her nipples were making tiny indentations in her top and Apollo was hard as a rock. He bent his head a fraction more and traced her stubborn little mouth with his. She jerked almost off balance and his arms snapped round her to steady her. She couldn't breathe then for excitement. It was the most extraordinary sensation. Suddenly she wanted what she hadn't wanted until that moment. She wanted to stretch up on tiptoe and claim the kiss he had teased her with and refused to give.

Apollo bit out a laugh, perceptive eyes mocking her. 'Stubborn and proud. That's dangerous in my vicinity because I'm stubborn and proud as hell too. We'd clash but we'd also have fireworks, not something I usually look for with a woman but I'd make an exception for you, *koukla mou.* I would enjoy making you eat every word of your defiance and your denial…'

Her blood ran cold in her veins because she believed him. Below the bed Hector uttered a soft little growl that she had never heard from him before.

Apollo laughed again with genuine appreciation. 'Aw, stop kidding yourself, dog! You're not going to attack. You're too scared even to come out from under the bed. What do you call him?' he asked, disconcerting her with that sudden change of subject.

'Hector.'

'Hector was a Trojan prince and a great army commander in Greek mythology. Did you know that?' he enquired lazily as he strolled out of the door.

'No, I didn't. I just thought the name suited him,' she mumbled weakly.

She didn't breathe again until she had closed the door and she rested back against it with eyes shut and the strangest sense of disappointment filtering through her. In the most disturbing way Apollo Metraxis had energised her. The threat gone, Hector scampered joyously out from below the bed and danced at her feet. She lifted him up, stroking what remained of his ragged little ears, and cuddled him. 'A Trojan prince, not just an ordinary dog, Hector. I named you well,' she whispered, burying her face in his tousled fur, feeling her lips tingle as she thought of that almost-but-not-quite kiss that had left her foolishly, mindlessly craving more.

Patrick Skyped her that evening, his thin face worn, eyes shadowed. 'I've got bad news,' he told her heavily. 'Maria's pregnant and she's not well.'

'Pregnant?' Pixie gasped in dismay.

Patrick grimaced. 'It wasn't planned but we want the baby. We've been together three years now,' he reminded his sister with a weak attempt at a smile. 'I just wish the pregnancy wasn't making her so ill because she can't stand on her feet all day in a shop in her current condition. I'm never here, I'm always working…who's going to look after her?'

'Give her my congratulations,' Pixie urged, concealing her feelings because she very well knew that her brother's pregnant partner could bring his entire debt repayment scheme tumbling down round their ears because it was a struggle for him to make his monthly payment as it was.

Her brother's blue eyes glittered. 'I hate asking but could you manage anything extra this month?'

'I'll see what I can do,' Pixie said thickly, not wanting him to realise that she could see the tears in his eyes.

A few minutes later the call was complete and Pixie felt as though she had received a punch in the stomach.

Patrick and Maria's financial situation was as fragile as a house built of cards. If one card fell, they would all fall. She groaned out loud. She couldn't afford to give Patrick any more money and she should have admitted that upfront. Unfortunately her panic-induced thoughts had flown straight to Apollo because she wanted her little brother to stay alive and in one piece and if he couldn't keep up those payments, he could well pay with his life.

Patrick was under threat and now there was Maria and a new baby on the way to consider as well, Pixie reflected wretchedly. How could she ignore their plight? How could she turn her back on them when Apollo had made it clear that if she did as he asked he would make all the bad things go away? And suddenly she was just desperate for those bad things to go away and for life to return to normal again.

Apollo as saviour? That concept didn't work. Apollo was more into helping himself than other people. In fact Pixie and her brother were more like chess pieces to be moved strategically on Apollo's master board. The human cost, the rights and wrongs and emotions didn't come into it for Apollo and how much simpler that must make his life, she thought enviously. She lifted the card and snatched up her phone.

I will be your Baby Mama if you settle my brother's debts, she texted with a sinking heart.

Ideals, she was learning, wouldn't be any comfort if her brother or Maria or the baby got hurt or were left alone in the world. Apollo had found her price and she felt humiliated, and even worse manipulated, for he had made her crave his mouth that afternoon and the memory of that unnerved her. It was one thing to defy Apollo, another thing entirely to contemplate being married to him and wholly within his power.

You won't regret it. We'll talk business the next time we meet.

Business, *not* marriage, she reflected uneasily, but maybe that was the right way to look at it, as an arrangement rather than a relationship. As a deal between two people rather than the intimacy normal between a married couple. He wouldn't really be her husband and she wouldn't really be his wife. Mostly they would be faking it…wouldn't they? Would that make it easier to bear?

CHAPTER FOUR

'IT'S QUITE SIMPLE,' Apollo murmured in a cold, dangerous tone. 'You pack up you and your dog and you'll be picked up this evening.'

'I can't just walk out on my job, and I'm supposed to give notice when I move out.'

'My staff will organise everything of that nature for you. You don't need to worry. I want you in London with me tonight, so that we can get on with the preparations.'

'What preparations?'

'You'll have to sign legal papers, see a doctor, buy clothes. There must be a dozen entries on the to-do list I've had drawn up for you. You're going to be very busy.'

Pixie thought about her brother and briefly closed her eyes, digging deep for composure. She had just put her life and her free will in Apollo's hands and the pressure was on *her* now. 'Where will I be staying?'

'At my apartment. It'll be more discreet than a hotel would be and I won't be there for most of the week. I'll be working in Athens.'

'OK.' Pixie forced herself to agree because she knew it was only the first step in another hundred or more steps when she would have to obediently fall in with Apollo's wishes. Dear heaven, had she ever hated a man so much?

Vito was one of the very few men Pixie had learned

to trust. She could see his love for her friend, Holly, every time he looked at his wife and his feelings for his son were equally obvious. But Pixie had had few such role models while she was growing up. Her own father had frequently resorted to domestic violence when he was drunk. He had beaten her mother and Pixie as well, calling her 'a mouthy little cow' for trying to interfere. When he wasn't in prison serving time for his burglaries, he had often taken his bad moods out on his family. Pixie had never had Holly's cosy, idealistic images of family life because she had experienced family life in the raw. Her father had married her mother when she fell pregnant but she had never seen any love or affection between them. Patrick had been born within a year of his sister's birth and her mother had found it a challenge to cope with two young kids.

By the time Pixie was eight years old, both children had been placed in a council run children's home because her mother had finally been imprisoned for her incessant shoplifting. Social workers had taken a very dim view of a mother trying to teach her children to steal. The council home and the various foster homes that followed had occasionally contained men with sexual designs on their charges. Pixie had been very young when she first learned to fear the opposite sex and the fact that she went on looking like a much younger child due to her lack of adolescent development had ensured that she had to remain on her guard around such men for years longer than most.

The foster home that had become the first real *home* for Pixie had been Sylvia and Maurice Ware's and she had gone to them when she was twelve. The semi-retired farmer and his wife had had a spacious farmhouse in the Devonshire countryside and they had been devoted guardians to the often traumatised children who had come to live with them. Now Maurice was dead, the farmhouse sold and Sylvia lived in sheltered accommodation but Pixie had never forgotten the debt she owed to the older couple for the love, kindness and understanding they had shown her. And it was in their home that she had met Holly and their friendship had been forged, even though Pixie was eighteen months younger.

Her possessions fitted into her one suitcase and a box she begged off the local corner shop. She left an apologetic message on her employer Sally's answering machine. What else could she do with Apollo calling all the shots? But being forced into such dangerous life changes genuinely frightened her. What would she do if Apollo decided that she wasn't suitable to be his wife after all? Where would she go? How would she find another job? She didn't trust Apollo and she didn't want to end up on the street, homeless and unemployed, particularly not with Hector to worry about.

A limousine arrived to collect her. The driver came to the door and carried out her luggage and then produced a pet carrier, which Hector refused to enter. Pixie protested and promised that the little dog would be quiet and well-behaved if he was allowed to travel on her lap. She climbed into the opulent car with an engulfing sense of detached disbelief. She'd had glimpses of Holly and Vito's wealth, had attended their wedding, had seen impressive photos of their Italian home, but Holly didn't wear much jewellery or particularly fancy clothes and, essentially, she hadn't *changed.* It was surprisingly easy to meet up with Holly and forget that she was the wife of a very rich man.

The luxurious interior of the limousine fascinated Pixie. It had a television and a phone and a bar. It was a long drive but there were regular stops to exercise Hector and an evening meal stop for Pixie at a very swanky hotel. It was only there that she noticed another car was accompanying them because it was one of the men in it who escorted her into the fancy dining room and urged her to choose whatever she liked from the menu. Pixie was so horrified by the prices on the menu and so scared that the bill would be handed to her at the end of the meal that even though she was starving she only dared to have soup, which came with a roll. Of course no one presented her with a bill. The big beefy bodyguard or whatever he was appeared to be there to take care of such necessities while Hector waited in the car.

By the time they finally arrived in London, Pixie was exhausted and living on her nerves. It was after ten in the evening and it was dark and, with Hector cradled in her arms, she left the limo in the underground car park and walked into a lift with the big beefy guy and his mate towering over her.

'What're your names?' she asked nervously.

'Theo and Dmitri, Miss Robinson. You're not really supposed to notice us,' Theo told her gently. 'We're here to take care of you but we're staff.'

It was yet another strong message that Apollo lived in a different world because Pixie could not imagine ever ignoring anyone in such a way. But at that moment she reminded herself that she had more pressing concerns. Would she see Apollo this evening? The lift stopped directly into a massive apartment foyer and she realised that it had to be a private lift only used by him and his employees.

A small, portly older man in a jacket approached her. 'I'm Manfred, Miss Robinson. I look after the apartment. Let me show you to your room.'

Pixie followed him across the foyer towards a corridor and on the way past saw into a large reception room where she glimpsed a lithe blonde beauty standing talking with a drink in her hand. One of Apollo's women? Probably, she thought. He always seemed to have a woman on the go. She would have to ask him what he planned to do after their marriage if they got that far because no way was she prepared to sleep with a man sleeping with other women at the same time. That wasn't negotiable yet the picture of a quiet, clean-living version of Apollo married refused to gel.

'This is the garden room,' Manfred announced grandly, walking across a big, lushly appointed bedroom to indicate the patio doors. He buzzed them open to show her the outside space. 'Perfect for the little dog…'

'Yes,' Pixie agreed in wonderment. Stepping out, she noticed that part of the roof garden was neatly and clearly temporarily fenced off, presumably to prevent Hector straying into the glimmering blue pool that lay beyond it.

'Can I get you any refreshments?' he asked cheerfully.

'I wouldn't say no to some sandwiches,' Pixie muttered apologetically.

Pixie unpacked while Hector explored the new environment and his own first private outside space. In one corner of the room sat a fur-lined pet bed with a roof. Hector sniffed all round it, finally decided it wasn't actively unfriendly and got into it. Manfred brought tea and sandwiches on a tray. Pixie went for a shower in the lovely bathroom, bemused to find herself dropped in the midst of such extreme comfort and luxury. Comfy in her shortie pyjamas, she curled up on the bed with her supper and ate.

Apollo had already told Lauren that he had an early start in the morning and that her uninvited visit was inconvenient. He had given her wine, made the kind of meaningless chit-chat that bored him and sidestepped a blatantly obvious invitation to have sex. He never brought his lovers back to his various properties. He took them to a hotel or went to their place because that meant that he could leave whenever he liked.

'You want me to leave, don't you?' Lauren said in a whiny little-girl voice that set his teeth on edge.

'Tonight doesn't suit me,' Apollo pointed out without apology. 'I have a busy schedule and I also have a guest staying.'

'Another woman?' she gasped.

And that was it for Apollo. Lauren had been in his life exactly two days. He hadn't yet slept with her and now he knew he never would because her attitude turned him off. Lauren stalked out in a snit, leaving Apollo free to indulge in his desire to see Pixie. Of course he wanted to see her, he reasoned with himself while his brain questioned *why* he would want to see her. But Pixie was very probably the woman he was going to marry and therefore infinitely more important than a casual hook-up like Lauren. And in any case he wanted to see if Hector liked his new hideaway bed.

With a brief knock on Pixie's bedroom door, Apollo opened it.

He was just in time to catch the look of fear on Pixie's face and the way she slammed back apprehensively against the headboard. 'Sorry, did I startle you?' he said, knowing that 'startled' didn't come near to covering her excessive reaction and wondering what had caused it.

Pale, Pixie suddenly reddened and unglued her spine from the headboard to straighten her narrow shoulders. 'It's all right,' she said with forced casualness. 'I thought you were entertaining?'

'No.' Apollo stared at her. She was wearing pyjamas and there was nothing elegant or alluring about them but, while his rational mind was telling him that, his body was reacting as if she were half naked. The nipples of her small breasts pushed against the thin cotton and her slender crossed legs were exposed yet he only had to look into her flushed and ridiculously appealing face and that bee-stung mouth and he was throbbing, grateful for the suit jacket he still wore as a cover.

'Well, I'm here,' Pixie pointed out nervously. 'Thanks for the bed for Hector.'

Apollo glanced at Hector, who had made himself as small and unnoticeable as possible at the back of the big bed, and a slanting, almost boyish grin flashed across his lean, strong face without warning. 'I thought he might as well hide in comfort.'

He looked amazing when he smiled like that, Pixie ruminated. She hadn't known he could smile like that or that he was a soft touch when it came to dogs, but he so obviously had not been joking when he said he often preferred animals to people. It gave him a more human side, made her a touch less unnerved by him. As for those dazzling, unexpectedly green eyes illuminating his hard dark features, it was a challenge to look away from them. But then of course he had appeal. He was a real player. Young, hot and rich, he was a target for hungry, ambitious and designing women, which was probably why he didn't like women very much. At least that was what she had privately decided about him even though she didn't know if it was true. And why should she care? Why was she even thinking about him in such a way? What Apollo Metraxis was really like shouldn't matter to her, should it?

And the need to stick to business belatedly impressed

her as a very good attitude to take because she did not want to be getting curious about Apollo and wondering what made him tick. Nor did she want to be admiring his stunning male beauty. None of that should matter to her, she told herself urgently.

'Do you mind telling me what you intend to do about my brother's debt?' she pressed tightly.

'If we go ahead and marry he can forget about it because I'll take care of it. If we stay married and you meet my conditions—'

'Getting pregnant?' she interrupted in dismay.

'No, that won't be on the table because it would be unreasonable. You may not conceive and if you don't I can hardly punish you for not doing so,' he conceded. 'As long as you try. That and confidentiality are really all I'm expecting from you. Whether we're successful or otherwise that debt will not come back to haunt your brother.'

'You're paying it off?'

'No, I'm taking over the payments,' Apollo lied without skipping a beat. 'Look on it as my method of ensuring you keep to your side of the bargain throughout our association.'

'It's not necessary to put that kind of pressure on me. I keep my promises,' Pixie argued, unhappy with what he was telling her.

'My tactics work,' Apollo countered levelly, feeling an unexpected stab of discomfiture for not telling her the truth, and the truth was that he already owned the debt in its entirety. After all, there was no way he could have entertained any kind of ongoing arrangement with a thug running an illegal gambling den.

Pixie swallowed hard on the angry, defiant response she wanted to make. When it came to the gambling debt, what he was offering was still much better than anything she could have hoped to achieve on her own. It would take the financial stress off Patrick and his partner and allow them to get on with their lives and concentrate on their coming baby. On the other hand Apollo's decision to maintain the 'carrot and stick' approach towards their marriage would put the weight of expectation squarely on Pixie's shoulders instead and it would worry her constantly that in some field she would fail to please and her loss of freedom and self-will would end up being worthless.

'I think that if you're prepared to marry me, you could be a little more trusting.'

'How can you say that? When I walked in you looked at me as though you expected me to attack you!' Apollo grated in condemnation. 'You don't trust me either.'

'It's nothing personal. I don't trust men generally.' Pixie lifted her chin. 'And why do I have to see a doctor?'

'Health check. Obviously there's no point in us marrying if it turns out that you may not be able to conceive.'

'So, presumably,' Pixie framed, 'you're being tested as well?'

'No.'

'Forty per cent of infertility problems are *male*,' Pixie pointed out. 'Not much point getting me tested if you're not going to get tested too.'

Apollo hadn't thought of that angle and for some inexplicable reason he realised that the suggestion that he might not be fertile really annoyed him. He opened the door. 'I'll see you tomorrow. By the way, *wear* the outfit I had put in the wardrobe for you.'

'Outfit?' she gasped, sliding off the bed and opening the wardrobe to see the blue dress and jacket that hung there in a garment bag and the silvery designer shoes and bag stowed beneath. 'What gives you the idea that you can tell me what to wear?'

'It's another milestone on the road to becoming my wife. Naturally I want you to look your best,' Apollo fielded, dragging his glittering gaze from his perusal of her slender thighs to jerk open the bedroom door again. Maybe he should've taken Lauren to bed, he reflected in annoyance, because he was deeply uneasy about the strength of Pixie's appeal. *Thee mou,* what was the matter with him? She wasn't a beauty but she was exceptionally pretty and there was something remarkably sexy about her as well, something that drew him on a level he didn't understand. Was it her expressive face? Those interestingly perky breasts? The tight bottom? The so touchable thighs and small, slender feet?

Did he feel sorry for her? Was that the source of her strange appeal? He didn't require a therapist to tell him that she suffered from low self-esteem. In the act of shutting the door, he turned and caught the filthy look she was shooting him while thinking herself unobserved and he strode down the corridor to his own bedroom laughing and feeling surprisingly upbeat for the first time since his father's death. No, he didn't feel sorry for Pixie, he *liked* that gutsy irreverent streak of hers even though he was out of necessity being forced to ensure that she reined it in. She really wasn't impressed by him. Or by his wealth. And when had he ever met with that attitude before in a woman? In truth it was a real first for him. The women he was accustomed to would have snatched the outfit out to check that it was designer and would then have praised his generosity with loads of gratitude and flattery to ensure that he did it again.

Pixie? *Not impressed.* Apollo grinned.

* * *

Pixie woke at seven to be greeted by Manfred drawing back the curtains and setting her breakfast down on a table by the window and stepping out through the patio doors to set down a dog dish for Hector. 'Mr Metraxis asks that you be ready for nine,' he told her quietly.

Pixie breakfasted like a king. She loved her food and had always had a healthy appetite. Staying in Apollo's palatial apartment was even better, she imagined, than staying in an exclusive hotel. After a shower, she dried her hair and took special care with her make-up before getting dressed.

She walked uncertainly into the huge main reception room and Apollo stared.

'Turn round,' he told her thickly, turning his fingers to emphasise the order.

Apollo was rapt. She was so incredibly dainty and feminine in that blue dress with the high heels accentuating her delicate ankles that he wanted to lift her off her feet and spin her round, and it was a weird prompting that bewildered him. She had the figure a model would kill for without the height.

'I like the dress,' he said, which wasn't surprising since he had personally selected it.

'It's elegant but I'm not used to wearing skirts or heels,' she complained. 'I'm more of a tomboy than a fashion queen.'

He took her to see a private gynaecologist. She was questioned, examined and scanned and blood tests were taken. The results would be in by the following morning. As she emerged she saw Apollo standing talking urgently into his phone. 'Did you have any idea? Well, no, I didn't think it through either...it's *not* funny, Vito. It was gross.'

Apollo finished the call and strode towards her with

all the eagerness of a male who could not get out of the plush surgery fast enough. 'Ready to go?'

Pixie was trying not to laugh because he had honestly sounded so shocked by what being tested had entailed and she thought it served him right after the process she had undergone without complaint. Evidently he did listen occasionally to a voice other than his own and he was playing fair at least.

'Where to now?' she prompted.

'My lawyers, after which you go shopping.'

'Oh? For what?'

'For a wedding dress obviously and all the rest of it. I'm putting you in the charge of a professional buyer and fashion stylist. She knows what you need as per my instructions. All you have to do is act like a mannequin.'

'But you haven't got the test results back yet.'

'Think positive...' Apollo bent down, his stubbled jaw line grazing her cheek a tiny bit, and every nerve in her body tightened like a string pulled taut. 'And I saw you smiling when you heard me talking to Vito,' he murmured huskily. 'No, I didn't enjoy being handed a porn mag but *ne*...yes, I had a fantasy and it was about you.'

As Apollo pressed her back into the limo, Pixie twisted her head back to gape at him. *'Me?'* she repeated in disbelief.

Green eyes roamed over her burning face with dark satisfaction. 'You, *koukla mou*.'

Luminous eyes taking on a faint bluish cast from the dress she wore, Pixie stared at him in astonishment. 'You're kidding?'

'Why would I be kidding? If I couldn't be attracted to you, how could we do this?'

It was a fair point but the idea that Apollo, all rippling male-muscle perfection and stunningly beautiful, could consider her attractive still stupefied Pixie. And while she stared, frozen to her seat, Apollo moved, scooping her off the seat and settling her down into his lap at a speed that thoroughly unnerved her. But then his mouth traced very gently over hers and that instinctive kick of fear that generally made her back away from men was soothed by that subtle approach, which seemed ridiculously unthreatening. Of course, it didn't dawn on her just at that moment that Apollo had an unequalled sensual skill set that allowed him to read women very easily.

The tip of his tongue traced her upper lip and something deep down inside just melted in Pixie. He followed that tactic up with a nibble at her full lower lip and she shivered, her whole body prickling with awareness to an almost painful degree. No man had ever made her feel anything like that before and she found it wildly seductive not to feel afraid. He teased her lips open and darted his tongue in lightly and a ball of erotic heat exploded in her pelvis and one of her hands flew up into his hair, feathering through the luxuriant strands to cup his well-shaped skull. She felt hot all over and curiously energised, almost as if someone had told her she could fly when all her life she had felt grounded and awkward.

His mouth was hard and yet his lips were soft and she was exploring every sensation with her brain and her body. He tasted so good, like water after a drought, like food after a famine. His mouth claimed hers with increasing pressure and her breasts ached inside her bra, liquid heat pushing between her thighs.

He was so warm she wanted to press into his lean, muscular frame and somehow meld with him. He framed her face with his hands and kissed her with steadily escalating passion and the hungry demand she recognised was thrilling rather than scary. She tipped her head back, allowing him all the access he wanted, jerking at each erotic plunge of his tongue and on fire for the next, which was why it was such a shock when without the smallest warning his hands dropped to her waist and he propelled her back into the seat he had snatched her off.

Blinking with disconcertion and sensual intoxication, Pixie looked at him with a frown of incomprehension as to why he had so abruptly stopped.

'For such a small woman you pack a hell of a punch!' Apollo growled accusingly, because he had been within an inch of ripping off her panties and bringing her down on his aching body, satisfying the raw need that had come at him out of nowhere. And he didn't like it, he didn't like it one bit because he had never been that close to losing control with a woman since he was a teen, and remembering that time when he had been little more than a boy toy for a mature woman's gratification brought him out in a cold sweat of revulsion.

'It was only a kiss,' she framed shakily between tingling lips, even though her body was telling her different and reacting in all sorts of disappointed ways to that sudden severance from his.

'I was ready to have you right here, right now!' Apollo grated through clenched white teeth, his jaw line rigid because he was so furious that for a few wildly exciting moments he had forgotten who he was and who she was and that the very last thing he had been thinking of was the bottom line.

And the bottom line was business, he reminded himself grimly, the business of satisfying his father's will and making the best he could out of being blackmailed into marriage and fatherhood.

'Here in the car?' Pixie gasped, looking ridiculously shocked by the concept. 'Would you have done that?'

And the very slight widening of his gorgeous green eyes fringed by those outrageously lush black lashes of his told her that he would have and indeed had probably had sex in a limo before. That brought her down to earth again with a timely thump. She was a virgin and he was a man whore and of course he had greater expectations and fewer boundaries than the average person. She wondered how often a first kiss had led into full sex for him and a shudder of distaste rippled through her, chasing off the last of the sexual heat he had evoked.

Aware that he had overreacted and exposed a certain sensitivity he had never ever exposed to anyone before, particularly not a woman, Apollo forced himself to shrug a careless shoulder. 'I suspect that you're likely to find living with me rather shocking. I like sex and I like a lot of it. Considering our current situation it's very positive that we light a fire together.'

Pixie shifted almost imperceptibly away from him to widen the gap between them. *I like sex and I like a lot of it.* It was quite an intimidating announcement for an inexperienced woman to absorb. Pixie's biggest secret, kept even from Holly, was that she had never actually *wanted* a man before. She had always been too wary around men to shake off that inhibition by the time she grew up. Usually the minute a man started touching her she wanted him to stop and feared how far he would try to go. But somehow that instinctive recoil, that fear, had been absent with Apollo and that worried her even while she told herself that it was just as well because there was no way on earth that she could somehow avoid consummating a marriage in which she had to try and conceive a child.

They arrived at a very fancy modern glass office building and, before they got out of the limo, Apollo turned to her to say, 'To all intents and purposes this has to seem like we're planning a normal marriage,' he warned her. 'You must *not* mention your brother's debt or anything of that nature.'

'OK,' Pixie muttered uncertainly.

'All you have to sign is a pre-nuptial agreement with a confidentiality clause included,' he revealed. 'You will have your own legal team to advise you.'

'My...*own*?' she whispered shakily, her eyes wide.

'To advise you of your best interests. You must've had access to legal advice to make the agreement stand up in court,' he explained. 'I know a lot about the subject because every one of my father's wives signed one of these agreements and half of them tried to wriggle out of it during the divorce negotiations.'

'I won't be wriggling anywhere,' Pixie mumbled.

'So, act like a girlfriend, not someone I hired!' Apollo advised in a warning aside.

'How would a girlfriend behave?' she whispered.

'I don't know. I've never had one, only sexual partners,' Apollo admitted, grasping her hand to urge her out of the limo.

'Never?' Pixie repeated incredulously.

'Just think about how a real bride-to-be would behave for this and behave accordingly.'

And an hour later, seated at a large conference table where the two sets of lawyers argued, often employing terms she didn't understand, Pixie took Apollo's advice and acted accordingly and accidentally brought the table to a standstill of silence.

'You mean...' she finally grasped '... I get financially punished if I'm unfaithful but Apollo *doesn't*? How is that fair? I won't accept that.'

That was the instant when Apollo appreciated once

again that Pixie could take advice too literally and that characteristically she was seizing on something none of his father's wives had even picked up on. Not only had he underestimated her intelligence, he had also seemingly overlooked what appeared to be a very moral take on infidelity and his heart sank because he had never planned to be faithful during his marriage. He had planned to be very discreet but *not* faithful because only once in his life had he been faithful to a woman and it brought back appalling memories of betrayal and stupidity.

'Fidelity isn't a negotiable concept,' Pixie declared with even greater clarity.

And every man at the table studied Pixie as though she had landed on it wearing wings and carrying a flaming sword of justice.

'If Apollo is unfaithful he has to suffer for it,' Pixie completed with satisfaction, wondering why Apollo wasn't looking impressed that she had finally spoken up and behaved as a real bride-to-be surely would have done.

Apollo compressed his firm sensual mouth and studied the table. In point of fact billionaires who married penniless women didn't expect to suffer in *any* way when they finally got bored, least of all financially. Was this Pixie's clever way of trying to increase her divorce settlement? It had to be the money she was thinking about, the profit, he reasoned and then he glanced up and Pixie nailed him with grey eyes like volcanic rock and he realised that the issue of actual fidelity was one he had completely forgotten to discuss. Breathing in deep, he suggested a break for coffee.

Shown into an empty office, he studied Pixie. 'I wasn't planning to be faithful,' he admitted bluntly.

'Then this arrangement dies now. I'm not willing to

have sex with a man at the same time as he is having sex with other women!' Pixie declared in a wrathful undertone of ringing disgust.

'You're forgetting that this is a business arrangement.'

'Business arrangements don't normally include sex!' Pixie shot back at him defensively.

A faint line of colour accentuated Apollo's supermodel cheekbones. 'We have an *extraordinary* arrangement.'

'But you don't get to sleep with other women and me at the same time!' Pixie told him doggedly. 'That's immoral and I refuse to be part of it.'

It was what was called an impasse and Apollo had very rarely met with anything similar. Just when he was within an ace of making the first move towards his goal of regaining his birthright too! He gritted his teeth. 'I'll *try* to be faithful,' he framed in a roughened undertone of frustration.

But Pixie was seriously disappointed in Apollo. She hated cheats and had even less time for married men who played away. And Apollo might not love her and she might not love him but it was not unreasonable for her to expect him to treat her with respect.

'It's not going to look much like a real marriage if you're still acting like the biggest man whore in Europe!' Pixie flashed back at him, watching temper flare like burning flames in Apollo's green eyes and watching him bite it back. And why had he bitten it back? Because she had only stated the truth, she suspected.

And eventually they signed the pre-nuptial agreement with an addendum that stated that the bridegroom would 'endeavour' to remain faithful but relations were strained right round the table, both legal teams well aware that wedding fever was at a low ebb just at that moment. Apollo was merely relieved by the knowledge that he was flying out to Athens that evening. He was also reluctantly recalling that Vito had warned him that Pixie could be hot-headed and difficult and wondering if only his haste had persuaded him to overlook that distinct drawback. What else could it have been?

But how could she be so naïve and unreasonable as to demand fidelity from him? He knew what he was, hell, even *she* knew what he was! But he had promised to try and he would try because he stuck to his word, even if it choked him. And on some strange level he was conscious that her stance had made him respect her. She had standards and nothing he could offer would sway her from them.

CHAPTER FIVE

PIXIE TWIRLED IN front of the full-length mirror and smiled hesitantly because her glossy reflection was unfamiliar. Having enjoyed the attentions of a make-up artist and a grooming day at a salon recommended by Holly, Pixie had never before enjoyed such a level of sophisticated presentation.

'I really did think you'd choose to wear white,' Holly confided.

'White would be wasted on Apollo,' Pixie replied, wrinkling her nose and making Holly laugh. 'If I ever get to have a *real* wedding, I'll wear white.'

'I still can't believe you're marrying him. I was really shocked when Vito told me.'

Pixie sat down on the end of the bed and studied her linked hands. 'There's still stuff you don't know about the deal I made with Apollo,' she admitted uncomfortably because she could not bring herself to admit that sex and conception were involved, fearing that Holly would think badly of her for being so desperate that she would agree to a demand of that nature.

Yet while remaining fearful of the judgement of others, Pixie had made peace with that condition on her own behalf. She had always planned to become a mother some day, to have a child who was absolutely her own to love and nurture and protect. To fulfil that longing while married and to be assured of a future income with which to raise that child might yet prove to be the best chance she would ever get to have a baby and give it the happy childhood she had personally missed out on.

After all, she was no great shakes at dating, she acknowledged ruefully. She had always had to force herself out of the door to even socialise with men and the few she had taken the risk of spending time with had turned her off the notion entirely. Consequently she had decided that, left to her own devices, it was perfectly possible that she would've stayed single and alone and would never have had the opportunity to settle down with a partner and have a family. On that basis, she had decided that her agreement with Apollo Metraxis might well have advantages she had initially overlooked because, however briefly, she would get to experience being a wife and, hopefully, a mother.

Apollo had shared the test results that had come back on one of his calls from Athens. They were both healthy and normal as far as the entry-level testing they had had could establish. There was no obvious reason why they shouldn't conceive as a couple. He was still rather cool and clipped with her in tone because she had not seen him since they had parted at odds after that legal meeting, but Pixie had no regrets on that score. His fidelity while they were trying to conceive, as far as she was concerned, was non-negotiable. It wasn't much to ask, she reflected with faint bitterness and resentment; shouldn't it be a simple question of respect and decency? Apollo couldn't escape every moral obligation by throwing the 'business arrangement' label at her. But how hard would he 'endeavour' to meet her expectations? As a promise, it might well not be worth the paper it was written on.

'Well, you've finally told me about Patrick and there can't be anything worse than the mess he's got himself into, so I fully understand *why* you're doing this,' Holly said, squeezing her friend's shoulder soothingly. 'But you should've come to me for help.'

'Patrick's my problem, *not* yours,' Pixie pointed out with a hint of fierceness because her friend's desire to be generous with her money seriously embarrassed her. 'And this way I won't owe anyone anything. Apollo needs me as much as I need him and I prefer it like that.'

'It's a pity he's so...*so*...' Holly struggled to find a word, her cheeks colouring because it was occurring to her that now Pixie was marrying Apollo, even though it wouldn't be a proper marriage, possibly a little tact was required.

'He's been very good to Hector,' Pixie murmured thoughtfully. 'You know, rich or not, I don't think Apollo had it easy growing up either. Five stepmothers...what must that have been like for a little boy?'

'He's strong. He survived just like us. I suppose what I really wanted to ask is...how will you cope with his women?'

Pixie reddened and her pretty pearlised nails dug into the fabric of her wedding gown.

'Don't go falling for him, Pixie,' Holly warned her anxiously. 'He dumps women the instant they get clingy or needy and he seems to have the sexual attention span of a firefly.'

'Oh, I don't think I'm in any danger of making *that* particular mistake,' Pixie responded in a more relaxed tone of quiet confidence.

She lusted after Apollo and that was all and, as he himself had commented, that was a positive in their situation. The truth that he could make a single kiss that irresistible had been very persuasive. For the first time ever Pixie wasn't in fear at the prospect of having sex. Until he had opened his big mouth and referred to having sex in the limousine Apollo had made sex seem warm and intimate rather than sleazy, potentially painful and scary. He had also made it incredibly exciting.

Pixie's thoughts drifted much the way her dreams had throughout the week leading up to her wedding day, dreams filled with humiliating X-rated images that disturbed her sleep and woke her up hot and breathless and feeling quite unlike her usual sensible self.

Manfred arrived to tell them that the limo had arrived. Her foster mother, Sylvia Ware, was meeting them at the hotel where the civil ceremony would be staged because Holly had arranged transportation for the older woman. But Holly, Vito and Sylvia, as well as Pixie's brother and his partner, would be the only guests because it was to be a very small, quiet wedding, appropriate for a male who not only abhorred publicity but had also recently buried his father. Apollo had initially said no to her brother's attendance but had surprised her by giving way after she had argued that she had to somehow explain why she was leaving the UK. She had agreed not to tell Patrick the truth though.

Before she went into the private function room where the celebrant was staging the ceremony, Pixie paused to twitch her hair straight in a convenient mirror and breathed in very deep. On every level the step she was about to take daunted her because every aspect of living with Apollo Metraxis would be frighteningly new to her and Pixie only ever felt safe with what was familiar and harmless. Sadly, Apollo didn't fit into either category. But, true to her nature, Pixie lifted her head high, straightened her spine and her eyes glittered with determination as Holly opened the door for her to enter the function room. Whatever she felt on the inside, however, Pixie would conceal. Showing nerves and insecurities in Apollo's radius would be like bleeding in the water near a killer shark.

Apollo's rampant impatience lifted when the door opened. She was five minutes late and for all of those five minutes he had wondered if she had got cold feet. Now with the opening of that door his natural cynicism reasserted its hold on him. Pixie was being very well rewarded for marrying him and when had he ever known a woman to turn her back on an opportunity to enrich herself? In his experience, money talked much louder than anything else. And then Pixie came into view.

And all such thoughts vanished at amazing speed from Apollo's mind. She was wearing bright pink, not white, and a short dress rather than a full-length one. And she looked exactly like a tiny, very elaborate porcelain doll in dainty heels. He stopped breathing, shimmering green eyes locked to her delicate face beneath the feathery, distinctly un-bridal fascinator crowning her golden head. For all her lack of height she looked ridiculously regal with her hair swept up, her skin glowing, silvery eyes wide and bright, bee-stung lips as pink as the gown. And in only a few more minutes she would be *his* woman, he reflected with a sudden deep satisfaction that was new to him. *His* in a way no other woman ever had been or would be in the future because there would be no more marriages ahead of him. He had learned from his father's mistakes that there was no perfect wife out there waiting if only you could find her, at least not if you were a Metraxis and richer than sin. But still Apollo could not look away from the vision his bride presented.

Pixie collided with emerald-green eyes that glittered like jewels below the thick black lashes longer than her own. Riveting. Powerful. *Hungry.* And she suffered a heady instant of disbelief that she could have that effect on Apollo, the notorious womaniser accustomed to females more beautiful than she could ever hope to be. She had tried so hard not to think of that aspect for comparisons of that nature were fruitless and would merely feed her anxieties in bed and out of bed with him. Colour ran riot up over her face because she had quite deliberately avoided reflecting on the end result of marrying Apollo… the wedding *night.* Would it be good or would her inexperience and his emotional detachment make it a disaster?

She reached his side and was dismayed to register that she was trembling. She had travelled in the space of seconds from telling herself that she was calm and composed to a jangling state of nerves that appalled her. As the celebrant began to read the wedding service, she forced herself to look up and encountered a searching look from Vito, who was smiling. Unnerved, she looked down again, her heart thumping very fast while Apollo threaded a ring onto her finger, his hand as warm and steady as hers was cold and shaky. *Lighten up, it's a business arrangement,* she reminded herself when the man and wife bit was pronounced and it was over and she believed she could relax again. At least she believed that for as long as it took Apollo to swing her round, his other arm sliding below her hips to lift her in what could only have been described as a caveman kiss.

He hauled her up to his level and his mouth crashed down on hers with passionate force. There was no warning, verbal or physical, simply that positively primeval public claiming that shocked Pixie anew. She had sensed the volatile nature pent up beneath the surface when Apollo had kissed her in his limousine but this kiss was a whole different experience. Before he had asked, this time he literally *took*, disdaining any preliminaries, both strong arms enclosed round her to keep her off the ground and raise her to his level. It took her breath away, it sent her heart thumping like a road drill, it stripped away every illusion that she had any form of control over him or herself. She could *taste* his sexual hunger and it speared through her like a heat-seeking missile, awakening every skin cell to raw new sensation.

It was wild and erotic and exciting but it was also ultimately terrifying for Pixie to feel unmanageable and wanton. For a frightening second, as he began lowering her back to the ground on legs that didn't feel they could possibly support her, she wanted to cling to his wide shoulders and stay exactly where she was. Instead she slid slowly down his big muscular body and not even his suit jacket could conceal the reality that he was as aroused as she was.

Shaken, she found her feet again, and Apollo closed a supportive arm round her lithe body. *His*, body and soul, whether she liked it or not. And he knew, he knew she wouldn't like it at all, and Apollo smiled with sudden blinding brilliance, raising a brow a little at his friend Vito's questioning appraisal and Holly's state of apparent incredulity. Pixie was his wife now and what happened between them was entirely his business and nothing to do with anyone else, he reflected with satisfaction.

Pixie glimpsed that smile and the colour already mantling her cheeks rocketed even higher, a pulse jumping at her collarbone because angry discomfiture was not far behind. With that kiss he had blown her cover story with Holly and she could see that even Vito was taken aback by Apollo's enthusiasm. In fact the only people not staring were Patrick, Maria and Sylvia, none of whom saw anything amiss with a passionate wedding kiss between the newly-weds. Pixie pulled away from Apollo to greet her foster mother, Sylvia, and thank her for her attendance, noting as she did that her brother was looking unusually stiff and troubled in comparison to his more usual carefree self.

Patrick kissed her cheek. 'What's wrong?' she whispered.

Holly tugged her away with an insistent hand on her arm. 'What haven't you told me?' she pressed in an undertone.

'Better you don't know,' Pixie whispered. 'Any idea what's up with my brother?'

'Vito said Apollo gave him a good talking to when he arrived,' her friend revealed. 'Not before time in my opinion. I think he frightened the life out of him about gambling.'

Fury shot through Pixie because she had always acted to the best of her ability as her brother's protector. It had hurt when they had ended up in separate foster homes, seeing each other only through occasional visits often set months apart. What did Apollo know about Patrick's life and what he had suffered? Or how proud Pixie was that her sibling had always had a job when so many other children who had been through the foster system ended up on the scrapheap of opportunity before they had even finished growing up? Yes, Patrick had got into trouble, and serious trouble at that, but that had happened two years ago and he had been paying for it ever since!

Apollo closed a big hand over hers and slotted a glass of wine into her other hand. 'We're eating now and then this nonsense will be over,' he framed with unhidden relief.

'What gave you the right to speak to my brother about his gambling?'

'He almost got you and himself killed the night you fell down those stairs,' Apollo countered with unblemished assurance. 'It was time someone showed him his boundaries.'

'That was not your right or your business,' Pixie hissed up at him like a stinging wasp, her anger unabated.

Apollo dealt her an unfathomable appraisal, his striking green eyes veiled. 'For as long as you remain my wife, everything that is your business will also be *mine*.'

'No, it isn't!' Pixie practically spat back at him in her ire.

'It's too late now to complain, *koukla mou.* That ring on your finger says very different,' Apollo spelt out without hesitation, and he swung round to stride back to Vito's side and laugh about something his friend was saying.

'Oh, dear,' Holly pronounced at her elbow. 'You're already fighting.'

Pixie was so enraged that she could hardly breathe and with difficulty she opened her mouth to say, 'Apparently, he regards a wedding ring on a woman's finger as something very like a slave collar.'

Holly giggled. 'That's only wishful thinking!'

And Pixie remembered her manners and asked after Holly's son, Angelo, who had remained in Italy with his nanny because his parents were only making a day trip to London. By the time that conversation concluded it was time to take their seats at the table and be served with the wedding breakfast. As time went on, Patrick's spirits picked up and he began to relax a little although his sister noticed he was visibly too scared to even look in Apollo's direction, never mind address him.

Sylvia insisted on making a very short speech, which

recounted a couple of tales about Holly and Pixie as teenagers, which made everybody laugh. Vito wished them well, showing no sign of being tempted to make an attack on the bride as Apollo had done with his speech on his friend's wedding day.

'Watch yourself with Apollo's temper,' Holly whispered anxiously over the coffee. 'Vito says he can be very volatile.'

'Think I already know that,' Pixie muttered. 'As well as dictatorial, manipulative and sexist. I could go right through the alphabet with him and not one word would be kind, but then right now I'm angry.'

'When he saw you in that dress he stared at you as if you'd jumped naked out of a Christmas cracker. It was quite funny.'

Obviously, he hated the dress. Well, Pixie didn't care about that. She had gone shopping with her official personal stylist and had overridden her to make her own selections because, had Apollo's recommendations ruled, she would have ended up dressed like a middle-aged lady without fashion sense. Evidently, he didn't want her wearing normal *young* clothes, he wanted her tricked out in longer skirts and high necks. Well, he could just go jump off the nearest cliff with that wish, Pixie thought resentfully.

Why should he think he had the right to dictate the very clothes she wore? Wasn't she already surrendering enough with her freedom and her control over her own body? She was her own person and always had been and marrying Apollo Metraxis was not about to change that reality…

CHAPTER SIX

As Pixie prepared to clamber dizzily out of the helicopter, Apollo vaulted out and took her by surprise by swinging back and scooping her off her feet and carrying her off the helipad.

'I can walk!' Pixie snapped freezingly, feeling like an idiot as the yacht crew hanging around the helipad stared in apparent surprise at what was happening before their eyes.

'If I put you down you have to take your shoes off and walk barefoot. No heels on the decks,' Apollo delivered unapologetically.

'If I take my shoes off, I shrink into something pocket-sized!' Pixie hissed in a most un-bridal manner between gritted teeth.

Apollo shrugged a very broad shoulder. 'That's the rule. Blame your parents for your genes, not me.'

Pixie breathed in so deep to restrain her temper that she was slightly surprised she didn't spontaneously combust like a balloon overfilled with air. 'Put me down, Apollo.'

Holding her up with one arm as if to emphasise how strong he was, he flipped off her six-inch shoes with the other hand and carefully lowered her to the polished perfection of the deck surface. Pixie shrank alarmingly in stature and flexed angry bare toes on the sun-warmed wood. 'You're a dictator insisting on bare feet,' she condemned.

'Some things aren't up for negotiation,' he pointed out quite unnecessarily, striding past her to greet his yacht captain and shake hands, responding in a flood of his native Greek with a wide smile.

Feeling not remotely bridal, Pixie had a bouquet thrust in her arms and managed a beamingly polite smile while Apollo translated the captain's good wishes on what she privately termed their matrimonial nightmare.

What else could she call it when Apollo seemed to be racing off the rails in his resolve to do exactly as he liked regardless of how she might feel about it? She was still furious that he had confronted her brother about a matter she considered to be none of Apollo's business. Having that source of resentment followed by a very long flight in a helicopter that made her feel sick to board Apollo's giant yacht, *Circe*, in the Mediterranean had not improved her outlook. The ring on her wedding finger already felt very much like the slave collar she had mocked.

Long brown fingers guided her by her shoulder in the direction she was expected to go and she wanted to jump up and down and scream in frustration. Apollo was making her feel like a glove puppet. Go here, sit there, *do that*! It was as if he had swallowed the manual of *How to be a Control Freak with your Wife* at the same moment he was told he was married. She had seriously underestimated how very forceful and domineering he could be unless you did *exactly* as you were told. And there was no room for complaint, which he ignored.

'We need to clear the air about your brother,' Apollo announced, urging her into a room fitted out like an office with built-in cabinets, shelves and a very large desk.

'I will only tell you this one more time…' Pixie framed quite shakily but loudly in her rage. 'My brother is none of your business!'

Once again, Apollo ignored that statement. He extracted a slim file from a drawer in the desk and tossed it across the desk. 'Patrick is *still* gambling. Small card games with low stakes but he has a problem and it needs to be dealt with.'

'That's a complete lie and very unjust!' Pixie exclaimed.

'Pixie, there's sibling loyalty and then there's complete stupidity. Show me that you understand the difference and read the file.'

Her face flaming red with angry embarrassment, Pixie grabbed the file and retreated to a chair.

Apollo studied her with an air of exasperation. Why couldn't she understand that it was *his* job as a husband to protect her? That was all he was doing, as well as sorting out a problem that would only get worse if it was ignored. He had no personal axe to grind when it came to his brother-in-law. But it was obvious that Patrick was weak and in need of firm guidance. That had to be sorted out before Pixie's brother got himself into an even bigger mess because Apollo would refuse to settle the younger man's gambling losses if he got into trouble again.

Pixie's shoulders hunched as she read the investigation report, which stated that Patrick often played card games in the evening after he finished work. Her heart sank to her toes, the colour draining from her face to leave her stiff and pale. Her brother had lied to her and she was hugely hurt by that reality. He had *sworn* he would never gamble again, he had *sworn* he was not addicted but the evidence in the file proved otherwise and it was a total slap in the face for her to have to learn that fact from Apollo, who had all the sensitivity of a hammer blow.

'I had him investigated only as a precaution. I will not allow Patrick's difficulties to cause trouble between us. I tackled him today—in a *private* location, by the way—for your benefit and that of his partner,' Apollo informed her on a pious note that made his bride's teeth grit. 'Your brother has agreed to see an addiction counsellor and after her assessment he will follow the advice he receives. Otherwise his gambling debts will come back to haunt him—'

Pixie leapt upright in consternation. 'No, but you promised *me*!'

'The carrot and the stick approach *work*, Pixie,' Apollo cut in very drily. 'He needs a reason to reform and the child on the way is an excellent source of pressure on him to change his ways.'

'Holding that debt over him is so cruel, Apollo,' Pixie framed unevenly, grey eyes wide with stinging tears and accusation.

'He needs professional treatment and support. You are his sister, *not* his mother,' Apollo pronounced with finality. 'I won't change my mind about this, so don't waste your energy arguing about it.'

But Pixie already knew that she was unlikely to get anywhere arguing. Apollo was a steamroller, who travelled in a dead straight line and it was simply your bad luck if you lay in his path because he wouldn't deviate from his course.

Unhappily, his comment about her being Patrick's sister and not his mother lingered longest with Pixie, stirring up memories she would have sooner left buried. From an early age Pixie had been urged to look after her little brother. Her mother had *loved* Patrick in a way she had not seemed able to love her older child and that had stayed true right to the end of the older woman's life when she'd begged her daughter to always support her younger sibling.

As a child, Patrick had got treats, praise, affection and smiles from their mother while Pixie had been denied all of those things and left wondering what it was about her that made her less loveable. As she'd matured, however, she had come to suspect that her mother had been one of those women who would always have idolised her son in preference to her daughter, indeed who saw something almost magical in the mother-son bond from which she jealously excluded everyone else.

A knock on the door sounded and Apollo yanked it open and four little furry feet surged across the floor to boisterously attack Pixie's ankles. Damp-eyed, she bent down and lifted Hector, who was crazy happy to be reunited with her after a twenty-four-hour absence. He planted excited doggy kisses over her chin and made her reluctantly laugh as she petted him to calm him down.

'You need to get changed for dinner now,' Apollo informed her, gratified to have scored a coup by reintroducing the dog at the optimum moment. But then Apollo very rarely left anything to chance. He had planned that reunion as a soother almost as soon as he'd discovered that Patrick Robinson was still gambling because he had known that he had to confront his bride-to-be with the realities of the situation.

If you knew how to handle women, you could avoid conflict. Apollo had been smoothly and cleverly handling women since he was a child because his comfort had depended on the relationship he had established with his stepmothers. He avoided dramas with lovers in much the same style. An expensive piece of jewellery or a new wardrobe could work a miracle with an angry, resentful woman. Pixie, however, so far seemed infuriatingly indifferent to her new clothes and lifestyle but he had not yet had the chance to test her in that line. She could simply be faking her lack of interest, striving to impress him. He studied her tear-streaked face, the grey eyes soft now as she petted the tatty little dog she undoubtedly loved. He liked that she liked animals. It was the first time in a very long time that Apollo had actively *liked* anything about a woman and it shook him.

'You deliberately let me think that Hector and I were going to be apart for weeks,' Pixie condemned. 'Why did you do that? The carrot and the stick approach with me as well?'

Apollo shrugged. 'I dislike arguments. I knew you would be upset about your brother. Hector's your reward for accepting that I'm doing right by Patrick.'

Pixie's delicate frame went rigid. 'Stop trying to manipulate me, Apollo. If you want me to do something just face me with it. Try being honest for a change.'

Even barefoot she contrived to stalk out of the office to join the yacht steward waiting outside for her to show her to the master suite. On the trek there she was shown the gym, the medical centre, the sauna and steam room and the cinema. *Circe* was a massive vessel with four decks and seemed to contain everything Apollo might require to live on it on a permanent basis. He hadn't offered to give her a grand tour as she had somehow expected and now she scolded herself for imagining he might want to do something that normal. He didn't care what she thought of his yacht. He had to know that she had never been on a yacht before and was already utterly overwhelmed by the sheer opulence of her surroundings.

The huge stateroom with the massive bed, private deck and en-suite intimidated her but not as much as the stewardess who greeted her in perfect English as

'*Mrs* Metraxis' and asked her what she intended to wear. From the closets, Pixie picked out a black silky catsuit. So, she had to change for dinner now. Strange the traditions Apollo took for granted, she reflected helplessly as she tried not to let her gaze linger on the giant bed.

She was a bag of nerves but a couple of drinks would steady her, she told herself urgently. This was not the time to fall apart. Apollo wasn't going to hurt her. He wasn't going to attack her. In addition, he might be detached and she might only be a means to an end but he wasn't tactless enough to wrestle her out of her bra and then ask in a disappointed tone where her boobs had gone, as had once happened to Pixie. That experience, added to the guy who had told her that her lack of curves just didn't rev his engine, had been sufficient to kill Pixie's desire to get naked with a man simply to experiment. If truth be known she had envied Holly for the greater sexual confidence that had allowed her friend to sleep with Vito the first day she met him because Pixie knew that in the same circumstances she would have panicked and ended up saying no.

Only no wasn't quite an option with a wedding ring on her finger on their wedding night, particularly not with a male programmed to try and get her pregnant as fast as possible. She practised smiling in the mirror as she renewed her make-up and straightened her hair. She breathed in deep and strong as she dressed and tried not to fret at the trailing hems of the pant legs, which she had expected to wear with six-inch heels. The stewardess provided her with deck shoes and she thrust her feet moodily into them to be escorted to the dining saloon.

And there was Apollo awaiting her, resplendent in a tailored white dinner jacket and narrow black trousers that moulded long, powerful thighs, long black hair flaring round his lean, darkly handsome bronzed face. Gorgeous as a movie star and very, very sexy, she told herself bracingly, but complex as an algebraic equation to someone who had never got the hang of algebra.

She looked like a kid in the trailing pantsuit, Apollo reflected with hidden amusement. Why hadn't it occurred to her to wear something short? Her starlight eyes flickered with nervous tension over him and moved away hurriedly and he wondered why she was on edge because a woman expecting to share his bed had never been on edge with Apollo before. In fact most were enthusiastic, sparkling and downright impatient because he had a reputation for never sending a woman away dissatisfied.

He could see her nipples through the fine fabric because she wasn't wearing a bra and the tiny pouting shape of her breasts made him unexpectedly so hard that he ached, and he was forced to shift position to ease his discomfort while the wine was poured.

'How long will we be on the yacht for?' Pixie asked tautly.

Apollo shrugged, striking green eyes veiled. 'For as long as it takes us to get bored. I set up *Circe* to enable me to work wherever I am. We'll go to Nexos when we leave the yacht.'

'Nexos?'

'The Greek island my grandfather bought for the Metraxis family,' he extended. 'Of course, he had six children, of whom my father was the eldest, and the family was much bigger in his day. My father only had me. I have hundreds of cousins.'

'Didn't your father want any more children?'

'It wasn't an option. He eventually discovered that cancer treatment he had in his thirties had left him sterile. Had he had a check sooner, all his wives wouldn't have wasted their time pursuing fertility treatment,' Apollo admitted wryly. 'That's why I had the check.'

Pixie finished her first glass of wine and watched it being refilled by the silent waiter attending them. It unnerved her having a conversation with staff around but Apollo contrived to act as though they were alone.

The food was out of this world but Pixie felt that for all the enjoyment it was giving her she might as well have been eating sawdust. As the waiter left the saloon to fetch the dessert course, Apollo dealt her a frown. 'That's your fourth glass of wine.'

'You're counting?' she gasped in dismay.

'Should you be drinking at all with the project we have in mind?'

'I didn't think of that.' Pixie set her glass down. 'I don't know.'

'We have a doctor on board. I'll ask him. Aside of that aspect, I'm not having sex with you if you're drunk. That's something I would never ever do, regardless of whether or not we are married,' Apollo declared grimly.

Pixie reddened as if she had been slapped. 'I'm just a little nervous.'

Apollo stared at her with clear incomprehension. 'Why would you be?'

And Pixie knew that it was her moment to tell him the truth. After all, hadn't she urged him simply to be honest with her? Yet here she was covering up something very basic about her. But how could she tell a legendary womaniser that she was a virgin? He would think she was a freak or that no man had ever asked. It would be horribly humiliating. But worst of all, it would give Apollo a glimpse of her most intimate insecurities about herself and that was what Pixie couldn't bear. He would see her fear, her weakness, and he was ruthless and cold and he would use it against her, she thought wretchedly.

'Are you still hungry?' Apollo prompted softly.

'No,' she told him truthfully.

In a split second, Apollo rose from his chair and strode down to scoop her up out of hers, depriving her so thoroughly of breath and brain power that she merely stared up at him in astonishment. 'Time to make a start on that project, *koukla mou*,' he teased.

'You can put me down to walk.'

'I don't want you tripping and breaking a leg.'

'Of course…that would interfere with the project,' Pixie voiced for herself.

'I'm not that cold-blooded,' Apollo parried with a sudden husky laugh, glancing down at her with brilliantly striking green eyes. 'At this moment all I'm thinking about is that you're my wife and I *want* you.'

Pixie didn't believe that and an edge of panic infiltrated her. 'I'm not that experienced,' she told him abruptly.

Apollo smiled down at her, his wide sensual mouth tilting. 'How many guys?'

'A few,' she lied hastily, her face colouring, eyes veiling. 'I'm kind of fussy.'

Apollo liked being told that and rationalised that far from liberated thought with the reminder that she was his wife and naturally he didn't want a wife who had anything like his own track record. He knew that was sexist but it was the way he felt and it was a knee-jerk reaction that took him by surprise.

It was beginning to bother him that Pixie inspired such uncharacteristic urges. She was his wife but not a proper wife, he reasoned, merely the wife he had never thought he would have in the matrimonial step he had sworn never to take. And she was only with him in the first place because he had saved Patrick from the thugs her cowardly little brother had chosen to tangle with. It was a timely reminder but something visceral inside him denied that reminder because all of a sudden he discovered that he didn't like that either. He liked it much more when he looked down into Pixie's luminous grey eyes and read the same hunger that he was experiencing.

As he settled her down on the huge bed Pixie studied him, loving the strong angle of his jaw line, the starkness of his well-defined cheekbones and the classic jut of his nose, not to mention the lush black velvet sweep of his lashes shadowing those riveting emerald-green eyes. Looking at Apollo had the strangest intoxicating effect on her and her lips tingled as if in recollection of the kiss they had shared earlier.

He backed off a step and shed his jacket, embarked on his shirt and her heart started beating very, very fast inside her ribcage as he exposed the hard slab of his stomach and the incredibly defined muscles indenting his broad chest. He was drop-dead beautiful to her wide gaze. The shirt went flying. There was nothing inhibited about the speed with which he was stripping and she tried and failed to swallow as the trousers were unzipped and Apollo got down to boxers that revealed almost more than they concealed. He was already aroused, which shook and surprised her, indicating as it did that he did want her as he had declared he did.

But then, he clearly suffered from a high libido, she reminded herself, and possibly he was merely in the mood for sex and she was the only woman available. Yes, that made more sense to her. She would just be another nick on a bedpost already so full of nicks that hers would vanish into the woodwork. She tugged at the sleeves of her catsuit but he forestalled her, lifting her up in an infuriatingly controlling way to turn her round and unzip the garment, sliding it off her stiff shoulders, tugging it down with all the smooth expertise of a male who could have stripped a woman out of the most intricate clothing in the dark without breaking a sweat.

Pixie trembled. He had even blocked her attempt to get a little tipsy. She was way more sober than she had planned to be, having assumed that the alcohol would make her less nervous. As it was she only felt the very slightest buzz from the wine she had imbibed before he made sobriety sound like her bounden duty.

Apollo was both disconcerted and enthralled by her sudden silence and submissive attitude for it was not at all what he had dimly expected from her. 'I'm not remotely kinky in bed if that's what you're worrying about,' he told her with amusement.

Pixie gulped. 'I'm not the slightest bit worried,' she assured him.

'Then why can't you relax and trust me?' Apollo enquired lazily, his dark deep drawl having already dropped in pitch and the vowel sounds roughened.

In mortification, Pixie closed her eyes. 'I'd really prefer the lights out...'

'Not my preference but if that's what it takes, *koukla mou.*' Apollo reached up to stab a button above the headboard and the stateroom was plunged into darkness although soft light emanated from the lights still illuminating the private deck beyond the windows.

His wicked mouth descended on the slope of her neck and she shivered, a different kind of tension entering her now that he no longer had an alarmingly bright view of her physical deficiencies. She quivered as long fingers expertly teased her straining nipples.

'I'm very small there,' she pointed out, unable to resist a ridiculous urge to draw his attention to the obvious.

'I like it,' Apollo growled next to her ear, nipping at her ear lobe, sending another shot of uncontrolled response darting through her.

'Men always want more, not less.'

Apollo arched his hips and ground his pelvis against her thigh. 'Does that feel like I'm low on sexual interest?' he asked silkily. 'Now, be quiet.'

And Pixie shut her mouth because she was embarrassed by the inappropriate comments spilling from her lips. He rested her against the soft pillows and employed his mouth on her breasts, sending increasingly powerful streams of sensation down into her pelvis. Her hips rocked of their own volition and that shocked her. She could feel herself getting hot and damp there and that shocked her almost as much as her sudden desire to join in and explore him. Of course, she didn't have the nerve. She lay there like a felled statue, settling for being hugely grateful not to be on the edge of a panic attack.

Apollo was wheeling out his entire repertory of foreplay in an attempt to win the fireworks response he had craved from their first kiss. He had never gone so slowly in his life with a woman. He had never had to because usually they were all over him, egging him on to the final act as if afraid he would lose interest if it took too long to get there. He kissed a line down a slender arm and smiled. There was just nothing of her and he would have to be very careful not to crush her. He caressed a tiny foot, flexed the toes, revelling in the novelty of that fragile daintiness. She might be small but everything was in perfect proportion. As he skimmed down her panties he reached up, fingers closing into her golden hair to raise her head and claim her lips again.

A gasp was wrenched from Pixie as he nuzzled her lips with his, brushed them gently apart and then went in for the kill with his tongue and it was as if the top of her head blew off. When Apollo kissed her she literally saw stars and heavenly galaxies. With every caressing, darting plunge of his tongue her temperature rocketed and her still hands finally rose and plunged into the depths of his hair. Finally getting that response energised Apollo's hunger.

There was so much he wanted to do that he didn't know where to begin but he knew he wanted it to be an unforgettable night for her. Why it had to be that way with her he didn't know or care, but then he had always responded very well to a challenge and in many ways Pixie had challenged him right from the start. Unimpressed, cool, indifferent. For the first time in his life Apollo wanted a needy, clingy woman and he didn't understand the desire or where it was coming from.

He spread her legs and shifted down the bed. Pixie froze as if he'd suddenly put the lights back on. He wanted to do *that*?

'I don't think I want that,' she told him hastily.

'You'll be surprised,' Apollo husked, ready to rise to yet another challenge and embarking on the venture with a long daring lick that made her squirm and gasp again. Satisfied, he settled in to drive her crazy. He would be the very best she had ever had in bed or he would die trying. Lack of interest would become craving. Coolness would become heat. Unimpressed would become awed.

Apollo touched her with expert delicacy that she knew she couldn't object to although she couldn't imagine that he could possibly *want* to do what he was doing. He slid a finger into her damp folds and she almost spontaneously combusted in shock and excitement and that was nothing compared to the intense feel of his mouth on the tiny bundle of nerves at the apex of her. All of a sudden control was something she couldn't reclaim because her body had a will of its own. Her hips ground into the mattress below her, her heartbeat thundered and she was breathing so loud she could hear it while the growing tightness deep down inside her was impossible to ignore. She could feel herself, reaching, straining, while the ripples of excitement grew closer and closer together and then an almost terrifying wave of ecstasy gripped her and she was flying and crying out and moaning all at the same time.

'When you come the next time, I want you to say my name,' Apollo growled in her ear while her body still trembled in shock from the sheer immensity of what he had made her experience.

'Never felt like that before,' Pixie mumbled unevenly.

'It will *always* feel like that with me,' Apollo assured her with great satisfaction as he slid over her, tilting her hips up to receive him, and drove down into her with an uninhibited groan of all-male need.

Pixie jerked back in shock from the sharp pain that assailed her and yelped in dismay.

But Apollo had already stopped. He raised himself higher on his arms to instantly withdraw from her again and folded back at her feet, the sheet tangled round him. His lean, darkly handsome face was a mask of disbelief. 'You're kidding me?'

Pixie sat up with a wince because she was sore and way more conscious of that private part of her than she wanted to be. She was still in too much shock to think because she had long dismissed as an old wives' tale the concept of a first sexual experience hurting and had been entirely unprepared to discover otherwise.

'A…*virgin*?' Apollo gritted in much the same tone of

disdain as he might have mentioned a rat on board his superyacht.

Anger began to lace her growing mortification. 'Why did you have to stop?' she gasped, stricken. 'Couldn't you just have got it over with?'

'Like you know so much about it?' Apollo virtually snarled at her as he vaulted off the bed with the air of a man who couldn't get away quickly enough from the scene of a disaster. A little warning voice at the back of Apollo's volatile head was warning him to tone it down but he was genuinely furious with Pixie for wrecking something with her silence that he had been determined to make special. Special…*really*? Where had that goal come from inside him? *Why?* He didn't know but he was still furious about the bombshell she had dealt him when he'd least expected it.

'Maybe I should have warned you,' Pixie framed tightly, recognising that he was sincerely annoyed with her.

'There's no maybe about it!' Apollo thundered back at her. 'I *hurt* you and how do you think that makes me feel? I gave you every opportunity to tell me and you didn't.'

'I thought you'd laugh at me.'

Apollo shot her a narrowed green glance. 'Do I look like I'm laughing?'

Pixie swallowed hard, her face burning at his raw derision. Clutching the sheet to her bare skin, she felt about an inch high while she watched him striding into the bathroom, over six feet of lean golden-skinned enraged male.

What did *he* have to be so annoyed about? She hadn't thought of her body as his business until they got into bed but then suddenly, she registered, it *had* become his business. Discomfiture gripped her. He was accustomed to experienced women and probably feeling out of his depth after she'd yelped cravenly at one small jab of pain. Really, could she possibly have made more of a fuss? Was it any wonder that he was angry?

Guilt stirring, Pixie slid out of bed and pulled on his shirt, because it was the nearest item of clothing that would cover her. She breathed in the scent of him almost unconsciously and sighed because she had screwed up, made a mountain out of what would probably have been a molehill had she simply been a little more frank in advance. But being frank on such a personal topic was something Pixie had never contrived to be, even with Holly.

As she appeared in the doorway Apollo glowered at her from the shower, standing there naked and unconcerned, water streaming from several jets down the length of his big bronzed body. Pixie stared and flushed. 'I'm sorry,' she said grudgingly. 'I should've warned you.'

'But instead of warning me, you actually *lied*!' Apollo condemned emphatically, still struggling to work out why he was so angry when he very rarely got angry about anything. A virgin—very unexpected but scarcely a hanging offence. That she had lied to him annoyed him more because, most ironically, she was the first woman he had ever believed to be more honest than was good for her.

'I said sorry. There's not much more I can do,' Pixie launched back at him a little louder, her temper rising. 'What do you want? Blood?'

'Already had that experience with you,' Apollo derided smooth as polished glass.

And that crack was the last straw for Pixie and she lost it. Her fingernails bit into her palms as her hands fisted and she shot a look of loathing at him that startled him. 'You're just reminding me why I don't like men and *why* I didn't warn you,' she framed jerkily, formerly suppressed emotion surging up through her slight body in a great heady surge.

'And why would that be?' Apollo demanded, switching off the water, grabbing up a towel and stalking out of the shower.

'Because you're threatening and selfish and mean! I put up with far too much of that growing up!' she told him in a screaming surge. '*Men* trying to catch me with my clothes off when I was in the bathroom or the bedroom…*men* trying to touch me places they shouldn't… *men* saying dirty stuff to me…'

Apollo had seemingly frozen where he stood. Not even the towel he had been using to dry himself was moving. 'What men?'

'Care staff in some of the children's homes I stayed in, foster fathers…sometimes the older boys in the homes,' she related shakily, caught up in the frightening memories of what she had endured over the years before she'd reached Sylvia's safe house and then eventually moved towards complete independence. 'So, don't be surprised I was still a virgin! Sex always seemed sleazy to me and I'm not apologising for it. Not everyone's obsessed with sex like you are!'

Listening, Apollo had lost all his natural colour and much of his cavalier attitude. His bone structure was very stark beneath his golden tan. 'You were abused,' he almost whispered the words.

'Not in the strictest sense of the word,' Pixie argued defensively. 'I learned to keep myself safe. I learned that what they were doing was wrong. Nobody ever actually managed to *do* anything but it put me off the physical stuff…'

'Obviously…naturally.' Apollo snatched in an almost ragged breath and veiled green eyes rested on her. 'Go back to bed and try to get some sleep. I won't be disturbing you.'

Taken aback, Pixie stared without comprehension at his tight, shuttered expression.

'I'm sorry I hurt you.'

'It was only a tiny hurt. I just wasn't expecting it,' she muttered awkwardly, but she could see that even that little hurt and the surprise of it had been a complete passion killer as far as he was concerned.

Apollo strode back into the bedroom and she heard him rummaging through the drawers in the dressing room. Moments later he stepped back into view sheathed in tight faded denim jeans and a white linen shirt and, without even pausing to button the shirt, he strode out of the stateroom. So much for their wedding night, Pixie thought wretchedly. Getting into bed he had definitely wanted her, lusted after her, and what had preceded the final act had been fantastic. He had given her an ecstasy she had not known she was capable of feeling. But all too quickly she had blown it…

CHAPTER SEVEN

WHAT WERE THE ODDS? Apollo asked himself as he sat on deck swigging from a bottle of Russian vodka, his black hair blowing back from his lean darkly attractive features, his green eyes very bright. What were the odds that he would end up with a woman who had also been abused? Whose attitude to sex had been inexorably twisted and spoiled by experiences that had happened when she was too young to handle them?

Not only had he hurt her physically, he had also *shouted* at her. Half a bottle further on, Apollo padded barefoot over to the rail. His wife was a virgin and he had acted like an idiot. Why? He was an arrogant jerk proud of his sexual skill and finesse…why not just admit that? He had been so determined to give her the fantasy and it had gone pear-shaped because she hadn't trusted him enough to tell him the truth. And how could he hold that against her when throughout his whole thirty years of life he had never told anyone but his father what had happened to him? He knew about that kind of secret; he *knew* about the shame and the self-doubt and the whole blame game. And even though he had seen slivers of low self-esteem and insecurity and anxiety in Pixie it had not once occurred to him that she too could be something of a victim, just like him.

She had deserved better, much better than he had given her. He had treated her like one of the good-time girls he normally enjoyed, confident and experienced women who wanted fun and thrills in and out of bed and as much luxury and cash as they could wheedle out of him. That had suited him because it left him in complete control at all times. But he wasn't in control with Pixie and that seriously disturbed him. He was clever, he was normally cool and logical and yet instead of being delighted that his wife had never been with another man he had shouted at her.

And paradoxically he *was* delighted because something about Pixie brought out a possessive vibe in him and that vibe of possessiveness had lit up and burned like a naked flame the instant he'd married her. Furthermore, since she had had the courage to tell him something as personal as what she had spilled out in her distress in the bathroom, he really did owe her, didn't he?

Apollo wove his path rather drunkenly back to his stateroom where he tripped over the clothes Pixie had gathered up and left in a heap directly in line with the door. The racket he made hitting the floor and his yell of surprise yanked her out of her miserable thoughts with a vengeance.

Fumbling for the bedside light, Pixie switched it on and stared in wonderment at Apollo sprawled in a heap on the floor. 'What happened to you?'

'I got drunk, 'Apollo informed her with very deliberate diction.

'After a…a crummy night that makes sense.'

'Don't be all English and polite and nice,' Apollo groaned, raking a hand through his tousled black hair. 'I wasn't.'

'But then you're not English,' Pixie parried, marvelling at the vision of her very controlled new husband in such a condition. His green eyes had a reckless glitter that unnerved her a little. Sober, he was a lot to handle. Drunk, he could well be more than she could manage.

'Never been with a virgin before,' he confided. 'I wanted it to be perfect and then it went wrong and I was furious. My ego, my pride, nothing to do with you. I was a…' He uttered a four-letter swear word.

'Pretty much,' she agreed more cheerfully after hearing that he had wanted their wedding night to be perfect, which was a hearteningly unexpected admission when deep down in advance of the bed business she had feared that he would not care a jot. She relaxed her stiff shoulders into the pillows while she studied him and decided that even drunk he was heartbreakingly gorgeous.

'My second stepmother beat me with a belt and left me covered with blood,' Apollo announced out of the blue.

Her jaw dropped. 'How old were you?'

'Six. I hated her.'

'I'm not surprised. What did your dad do?'

'He divorced her because of it. He was very shocked… but then he was sort of naïve about how cruel women can be,' Apollo told her as he drank out of the bottle still clutched in one big bronzed hand, lean muscles rippling to draw her attention to the intricate dragon tattoo adorning his arm. 'He didn't appreciate that *I* was the biggest problem in his remarriages.'

'How?' Pixie asked, wondering if she should try to get the bottle off him or just close her eyes to it. He wasn't acting like himself. He might hate her tomorrow for having seen him in such a vulnerable mood.

'When a woman marries a very rich man *she* wants to be the one who produces his son and heir but I was already there and the apple of my father's eye.'

'By the sound of that beating you got, he wasn't looking after his apple very well.'

Apollo closed his eyes, black lashes almost hitting his cheekbones. 'He married my third stepmother when I was eleven. She was a very beautiful Scandinavian and the only one who seemed to take a genuine interest in me. Never having had a mother, I was probably starved of affection.' His shapely mouth quirked. 'She would come and visit me at school and stuff. My father was very pleased and encouraged her every step of the way.'

'So?' Pixie prodded, sensing the tripwire coming in the savage tension bracketing his beautiful mouth, the warning that all could not have been as cosy as he was making it sound.

'Basically she was grooming me for sex. She liked adolescent boys…'

'You were eleven!' Pixie condemned. 'Surely you weren't capable.'

'By the time she took me to bed I was thirteen. It went on for two years. She took me out of school to city hotels. It was sordid and deviant and I was betraying my own father but…*but* she was my first love and I was fool enough to worship the ground she walked on. I was her *pet*,' he completed in disgust.

Pixie leapt out of bed and darted across the floor to kneel down in front of him. 'You were…what age?'

'Fifteen when I got caught with her.'

'For two years a perverted woman preyed on you.'

'I wasn't even her only one,' Apollo bit out in a slurring undertone. 'She'd been meeting up with the son of a local fisherman on the beach. It was *his* father who went to mine and tipped him off about what she was like.'

Pixie shifted until she was behind him and wrapped

her arms round his rigid shoulders. 'You were just a kid. You didn't know any better.'

'I definitely knew it was wrong to have sex with my father's wife,' Apollo broke in curtly. 'I don't deserve forgiveness for that but he still forgave me.'

'Because he loved you,' Pixie reasoned. 'And he knew his wife was using you for her own warped reasons. I'm so sorry I called you a man whore. You had a really screwed-up adolescence and of course it affected you.'

Apollo reached behind himself to yank her round and tumble her down into his lap. 'I never told anyone about that before...until you told me tonight about growing up in care with men trying to hit on you or spy on you or whatever,' he mumbled into her hair, the words slurring. 'Now I think I need to go to bed before I fall asleep on top of you, *koukla mou*.'

Pixie got up and removed the bottle while he stripped where he stood and, only staggering very slightly, fell like a tree into the bed. He slept almost immediately and she watched him in the half-light for long minutes, thinking how wrong she had been about him once and how much better she now knew him. Yet with what he had revealed he seemed more maddeningly complex than ever and without a doubt the man she had married in a business arrangement absolutely fascinated her. She brushed his tumbled black hair back from his brow and slid into the other side of the bed, hesitating only a moment before edging closer to take advantage of Apollo, whose natural temperature seemed to be the equivalent of a furnace.

She surfaced to dawn very, very slowly, the insistence of her body awakening her to a sweet flood of sensations. It was still so novel for her to feel such things that she knew instantly it was Apollo touching her and just as quickly she relaxed. Her nipples had tightened into needy little buds and the delicate place where his clever fingers were playing was embarrassingly sensitive and wet.

'You awake now?' he prompted gruffly in her ear.

'Yeah…' she framed weakly, her hips moving all on their own because the magical way he touched her made her ache, need and want all over again.

Apollo shifted over her, all rippling muscle and ferocious control. Green eyes glittered down at her, his lean, strong face taut and dark with stubble. She felt him at the heart of her and anxiety screamed that there was too much of him for what little there was of her so it was a struggle to force herself not to stiffen. Fortunately, he went slow—achingly slow—and she gradually stretched around his fullness, tender tissue reacting with unexpected pleasure to the source of that amazing friction. He shifted his hips, moved and a rush of exhilarating feelings engulfed her and her head fell back, eyes wide with surprise.

'Didn't want to give you the chance to get all nervous again,' Apollo admitted. 'Like it was likely to be some sort of punishment.'

'Definitely…*not*…punishment,' she gasped breathlessly, her body rising to meet the gathering power of his, excitement pooling like liquid fire in her pelvis.

'Just sex,' he told her.

And had she still had breath to disagree she would have done but she couldn't breathe against the rising tide of intoxicating excitement. Little undulating tingles of intense arousal were travelling in tightening bands through her trembling length. He was inside her and over her and nothing had ever felt that good or that powerful. Apollo smiled down at her, a smile ablaze with male satisfaction and, for once, she didn't mind his assurance. He gathered up her legs and angled her back, rising higher, thrusting faster, deeper, forcing little moans and cries from her parted lips that she couldn't hold back. The excitement intensified, sensation tumbling on sensation until a sensual explosion detonated deep within her and she went flying high and free on an electrifying surge of pleasure.

Apollo groaned his appreciation into her hair and she wrapped her arms round him. It was automatic, instinctive, something of a shock when he broke immediately free and imposed space between them. His lean, darkly handsome face had shuttered. 'I can't do that stuff,' he muttered semi-apologetically, his beautifully shaped mouth momentarily rigid with tension.

And Pixie forced a smile she didn't feel and shifted back in turn because she got it, she really did get it after what he had explained the night before. A child crying out for maternal affection, initially given it only to discover that it was an evil deception being utilised to gain his trust and love.

She swallowed the thickness in her throat and fought a very strong urge to hug him. He was the only man who had ever had that much power over her and momentarily it scared her. Sometimes Apollo made her want to kick him very hard and then equally suddenly she wanted to put her arms round him instead, even though she knew he didn't want that, couldn't handle that... It wasn't only her body he could make fly out of control: somehow he was reaching her emotions as well, and she knew that was dangerous and she tensed.

Apollo was intensely uncomfortable for a male accustomed to feeling at home in virtually every situation. He very rarely drank to excess and when he did he could still control his tongue, yet inexplicably he had lost control the night before and confided his deepest secrets. He understood that her experiences had reanimated memories he had suppressed and that that had destabilised him but that didn't mean he had to like his own weakness. He really didn't like that sudden feeling of being exposed and vulnerable because it reminded him too much of his lost childhood. For that reason it felt good to have a distraction available.

'I've got something for you,' he told her, reaching into the drawer by the bed to produce the jewellery case he had stashed there several days before. Apollo always thought out everything well in advance, preparing for every eventuality if he could. And she *deserved* a gift much more than the women who usually shared his bed.

The wedding night, after all, had been pretty much disastrous and his getting drunk and telling all in such a girly fashion, Apollo reflected grimly, had crowned the disaster. She had tolerated it all and in spite of everything that had gone wrong she had still lain back trustingly for him to claim her body even though she had feared that consummation.

Taken aback, Pixie stared down in astonishment at the case and then carefully opened it. A breathtaking bracelet ran in a river of glittering diamonds across the velvet inset. 'For me?'

'Wedding present,' Apollo pronounced with relief as he leapt out of bed with alacrity and headed for the shower, convinced that he had done the very best that he could to be thoughtful and decent.

'It's gorgeous and I suppose I need some jewellery to make me look like a proper rich wife,' Pixie murmured uncertainly, battling to rise above hurt feelings she knew she had no right to experience. 'But this was a bad time to give it to me.'

Apollo's long lashes fanned down in disbelief and

he gritted his white teeth before he swung back to her. 'How so?'

Pixie contemplated him as he stood there, buck naked, bronzed and very Greek godlike in his physique. He was without a doubt the most physically beautiful male she would ever be with but, time and time again, he confounded her and wounded her. 'I'm not some whore you have to pay for a one-night stand.'

'I've never been with a professional,' Apollo said icily. 'I gave you a gift. Thanks would have been the appropriate response.'

'It's just the way *this* makes me feel,' Pixie began, struggling to verbalise what she didn't quite understand herself.

'We have a business arrangement,' Apollo shot back at her unapologetically. 'Think of it as business.'

'I can't think of my body as business. I'm not sure what that would make me,' Pixie admitted unhappily. 'But I need more respect than you're giving me if we're going to be stuck together like this for months. I don't think that's too much to ask. Obviously you can't even bring yourself to put your arms round me after sex. I'm not going to turn clingy or needy, Apollo. I'm not about to fall in love with you or the things you can buy me either. I know this marriage isn't real.'

A whine sounded from below the bed.

'Shush, dog,' Apollo groaned in raw frustration. 'You've been walked, you've been fed and watered. Stay out of this…she's enough to handle without your input.'

Pixie had to bite her tongue not to comment on the reality that she had overlooked her beloved pet's needs and Apollo had not. Instead she forced herself to continue. 'Couldn't we try friendship if we can't have anything else that might make you feel threatened?'

Apollo flung back his arrogant dark head and green eyes radiated emerald fire in the sunlight. 'You do *not* make me feel threatened.'

Pixie surrendered and said exactly what was on her mind. 'Don't punish me because you talked too much for your own comfort last night.'

And there it was in a nutshell, what Apollo Metraxis absolutely couldn't *stand* about Pixie. Somehow, *Thee mou*, she saw beyond the surface and saw right *through* him and it was the most unnerving experience he had had in many years. Without another word, Apollo strode into the shower, hit every dial, turned up the pressure and refused to think by blanking out everything, a trick he had learned as a child to stay in control. He held himself straight and taut until the confusion and bewilderment and seething frustration drained fully away with the swirling water.

Suppressing a groan of equal frustration, Pixie tunnelled back down into the bed and made no objection when Hector jumped up to tuck himself in next to her body. Hopefully Apollo would think she was sleeping in. Instead of sleeping, however, she was counting pluses, a habit she had formed as a child to make a grey day look sunnier. Number one, she enumerated, they had done the sex thing and it had been…amazing. Number two, Apollo was damaged but at least he had explained why, even if he did regret it. Number three, he was *trying* to make the marriage work but he hadn't a clue how to meet such a challenge. Female partners who whooped over his financial generosity and who only lasted for a two-week session of nightly sex didn't provide a man with much of an education on how to make a woman feel happy, respected and secure. Was she expecting too much from him? This was supposed to be a business arrangement, she reminded herself ruefully. Maybe *she* was being unreasonable…

Pixie breakfasted alone on the polished deck with Hector at her feet: Apollo was working. He had *phoned* her to make that announcement in a very detached voice that suggested he suspected he could be dealing with a potential screaming shrew. As far as avoidance techniques went, Apollo had nothing whatsoever to learn. When her phone went off again she answered it unhurriedly, assuming there was something he wished to tell her, but this time it wasn't Apollo, it was Holly.

'Vito and I are flying out to join you this afternoon!' Holly exclaimed excitedly. 'What do you think?'

Pixie rolled her eyes. 'The more the merrier,' she quipped, oddly hurt that Apollo had to bring in other people to create yet another barrier between them within a day of the wedding. Was she really that unbearable? She flexed her fingers against her flat stomach and prayed to get pregnant *fast*. The sooner she and Apollo escaped the situation they were in and separated, the better it would be. If they weren't living together and sharing a bed, it would be easier to stick to a businesslike attitude, she reasoned, wondering why her heart now felt as heavy as lead.

'We're all heading to some nightclub on Corfu tonight,' Holly told her. 'Of course, you'll already know that…sorry, I'm talking a mile a minute here.'

Quite unaware that yet another attempt to please Pixie had bombed dismally, Apollo stayed in his office on board until he got word that their guests were arriving.

'I promise not to ask any awkward questions,' Holly whispered as she settled on the end of the bed in Apollo and Pixie's stateroom. 'But you don't look happy and I can't imagine we'd be getting hauled in last minute if you were. Am I allowed to ask about that?'

Pixie grimaced. 'No. I'm sorry.'

'No need to be sorry but you sound attached…and the weird thing is Apollo is sounding attached too—'

'No, that's definitely not happening,' Pixie cut in with confidence.

'Apollo told Vito he wanted us here because he thought it would please you. Vito's never known him to make that much effort for a woman.'

Unimpressed, Pixie shrugged and watched Holly pet Hector while Angelo explored the room in the vain hope of finding something to play with. Bending down, she scooped her godson up intending to get reacquainted with the adorable toddler.

'So, what are you wearing tonight?' Holly prompted, taking the hint.

Relieved by the change of subject, Pixie showed off her outfit.

'My goodness, I'll look so old-fashioned next to you. What time are you getting your hair done?'

'I'm doing my own hair,' Pixie countered in surprise.

'You've got a beauty salon on board and you're *still* going to do it yourself?'

As soon as Holly had realised that Pixie hadn't even known the *Circe* had a full-time grooming parlour for guests and had commented bluntly on Apollo's deficiencies as a husband and a host, the two women set off on an exploration tour designed to satisfy both and entertain Angelo.

Hours later, after a convivial dinner during which Apollo contrived to ignore the reality that he had a wife seated at the same table, which resulted in Pixie going to even more extreme lengths to ignore him, Pixie emerged on the lower deck, fully dressed and ready to board the motor boat waiting to whisk them out to the island of Corfu.

Apollo studied his wife in consternation, his lean dark face taut and cool. 'I don't like the clothing,' he said baldly.

Vito actually flinched and walked Holly over to the deck rail several yards away.

Pixie jerked a narrow bare shoulder in dismissal of the comment. She wore a skintight cerise-pink leather corset and a fitted black pencil skirt with very high heels. It was young and hip and she didn't much care what he thought about it. 'You can command everything else, Apollo, but *not* what I wear. What's your objection anyway?'

His strong jaw line squared. 'You're showing too much of your body.'

'I've heard you've been seen with women who don't even bother with underwear.'

'You're different…you're my wife,' Apollo declared grimly. 'I don't want other men looking at my wife.'

'Tough,' Pixie commented with a combative glint in her grey eyes. 'You're a Neanderthal in a suit.'

'If we didn't have guests, I wouldn't allow you off the boat!' he growled half under his breath.

What a complete hypocrite he was! Pixie thought in wonderment, helpless amusement lacing her defiance. Apollo was a living legend for entertaining women who looked as though they had left half their outfit at home to maximise the exposure of their perfect bodies.

A couple of hours later, amusement had become the last thing on Pixie's mind. She was huddled in the luxury

VIP cloakroom of the club with Holly. 'I'm sorry you've been dragged into this,' she muttered apologetically.

'What? Watching Apollo behave badly? I shouldn't say it but it's his favourite pastime.'

Pixie tossed her head, golden blonde hair dancing round her shoulders, her piquant little face vivid with anger and mortification. 'I can behave badly too…'

Holly pulled a face. 'But provocation is not the road I would take with Apollo.'

Pixie, however, was past being polite and low-key and sensible. Since their arrival at the nightclub Apollo had been swamped by women. He was extremely well-known on the club circuit and he had not made a single attempt to deter the rapacious females trying to pick him up. Pixie had watched in wooden silence while other women pitched themselves onto her husband's lap, danced in front of him in very suggestive ways and squeezed up close to him. He had bought them drinks and chatted to them as if Pixie were the invisible woman and she had had enough of his treatment. She had also learned why he made no effort with her. From what she could see by the over-eager girls surrounding him, Apollo had never *had* to make an effort. He was very hot and very rich and acting like a kid let loose in a candy shop was the norm for him.

Pixie took her cocktail over to the VIP rail and watched the dancers because she loved to dance. Much good it was doing her though, she reflected moodily, wincing at the high-pitched giggling travelling from their crowded table. She wanted to empty entire ice buckets over Apollo and then kick him from one end of *Circe* to the other. Friends, she had suggested mildly, and *this* was the answer he was giving her? And why did she care? Why on earth did she care? She glanced at him out of the corner of her eye and watched a woman run her fingers down his broad chest and her teeth clenched with something that felt very like rage.

'Would you like to dance?' a faintly accented and unfamiliar voice said from behind her.

Pixie spun round and found herself virtually eye to eye with a black-haired good-looking young man with very dark eyes and an Eastern cast of feature and she smiled. Vito had asked her to dance and she had said no, recognising pity when she saw it, and she had said no to Holly too, but a total stranger was a perfectly acceptable substitute for a husband who was ignoring her while simultaneously outraging her sense of decency.

'Yes, thank you…' Pixie acquiesced, noticing how all four of the bodyguards who had accompanied their party from the yacht all rose as one at a nearby table. With determination she smiled to let them know that she was pleased to have company and not in need of rescue.

'I am Saeed,' her companion informed her.

'I'm Pixie,' she said cheerfully, preceding him down the stairs, noting that two of Apollo's bodyguards were now taking up position at the edge of the dance floor alongside two large men of a similar look.

'Where's Pixie?' Apollo asked Holly abruptly.

'Dancing,' Holly announced somewhat smugly.

'With another man?' Apollo demanded with savage incredulity and he flew upright.

Vito sprang up as well and accompanied his friend to the rail that overlooked the floor below. 'You can't thump him. He holds diplomatic status and he's half your size. It would make you look bad.'

At his elbow, Apollo swore wrathfully in four different languages as he finally picked out his wife and her partner from the crowd. He watched Pixie wriggle her diminutive behind while her partner gripped her hips and drew her close. Blinding rage filled him as the other man bent his wife back in a dip that brought their bodies into intimate contact and he strode down the stairs with Vito flying to keep pace with him.

'He's an Arab prince...don't hit him and cause a scene!' Vito warned.

Apollo's powerful hands coiled into fists of fury. What the hell did Pixie think she was playing at? She was his wife and she wasn't allowed to let *any* other man touch her body! He never ever lost his temper, he reminded himself fiercely, but there she was, twitching every inch of that lithe, dainty little body and the Arab Prince wasn't the only one noticing that tight skirt and that fitted little top that showed the slope of her gorgeous breasts. In an almighty storm of rage Apollo acted in what for him was a very diplomatic manner. He stepped up behind Pixie and hauled her off her feet and threw her over his shoulder.

'She's my wife!' he grated down at the startled Prince, who was the same size as Pixie in her heels, which wasn't very tall, and with that clear announcement of his God-given right to interfere Apollo strode off for the exit.

It took several annoying seconds for Pixie to realise what was happening but she instantly recognised Apollo's scent. She pounded his back with clenched fists and screamed at him full volume, 'What the hell do you think you're doing? Put me down right this minute!'

His bodyguards studiously not looking near either of them, Apollo stuffed his wife in the limo that would take them back to the harbour. Like a spitting cat, Pixie launched herself at him to try and get back out of the car again. 'I want to go back and join Vito and Holly!' she yelled.

Apollo drew in a deep shuddering breath and said as mildly as he could, 'You're going back to the yacht and if that's how you intend to behave when I take you out it'll be a long time before you get out again.'

'You can forget that option!' Pixie railed at him, frantically trying to get out of the other side of the car only to be foiled by the automatic locks. 'Let me out!'

'No,' Apollo decreed, temper moderated by the simple fact that he had her back again where she should be. 'You shouldn't have let him touch you like that.'

'Are you for real?' Pixie screamed at him. 'You've had women throwing themselves at you and pawing you all evening!'

Apollo shot her a riveting green glance of near wonderment. 'That approach works on other women…what's wrong with you?'

'What's *right* with me is that I'm not about to let you walk all over me!' Pixie hissed back. 'Anything you can do I can do too and I will. I'll throw myself at every man in my radius if it annoys you enough… I hate you, Apollo… I *hate* you!'

Apollo watched her stalk like a miniature warrior onto the motorboat and sit down as far as she could get from him. Marriage promised to be a great deal more challenging than he had ever appreciated, he conceded, still lightheaded from the sheer amount of rage that had flooded him when he'd seen the Prince put his hands on her. How dared he? He gritted his even white teeth while he fought the lingering pulses of fury.

With a flourish intended to convey sarcasm, Pixie whipped off her shoes before she boarded the yacht. 'And we abandoned our guests on our night out,' she remarked in a stinging tone. 'Some hosts we make.'

'If you think Holly and Vito want to come back and find themselves in the middle of a marital spat, you're mental. They'll stay out until dawn,' Apollo forecast, grim-mouthed.

CHAPTER EIGHT

PIXIE SLUNG HER shoes across their stateroom in a gesture of frustrated fury. Apollo had acted like a total ass all evening and then somehow made a fool of her as if *she* were the one in the wrong? How was that fair? How was she supposed to forgive him for that? How was she supposed to cope with being married to such a maniac? So much for the business arrangement!

The door clicked open and Pixie spun. 'I'm not sleeping in here with you tonight.'

Apollo simply depressed the lock and studied her. 'You're not sleeping anyplace else.'

'You've got *ten* guest cabins. What is the matter with you?' Pixie exclaimed furiously. 'What do you want from me?'

Apollo surveyed her steadily, concealing his growing bewilderment at his own actions with difficulty. He had lost his head and he didn't ever do that.

'Are you going to answer me?' Pixie asked impatiently, one hand planted on her hip while her foot tapped cheekily on the floor.

He just wanted her. Somehow she was like a missing puzzle piece he had to have at any price. The sex had been amazing. It was the fireworks and the sex that attracted him. She was having the weirdest effect on him. Problem solved and sorted, he told himself stubbornly.

'Any time soon?' Pixie prodded in frustration. 'Like… tonight?'

Apollo unbuttoned his shirt for want of anything better to do. A knock sounded on the door and he answered it. Hector raced in, paused in horror at the sight of Apollo, gave him a very wide berth and shot trembling below the bed. Apollo locked the door again. 'You're my wife,' he told her finally, and as far as he was concerned at that moment that covered everything he needed to say.

Pixie was perplexed by that response. 'But not a real wife…'

'We're legally married, having sex and I'm trying to get you pregnant. How could it be any *more* real?' Apollo enquired. 'Tonight I felt married.'

Her smooth brow indented, grey eyes shimmering with indignation. 'Well, if that's how you behave when you're married, I wouldn't like to have been around when you were still single.'

'I wasn't expecting you to hit back,' he admitted with startling abruptness, his beautiful wilful mouth curling with a sudden amusement that enraged her even more. 'Clever move, *koukla mou.* Guaranteed to get a rise out of a guy as basic as me.'

Her breasts swelled temptingly over the top of the corset as she breathed in very, very deeply. 'You think it was some kind of strategy to get your attention back?' she shouted at him in disbelief.

'It worked,' Apollo pointed out drily. 'So, presumably it was deliberate?'

'No, it freakin' well wasn't deliberate!' Pixie launched at him, bending to scoop up a shoe and hurl it at him in furious rebuttal of that conviction. 'How dare you be so big-headed that you can think that?'

'I'll let it go this once,' Apollo murmured silkily. 'But if you ever let another guy touch you like that again you'll pay for it.'

'Threatening violence now?' Pixie questioned, scooping the other shoe and holding it like a weapon.

'No, you're rather more violent than I am. You've already punched me once and now you're throwing stuff at me,' Apollo pointed out deadpan.

Pixie threw the second shoe but he was quick on his feet and she missed. Hector started to whine below the bed.

'I can allow you to do a lot of things I haven't allowed a woman to do before, *koukla mou*,' Apollo intoned as he strode forward, 'but I really can't stand by and allow you to frighten that dog!'

Hauling her up into his arms, Apollo sat down on the bed. 'Settle down,' he instructed, pinning an arm round her to stop hers from flailing. 'You've got my full attention.'

'And now I don't *want* it!' Pixie yelled at him, so wound up with emotion she almost felt tearful over her inability to express herself.

'I'm afraid you're stuck with it,' Apollo told her, dropping his arm to frame her face with big controlling hands. 'I want you.'

'No!' Pixie snapped, striving to clamber off him again.

'You want me too, you just won't admit it,' Apollo opined in frustration.

'Do you ever listen to yourself? Marvel at the little megalomaniac remarks you make?'

His beautiful stubborn mouth claimed hers in a scorching kiss and her temperature rose like a rocket.

She felt hot, she felt faint, she spread her hands against his shoulders and, meeting shirt fabric, slid her fingers beneath the parted edges to find warm brown skin. His tongue dipped and plunged and one of her hands delved into his luxuriant black hair. As she knelt over him, he pushed up her skirt and ground her hips down on him. Suddenly she was achingly aware of the long hard thrust of him behind his zip. Liquid warmth surged between her thighs and she gasped, her nipples swelling and tightening. Yanking down the zip on her top, Apollo cast it aside and bent her slender body back over one arm to suck at a pretty pouting nipple, a manoeuvre that dragged an agonised moan from low in her throat.

'I'm not speaking to you!' Pixie exclaimed in consternation.

'Since when was speech required?' Apollo groaned, reaching with difficulty below her skirt to rip at the fragile lace of her panties and then touch her with frighteningly knowing fingers in the exact spot she could least resist.

'Apollo!' Pixie muttered furiously, helpless in the grip of the sensations flooding her and blaming him for the fact.

He met her shaken eyes and he smiled with sudden brilliance. 'I want you much more than I've ever wanted any other woman,' he breathed in a raw and shaken undertone.

Oh, the combination of that smile and those tantalising words, it left Pixie dizzy and without her conscious volition her arms slid round his neck and she leant against him, momentarily hiding her face, her thoughts in a messy whirl. *What's wrong with me? Why do I still want him? What happened to the anger?*

Lifting her head, she clashed with black-lashed gorgeous green and her heart gave a hop, skip and a jump as though he had hit a switch. And she told herself she couldn't *possibly* be falling for him. No, she was too sensible and not at all the type who would build herself up knowing she would only be broken down by the end of the relationship. It was lust, wild, wicked lust, and it was merely hitting her harder because she was a late developer.

Apollo stroked her, teased her tingling core, reducing her defences to forgotten rubble until all she wanted, all she craved, was for the ravaging, greedy hunger to be sated. He tipped her back, removed the tight skirt to the accompaniment of a ripping sound that implied damage, unzipped and came down on her without even undressing. 'Can't wait,' he growled. 'Have to have you now.'

He pushed into her with scant ceremony but that hard, driving fullness was absolutely what her body needed and desired just then. A cry of compliance left her lips, followed by an ecstatic sigh of gratification when he moved. He changed position to hit her at another angle and she jerked and moaned with pleasure, hearing herself, inwardly cringing for herself but wanting him and that feeling so powerfully she couldn't fight her own hunger. The waves of pleasure rolled faster and faster, the sensual power of him overwhelming. Her climax engulfed her like an avalanche driving all before it, emptying her of thought, breaking her down into a blissful bundle of pure satisfaction. In the aftermath she was weighted to the bed by Apollo and she decided she might never want to move again.

He scooped her up and slotted her into bed, kneeling over her to almost frantically wrench himself out of what remained of his clothing. That achieved, he crushed her mouth under his again. 'Hope you're not tired,' he breathed in a driven undertone. 'I think I could go all night…'

They were at peace again. Apollo told himself that that had been his ultimate goal but he already knew that what he craved most was the joy of sinking into her honeyed depths again. There was simply something about her, something that acted on him like an aphrodisiac. He wasn't going to think about it. Why should he? What was the point? Fabulous sex didn't need to be dissected: it simply *was*. Gritting his teeth, he slowly edged an arm round her and she didn't need much of an invitation after that. In fact she scooted across the divide between them and clamped to the side of him like a landmine, doing all the work for him, he conceded in relief.

'Women like hugs,' Vito had told him as if it were some great secret known only to the precious few. Apollo didn't like hugging women but he believed he could learn to pretend that he did…particularly if it encouraged sex, he reflected with a sudden wolfish grin. *Be nice,* Holly had told him without much apparent hope that he could possibly deliver on that suggestion.

But when it came to strategy, Apollo was very much on a level with Vito in business. He had misjudged his audience when he'd waited for Pixie to throw a jealous scene at the club, had actually felt pretty offended when she'd failed to deliver on that front but he wouldn't make that mistake again. No, he would listen and observe and learn until their marriage became much more civilised and both of them got what they wanted out of the arrangement. That was the rational approach and designed to provide the most desirable result, he reasoned with satisfaction.

While Apollo was deliberating with what he believed to be perfect rationality, Pixie was feeling as irrational as a bunch of dandelion seeds left to blow hither and thither in the wind. She had no guidance, no foundation stone for the strong feelings that assailed her when Apollo, apparently quite naturally, wrapped both arms tightly around her. He made her feel safe. He made her feel as if he cared. He made her feel as if she was indeed special. And even though the common sense in her hind brain was already sneering that she was nothing in comparison with the leggy, glamorous underwear models of the type he favoured, she was happy for the first time in a long time, happy instead of just getting through the day…

She decided she wasn't going to waste energy worrying or picking herself apart with self-loathing criticisms. He was right on one thing: she wanted *him*. And if their marriage was to work on any level they had to have that chemistry and use it accordingly. A lean hand smoothed down her spine and she quivered and stopped thinking altogether.

Apollo had already laid the trail and Hector was becoming an old hand at following treat trails.

The scruffy little animal crept out from his roofed hidey hole of a basket and snuffled up the treats, inching half under Apollo's desk while Apollo pretended to ignore his progress. Every week the little terrier dared to move a little closer to the male who terrified him—not that Apollo took that personally. Hector was uniformly terrified of every man that came into his vicinity and considerably more trusting of the female sex. He had first bonded with Pixie in the vet surgery where his injuries had been tended. Pixie had worked next door and, being friendly with the veterinary nurse, had often visited the homeless dogs in their cages. Although Pixie had worked and did not have a garden, the vet had deemed her a good prospective owner because Hector had taken to her immediately.

At least, though, Hector was rather more predictable than Pixie, Apollo conceded with a frown.

He could see that Pixie didn't really trust anything he said. It was as if she was fully convinced that he could never be anything other than a womaniser, as if she believed he carried some genetic flaw that made him unsuitable for any other purpose, and it was quietly driving him crazy. He had never met a woman so resistant to his attempts to change her mind about him. In bed, she was his perfect match, the only woman he had ever met as highly sexed as he was, but beyond that bedroom door she was blind to his best efforts. He tossed a squeaky toy across the desk in Hector's direction. He was expecting the dog to run away from it but Hector took him by surprise and pounced with apparent glee on the toy and pummelled it with his paws, seemingly pleased by the frantic squeaking that resulted.

Pixie stretched a daring toe out of the bed and slowly sat up, checking her newly unreliable body for the roiling wave of sickness that had attacked her on several occasions throughout the week. Even though she stood up equally slowly, that was still when the nausea hit and with a groan she raced for the bathroom. After a shower she got dressed, her stomach restored to normality again. Was she pregnant? If she was, she could only be at a very early stage and she doubted that she could already be suffering from nausea. Her hopes, after all, had been dashed after the first couple of weeks of their marriage passed and her cycle kicked in as normal. It had seemed incredible to her even then that all that sex hadn't led straight to conception. This time, however, her period was a little late but not late enough to risk raising false hopes, so she had said nothing to Apollo as yet.

A false alarm would be embarrassing but what was really bothering her was the disturbing suspicion that even if she *had* conceived she still wouldn't want to rush into telling him. And why would that be?

Pixie coloured as she pulled on shorts and a tee and then dried her hair. No, she still wasn't using the onboard beauty salon for that because she had always liked doing her own hair. She was using it for other services though, she conceded, glancing at her perfectly manicured nails and equally well-groomed brows. Apollo's wealthy lifestyle was slowly but surely overtaking the former ordinary informality of hers. It scared her to accept that she was becoming accustomed to wearing designer clothes and expensive jewellery. Apollo called it 'looking the part' and she had to agree that nobody would take their marriage seriously if she went around dressed like a beggar or a bag lady. But even so, sometimes she felt as though she was losing an essential part of herself and that would have to be her independence.

Of course, everything would change if she *was* pregnant, she told herself unhappily. Apollo would reclaim his previous life and return happily to acting like the biggest man whore in Europe. After all, once a pregnancy was achieved there would be no reason for him to stay with Pixie or settle for having only one woman in his life. There wouldn't even be a reason for him to share a bed with her any longer…it would be the effective end of their supposed marriage.

And there it was. The sad truth that lay at the heart of her anxieties. She was hopelessly in love with a husband who wasn't a real husband. She had learned so much about Apollo over the past six weeks and he was not at all like the playboy he was depicted as in the tabloids and on the gossip sites on the Internet. She had always wondered why he and Vito, who was rather serious in nature, were such close friends when at first glance as men they were so very unalike. And in temperament, family background and outlook they *were* very different but not anything like as different as Pixie had originally assumed.

Apollo supported loads of charities and the main one, she had discovered, was a charity for abused children. But the charitable cause possibly closest to his heart was an abandoned pets' sanctuary he had set up in Athens. On the Metraxis island of Nexos he had also established a therapy centre where the more damaged animals were rehabilitated and she couldn't wait to visit it and possibly pick up a few tips from the professionals there on how best to handle Hector's fear. It was hard facts of that nature that had begun to eradicate Pixie's former hostile distrust of Apollo.

Ever since that evening at the nightclub when they had both lost their tempers, the mood had changed between them. They had not been apart for even a night since then. Pixie's mouth quirked. She wasn't sure Apollo could get by one night without sex. Or that she could. Indeed the stormy fizzing passion they shared in bed thrilled her almost as much as it could still unnerve her. Naturally they still fought on occasion but in every way their relationship seemed so normal that it was a continual battle for Pixie to remember that their marriage wasn't really a marriage at all, but a business arrangement with the ultimate goal of conception and a very firm end date.

Her brother, Patrick, however, wasn't aware of those facts and brother and sister talked regularly on the phone. Since the wedding her brother had become more honest, finally admitting that he did have a problem with gambling. Patrick was now seeing an addiction counsellor and attending Gamblers Anonymous on a regular basis. Although Pixie had been furious when she'd realised that Apollo had confronted her brother about his issues without consulting her, she had changed her mind on that score, deciding that even though she hadn't liked Apollo's methods his approach had been the right one. After all, but for Apollo's intervention she wouldn't even have known that her sibling was still gambling. Furthermore, given advice and support, Patrick now had a much better chance of overcoming his gambling dependency and living a happier and much safer life.

It probably wasn't even slightly surprising that she had fallen so hard for Apollo, Pixie reflected ruefully. He was her first lover, her first *everything* and like any legendary stud he had buckets of charisma when he tried to impress. And that was what she couldn't afford to forget, Pixie reminded herself doggedly: Apollo was *faking* it for her benefit and his. Did he think that she was so stupid that she didn't know that?

Obviously every seemingly concerned or pleasant thing he had done around her was a giant fake!

After all, the stress and strain of a bad relationship could prevent her from getting pregnant while simple strife would keep her out of his bed. So, when she had dived off the top deck of *Circe* to surprise him because she was a very proficient swimmer and diver and Apollo had gone ballistic at the supposed dangerous risk he had deemed her to have taken, his evident concern for what might have happened to her couldn't possibly have been genuine. If she killed herself diving it would be inconvenient for him but with his resources and attraction he would quickly replace her, Pixie thought, miserably melodramatic in the mood she was in.

In the same way, the many trips they had shared, stopping off to swim and picnic in secluded coves and explore enchanting little villages on various Greek islands were not to be taken too seriously. Apollo enjoyed showing off the beauties of his homeland and was a great deal better educated than she had initially appreciated. She had discovered that he could give her chapter and verse on every ancient Greek or Roman site they came on. Her fingers fiddled restively with the little gold and diamond tiger pendant she wore. He had given her that a week after that nightclub scene, telling her that she was much more than a kitten with claws. Since she had scored his back in the heat of passion with her nails the night before he had given it to her she had laughed in appreciation. And that had annoyed Apollo, something she seemed to do sometimes without even meaning to, she acknowledged with regret.

But then, undeniably, Apollo was mercurial and volatile, passionate and outspoken and still in many ways a mystery and a contradiction to Pixie. He was a billionaire with every luxury at his command and yet he could picnic on a beach quite happily with a rough bottle of the village vino, home-baked bread and a salad scattered with the salty local cheese. He clearly loved dogs and could have owned a select pack of pedigreed animals without any need of therapy, but he had not owned a dog since childhood and seemed to prefer to spend his time trying to win Hector's trust. And Hector was the most ordinary of ordinary little terriers with the scrappy stubborn nature of his breed and he was extremely reluctant to change his defensive habits.

The door opened and Pixie scrambled up as her dog trailed after Apollo into the room. Hector wouldn't go *to* Apollo but he was quite happy to follow him at a safe distance. Clad in tailored chino pants and an open-necked black shirt, Apollo slanted her a reproving grin. 'What's with all this sleeping in every morning? You didn't join me for breakfast again,' he complained.

'Maybe you're wearing me out,' Pixie quipped.

His green eyes gleamed like jewels fringed by lush black lashes in his lean, strong face. 'Am I too demanding?' he suddenly asked with a frown.

And Pixie went pink, dismay assailing her because she had been teasing. 'No more than I am,' she muttered, her eyes veiling as she remembered wakening him up at some time of the night and taking thorough advantage of his lean, hard body to satisfy the need that never entirely receded in his radius.

Apollo wrapped a careless arm round her shoulders. 'I do like an honest woman,' he confessed with husky sensual recollection.

'No, what you like is being my only object of desire,' Pixie corrected, her body sliding into the lean, hard embrace of his as if it were programmed to do so.

He bent his dark head and claimed her bee-stung mouth with a hungry thoroughness that tightened her nipples and ran like fire to the heart of her and she trembled against his hard, muscular frame, suddenly weak again in a way she hated. She denied herself the desire to put her arms round him. She didn't want Apollo to know how she felt about him because that would inevitably make their relationship uncomfortable. Hadn't she promised him that she wouldn't turn clingy or needy? And that she had no intention of falling for him? Even worse, she thought painfully, she had truly believed she could deliver on those pledges of faith in his undesirability.

Her incredibly tender breasts ached with a mixture of oversensitivity and swelling desire when he crushed her to him with sudden force and for a split second she knew he could have done anything he wanted with her because she had no resistance and no longer any defences to fall back on to support her.

It was disconcerting when Apollo set her back from him in an uncharacteristic move of restraint. 'No,' he breathed in a fractured undertone. 'I came down to bring you up on deck. I want you to see the island for the first time as we come into harbour.'

And Pixie understood why he had backed off even though it did make her feel a little like an overdose of sugar being rejected by someone who had decided to go on a diet. In truth she had always accepted, she thought ruefully, that Apollo *could* resist her if he chose to do so and naturally that hurt her pride and her heart, but it was also a fact of life she had better learn to live with. After all, if she had already conceived she suspected their actual future as a couple could be measured in days rather than months.

Furthermore, the island of Nexos, the home of the Metraxis family for several generations, was hugely important to Apollo and probably one of the main reasons he had married her. Without a wife and a child he could not securely claim his heritage.

Pixie stood out on deck with the bright blue sky above her and the sun beating down while *Circe* powered more slowly than usual towards the island spread before them. Apollo slid his arms round her from behind and she leant back against him to be more comfortable, her keen and curious gaze scanning the pine trees edging the sandy beach at one end of the island and the rocky cliffs towering at the other. In the middle there was greenery and silvery olive groves and a fair-sized village climbing the hill behind the harbour—little white cube houses stretching in all directions while a little domed stone church presided over the flat land at the water's edge.

'It's beautiful,' she murmured dreamily.

'I didn't properly appreciate Nexos as my home until I thought about losing it,' Apollo intoned grimly. 'If I'd confided more in my father he would not have left that will as his final testament to me.'

'It doesn't matter now, not really,' Pixie reasoned, hopelessly eager to provide comfort when she recognised the emotional undertow of regret in his dark deep drawl. 'Maybe your father simply knew what bait to put on the hook.'

Apollo burst out laughing without the smallest warning and gazed down at the top of her golden head. 'I doubt if he appreciated you would be less than five foot tall and a hairdresser. A talented one though, I must admit, *koukla mou*,' he added, clearly worried that he had hurt her feelings and that she had interpreted that reminder of her more humble beginnings as a put-down. 'As bait you have proved as efficient as a torpedo under the water line.'

Destructive? Was that how he saw her? Was that because he had confided in her about his evil stepmothers? Or because he had shown her that he was as vulnerable as any other human being in childhood? And as amazingly loveable, she conceded wretchedly, worry dragging her down again along with the fear of the separation she saw waiting on the horizon.

CHAPTER NINE

'YOU SHOULD CHANGE before we disembark,' Apollo urged. 'The press will be waiting at the harbour.'

'The *press*?' Pixie emphasised, eyes flying wide. 'Why would they be waiting?'

'I issued a press release about our marriage last week,' Apollo admitted. 'They'll want a photo since I saw no reason to be that generous.'

'I thought Nexos was a private island,' Pixie admitted tautly, disconcerted at the prospect of camera lenses being trained on her for she had yet to be photographed in Apollo's company. That was undoubtedly because Apollo hated the paparazzi and knew exactly where to go to avoid attracting that kind of attention.

'It is but not as private as it was in my grandfather's day. The islanders need to make a living and my father began letting tourists in twenty years ago. I accelerated that process by building an eco-resort on the other side of the island,' he revealed calmly. 'The years of the locals getting by fishing and farming are long gone. Not unnaturally their children want more.'

'And even if that infringes on your privacy on your island you let them have it,' Pixie remarked in surprise.

'It doesn't infringe. The Metraxis estate is very secure but owning an island with an indigenous population comes with responsibility. The people have to have a future they can count on for their children or the younger generation will leave. My father didn't really grasp that reality.'

Pixie stepped into the motor launch twenty minutes later, clad in print silk trousers with a toning shirt worn over a camisole and a sunhat that she had to hang onto as the launch sped across the gleaming clear turquoise water into the harbour. She tensed when she saw just how many people seemed to be grouped there ready to greet them. It dawned on her that in her guise as Apollo's wife she probably seemed a much more important person to the locals than she actually was.

'Don't answer any questions whatsoever. Ignore the cameras,' Apollo urged, lifting her into his arms to carry her off the launch before she could make for the steps under her own steam.

Flushed and uneasy, Pixie regained her feet and Apollo's bodyguards swung into action to keep the photographers at a careful distance. With the indolent cool of a male accustomed to the press invading his privacy, Apollo dropped an arm round her shoulders and walked her off the marina at an unhurried pace. He exchanged greetings in his own language with several people but he did not once pause in his determined progress towards the four-wheel drive parked in readiness beyond the crush.

Pixie, however, had never been so uneasily conscious of being the centre of attention and she was hopelessly intimidated by the shouted questions and comments in different languages. She felt the wall of stares being directed at her and her tummy gave a sick lurch. She suspected that she had to be a pretty disappointing spectacle for people who had probably expected Apollo to marry an heiress or a model and, at the very least, someone famous, incredibly beautiful and photogenic. Possessing none of those gifts, she felt horribly exposed and all the more aware that she was a fake wife, pregnant or otherwise.

Only when they were inside the car did she breathe again.

'See…that wasn't so bad,' Apollo pointed out with a shrug that perfectly illustrated his indifference to that amount of concentrated interest and speculation.

'I'll take your word for it… I found it tough,' Pixie responded honestly. 'I'm not used to being looked at like that and knowing I am a totally phony wife doesn't add to my confidence.'

'When will you listen to me?' Apollo shot back at her in exasperation. 'You're my *legal* wife!'

Pixie breathed in slow and deep to calm her racing nerves and turned her head to look out of the car windows. Apollo had taught her that a legal wife still wasn't a *real* wife.

'And you will never leave our estate without bodyguards…is that understood? Not even for a walk down into the village,' Apollo specified.

'Is that level of security really necessary?' 'Our' estate, he had said, she noted in surprise, and then wrote it off as either a slip of the tongue or a comment designed to make her feel more relaxed about their living arrangements.

'There's always a risk of paparazzi in the village or even a tourist photographing you to make a profit. My security team are trained to handle all that and ensure that nobody gets to bother you.'

The car was travelling up a steep incline and electric gates whirred back while Pixie gazed at the big white rambling villa at the top of the hill. It was certainly large but it wasn't anywhere near as massive as Vito's giant palazzo in Tuscany and she was relieved. As she stepped out, one of the bodyguards lifted Hector's carrier from the four-wheel drive and set it down to release him. Hector raced out and gambolled round Pixie's ankles, relieved to have escaped his brief imprisonment.

They walked into a grand marble-floored space with staircases sweeping down on either side of the hall and a very opulent chandelier. A housekeeper, dressed in black with a white apron, greeted them and was introduced as Olympia. Apollo spoke to her at length in Greek while Pixie succumbed to curiosity and crossed the hall to peep into rooms. She had never seen so many dead white walls in her life or such bland furnishings. Indeed the interior had the appearance of a house that served as a show home.

Apollo frowned as he examined her expressive face. 'You don't like it? Then you can change it. I had it all stripped, painted and refurnished while my father was ill. Every one of his wives had different decorating ideas and favourite rooms and the house was a mess of clashing colours and styles. When he was well enough to come down for dinner I realised that the décor awakened unfortunate memories so I wiped the slate clean for his benefit.'

'Well, all that white and beige is certainly clean,' Pixie assured him gently, rather touched by his thoughtfulness on his ailing father's behalf.

'I'll show you round,' he proffered, walking her from room to room, and there really was very little to look at in the big colourless rooms. There were no photographs, no ornaments, only an occasional vase of beautiful flowers.

'I thought the house would be much larger,' she confided as he walked her upstairs. 'Holly said you had a lot of relatives.'

'Relatives and friends use the guest cottages behind

the house. My grandfather and my father preferred to have only family members lodge in the actual house. Vito and Holly stayed here with me for the funeral because Vito is the closest thing I have to a brother,' he admitted quietly, his handsome mouth quirking. 'But don't go repeating that or he'll get too big for his boots.'

Pixie laughed as he showed her into a spacious bedroom with a balcony running the entire length. The pale curtains beside the open doors streamed back in the breeze coming in off the ocean. She stepped outside to appreciate the incredible bird's eye view of Nexos and the sea and understood exactly why Apollo's grandfather had chosen that spot to build his family home. 'It is really gorgeous,' she murmured. 'But this place could definitely do with some pictures on the walls and other stuff just to take the bare look away.'

'The canvases are stored in the basement but run it by me before you have anything rehung,' Apollo countered. 'There are portraits of the ex-wives, which I have no desire to see again…and certain artworks fall into the same category,' he completed tight-mouthed.

Pixie rested a tiny hand on his. 'This is your home. The ex-wives are gone now and won't be coming back, so forget about them.'

Apollo bit out an embittered laugh. 'Only if I contrive to produce a child…and who knows whether or not that will be possible?'

Pixie pinned her lips together and stared out to sea and then she couldn't hold the words bubbling on her tongue back any longer. 'There may be a slim chance that this month…well, don't go getting excited yet *but* I am a little late…'

Apollo stared down at her transfixed by even the slender possibility that she had outlined. 'And you didn't even mention it to me until now?' he demanded in seething disbelief.

'Because we don't need to put ourselves through some silly false alarm, do we?' Pixie appealed.

Apollo shook his head as if he couldn't identify with that attitude. His black hair blew back from his lean bronzed features as he leant back against the glass barrier, his green eyes jewel bright in the sunlight. He dug out his phone, stabbed buttons with impatience and started talking in fast Greek while she watched, frowning in bewilderment.

'Dr Floros will come up with a test for us this afternoon.'

'But I'm only a couple of days late,' Pixie protested.

'Even *I* know that that's usually soon enough to tell us one way or the other,' Apollo pronounced. 'Why sit around wondering any longer?'

Well, you chose to open your big mouth and spill, Pixie censured herself unhappily. He would either be very pleased or very disappointed. It was out of her hands now.

'You have to learn the habit of *sharing* these things with me,' Apollo breathed in an almost raw undertone, green eyes veiled and narrowed as he stared down at her.

'Didn't I just do that?'

'Obviously you've been thinking about this on your own for a few days and that's not how I want you to behave, *koukla mou*. The minute anything worries you bring it to me.'

But even as Apollo gazed down at Pixie, his big frame was stiffening and he was losing colour because ill-starred memories were being stirred up by their predicament. He had quite deliberately closed out the awareness that sometimes women died in childbirth: his mother had. More than once his father, Vassilis had discussed that tragedy with his son. Vassilis had idolised Apollo's mother and he had never really come to terms with losing her in such terrible circumstances. At the moment when he should have been happiest with his wife and his newborn child he had been plunged into grief.

'What's wrong?' Pixie asked abruptly, watching sharp tension tighten the sculpted lines of Apollo's lean, hard face.

'Nothing. I forgot,' Apollo said equally abruptly, 'I have a couple of work calls to make. Will you be all right settling in here on your own?'

'Of course I will be.'

Apollo strode down the stairs like a hungry lion in search of prey. If Pixie was pregnant, there would be no home birth, he reasoned with immediate resolve. No, she was going to a fully equipped hospital regardless of how she felt about that decision. He would also engage a standby medical team. He wouldn't take any risks with her because he was too conscious that something quite unexpected could happen during a birth. He wouldn't mention that to Pixie though. He wasn't that stupid. He didn't want her worrying and certainly not to the extent *he* was suddenly worrying.

For a split second he was grudgingly amused by his own attitude. He had married Pixie to have a child and now that there was a chance they might have succeeded at step one, he was suddenly awash with anxiety. She was so small…and the baby could be big as he had been… and now he needed a drink.

By the time Pixie had watched her luggage being unpacked, enjoyed a cup of tea on the shaded terrace alone and even taken Hector for a walk through the meandering gardens with tree-lined paths alone, she had accepted that Apollo was not as excited by the concept of becoming a father as she was excited about becoming a mother. He had vanished like Scotch mist and she felt that they did not have the kind of marriage that empowered her to go looking for him as a normal wife might have done. Looking for Apollo any place struck Pixie as clingy and she refused to act clingy.

Dr Floros arrived, middle-aged and bearded and relentlessly cheerful even in the face of Apollo's grave demeanour. Yes, Apollo had finally reappeared and Pixie could not help but notice that her husband was as grim as a pall-bearer in comparison to the chirpy medical man. Maybe the actual prospect of a child was a little sobering for a playboy, Pixie reasoned uncertainly as she took the test and vanished into the palatial cloakroom on the ground floor. It would be foolish of her to think that he had lost his original enthusiasm for conception. That wasn't possible, was it?

'My wife is very small in size,' Apollo remarked to the doctor while Pixie was absent.

'Nature has a wonderful way of taking such differences into account,' Dr Floros assured him without concern. 'I'll take a blood test as well if the result is positive.'

Pixie watched the test wand change colour, but since the packaging and instructions were in Greek she had no idea what was a positive and what was a negative and had to return in continuing ignorance to the two men.

Dr Floros beamed before she even reached them. 'Congratulations!' he pronounced in English.

Pixie felt a little dizzy at the confirmation that she was going to be a mother and she sat down hurriedly, her attention locked to Apollo's lean, strong face. He froze, betraying nothing, neither smiling nor even wincing in reaction and she wanted to slap him for it. Apollo explained about the blood test and Pixie stood up a little nervously because she didn't like needles. Indeed Dr Floros only got as far as flourishing his syringe before Pixie felt faint, her knees wobbling so obviously that Apollo gripped her to steady her.

'Are you all right?'

And no, she wasn't all right because at that point she fainted and resurfaced lying on a sofa.

'Don't look at the needle...' Apollo urged, quick as always to identify the source of her fear, and he crouched down beside her and held her hand as tightly as if she were drowning.

The test was done. She apologised to the doctor and he said it was probably the combination of the good news and stress that had made her pass out. Dr Floros departed and Apollo reappeared with Olympia carrying a pot of tea.

'You could say something now,' Pixie prompted when they were finally alone.

Apollo frowned. 'About what?'

'Well, it did only take us six weeks...you could look happy, look *pleased*!' Pixie emphasised in annoyance.

'I am pleased,' Apollo assured her unconvincingly. 'But not if it makes you ill and you collapse like that. That was scary.'

'I didn't exactly enjoy it. I hate needles and injections and I felt so dizzy and then everything went dark,' Pixie explained rather curtly. 'I'm not about to be ill. I'm simply pregnant and there are a few symptoms that come with that. Dizziness is one of them. Holly was always getting light-headed.'

'Luckily we have a lift, so you won't have to use the stairs.'

Pixie studied him in wonderment. 'You expect me to use a lift to go up or down one floor? Are you crazy?'

'You could *fall* on the stairs,' Apollo traded with deadly seriousness.

'Thank you, Mr Cheerful.' Pixie rested her head back and tried to imagine becoming a mother. She wasn't about to let Apollo's strange lack of enthusiasm take the edge off her sense of joy and achievement. A baby, a darling, gorgeous little baby who was hers *and* his. She couldn't keep Apollo but she *could* keep their baby. She was happy, really, really happy about that aspect and suspected it would be something of a comfort in the future when Apollo was no longer a constant part of her life.

There would be a divorce first, she reminded herself doggedly. Then she would have to get accustomed to seeing him with other women in tabloid pictures, knowing he was sharing a bed with them while also knowing exactly what he was doing with them there. Doubtless he would phone her to keep up to date with their child's development and from time to time he would visit in person until the child was old enough to go and visit him. It would all be very civilised and polite but she was already painfully aware that losing Apollo would smash her heart to smithereens!

Apollo studied the tears rolling down Pixie's cheeks as she stared up at the ceiling. She wasn't happy about being pregnant and he wondered why he had expected otherwise. She liked kids, he knew she did, but then they weren't having a child in the most ideal circumstances, he reminded himself grimly. She was having a child she would pretty much raise alone and possibly she felt trapped because at her age most women were young, single and free as the air.

A chilling shot of rage assailed Apollo at the image of

Pixie reclaiming her freedom after a divorce and becoming intimate with another man. He had the strangest possessive feelings where she was concerned, he conceded in bemusement. For some reason too he was feeling as exhausted as if he had climbed a mountain. Somehow Pixie being pregnant was incredibly stressful. No, worse than stressful, *frightening*, he adjusted in consternation. For the first time it occurred to him that Vito had been saved from such concerns by only entering his son Angelo's life when the baby was already six months old. Was it normal for a first-time father to feel on the edge of panic? He crushed the reaction and went into denial.

'By the way, we're having a big party here in a few weeks,' Apollo announced in a determined change of subject. 'I organised it last month.'

'Thanks for sharing *after* the event,' Pixie said sarcastically.

'I've invited friends and family here to celebrate our marriage but I didn't fancy a wedding-type event,' Apollo confided with a cynical twist of his mouth. 'I settled on a fancy-dress party for a theme.'

'Oh, joy…' Pixie mumbled sleepily as she turned her face into a cushion, presenting him with her narrow back.

'I've taken care of our outfits,' Apollo told her with pride, relieved she would not be put to the worry of wondering what she should wear and very much hoping that she would appreciate the amount of trouble he had gone to.

'Your way or the highway,' Pixie whispered unappreciatively. 'Don't worry. I knew what a control freak you were the day I married you.'

Apollo surveyed Hector, who was seated on the rug, his little face seemingly anxious. *You and me too, buddy,* Apollo thought wryly while he wondered if it was possible that Pixie could roll off the sofa and hurt herself while she slept. For the first time in his life concern was weighing him down like a big grey cloud closing out the sun. He had never truly had to worry about anyone but his father but now he had a wife and a child on the way. He thought it extraordinary that achieving the pregnancy required to fulfil the terms of his father's will should suddenly and quite inexplicably feel, not like a prize, but more like a poisoned chalice.

Apollo came to bed in the early hours. Having persuaded herself that he might not even choose to still share the same room, Pixie was lying sleepless watching the moonlight glimmer through the shadows. She listened to him in the shower, watched him stride naked towards the bed and sensual heat curled low in her body because she could see that he was aroused.

Apollo slid quietly into bed and lay there, thoroughly irritated by the throbbing at his groin. Pixie was pregnant, fragile and definitely *off-limits*. But it was as if she had lit a fire in him the first time they had had sex. It was a fire only she could seem to cool and that knowledge seriously disturbed him. Throughout his adult life Apollo had viewed sex as a casual diversion from more important activities. Sex had always been easily available and his libido had never homed in on one particular woman. His life had been wonderfully simple, he reflected grimly. He would see a woman he wanted, enjoy her for a while and when he got bored move on to the next. And now, for some peculiar reason, he wasn't getting bored any more...and he was feeling urges he had no desire to feel.

Pixie shifted across the bed inch by inch, wishing it weren't quite so big. Her hand settled on the male shoulder furthest from her and slowly drifted down over Apollo's magnificent torso. She smiled as she felt his hard muscles ripple and tense across his abdomen.

He turned towards her and his eyes glittered in the moonlight. 'We shouldn't,' he breathed with sudden amusement.

'Don't be silly,' Pixie whispered, her tiny hand heading further south to find the long, jutting length of him and stroke. 'I'm pregnant, not breakable.'

Apollo groaned out loud and arched his lean hips while watching her slide below the sheet to administer an even more potent invitation and that fast his once renowned self-control broke like a dam breaking its banks. He tugged Pixie up to him with shuddering impatience and rolled her under him while his hungry mouth tasted hers with heated urgency.

'That's more like it,' Pixie commented a shade smugly as she gazed up at him, her fingers skimming caressingly through his damp, tousled hair. She felt lighter than air at the ego-boosting confirmation that he still wanted her. Intelligence warned her that he was a young healthy male, who was usually in the mood for sex, but she refused to think about that angle, choosing to concentrate instead on the soothing conviction that pregnancy wasn't quite the turn-off she had feared.

'There is only one way this can continue,' Apollo decreed, resting her back against the pillows. 'You lie there… *I* do the work, *koukla mou*.'

And it was amazing, she thought much later, drifting into an exhausted and gratified sleep, but then it always was amazing with Apollo.

Apollo held her while she slept and marvelled at how natural it had become to hold her close. One large hand splayed across her flat stomach. How had he ever believed that he could walk away untouched after conception occurred? How had he credited that he could bring a child into the world and not want to play a full part in his son or daughter's life? The unquestioning arrogance of those selfish assumptions belatedly savaged his view of himself. As fond memories of moments with his own father while he was still a little boy drifted through his mind he finally understood Vassilis Metraxis's almost primitive need to safeguard the continuation of the family line, and he also grasped that walking away at any stage from his own child wasn't an option he would ever be able to live with.

CHAPTER TEN

THREE WEEKS LATER, Pixie blinked sleepily into wakefulness and finally sat up to make a grab for the phone ringing while ruefully contemplating the empty space beside her. It was forty-eight hours since Apollo had flown to London on business. Pixie would have accompanied him had the whole household not been in chaos getting ready for the big party the following day. With the housekeeper, Olympia, presenting Pixie with query after query it had slowly dawned on her that she needed to stay on Nexos to take charge.

'Nonsense,' Apollo had declared without hesitation. 'These matters have been managed without a wife's input for years.'

But during that conversation Pixie had had to race off and be horribly sick, which had driven home hard another drawback. Hours of travel with her current delicate stomach would make her miserable and she was in no hurry to face Apollo with the repugnant downside of pregnancy. She was being ill an awful lot more than she had ever expected because her morning sickness seemed to attack at all times of the day. For that reason she had used the party arrangements as an excuse because she didn't want Apollo to realise just how sick she was. While in her head she knew she should be sharing her suffering with him because he was an adult, it was a struggle to overcome her reluctance. He would fuss and she hated fuss and didn't want to be treated like an invalid. In any case they had arranged for Pixie to have her first scan that very afternoon and she planned to ask the visiting gynaecologist then about her seemingly excessive sickness.

Pixie put the phone to her ear.

'Pixie?' Holly exclaimed before bursting into a mile-a-minute speech that left Pixie, who was still drowsy, none the wiser.

'Sorry, I didn't catch all that,' she confided.

'You've seen that stupid story already, haven't you?' Holly groaned. 'Your voice sounds weird…you've been crying…'

A cold feeling slid down Pixie's spine while she leant back against the pillows, striving to overcome the nausea beginning to creep over her. It would've been easier for her to simply admit that she was pregnant and sick but her best friend would be arriving the next day for the party and she wanted to save her baby news until she saw her in person. 'What story?'

'Vito insists it's untrue…well, with that particular girl.'

'Can I phone you back, Holly?' Pixie gasped, cutting off the call and leaping from the bed in wild haste to charge for the bathroom.

Afterwards, she rested her brow down on the welcome coldness of the marble vanity counter and tried to muster the energy to clean her teeth. Oh, dear, she thought limply, it had not occurred to her that pregnancy would be quite so challenging. Certainly Holly had had a few upsets during her pregnancy but nothing similar to what Pixie was encountering.

And what had Holly been referring to? Some story in a newspaper? About Vito? No, why would she be phoning Pixie if it had been about Vito? And why would Holly think she had been *crying* about something? The chilled feeling of foreboding returned and as Pixie's brain began to function again she reached for the tablet by the bed and put Apollo's name in the search engine. The usual flock of references came up. She knew from experience that if she wanted to she could now access images of herself arriving on Nexos looking like a skinny bird in a very big sun hat that covered her face almost completely...

She sat on the edge of the bed while a tabloid page formed under the title 'Leopards don't change their spots...' And with perspiration breaking out on her clammy skin she read about how the newly married Apollo Metraxis had been pictured entering his apartment building with a very beautiful girl and emerging with her still in tow the following morning. For a few moments she thought she would be sick again but she fought the urge fiercely.

So, what she had always expected to happen *had* happened within only a few months of their wedding. It was no big deal, she told herself squarely and, casting the tablet aside, she went for a shower. Apollo had said he would try to be faithful but the very first time he had had to leave her behind he had found alternative entertainment of the sort he was most accustomed to enjoying. His behaviour sent a powerful message. Clearly, Pixie was no more important or special to him than any other woman he had slept with. How could she ever have thought otherwise?

And Izzy Jerome *was* a very beautiful girl with long corn-blonde hair and endless legs. She was also famous, a fairly recently discovered model/celebrity. Apollo's type in every way. Well, she wasn't about to make a giant scene over Izzy or do anything silly, Pixie warned herself severely. It was time to default to their original marriage setting in which they shared a business arrangement and nothing else. At least she could save face that way, she reasoned in despair, a sudden convulsive sob creeping up on her and squeezing her throat painfully tight.

But she wasn't going to cry over Apollo, Pixie told herself angrily. He wasn't worth her tears. He was selfish and shallow and his betrayal had literally been written in the stars because she had always been well aware that leopards didn't change their spots. The phone was ringing again somewhere in the distance but she ignored it, sitting on the shower seat while the water beat down on her and washed away the shameful tears. A sob escaped her straining lungs and she clenched her teeth in frustration. There was no way she was prepared to greet Apollo with red-rimmed eyes that would tell him just how badly he had hurt her.

And willpower did finally triumph over the tears. She switched off the shower and stepped out to grab a towel but only minutes later found herself throwing up again. Utterly wretched, she curled up on the cold floor for several minutes with Hector nuzzling against her legs. She petted him with a shaking hand. She felt dizzy and sick and dreadful but she wasn't about to show it. Apollo had done her a favour, she reasoned miserably. Her body was already changing. Her breasts had swelled, her waist had thickened and her tummy was no longer perfectly flat. Apollo would soon have lost interest in her anyway and it was better that it happened sooner rather than later.

After all, she had to learn to be independent again and stand on her own feet. Her baby would need her to be strong and brave. She had to cope and rise above the terrible hurt trying to overwhelm her common sense. He didn't love her; he had *never* loved her. The only woman Apollo had ever loved had been the evil stepmother who used him when he was far too young and immature to protect himself and had destroyed his trust and his ability to love. Was it any wonder that he had never had a serious relationship with a woman since then?

Slowly, clumsily, Pixie got herself upright again and began to dry her hair. Apollo would be home in a couple of hours with the gynaecologist he was flying out from London with him and she refused to humiliate herself by behaving like an emotional wreck and letting him appreciate what a fool she had been where he was concerned. Her pride would never recover from such an exposure. And how could she have fallen madly in love with a male programmed from the outset to break her heart? How stupid was that?

And even worse she had that wretched party to get through. As if that was not enough Apollo had contrived to destroy Christmas for her as well for the two of them had been invited to celebrate Christmas with Vito and Holly in Tuscany. Of course she would cry off now. She had no plans to take the shine off the festivities by attending as a betrayed and broken-hearted wife, who had nowhere else to go over Christmas. Apollo would probably take Izzy Jerome with him instead. Of course, Izzy might not still be Apollo's flavour of the month in three weeks' time, she thought wretchedly. His interest in a woman rarely lasted that long.

Squeezing herself into a stretchy skirt, Pixie blinked back fresh tears. Why was she putting on weight so fast? According to what she had read she was supposed to be gaining weight very gradually, not piling it on as though she had been eating for an entire rugby team!

In London, Apollo paced beside his private jet while he spoke to Vito. Who could ever have guessed that marriage could be so stressful? His life pre-Pixie now seemed free as the air, a time of immaturity and egotism. Back then nothing had bothered him very much, not the scandals, not the grasping women, not even the horrendous rumours and gossip about his lifestyle. He hadn't had to explain himself or defend his reputation to anyone because he truthfully hadn't cared what anyone thought about him. It hadn't mattered as long as he knew that he had done no wrong. But now he had Pixie and everything had changed out of all recognition. He had a wife who was pregnant and vulnerable and innately distrustful of him.

'The way the paparazzi follow you around it was bound to happen,' Vito contended. 'And now that you've achieved your objectives and she's pregnant...does it really matter?'

Pure rage slivered through Apollo. 'If it hurts her, it matters,' he breathed in a raw undertone. '*Of course*, it matters!'

'You don't sound quite as detached as you usually do,' his friend commented.

'Look, I'll talk to you tomorrow,' Apollo concluded, ending the call in sheer frustration.

Obviously, he wasn't detached. He was in turmoil. He was thinking things he'd never thought. He was feeling things he had never allowed himself to feel and the result was a state of mind dangerously close to panic. He boarded the jet with the fancy gynaecologist and his small team, yet another source of worry to be dealt with. Dr Floros had suggested that he call in a consultant when Pixie's blood tests had come back with an unexpectedly high count and the result had been forwarded to London. The scan would hopefully reveal whether or not there was any cause for concern. Apollo had persuaded the island doctor not to reveal that fact to Pixie in advance of the scan, lest it upset her, but he knew the older man was planning to share the result with her the following day.

When had his life become so impossibly complicated? An image of Pixie on their wedding day was superimposed over his troubled thoughts. But no, he reasoned, it had started even before then. From the very first day when she'd punched him Pixie had been different. She wasn't impressed by him, she was never impressed by him…except occasionally in bed, he conceded abstractedly, a shadowy smile briefly relaxing the tense line of his sensual mouth.

Unlike other women, Pixie had only ever treated him as an equal. She judged him by the same rules she applied to everyone else. She didn't make excuses for him or handle him with kid gloves. She didn't believe that his vast wealth entitled him to special treatment. In fact she demanded more from him than any woman had ever demanded, only her currency of choice wasn't cash or gifts. Apollo had learnt the hard way that cash or gifts were easy to give while everything else was a challenge demanding more than he was usually prepared to give.

During the flight random memories drifted through his mind. Pixie, grinning with triumph and punching the air after that insane dive she had made from the top deck of *Circe*. Pixie staring dreamily out to sea as the sun went down in splendour, saying, 'You really don't appreciate how lucky you are to see this every day.' Pixie wandering round the picturesque narrow village streets on Nexos, admiring colourful flowerboxes, sleeping cats, starlit eyes wide with interest while she drank lemonade in the café overlooking the harbour and watched the fishermen bringing in their catch. She made everything fresh, Apollo acknowledged in growing bewilderment; she made him see things through less jaded eyes.

Pixie could feel her facial muscles lock as she descended the stairs to welcome the arrivals. She refused to look at Apollo but she was seethingly conscious of him standing back in a stylishly crumpled beige linen suit teamed with a white tee shirt. She showed the doctor, the technician and the nurse into the room where their equipment could be set up and Olympia brought a tray of tea and snacks out to the terrace for them.

'Pixie…' Apollo said then, having demonstrated unusual patience for such an impatient man. 'Could I have a word?'

No, no way, she wanted to scream at him but she couldn't let herself scream. There would be no discussion about Izzy Jerome or about the promise he had given about *trying* to stay faithful. What was done was done and there was really nothing more to say. All she had to do now was draw a line under their marriage as such and default to the useful guidelines printed in her prenuptial contract.

'Your office,' she suggested, stealing an involuntary glance at him.

He hadn't shaved and he was still gorgeous. Dark stubble shadowed his strong jaw line and outlined his superbly kissable lips. His black hair was messy, his stunning green eyes glittering warily below his black velvet lashes. He was sexy as sin and a pang of wanton lust pierced her pelvis. Guilty colour washed her pallor away. He had cheated on her with a blonde beauty, so how could she still respond to him on a physical level? Self-loathing inflamed her while she picked her passage through the team of caterers fussing over the chairs that were being carried into the ballroom where the party would be held.

The mere prospect of the party made her grit her teeth. All those people would be attending primarily to see her in her role as the wife of Apollo Metraxis, people who would know he was already playing away with another woman, and yet Pixie would have to pretend that nothing was wrong because that was what she had agreed to do when she chose to marry him. Luckily pretending, however, would allow her to retain a certain dignity, she reminded herself doggedly.

Her visceral reaction was to scream, shout and claw at Apollo and from the curious glances he was angling at her she could see that a major scene was what he expected. But Pixie was determined not to lower herself to that level. Whatever else he was, Apollo was the father of her child and, whether she liked it or not, he would remain a feature of her life for many years in the future. She was determined not to embarrass herself in front of him by revealing that she had made the mistake of becoming emotionally involved.

'I'm relieved that you're giving us the chance to talk before Mr Rollins gives you the scan,' Apollo murmured in an unusually quiet voice.

Was he ashamed? No, Apollo didn't do shame or fidelity when it came to sex, she reasoned painfully. He was probably genuinely grateful that she wasn't making a big scene.

Pixie stationed herself by the window that looked across the sloping gardens and over the top of the trees and out to sea. She steeled her spine. 'I want us to separate—'

'No,' Apollo interrupted immediately.

'It's in the pre-nup agreement,' Pixie reminded him. 'Once I'm pregnant I can if I wish ask to live separately and I would like to return to the UK as soon as it can be arranged.'

Apollo was powerfully knocked off balance by that announcement. Yes, that was in the agreement because before he married her he had assumed that he would want his freedom back as soon as possible. Had ever a man been so bloody stupid and blind? he railed at himself in furious frustration. 'That is exactly what I *don't* want.'

Pixie rested icy grey eyes on his lean bronzed face. 'I don't care what you want.'

'You're not even giving me a chance to explain?'

'No, that kind of discussion would challenge my ability to be civil to you,' Pixie admitted hoarsely, because inside herself where it didn't show she was breaking apart. She hated him and yet she still wanted to be near him. She loathed him for betraying her and yet her weak, wanton body still hummed in direct response to the insanely hot attraction he exuded. The very thought of not seeing Apollo again for months on end threatened to rip her into tiny pieces but she knew the difference between right and wrong and she knew what she had to do to restore the boundaries she needed to feel safe.

And she could never *ever* feel safe with an unfaithful man. It didn't matter that it had only happened once, what mattered was that she had made the mistake of thinking of their marriage as a real marriage and now she was being destroyed because she loved him. But he hadn't asked her for her love or her possessiveness and he had even warned her that fidelity would be a struggle for him. How far in those circumstances could she blame him for what he had done? She had fallen for him and that was her mistake, not his.

'This is crazy…' Apollo breathed with sudden rawness, big brown hands settling over her slight shoulders. 'You won't even look at me!'

'I'm being polite.'

'That isn't you... I don't *know* you like this!' Apollo growled in frustration. 'Shout at me, kick me...whatever!'

'Why would I do that?' Pixie forced a frozen little smile to her lips. 'We've enjoyed a successful business arrangement. My brother is safe and learning how to live without gambling and I'm carrying a baby I want very much. Now you can return to the freewheeling life you prefer.'

Even though his temper was cruelly challenged by that speech, his big hands withdrew from her tense shoulders and dropped away to slowly ball into fists by his sides because he genuinely didn't want to argue with her and upset her. 'Mr Rollins should be ready for you now,' he pronounced with savage quietness.

Pixie chewed at her full lower lip, blaming him for the fact that the scan she had been eager to have had now been horribly overshadowed by his betrayal and her heartbreak. But maybe seeing the shape of her baby on a screen would restore her and cure the agony clawing up inside her. It hurt so much not to have Apollo any more. It hurt not to be able to allow herself to touch him. But a kick, never mind a kiss, would have released the pent-up rage and hurt she was holding back.

She wanted to tell him that she had gone down to the animal rehabilitation centre on the outskirts of the village while he was away and had met the staff and occupants as well as spotting a little dog very similar to Hector. She had wanted to share that with Apollo but then she wanted to share *everything* with Apollo, had in fact got used to treating him like her best friend, and in the wake of his infidelity that was a really terrifying revelation. What had happened to her pride? But now she could feel the new distance forming inside her and she clung to that barrier in desperation.

Having set up the equipment, the nurse and the technician were ready to give Pixie her scan. She got up on the mobile examination table, rested her head back on the pillow and pushed down her skirt to expose her tummy while the consultant talked smoothly about what she could expect to see. He referred to her blood test, which surprised her. Clearly he had consulted the island doctor for that result and she wondered why.

The gel the technician put on her stomach was cool and she shivered, eyes flying wide when Apollo moved forward and closed a hand over her knotted fingers. The amazing racing sound of the baby's heartbeat filled the silence and she smiled in sheer wonder. The wand moved and then the heartbeat surged again.

'Two babies, Mrs Metraxis.'

'Two?' she echoed in astonishment.

'Twins. I suspected a multiple pregnancy when I saw the results of your first blood test…'

Shocked, Pixie locked her eyes to the screen while the consultant outlined the shadowy forms of her children. Children, not one child as she had simply assumed. It was an enormous change to get her head around. She wondered if that explained the heavy nausea she was enduring and the physical changes that were already altering her body.

Apollo studied the screen in horror. Two of them? Two babies struggling to make space in Pixie's tiny body? How could that be? That had to make everything more dangerous.

Pixie yanked her hand from Apollo's because he was crushing her fingers. She glanced up at him, reading the raw tension etched in his hard features. He wasn't pleased. But then why would he be? He had only needed one child and two would presumably be more hassle and expense. The nurse wiped off the gel and helped her back to her feet. She took a seat for yet another blood test and shut her eyes tight sooner than see the needle while Apollo took up position behind her and rested his hands down heavily on her shoulders.

She told the consultant about her frequent nausea. He explained that that could occur in a twin pregnancy and that it should settle down by the end of her first trimester, but that if it began to impact on her health she would need support. He mentioned that the twins each had their own placenta, which lessened the chance of complications. The information he gave her was very practical and Pixie was happy to thank him and leave while Apollo demonstrated a dismaying eagerness to stay behind and talk to the medical team.

Apollo's blood had run cold throughout his entire body when the word 'complications' struck him like blow. He felt sick. Mr Rollins informed him unasked that sex was still perfectly fine. Ironically, Apollo had never felt less horny and he was suddenly feeling very guilty. If anything went wrong it would be his fault. He had planned this pregnancy, done everything possible to make it happen and now that he had he was discovering that he had hitched a ride on a rocket that he could no longer control. Not since his troubled childhood had he been made to feel so helpless. By the time the medical team departed on the helicopter to head back to the airport, Apollo was in a seriously sombre mood.

Pixie settled down happily with a pot of tea on the shaded terrace with Hector at her feet. Two babies, my goodness, weren't they going to be a handful? She was in shock but, after hearing her babies' heartbeats, she was excited and pleased as well. She sipped her tea and wondered if the twins would be identical or non-identical and whether they would be boys or girls or even one of each. It was a huge relief to have something other than Apollo to think about.

Apollo strode out onto the terrace and surveyed her. 'I can't let you leave me,' he intoned grimly. 'I *have* to be part of this. They are my children too. I need to be sure you're healthy and looking after yourself.'

'What about what I need?' Pixie countered, eyes narrowing as she looked back at him because he was standing in sunlight, tall and bronzed and muscular as a god in stature and so beautiful he didn't seem quite real to her.

'You need my support.'

'No, I don't. I've been independent all my life,' Pixie traded without hesitation.

Apollo leant back against the low wall separating the terrace from the garden and tossed a squeaky toy at Hector, who bounded after it with glee. 'I don't want you to be independent.'

'Tough. We made a business arrangement,' Pixie reminded him. 'Getting pregnant is my get-out-of-jail-free card and I'm playing it.'

'You're being unreasonable.'

'I love the island. I like my life here but this is *your* house, *your* island and I don't want to live in your house on your island,' Pixie explained without apology.

Apollo breathed in slow and deep and practised a patience that he was in no way accustomed to practising. 'We'll discuss it after the party tomorrow.'

Her life had fallen apart, Pixie thought, suddenly losing the high of finding out that she was carrying two babies. She was about to become a single mum, which most poignantly was something she had once sworn she would never be. But that was life, she told herself, knocking you back on your heels and changing things without warning. And she would be a liar if she argued that she couldn't have foreseen the breakdown of their marriage. After all, that breakdown had been foreseen in the prenuptial agreement she had signed and all the conditions for that breakdown laid out in advance. She had read the terms and she had even read the small print. She knew that she had rights and that Apollo couldn't ignore them.

Apollo crossed the tiles towards her and studied her with gorgeous glittering green eyes. 'I don't want this marriage to end. I don't want a divorce,' he declared. 'I don't want you to leave Nexos either.'

After a noisy pummelling session with his squeaky toy, Hector sneaked across the floor and hovered uneasily near Apollo's feet before he gingerly dropped the toy there. Muttering something shaken in Greek, Apollo stilled and then he bent, scooped it up and threw it and Hector went careening after it. 'He brought the toy to me. He *finally* brought it to me!' he exclaimed in amazement.

'I never said my dog had good taste,' Pixie remarked, in no mood to be captivated.

The following morning, the day of the party, Pixie was following her usual routine of being horrendously sick when Apollo joined her in the bathroom. 'Go away!' she shrieked furiously.

'No, this is my business,' Apollo declared, crouching down to loop her hair out of the way and support her.

'I *hate* you!' Pixie snapped with pure venom because it was the last straw that he should witness her in such a state when all her defences were down, and there were many more such tart exchanges before her stomach settled again.

Having cleaned her up with unblemished cool, Apollo carried her back to bed. 'Do you want me to cancel the party?'

'You can't. Half our guests are already on their way,' she groaned. 'I'll be fine once Holly gets here.'

'I haven't had sex with anyone but you since we got married,' Apollo announced just when she was least expecting any reference to that burning issue.

'Don't believe you,' Pixie gasped, turning over on her side to avoid looking at him. 'Nobody would believe you. I'm not stupid. It's what you do, it's who you are…you probably can't even help it.'

'It's not who I am!' Apollo bit out hotly from between clenched white teeth, his eyes emerald bright and accusing. 'The least you can do is give me the chance to explain.'

Pixie closed her eyes tight and played dead. His sudden anger had unnerved her. She didn't fear him but right then she didn't feel equal to the challenge of such an emotive confrontation. In fact suddenly all she wanted was Holly's reassuringly soothing presence. Tears stung her eyes behind the lowered lids.

'Izzy is Jeremy Slater's kid sister. Vito and I went to school with Jeremy. Although you haven't met him yet, he's a close friend. Izzy was at a dinner I attended. I've met her before and she asked me for a lift because she was visiting someone with an apartment in the same building as my London penthouse. I thought nothing of it,' Apollo admitted grittily. 'I wasn't particularly surprised either when the paparazzi jumped out to photograph us when we arrived because Izzy's every move is currently prime fodder for the tabloid newspapers.'

'So, according to you, you simply gave her a lift,' Pixie recited. 'How does that explain her still being with you the next morning?'

'She spent the night with whoever she was visiting. She phoned me first thing and asked me if I could drop her off on my way into the office. She was waiting for me in the lobby and we left the building together.'

'When you were caught on camera again. Why didn't your bodyguards intervene?'

'Because I suspected that Izzy was using me to raise her own profile and, not having thought through the situation, I saw no harm in it and waved them back,' Apollo ground out angrily.

His explanation covered the facts but his generosity towards Izzy Jerome's craving for publicity when he himself loathed paparazzi attention infuriated her. Since when had Apollo not 'thought through' a situation? He must've realised how the press would present those photos, one taken the night before, the next early the next morning.

'I'm sorry,' she pronounced flatly. 'I don't believe you.'

The door thudded closed on his exit and only then did her tension ease a little yet she had never felt so empty. She had not realised that she could love anyone as much as she loved Apollo and she had not realised that losing someone could hurt so much that it hurt to breathe. And it was a lesson she truly wished she had not had to learn. She had lain awake a long time the night before. Apollo had presumably slept in another room and ironically his absence had distressed her as much as his presence would have done. It was as though she were being ripped slowly apart, divided between wanting him and not wanting him.

Vito and Holly arrived mid-afternoon. As soon as

Pixie heard Holly's bright voice echoing up from the hall she called down to her friend from the upper landing. Apollo and Vito looked up. Pixie reddened and waved to excuse herself for not having gone downstairs to welcome their guests.

'I'm pregnant,' she told Holly baldly. 'And, yes, it was planned.'

'Is that why Apollo is looking a little ragged round the edges?'

'No… I think that was caused by the doctor telling us that we're having twins.'

'Twins?' Holly squealed in excitement. 'When are you due?'

As the friends shared due dates, because Holly was expecting her second child, they went downstairs by a service staircase and settled down with cool drinks in the orangery with its tall shady plants and softly playing indoor fountain.

'Vito told me about the will and that you were planning to have a child with Apollo,' Holly confided then.

Pixie sighed heavily.

'And you broke the rules, didn't you?' Holly whispered, anxiously searching Pixie's tense little face and shadowed eyes. 'You went and fell madly in love with his fancy-ass yacht.'

Pixie didn't trust herself to laugh or speak and she jerked her chin down in confirmation.

Holly groaned out loud.

'I wanted a child and because I wasn't very good at… er…dating I thought that Apollo could be my best chance of ever having one,' Pixie admitted very quietly. 'I should tell you now…we are separating after the party.'

'Is it really that cut and dried? I mean, even Vito, who generally assumes the worst of Apollo when women are involved, thinks that there's no way that Apollo would have slept with Izzy Jerome. She's Jeremy's kid sister and sisters are off-limits between friends. And Apollo has *un*invited Izzy from your party,' Holly completed with satisfaction.

'Izzy Jerome was on the guest list?' Pixie gasped in dismay.

'She's not any more,' Holly emphasised. 'I don't think he is involved with her. She's very young, you know, still a teenager.'

'It doesn't matter.' Pixie lifted her head high and sipped at her drink. 'The best way forward for us now is for us to go our separate ways. That was planned from the start.'

Holly shook her head. 'I can't believe you signed up for that. I thought you hated him.'

Pixie said nothing because there was a sour taste in her mouth. Only days had passed since she had planned to tell her friend how very different Apollo was from his public image but recent events had proved her wrong in all her assumptions. In truth she supposed that she had stupidly idealised Apollo to justify the reality that she had fallen in love with him.

'Let me see what you're wearing tonight,' Holly urged in a welcome change of subject.

Pixie took her up to the bedroom to show her the long scarlet dress in its garment bag. 'Apollo had it designed and I don't like it much...it's a wee bit slutty, don't you think? I have no idea what he's wearing.'

Holly skimmed a thoughtful fingertip over the black corset lacing round the bust line. 'Gangster's moll?'

'Well, at least there's no fairy wings included,' Pixie commented flatly. 'But there is a very ornate piece of valuable jewellery which he brought back from London and he evidently expects me to wear it with the costume.'

Pixie opened the worn leather box on the dressing table and listened to Holly ooh and ah over the fabulously flamboyant ruby necklace and drop earrings. She turned her head and glanced back at the red dress again. There was something about it, something eerily familiar but she couldn't pin down what it was.

Dressing for dinner, she donned the costume. She decided it was fortunate that pregnancy had swelled her boobs because the gathered, dipping neckline positively demanded a glimpse of bosom. She tightened the laces, noting with wry appreciation that she finally had the chest she had long dreamt of having. But like her marriage to Apollo, it was an illusion, she thought morosely, for when she had finally delivered her twins she would probably return to being pretty much flat-chested again.

Apollo strode in and she stopped dead to stare at him. He was tricked out like a pirate in tall black boots and fitted breeches with a white ruffled shirt and a sword. And being Apollo and fantastically handsome, he looked spectacular and electrifyingly sexy.

'I gather that I'm a pirate's lady,' Pixie guessed.

'A pirate's treasure,' Apollo quipped. 'You're not wearing the rubies.'

He extracted the necklace from the box and handed her the earrings. 'This set belonged to my mother. It hasn't been worn since she died. I had it cleaned and reset for you in London.'

The eye-catching rubies settled coolly against her skin and she slowly attached the earrings, watching them gleam with inner fire as they swung in the lamp light. 'Thanks,' she said stiltedly.

A very large dinner party awaited them on the ground

floor. With surprising formality Apollo brought his relatives forward one by one to meet Pixie. There were innumerable aunties and uncles and cousins. She marvelled at his calm control under stress and his polished manners. He was essentially behaving like a proud new husband. Nobody could ever have guessed that that dream was already dead and buried. It had been a dream, she reminded herself doggedly, a dream that could never have become reality with Apollo Metraxis in a leading role.

In the ballroom she watched Apollo socialising and frowned. It wasn't fair that she could barely drag her eyes off his tall, powerful physique; it wasn't right or decent that she still felt his magnetic pull. And Apollo dressed up like a pirate was pure perfect fantasy. The arrogant tilt of his dark head, the breadth of his shoulders, his narrow waist and lean, tight hips, the long muscular line of his thighs in skin-tight pants. Her mouth ran dry watching him and her weakness filled her with self-loathing.

Apollo, meanwhile, was in a filthy mood. The planning had gone perfectly but the timing had gone seriously askew. He should have known better; he should have known not to waste his time trying to be something he was not. Since when had he been romantic? What did he even *know* about being romantic? And in any case, she hadn't even *noticed*, which said all that needed to be said. He had taken the cover of her battered romantic paperback and had the outfits copied. Even the costume designer had gazed at him as though he were crazy and he felt like an idiot for going for the pirate theme. Even so, he wasn't going down without a fight.

'I'm no good at slow dances,' Pixie protested when Apollo slowly raised her out of her seat and took her away from Holly, whom she had clung to throughout the evening.

'So, stand on my feet,' Apollo advised, wrapping her slender body into his arms with the kind of strength she couldn't fight without making a scene.

Murderously conscious that their guests were watching them, Pixie pressed her face against his chest and breathed in deep. He smelled so good she wanted to bottle him. Her fingers spread across his powerful shoulders and she drifted in a world of inner pain, wavering wildly between hating and craving and loving. She had missed him so much when he was away from her in London and now she had a whole future of missing him ahead of her.

'I won't agree to a separation,' Apollo breathed softly above her head.

'I don't need your agreement. I'll just leave.'

He went rigid in her arms and missed a step. Pixie was fighting back tears, reminding herself that they were in the middle of a party, that they were the centre of attention as much because she was a new bride as because the bridegroom had been outed as a cheat little more than forty-eight hours previously.

'I'll buy you a house in London…but you stay safe *here* until I have that organised for you.'

'I don't need your help.'

'I'll call you when I've set up the house and you can fly out and give me your opinion.'

Pixie swallowed back a sudden inexplicable sob because, without warning, Apollo had stopped fighting her and had backed off. Instead of feeling relieved, she felt more lost and alone than ever. They really were splitting up. Their marriage was over.

The three weeks that followed were a walking blur for Pixie. Apollo had left Nexos as soon as the last of their guests had departed. He had not attempted to have another serious conversation with her. Those last words exchanged on the dance floor, with her ridiculous threat to just walk out, lingered with her. Yes, she could walk out, she conceded, but she couldn't just walk away from her feelings, the painful feelings that accompanied her everywhere no matter where she was or what she was doing. She couldn't stop thinking about Apollo or fighting off the suspicion that she had condemned him on the basis of his reputation rather than on the evidence.

So preoccupied was she that she barely noticed that her bouts of sickness were fading away. She had to move into maternity clothes rather sooner than she had hoped because most of her fashionable outfits were too fitted to cope with her swollen breasts and vanishing waistline. She purchased new clothes online, loose-cut separates picked for comfort rather than elegance. With Apollo absent she discovered that she didn't care what she looked like. He phoned every week to civilly enquire after her health, and when he asked her if she could join him in London on a certain date her heart sank, because once he showed her the house he expected her to occupy she assumed that the dust would settle on their official separation. Evidently he had accepted that their relationship, their intimacy, was over now.

And wasn't that what she had wanted? How could she move forward without putting their marriage behind her? Apollo had denied infidelity but he hadn't put up much of a fight against her disbelief, had he? But like a sneaky snake in the grass in the back of her mind lurked the dangerous thought that she could, if she wanted, offer him a second chance. She was so ashamed of that indefensible thought that it woke her up at night in a cold sweat. She understood that her brain was struggling to find a solution to her unending grief and sense of deep loss and she knew that the forgiving approach worked for some couples but she knew it would never work for her. Nor would it work for a male like Apollo, who needed strong boundaries and punishing consequences because he wouldn't respect anything else.

Pixie arrived back in London late afternoon in late December with Hector in tow. A limo met her at the airport and whisked her back to the penthouse apartment. Apollo was flying in from LA and had told her that he would not be arriving until shortly before their scheduled meeting. That was why it was a surprise for Pixie to be curled up on a sofa with her dog in front of the television and suddenly be told by Manfred that she had visitors. As she stood up Hector bolted for cover under a chair.

A tall man with prematurely greying dark hair walked in with an oddly self-conscious air but Pixie's attention leapt straight off him towards the highly recognisable youthful blonde accompanying him.

'I'm Jeremy Slater and I apologise for walking in on you like this but my sister has something she has to say to you,' the man told her stiffly. 'Izzy...you have the floor...'

The tall, slender blonde fixed strained blue eyes on Pixie and burst into immediate speech. 'I'm really sorry for what I did. I set Apollo up as cover. I knew he was married but I didn't think about that. I'm afraid I was only thinking about what suited me.'

Pixie was frowning in bewilderment. *'You set Apollo up?'* she repeated blankly.

'I knew that if I was spotted with Apollo, the paps would assume that we were together and that they wouldn't look any more closely into who I was staying with in that building,' she spelled out tautly.

'What my sister *isn't* saying,' Jeremy interposed drily, 'is that she has been involved with a famous actor, who keeps an apartment in Apollo's building. As that man is married, both my sister and he wished to keep their relationship out of the public eye.'

'I didn't intend to cause anyone any trouble,' Izzy said pleadingly.

'But you weren't too concerned when you did cause that trouble,' Pixie pointed out, her stomach churning with shock. 'I can see that I have your brother to thank for this explanation being made.'

'I couldn't stand back and let Apollo take the fall for something he didn't do,' Jeremy declared cheerfully. 'He's been guilty as charged so often and I'm certain that that means that he suffers in the credibility stakes.'

'Yes,' Pixie agreed, her face hot with shame because even she hadn't really listened to Apollo when he'd said he was innocent.

She hadn't asked the relevant questions and she hadn't asked if he could prove his story. In fact she hadn't given him a fair hearing in any way and in retrospect that acknowledgement humbled her. In common with any other bystander she had indeed assumed that he was guilty as charged, but she had had much less excuse than other people because she had lived with Apollo for months and knew that he was something more, something deeper than the heartless womaniser he appeared to be in public.

Jeremy and Izzy departed soon afterwards with Jeremy remarking that he hoped they would soon meet in more sociable circumstances. His sister, however, said nothing, probably guessing that Pixie never wanted to see her again if she could help it.

After that visit, Pixie went to bed but of course she couldn't sleep. She had never trusted Apollo and had essentially regarded her distrust as a trait that strengthened her. Only now was she seeing the downside of that outlook. Looking for the worst and always expecting the worst from a man was not a healthy approach and it was unfair. Even worse, using distrust as a first line of defence had crucially blinded her to what was actually happening in their marriage. She should have recognised how far Apollo had already drifted from his original blueprint for a marriage that was a business arrangement. Time after time he had done things, *said* things that defied that blueprint and she had ignored that reality. After all, *she* had changed—why shouldn't he have changed too?

The next morning it was a struggle for Pixie to eat any breakfast. She had forced a separation on Apollo and had voluntarily given him back his freedom. She had well and truly proved to be her own worst enemy. Pride and distrust had driven her into rejecting the man she loved. Could he forgive her for that? Could he forgive her for misjudging him?

Would her misjudgement and their marriage even matter to him now? After all, his inheritance would soon be fully his because by the time their children were born he would have met the exact terms of his father's will. Nowhere in that will did it state that Apollo had to be still living with his wife.

A limousine collected her at half past nine, wafting her through streets soon to be thronged with Christmas shoppers. Shop windows were bright with decorations and sparkle. Pixie had dressed with care and not in one of her less than flattering maternity outfits. She had put on a green dress. True it was a little tight over her bust but it gave her a shape and her legs were the same as they had always been. In truth, she reflected unhappily as the car drew up outside a smart city town house in a tree-lined Georgian square with a private park, she would never be able to hold a candle to the likes of Izzy Jerome in looks. On board *Circe*, she had marvelled at Apollo's insatiable hunger for her and revelled in it. Now, she had to ask herself if she had anything more substantial to offer a male of his sophistication…

Apollo opened the door of the house himself, which shook her because he almost always had staff around to take care of such tasks.

Pixie stepped over the threshold. She glanced up at him, encountering shimmering green eyes below lashes as rich and dark as black lace, and her heartbeat raced, butterflies unleashed to fly free in her stomach. 'Apollo…' she acknowledged jerkily.

She came to a halt to stare in wide-eyed amazement at the lavish Christmas tree in the hall and the glorious trails of holly festooning the hall fireplace and the stairs. 'Oh, my goodness, this house…it's all decorated for Christmas,' she muttered inanely. 'And it's still furnished.'

'Relax. The furniture and the decorations are mine. This house was rented out for years. My father owned it but he didn't use it and it was too large for me to use while I was still single,' Apollo told her, gently but firmly urging her down into the armchair set by the small crackling fire in the hearth. 'Sit down and stop stressing.'

Pixie sat but she couldn't stop stressing. Apollo was exquisitely well-dressed in a formal navy suit, cuff links glinting at the cuffs of a fine white shirt, and she remembered him dressed like a pirate and every skin cell leapt up in sensual recollection. 'You want me to live in your father's house? I thought I was supposed to live in a house you bought me?'

Apollo dealt her an impassive appraisal that told her nothing about his mood. 'I understand that Jeremy called on you with Izzy last night,' he remarked stiffly.

Pixie flinched and paled, unnerved by that reminder. Of course, it had been foolish of her not to appreciate that his friend would naturally have told him about that visit. 'Yes, I'm so, so sorry. I misjudged you and refused to listen and there's no excuse for that, is there?'

'Perhaps there is,' Apollo conceded, sharply disconcerting her with that measured response. 'Maybe if I'd said more sooner, you *would* have wanted to listen to what I had to say.'

Sick with nerves, Pixie curled her hands tightly together. 'I'm really sorry,' she said shakily again. 'I didn't give you a chance.'

'I have a bad reputation with women,' Apollo allowed reflectively. 'But in one sense it's unjustified. I have always ended one relationship before I embark on another. I don't do crossovers or betrayals. That's a small point but that's how I live. I don't cheat on anyone.'

Her nails dug into her palms because she was so very tense and afraid of saying the wrong thing. She had said she was sorry but she didn't want to keep on saying sorry and she didn't want to crawl either. 'I understand.'

'We were talking about this house,' Apollo reminded her, lounging elegantly back against the marble console table behind him.

'Y-yes,' she stammered.

'I want you to live here with me. With twins on the horizon we definitely need a spacious family house.'

Her smooth brow indented as she struggled to understand. 'Are you saying that you can forgive me for the way I behaved on Nexos?'

'There are still things that you have to forgive me for,' Apollo told her tautly. 'When we first married I pretended that I was still holding your brother's debt over you because I saw that debt as a guarantee that you would do as you were told.'

Her smooth brow furrowed. 'You pretended? In what way?'

'I paid off the debt in its entirety before our marriage. I didn't want any further dealings with the thug your brother owed that money to,' he admitted.

Pixie nodded understanding. 'The carrot and the stick approach again…right? Well, you're good at faking.'

'Thank you,' Apollo murmured wryly. 'I should've been more honest with you though.'

'We both hugged our secrets back then. It takes time to learn to trust someone.'

'You're the first woman I've ever trusted,' Apollo admitted. 'You know the worst of me. You've seen the bad stuff. Give me a chance to show you the good things I can do.'

Pixie unfroze and stared up at him. 'You *are* willing to forgive me for misjudging you,' she suddenly appreciated in wonderment.

His smile slanted into a heart-stopping grin. 'As I can't live without you I don't think I have much choice about that.'

'You can't live,' she began incredulously, '*without* me?'

'I've got remarkably used to having you and Hector around,' Apollo told her almost flippantly.

'H-have you?' Pixie mumbled uncertainly.

'Even though trying to plant an idea in your head is sometimes like drilling through concrete.'

'What idea were you trying to plant?'

'That we could be happy together and stay together and married for ever.'

'You don't do for ever,' Pixie argued, her voice taking on a shrill edge of disbelief.

'But then I met you and ever since then everything I *thought* I knew has been proven wrong,' Apollo admitted gravely. 'That unnerved me...but there it is. You've turned my life upside down and, strangest of all, I've discovered that I *like* it this way.'

Pixie's mouth had run dry. 'I'm not sure I understand.'

Apollo reached down a lean brown hand towards hers and in a sudden movement she grasped it. He tugged her upright. 'I want to show you something and ask you a special question.'

Blinking rapidly, her heart hammering inside her chest, Pixie let him urge her upstairs. He pushed open the door on a bedroom but her attention leapt straight to the garment hanging in front of a wardrobe. 'What's that?' she gasped, for it looked remarkably like a white wedding dress.

Apollo dropped fluidly down on one knee while she stared at him as if he had lost his wits, her grey eyes huge and questioning. 'Pixie...will you marry me?'

'Wh-what?' she stuttered shakily.

'I'm trying to do it right this time. I love you,' Apollo breathed huskily. 'Will you marry me?'

'But we're already married,' she whispered in a small voice. 'You...*love*...me?'

'Much more than I ever thought I could love anyone.'

And the power in Pixie's legs just went and she dropped down on her knees in front of him. 'You mean it...you're not just saying it?'

Apollo flipped open the small jewellery box in his hand and extracted a ruby ring. 'And this is the ruby ring I intended to give you before the fancy dress party but sadly it would have been the wrong time.'

Pixie watched in reverence as he eased the glorious

ring onto her wedding finger. 'Is this an engagement ring?' she whispered.

With an impatient groan, Apollo leapt back upright and bent to scoop Pixie up and plant her at the foot of the bed. 'Yes, it is, and we need to start moving quickly. That is if you're willing to stay married to me?'

'Yes, I am… I'm kind of…' Pixie hesitated and then lifted her bemused head high to look up at him '…attached to you, *so* attached I can't bear having you out of my sight and the last few weeks have been sheer *hell*,' she admitted feelingly. 'I don't know when it happened because I started out convinced I hated you and somewhere along the way I fell madly in love with you.'

Sheer relief rippled through Apollo's lean, powerful frame. '*Thee mou*...you made me wait for that, you little witch. Would you like me to help you put on your wedding gown?'

Another wave of bewilderment rocked Pixie. 'Why would I put on a wedding gown?'

'Because your very romantic husband wants to take you to a church to renew our vows…and this time, we'll mean *every* word and every promise, *koukla mou*. I wanted to see you in a white dress.'

Pixie felt as though her brain had gone on holiday. She was poleaxed by that information.

Apollo lifted her off the bed and unzipped her dress, pushing it off her shoulders until it slid down her arms and dropped to the rug. 'I like the lingerie,' he growled soft and low.

'We're going to renew our vows? You've actually arranged that?' she exclaimed as her brain absorbed that incredible concept. 'Oh, I like that. I *like* that idea very much…'

'And then we're going to fly out to Tuscany to spend Christmas with Vito and Holly.'

All of a sudden, Pixie became a ball of energy. She whirled away from him, a slender vision in white lace underpinnings, and yanked the wedding dress off the wardrobe at speed. 'I hope it fits.'

'I told the designer you were pregnant and she made allowances.'

Pixie wrenched off the bag and dived into the wedding gown as if her life depended on it and indeed at that moment it felt as if her life did depend on it. Apollo was making all her dreams come true at once. He was trying to rewrite their history and she adored him for that piece of unashamed sentimentality. He was, after all, offering her the white wedding dress and the church she had once dreamt of. He loved her. Could she truly believe that? The ruby sparkled enticingly on her finger and she heaved a happy sigh. When Apollo began organising church blessings and getting down on bended knee to propose, it was time to take him very seriously indeed, she thought happily.

It was an exquisitely delicate and elegant lace dress and Apollo was fantastic at doing up hooks. Dainty pearlised shoes completed the ensemble and she dug her feet into them with a sigh. 'You've thought of everything.'

'I had to organise it all in advance even though I was scared you would say no. My first romantic scenario fell very flat,' Apollo pointed out in his own defence. 'Your bouquet is downstairs.'

'What *first* romantic scenario?' she prompted with a frown.

'The one where I had the cover of your bodice-ripping paperback copied for our fancy dress costumes,' Apollo extended. 'The one where I dressed up as a stupid pirate and you were *supposed* to recognise the outfits from the book cover.'

Pixie gasped and her grey eyes widened to their fullest extent. She recalled that sense of familiarity when she had seen the red dress he had had designed for her and she grinned. 'It was the first romance I ever read. I bought it at a church jumble sale...but when I got older, I didn't think it was realistic to believe I could ever meet a man as swoonworthy as the hero...and here you are, Apollo Metraxis, and you're hotter than the fires of hell!'

'Even so, you didn't notice,' he reminded her doggedly.

'I definitely noticed how sexy you looked,' she confided, her cheeks turning pink, and her heart literally sang at the image of Apollo going to so much trouble in an effort to be romantic and please her. 'Breeches and knee boots are a great look on you, so maybe you'll put that on again for me some day and I faithfully promise to demonstrate my appreciation. That night, I'm afraid I was too locked into the hurt of the Izzy business to notice. I'm sorry.'

'And I'm sorry you were hurt,' Apollo confided tenderly as he urged her back down the stairs, grabbed the bridal bouquet out of another room and planted it into her hands. 'Let's get to the church, Mrs Metraxis...'

And the little ceremony was glorious and everything Pixie could have dreamt of it being. She could see the love in Apollo's brilliant green eyes and when he actually paused afterwards on the church steps and posed with his arm round her for the paparazzi, he smiled with even greater brilliance and a level of happiness he had never known before.

'What time are Vito and Holly expecting us?' Pixie whispered as they climbed into the waiting car.

'My social secretary rang them to let them know we

wouldn't be arriving until later,' Apollo revealed. 'I don't want to share you just yet. I want a few hours to privately appreciate my very beautiful, pregnant-with-twins wife.'

'And how do you feel about the babies?'

'Over the moon now that we'll be in London with the best possible medical care on the doorstep,' Apollo told her, drawing her close, the heat of his big frame sending a little pulse of fiery awareness through her. 'I was worrying far too much and your consultant reassured me. You'll be in the best possible hands for the duration of your pregnancy.'

'*Your* hands,' Pixie muttered, pressing his palm against her cheek in a loving gesture. 'You'll look after me… I know you will.'

'You're my whole world and our children are part of us both. I can't believe I ever thought I'd be able to walk away and take a back seat in their lives.'

'Well, you won't be walking away any place now,' Pixie said cheerfully, resting shining eyes on him. 'I love you, Apollo, and there's no escape.'

'And you're the love I didn't believe existed as well as the most amazing woman I've ever met,' he growled, claiming her parted lips with his in a long, deep, hungry kiss of possession that thrilled her right down to her toes. 'Where else will I find a woman insane enough to dive off the top of my yacht? And expect me to be pleased? Or threaten me with a miniature Arab Prince as a rival?'

EPILOGUE

AT SIXTEEN MONTHS OLD, Sofia Metraxis was a force to be reckoned with. She ran over to her brother, Tobias, swiped his toy truck off him and sat back to bat away his attempts to retrieve it.

'That wasn't nice,' Pixie said, scooping up Tobias, who was crying over the loss of his favourite toy.

'You don't do nice, do you, Alpha baby?' Apollo chuckled, lifting his daughter and exchanging the truck for another toy to return it to Tobias.

'She's just cheeky,' Pixie contended.

'And bossy…wonder where she gets that from,' Apollo teased, watching Tobias stop crying to play with his truck. 'I can't get over how different they are.'

And the twins were. Tobias was the quieter twin, clever and thoughtful and methodical even in play. Sofia was all bells and whistles and complaints and needed rather less sleep. Together the two children had transformed their parents' lives, ensuring that Apollo and Pixie spent more time enjoying the wide open spaces and beaches available on Nexos than in their comfortable London town house.

Pixie had spent all of her pregnancy in London. Only after the birth of the twins had Apollo admitted that his own mother had died in childbirth and that that was the main reason he had been so concerned about her. Luckily the twins had been born only a couple of weeks early by a C-section and neither they nor Pixie had had any health concerns. Her brother's little boy had been born in the summer and Patrick and his little family now lived in Scotland where Apollo had found her brother a better-paying job. Patrick was still attending Gamblers Anonymous meetings regularly.

Springing upright, Apollo closed a hand over Pixie's and walked her out to the landing, leaving the twins in the care of their nannies. 'I have a present for you,' he proffered.

'Now? But tomorrow is Christmas Day!' she protested.

'Every day feels like Christmas with you, *agapi mou*,' Apollo traded. 'And Vito and Holly will be arriving in a couple of hours.'

'My goodness, is it that time already?' Pixie asked in an anxious voice. 'I should check the—'

'No,' Apollo stated firmly. 'You don't need to check anything. The house is decked out like a Christmas fair. The gifts are wrapped and our staff have mealtimes covered.'

Pixie gazed down at her gorgeous sparkling Christmas tree in the hall and she slowly smiled. He was right. Everything was done. It had become a tradition that every year the two young families shared Christmas and this year it was Apollo and Pixie who were playing host because Holly was pregnant again with her third child and she wanted to take it easy and be a guest. And although Pixie and Holly didn't compete over who could put on the best festive show, high expectations did add a certain inevitable stress to the preparations. In any case, the whole house was looking marvellous. Holly was good at design and she had put together some colour schemes for the island villa and it was a much more welcoming house now that the bland beiges had been swept away and replaced with clear bright and subtle colours.

'Bed?' Pixie whispered to her husband because the arrival of guests, even if they were best friends, did put certain restrictions on what they could and couldn't do.

'You see, this is why I want to be married to you for ever and ever,' Apollo declared as he swept her up into his arms. 'You think like I do...'

Sometimes he was naïve, Pixie thought fondly. It wasn't that she thought the same way as he did. It was more simply that she could never resist his sex appeal. He was dressed down for the day too in well-washed jeans and a sweater, but her amazing male still took her breath away with one wicked, wolfish smile. He just made her happy. In bed, out of bed, as a husband, as a father, he was all she had ever dreamt of and a couple of years of marriage had only increased his pulling power. His patient approach with Hector had taught her a lot about the man she had married. At heart he was kind and loving and good.

Hector and his little Greek shadow, another terrier called Sausage, followed them upstairs.

Apollo slid a diamond eternity ring onto Pixie's already crowded finger. Her hands sparkled with a plethora of rings and she chose which ones to wear every morning. He liked to buy her stuff and she knew it was because she was rarely out of her husband's thoughts when he was away from her. He kept his business trips brief and, if he could, took them all out on the yacht and did business on *Circe* where he could still have his family around him.

'It's beautiful,' she told him gently, grey eyes silver bright with love and understanding because she had gradually come to see that having his own family meant everything to Apollo. He had longed to have a loving family when he was a child and had been sadly disillusioned by his father's disastrous remarriages. Creating his own family as an adult had given him a kind of rebirth, allowing him to grow into the man he might have become had he had a less dysfunctional childhood.

'No, you're the jewel who outshines every setting,' Apollo insisted, claiming her soft mouth in a hungry, demanding kiss that sent little shivers quivering through her. He pinned her to the bed, gazing down at her with unashamed satisfaction. 'Do you think Vito and Holly are aiming for a football team in the kid department?' he asked curiously.

'I wouldn't be surprised,' she said with a grin. 'But it'll be a year or two before I want another one. Tobias and Sofia are exhausting.'

'Almost as demanding as their mother,' Apollo groaned, intercepting the fingers running along a lean, muscular thigh and carrying her tiny hand to a rather more responsive area. 'But I *love* that about you.'

Pixie looked up into glittering green enticement fringed by black. 'I love you, Apollo.'

'Isn't that fortunate? Because I'm keeping you for ever,' he admitted thickly.

And later when their guests had arrived and every room seemed to be awash with overexcited exploring children and equally excited dogs, the adults settled down with drinks and snacks and Pixie curled comfortably up beneath Apollo's protective arm and admired the sparkling lanterns glowing on the Christmas tree. It promised to be another wonderful Christmas and she was sincerely grateful for the happy ending she had found with the man she loved.

* * * * *

Don't miss the first part of the
CHRISTMAS WITH A TYCOON *duet*
THE ITALIAN'S CHRISTMAS CHILD
Available now!

If you enjoyed this story from Lynne Graham,
look out for these other great reads!
BOUGHT FOR THE GREEK'S REVENGE
THE SICILIAN'S STOLEN SON
LEONETTI'S HOUSEKEEPER BRIDE
THE SHEIKH'S SECRET BABIES
Available now!

'Here he is at last. Arden, I'd like to present you to my cousin Idris— Sheikh of Zahrat.'

Arden widened her smile, determined not to be overawed by meeting her very first and no doubt last sheikh. Coming to this formal reception, surrounded by VIPs who oozed money and privilege, had already tested her nerves.

She turned, tilting her head to look up, and felt the world drop away.

His face was severely sculpted, as if scored by desert winds. Yet there was beauty in those high cheekbones and in his firm yet sensual mouth. His nose and jaw were honed and strong. The harsh angle of those beetling black brows intimidated. So did the wide flare of his nostrils, as if the Sheikh had scented something unexpected.

Shock dragged at her, loosening her knees till her legs felt like rubber.

His eyes…

Dark as a midnight storm, those eyes fixed on her instinctive movement as she clutched Hamid for support. Slowly they lifted again to clash with hers, disdain clear in that haughty stare.

A shuddering wave of disquiet rolled through her as she blinked up, telling herself it wasn't possible. It couldn't be.

Despite the frantic messages her body was sending her, she *couldn't* know this man.

Yet her brain wouldn't listen to reason. It told her it was *him*. The man who'd changed her life.

Secret Heirs of Billionaires

There are some things money can't buy...

Living life at lightning pace, these magnates are no strangers to stakes at their highest. It seems they've got it all… That is until they find out that there's an unplanned item to add to their list of accomplishments!

Achieved:

1. Successful business empire

2. Beautiful women in their bed

3. *An heir to bear their name...?*

Though every billionaire needs to leave his legacy in safe hands, discovering a secret heir shakes up his carefully orchestrated plan in more ways than one!

Uncover their secrets in:

Unwrapping the Castelli Secret by Caitlin Crews

Brunetti's Secret Son by Maya Blake

The Secret to Marrying Marchesi by Amanda Cinelli

Demetriou Demands His Child by Kate Hewitt

Look out for more stories in the **Secret Heirs of Billionaires** series coming soon!

THE DESERT KING'S SECRET HEIR

BY

ANNIE WEST

MILLS & BOON

First Published in Great Britain 2016
By Mills & Boon, an imprint of HarperCollins*Publishers*
1 London Bridge Street, London, SE1 9GF

ISBN: 978-0-263-92140-3

Our policy is to use papers that are natural, renewable and recyclable products and made from wood grown in sustainable forests. The logging and manufacturing processes conform to the legal environmental regulations of the country of origin.

Printed and bound in Spain
by CPI, Barcelona

Growing up near the beach, **Annie West** spent lots of time observing tall, burnished lifeguards—early research! Now she spends her days fantasising about gorgeous men and their love-lives. Annie has been a reader all her life. She also loves travel, long walks, good company and great food. You can contact her at annie@annie-west.com or via PO Box 1041, Warners Bay, NSW 2282, Australia.

Books by Annie West

Mills & Boon Modern Romance

The Flaw in Raffaele's Revenge
Seducing His Enemy's Daughter
Damaso Claims His Heir
Imprisoned by a Vow
Captive in the Spotlight
Defying Her Desert Duty

One Night With Consequences

A Vow to Secure His Legacy

Seven Sexy Sins

The Sinner's Marriage Redemption

Desert Vows

The Sheikh's Princess Bride
The Sultan's Harem Bride

At His Service

An Enticing Debt to Pay

Dark-Hearted Tycoons

Undone by His Touch

Visit the Author Profile page at millsandboon.co.uk for more titles.

This book is dedicated to the wonderful men in my family
across three generations:
all heroic in their own way.
What excellent role models for my heroes!

CHAPTER ONE

'LET ME BE the first to congratulate you, Cousin. May you and your Princess be happy all your days.'

Hamid beamed with such goodwill Idris felt his own mouth kick up in a rare smile. They might not be close but Idris had missed his older cousin as they'd carved separate lives for themselves, Idris in Zahrat and Hamid as a UK-based academic.

'Not my Princess yet, Hamid.' He kept his voice soft, aware that, despite the chatter of a few hundred VIPs, there were plenty of ears eager for news of his impending nuptials.

Hamid's eyes widened behind rimless glasses. 'Have I put my foot in it? I'd heard—'

'You heard correctly.' Idris paused, tugging in a breath before it lengthened into a sigh. He had to conquer this sense of constraint whenever he thought of his upcoming marriage.

No one forced his hand. He was Sheikh Idris Baddour, supreme ruler of Zahrat, protector of the weak, defender of his nation. His word was law in his own country and, for that matter, here in his opulent London embassy.

Yet he hadn't chosen marriage. It had chosen him—a necessary arrangement. To cement stability in his region. To ensure the line of succession. To prove that, despite his modern reformist ways, he respected the traditions of his people. So much rode on his wedding.

Change had been hard won in Zahrat. A willingness to conform in the matter of a suitable, dynastically necessary marriage would win over the last of the old guard who'd fretted over his reforms. They'd viewed him as an unseasoned pup when he'd taken over at just twenty-six. After four years they knew better. But there was no escaping the fact this wedding would achieve what strong leadership and diplomacy hadn't.

'It's not official yet,' he murmured to Hamid. 'You know how slowly such negotiations proceed.'

'You're a lucky man. Princess Ghizlan is beautiful and intelligent. She'll make you a perfect wife.'

Idris glanced to the woman holding court nearby. Resplendent in a blood-red evening gown that clung to a perfect hourglass figure, she was the stuff of male fantasy. Add her bred-in-the-bone understanding of Middle Eastern politics and her charming yet assured manner and he knew he was a lucky man.

Pity he didn't feel like one.

Even the thought of acquainting himself with that lush body didn't excite him.

What did that say about his libido?

Too many hours brokering peace negotiations with not one but two difficult neighbouring countries. Too many evenings strategising to push reform in a nation still catching up with the twenty-first century.

And before that too many shallow sexual encounters with women who were accommodating but unimportant.

'Thank you, Hamid. I'm sure she will.' As the daughter of a neighbouring ruler and a means to ensure long-term peace, Ghizlan would be invaluable. As the prospective mother of a brood of children she'd be priceless. Those children would ensure his sheikhdom wasn't racked by the disruption it had faced when his uncle died without a son.

Idris told himself his lack of enthusiasm would evaporate once he and Ghizlan shared a bed. He tried to picture her there, her ebony hair spread on the pillow. But to his chagrin his mind inserted an image of hair the colour of a sunburst. Of curling locks soft as down.

'You'll have to come home for the ceremony. It will be good to have you there for a while instead of buried in this cold, grey place.'

Hamid smiled. 'You're biased. There's much to be said for England.'

'Of course there is. It's an admirable country.' Idris glanced around, reminding himself they might be overheard.

Hamid's smile became a chuckle. 'It's got a lot going for it.' He leaned even closer, his voice dropping further. 'Including a very special woman. Someone I want you to meet.'

Idris felt his eyes widen. Hamid with a serious girlfriend? 'She must be out of the ordinary.'

One thing the men in his family excelled at was avoiding commitment to women. He'd been a case in point until political necessity forced his hand. His father had been famous for sowing his wild oats, even after marriage. And their uncle, the previous Sheikh, had been too busy enjoying the charms of his mistresses to father a child with his long-suffering spouse.

'She is. Enough to make me rethink my life.'

'Another academic?'

'Nothing so dull.'

Idris stared. Hamid lived for his research. That was why he'd been passed over for the throne when their uncle died. Everyone, Hamid included, acknowledged he was too absorbed in history to excel at running a nation.

'Will I meet this paragon tonight?'

Hamid nodded, his eyes alight. 'She's just gone to freshen up before—ah, there she is.' He gestured to the far end of the room. 'Isn't she lovely?'

Only a man besotted would expect him to identify an unknown woman in that crowd. Idris followed Hamid's eager gaze. Was it the tall brunette in black? The svelte blonde in beads and diamonds? Surely not the woman with the braying laugh and the oversized rings flashing like beacons beneath the chandelier?

The crowd shifted and he caught a sliver of silk in softest green, skin as pale as milk and hair that shone like the sky at dawn, rose and gold together.

His pulse thudded once, hard enough to stall his breath. Low in his belly an unfamiliar sensation eddied. A sensation that made his nape prickle.

Then his view was blocked by a couple of men in dinner jackets.

'Which one is she?' His voice echoed strangely, no doubt due to the acoustics of the filled-to-capacity ballroom.

For a second he'd experienced something he hadn't felt in years. A tug of attraction so strong he'd convinced himself it hadn't been real, that imagination had turned a brief interlude into something almost…significant. No doubt because of the dark, relentlessly tough days that had followed. She'd been the one lover he'd had to put aside before his passion was spent. That explained the illusion she was different from the rest.

But the woman he'd known had had a cloud of vibrant curls, not that sleek, conformist chignon.

'I can't see her now. I'll go and fetch her. Unless—' Hamid's smile turned conspiratorial '—you'd like a break from the formalities.'

Tradition decreed that the ruler received his guests on the raised royal dais, complete with a gilded, velvet-cushioned throne for formal audiences. Idris was about to say he'd wait here when something made him pause. How long since he'd allowed himself the luxury of doing something he wanted, not because it was his duty?

Idris's eyes flicked to Ghizlan, easily holding her own with a minor royal and some politicians. As if sensing his regard she looked up, smiled slightly then turned back to her companions.

No doubt about it, she'd make a suitable queen—capable and helpful. Not clinging or needy. Not demanding his attention as too many ex-lovers had done.

Idris turned to Hamid. 'Lead on, Cousin. I'm agog to meet this woman who's captured your heart.'

They wove through the crowd till Hamid halted beside the woman in green. The woman with creamy skin and strawberry-blonde hair and a supple, delicate figure. Idris's attention caught on the lustre of her dress, clinging to her hips and pert bottom.

He stilled, struck by a sensation of déjà vu so strong it eclipsed all else. She said something to his cousin in a soft, lilting voice.

A voice Idris knew.

He frowned, watching Hamid bend his head towards her, seeing her turn a little more so she was in profile.

The conversations around them became white noise, a buzz like swarming insects.

His vision telescoped.

Her lush lips.

Her neat nose.

Her slender, delicate throat.

Two facts hammered into his brain. He knew her, remembered her better than any of the multitude of women who'd once paraded in and out of his life.

And that strange feeling surging up from his gullet and choking his throat with bile was more than surprise or disbelief at the coincidence of meeting her again.

It was fury at the idea she belonged to Hamid.

'Here he is at last. Arden, I'd like to present you to my cousin Idris, Sheikh of Zahrat.'

Arden widened her smile, determined not to be overawed by meeting her very first and no doubt last sheikh. Coming to this formal reception, surrounded by VIPs who oozed money and privilege, had already tested her nerves.

She turned, tilting her head to look up, and felt the world drop away.

His face was severely sculpted as if scored by desert winds. Yet there was beauty in those high cheekbones and his firm yet sensual mouth. His nose and jaw were honed and strong. The harsh angle of those beetling black brows intimidated. So did the wide flare of his nostrils, as if the Sheikh scented something unexpected.

Shock dragged at her, loosening her knees till her legs felt like rubber.

His eyes…

Dark as a midnight storm, those eyes fixed on her instinctive movement as she clutched at Hamid for support. Slowly they lifted again to clash with hers, disdain clear in that haughty stare.

A shuddering wave of disquiet rolled through her as she blinked up, telling herself it wasn't possible. It couldn't be.

Despite the frantic messages her body was sending her, she *couldn't* know this man.

Yet her brain wouldn't listen to reason. It told her it was *him*. The man who'd changed her life.

Heat seared from scalp to toe. Then just as quickly it vanished, leaving her so cold she wouldn't be surprised to hear the crackle of ice forming along her bones, weighing her down.

Her grip on Hamid's arm grew desperate as tiny spots formed and blurred before her eyes. She felt as if she'd slipped out of the real world and into an alternate reality. One where dreams did come true, but so distorted as to be almost unrecognisable.

It wasn't him. It couldn't be. Yet her gaze dropped to his collarbone. Did he have a scar there?

Of course he didn't. This man was tougher, far more daunting than Shakil. She'd bet he didn't do easy, charming smiles. Instead he wore royal authority like a cloak.

Yet she could almost hear herself asking, *Excuse me, Your Highness, would you mind undoing that exquisitely tailored suit and tie so I can check if you have a scar from a riding accident?*

'Arden, are you okay?' Hamid's voice was concerned, his hand warm as it closed over hers.

His touch jerked her back to reality. She slipped her hand from his arm and locked her wobbly knees.

Tonight had revealed, to her astonishment, that Hamid now thought of himself as more than a friend. She couldn't let him labour under that illusion, no matter how grateful she was to him.

'I'm…' She cleared her throat, hesitating. What could she say? *I'm reeling with shock?* 'I'll be all right.'

Yet her gaze clung to that of the man towering before her as if he was some sort of miracle.

It was that realisation that snapped her back to reality. He wasn't Shakil. If he *had* been Shakil, he'd be no miracle, just another of life's tough lessons. A man who'd used her and tossed her aside.

'It's a pleasure to meet you, Your Highness.' Her voice sounded wispy but she persevered. 'I hope you're enjoying your stay in London.'

Belatedly she wondered if she was supposed to curtsey. Had she offended him? His flesh looked drawn too tight and she glimpsed the rigid line of a tendon standing proud in his neck. He looked ready for battle, not a society meet and greet.

For long seconds silence stretched, as if he didn't want to acknowledge her. She felt her eyebrows pucker into a frown. Beside her Hamid's head swung sharply towards the Sheikh.

'Welcome to my embassy, Ms…'

That voice. He had the same voice.

'Wills, Arden Wills.' Hamid spoke since Arden's voice had disappeared, sucked away by the tidal wave of horror that seized her lungs and stopped her breath.

'Ms Wills.' The Sheikh paused and she glimpsed what almost looked like confusion in those dark eyes, as if he wasn't used to pronouncing such a commonplace name.

But Arden was too busy grappling with her own response to Hamid's cousin. He looked and sounded exactly like Shakil. Or as Shakil would if he'd sloughed off his laid-back, live-for-the-moment attitude and aged a few years.

This man had a thinner face, which accentuated his superb bone structure. And his expression was grim, far harder than anything Shakil had ever worn. Shakil had been a lover not a fighter and this man looked, despite his western tailoring, as if he'd be at home on a warhorse, a scimitar in his hand as he galloped into battle.

Arden shivered, clammy palms skimmed her bare arms as she tried to ease the tension drawing gooseflesh there.

He said something. She saw his lips move, but there was a weird echoing in her head and she couldn't make out his words.

She blinked, swaying forwards, stumbling and steadying herself, drawn unwillingly by his dark velvet gaze.

Hamid pulled her against his side. 'I'm sorry. I shouldn't have insisted you come tonight. Your condition is too delicate.'

Arden stiffened in his hold, dimly noting the Sheikh's sharply indrawn breath. Hamid was a dear friend but he had no right to feel proprietorial. Besides, it was a long time since she'd craved any man's touch.

'I'm perfectly healthy,' she murmured, trying to inject power into the words. The flu had knocked her but she was almost back to normal. Yet her recent illness provided a perfect explanation for her woozy head and unsteady legs.

She moved a half step away so he had to drop his arm. Gathering the shreds of her composure, she met the Sheikh's midnight eyes again, instinctively fighting the awareness thundering through her, and the crazy idea she knew him. That wasn't possible. Shakil had been a student, not a sheikh.

'Thank you for the welcome, Your Highness. It's a beautiful party.' Yet she'd never wanted to leave anywhere with such urgency.

It felt as if he delved right into her thoughts with that unblinking regard. It took all her control not to shift under his scrutiny.

'Are you sure you're well, Ms Wills? You look unsteady on your feet.'

Her smile grew strained and she felt the tug of it as her face stiffened.

'Thank you for your concern. It's only tiredness after a long week.' Heat flushed her cheeks at the realisation she'd actually come close to collapsing for the first time in her life. 'I'm very sorry but I think it best if I leave. No, really, Hamid, I'm okay by myself.'

But Hamid would have none of that. Nothing would satisfy him but to see her home.

'Idris doesn't mind, do you, Cousin?' He didn't wait for an answer but went on. 'I'll at least see you back to the house then return.'

From the corner of her vision Arden registered the sharp lift of the Sheikh's eyebrows, but she had more to worry about than whether she offended by leaving his party early.

Like how she could kindly but effectively stave off Hamid's sudden romantic interest without straining their friendship.

Like how Sheikh Idris could be so uncannily like the man who'd torn her world apart.

And, most important of all, why it was that even after four years she felt sick with longing for the man who'd all but destroyed her.

A night without sleep did nothing for Arden's equilibrium. The fact it was Sunday, the one day of the week she could sleep in instead of heading in to work at the florist's shop, should have been a welcome pleasure. Instead she longed for the organised chaos of her workday race to get out the door.

Anything to distract from the worries that had descended last night. And worse, the memories, the longings that had haunted each sleepless hour.

Life had taught her the dangers of sexual desire, and worse, of falling in love. Of believing she was special to someone.

For four years she'd known she'd been a naïve fool. Brutal reality had proven it. Yet that hadn't stopped the restlessness, the yearning that slammed into her like a runaway truck the moment she'd looked up into the eyes of Sheikh Idris of Zahrat.

Even now, in the thin light of morning, part of her was convinced he was Shakil. A Shakil who'd perhaps suffered a head injury and forgotten her, like a hero in an old movie with convenient amnesia. A Shakil who'd spent years searching desperately for her, ignoring all other women in his quest to find her.

Sure. And her fairy godmother was due any minute, complete with magic wand and a pumpkin carriage.

Shakil could have found her if he'd wanted. *She* hadn't lied about her identity.

He'd taken pleasure in seducing a gullible young Englishwoman, starry-eyed and innocent, on her first overseas vacation.

Arden shivered and hunched her shoulders, rubbing her hands up her arms.

She was *not* giving in to fantasy. She'd done with that years ago. As for the Sheikh looking like Shakil—it was wishful thinking. Wasn't it Hamid's almost familiar looks that had drawn her to him that day at the British Museum? That and his kind smile and the earnest, self-effacing way he spoke to her about the elaborately beautiful perfume bottles and jewellery at the special exhibition of Zahrati antiquities.

He'd reminded her of Shakil. A quieter, more reserved Shakil. So was it any wonder his cousin the Sheikh had a similar effect? Maybe crisp dark hair, chiselled features and broad shoulders were common traits among the men of their country.

Right now she'd had enough of Zahrati men to last a lifetime. Even Hamid, who'd suddenly turned from friend and landlord to would-be boyfriend. When had that happened? How had she not seen it coming?

Setting her jaw, Arden grabbed an old pullover and shrugged it on, then cautiously opened the cleaning cupboard, careful not to make too much noise. At least, as the only one awake, she had time to ponder what to do about Hamid and his sudden possessiveness.

Grabbing a cloth and the brass polish, she unlatched the front door and stepped outside, pulling it to behind her. She always thought better when she worked. Rubbing the brass door knocker and letter box would be a start.

But she hadn't begun when she heard footsteps descend to the pavement from the main house door above her basement flat. A man's steps. Arden took the lid off the polish and concentrated on swiping some across the door knocker. She should have waited till she was sure Hamid had left. But she'd felt claustrophobic, cooped up inside with her whirling thoughts.

'Arden.' The voice, low and soft as smoke, wafted around her, encircling like an embrace.

She blinked and stared at the glossy black paint on the door a few inches from her nose. She was imagining it. She'd been thinking of Shakil all night and—

Footsteps sounded on the steps leading down to the tiny courtyard in front of her basement home.

She stiffened, her shoulders inching high. This wasn't imagination. This was real.

Arden swung around and the tin of polish clattered to the flagstones.

CHAPTER TWO

HUGE EYES FIXED on him. Eyes as bright as the precious aquamarines in his royal treasury. Eyes the clear green-blue of the sea off the coast of Zahrat.

How often through the years had he dreamed of those remarkable eyes? Of hair like spun rose gold, falling in silken waves across creamy shoulders.

For a second Idris could only stare. He'd been prepared for this meeting. He'd cancelled breakfast with Ghizlan and their respective ambassadors to come here. Yet the abrupt surge of hunger as he watched Arden Wills mocked the belief he was in command of this situation.

Where was his self-control? How could he lust after a woman who belonged to someone else?

To his own cousin?

Where was his sense, coming here when he should be with the woman to whom he was about to pledge his life?

Idris didn't do impulsive any more. Or self-centred. Not for years. Yet he'd been both, seeking out this woman to confirm for himself what Hamid had implied last night—that they lived together.

A ripple of anger snaked through him, growing to gut-wrenching revulsion at the idea of her with his cousin.

'What are you doing here?' Her voice was husky, evoking long ago memories of her crying out his name in ecstasy. Of her beguiling, artless passion. Of how she'd made him feel for a short time, like someone other than the carefree, self-absorbed youth he'd been.

How could such ancient memories feel so fresh? So appallingly seductive?

It had only been a holiday romance, short-term fun such as he'd had numerous times. Why did it feel different?

Because it *had* been different. For the first time ever he'd planned to extend a casual affair. He hadn't been ready to leave her.

'Hamid's away.' Was that provocative tilt of her jaw deliberate, or as unconscious as the way her fingers threaded together?

Satisfaction stirred. It was beneath him perhaps, but reassuring to discover he wasn't the only one on edge. Idris was used to being sure of his direction, always in command. Doubt was foreign to him.

'I didn't come here to see Hamid.'

Those eyes grew huge in a face that looked even milkier than before. Hamid had talked of her being *delicate*. Was that code for pregnant? Was that why she looked like a puff of wind would knock her over?

Jealousy, a growling caged beast, circled in his belly. It didn't matter that he had no right to feel it. Idris had stopped, somewhere around four this morning, trying to tell himself he felt nothing for Arden Wills. He was a pragmatist. The fact was he did *feel*. He was here to sort out why and then, with clinical precision, to put an end to it.

'You should sit. You don't look well.'

'I'm perfectly fine.' She crossed her arms, making Idris aware of the swell of plump breasts under her shapeless pullover. Had her breasts always been like that? He remembered them as delectable, but—

'I'm up here.' A palm waved in front of his eyes and, for the first time he could recall, Idris felt embarrassment at being caught ogling. Heat flushed his face. It wasn't a sensation to which he was accustomed.

When he lifted his gaze he saw a matching bright pink stain on her cheeks. Annoyance? Embarrassment? Or something akin to the untimely, unwanted attraction he couldn't quash?

'I came to see you.' His voice dropped to a primal, darkly possessive note he couldn't hide.

'Me?' Now she was on the back foot and, ridiculously, it pleased Idris. He hated the sensation, since last night, that he careered out of control.

'You. Shall we go inside?'

Her folded arms dropped, spreading out a little from her body, almost as if she'd bar his entry to the house. 'No. We can speak here.'

Idris scowled. 'Surely even in Britain one invites guests inside?'

Her mouth tightened but she remained defiant. 'I prefer to stay outside. It's…better.' She took a step back. To prevent him hauling the door open?

Idris felt his head snap back as if he'd been slapped. Did she have so little faith in his chivalry? Was she really afraid to be alone with him?

He was torn between delight at the idea he wasn't the only one feeling the burn of rekindled lust and horror that his feelings were reciprocated and therefore harder to quell.

'I have a key to Hamid's house, if you'd like me to let you in upstairs. Since you're his cousin, I'm sure he wouldn't mind.'

Idris jerked his gaze up to the glossy black door a level above them, and then to the one behind Arden, noting for the first time the brass street number with a small but significant letter A beside it. The relief washing through him was palpable.

'You live in a basement flat? You don't live together?'

She drew herself up till she almost topped his shoulder. Idris told himself the movement wasn't endearing, yet he felt a little corkscrewing twist of pleasure that punctured his satisfaction in an instant.

'We don't live together. Hamid is my landlord.'

Yet that didn't mean they weren't lovers. For all Hamid's devotion to history and old books, he, like every other male in their family, had a penchant for a pretty face and a delectable female body. Besides, there'd been no mistaking Hamid's proprietorial attitude last night, or his meaning when he'd spoken about a *special* woman in his life.

'It's you I came to see.'

She shook her head and a froth of hair swung around her, the colour of the desert at sunrise. Last night he'd been thrown by the smoothly conventional way she'd worn it. This was the woman he recalled, with a riot of loose curls that made his palms itch to feel all that silken softness.

'Why?'

Was she being deliberately obtuse?

'Perhaps to talk over old times?'

There was a thud as she fell back against the solid door, her face a study in shock.

'It *is* you! You were at Santorini.'

Idris stared. 'You thought I was someone else? You didn't remember me?'

It was impossible. He might have had more lovers than he could remember, but the idea Arden Wills had forgotten him was inconceivable.

Especially when his recall of her was disturbingly detailed. After four years he still remembered the little snuffling sigh she made in her sleep as she snuggled, naked, against him. The feel of her slick, untried body when they'd made love the first time returned to him time and again in his dreams. He'd almost exploded disgracefully early at the sheer erotic enticement of her delicate, tight body and the knowledge he was the first man to introduce her to ecstasy. Doing his duty and walking away from her had been amazingly difficult.

'I thought…' She shook her head, frowning. 'How can you be a sheikh? You were a student.'

'Ex-student—I'd just finished a graduate degree in the States when we met. As for becoming Sheikh—' he shrugged '—my uncle died. It was his wish that I succeed him and that wish was ratified soon after his death.'

It sounded easy, but the reality had been anything but. He was a different man to the one he'd been four years ago. Responsibility for a country that had suffered so long because of its ruler's neglect had transformed him. He carried the burden of changing his homeland into one ready to face the future instead of dwelling on the past. This morning was the first time in years he'd carved time to do something simply because he wished it. His secretary's disbelieving look when he'd altered his schedule had spoken volumes.

Idris took a step closer, his nostrils flaring at the astringent smell of metal polish and something more delicate that tickled his memory—the scent of orange blossom.

'Come, let's take this conversation indoors where we can—'

'No!' Her eyes were round as saucers and if it weren't ridiculous he'd say she was shaking.

That brought him up short. He might be supreme ruler of his kingdom and an emerging force in regional politics, but he wasn't the sort of man who deliberately intimidated women.

'I have nothing to say to you, *Your Highness*.' She all but sneered his title and Idris scowled. It hit him suddenly that, for all they'd shared, there was a lot he'd never learned about her.

'You have a problem with royalty?'

She tossed her head back. He couldn't remember her being feisty before, just warm and eager for him. 'I have a problem with men who lie about who they are.'

Idris's hands clenched and his jaw hardened. He wasn't used to having his will crossed, much less his honour impugned. The fact they were having this conversation metres from a public footpath, albeit in a quiet square, incensed him.

His fingers itched with the urge to haul this spitfire of a woman into his arms and barge through the door into her private domain.

Except he knew in the most primitive, instinctive part of his brain that if he touched her he was in danger of unleashing something far better left alone.

He'd come here to satisfy his curiosity and put an end, somehow, to the nagging sense of unfinished business between them.

He was about to become betrothed to a beautiful, diplomatically desirable princess. Their match was eagerly awaited by both nations. Getting involved in any way with Arden Wills would be a mistake of enormous proportions. Giving in to the dark urge to lay hands on her and remind her how it had been between them with a short, satisfying lesson in physical compatibility would be madness.

And so tempting.

'I never lied,' he said through gritted teeth.

Dark gold eyebrows rose in a deliberately offensive show of disbelief that stirred the anger in his belly.

'No? So you're telling me you're not Sheikh Idris? Your name is actually Shakil?'

'Ah.' He'd forgotten that.

'Yes, ah!' She made it an accusation, looking down that little nose of hers as if he were some lowlife instead of a paragon of duty and honour. No one had ever looked at him that way.

'I used Shakil when we met because—'

'Because you didn't want me finding you again.' The words spat out like poisoned darts. 'You had no intention of following through on that promise to meet again, did you? You'd already wiped your hands of me.'

'You accuse me of lying?' No man, or woman, for that matter, had ever doubted his word.

Arden crossed her arms over her chest and tipped her chin up in a supercilious expression as full of hauteur as that of any blue-blooded princess. 'If the shoe fits.'

Idris took a step closer before his brain kicked into gear and screamed a warning. Ire overcame the seductive tug of that orange blossom scent. Caution disappeared on the crisp breeze eddying down from street level.

'Shakil was my family nickname. Ask Hamid.' It meant *handsome* and was one he discouraged, but back then it had been a handy pseudonym. He heaved a deep breath, telling himself he didn't care that the movement reduced the distance between them. Or that his nostrils flared as the scent of warm female flesh mingled with the fragrance of orange blossom. 'I used Shakil on vacation to avoid being recognised. There'd been a lot of media speculation about me and I wanted to be incognito for a while. I was Shakil to everyone I met on that trip. Not just you.'

He'd grown tired of people clamouring for attention because of his royal ties and wealth. Merging into the holiday throng in Greece as Shakil had been a delicious freedom. And it had been a heady delight knowing that when pretty little Arden had smiled at him in that bar on Santorini there'd been stars, not dollar signs in her eyes. She saw simply the man, not the shadow of his family connections and how she might benefit from them.

Was it any wonder he remembered their affair as special?

Still she didn't look convinced.

'As for not turning up at the rendezvous that last afternoon—you can hardly hold me to account. You didn't show.'

A phone call had hauled him out of Arden's bed and back to the upmarket hotel room where he hadn't spent a single night for the week since he'd met her. All he'd known at first was something important had happened and he needed privacy to talk with his uncle's closest advisers. It was only when he was alone in his hotel that he'd learned about his uncle's heart attack, the fact his life hung by a thread, and that he'd named Idris his heir.

There'd been no question of returning to the rendezvous with Arden—three o'clock by the church—even if she had decided to accept his invitation to an extended vacation in Paris. There'd been no question of Paris or a lover, not when he was urgently needed at home.

And if he'd been fleetingly disappointed that she'd thought better of accepting his offer, he'd known it made things easier given the enormity of what he faced. He had enough experience of clinging women to know severing ties could be tiresome.

'You went to the church to meet me?' Her words held a breathless quality and there was something in her eyes he couldn't read.

'I had to fly home urgently. I sent someone instead.'

There was a tiny thud as her head rocked back against the door. Her eyes closed and her mouth twisted. Idris frowned at what looked like pain on her features.

'Are you okay?'

'Fine.' Finally she opened her eyes. 'Absolutely fine.'

She didn't look it. She looked... He couldn't put a name to that expression, yet he felt an echo of it slap him hard in the chest.

'He didn't wait long.'

'Sorry?'

'Your friend. He didn't stay long.'

'You're saying you *did* go to the rendezvous?' To say goodbye or accept his offer of a longer affair? For a moment Idris wondered, until he reminded himself it was history, done and dusted.

'I was late.'

It was on the tip of his tongue to ask why. Second thoughts? A last-minute dash? He pictured her running through the narrow streets of Thera, between the white-washed buildings she'd so enjoyed exploring. Her hair would be down like now, and her summer skirt floating around those lissom legs.

He chose to say nothing. What was there to say now, after four years? What was done was done.

Except, remarkably, it seemed that what they'd shared in that sultry week in Santorini hadn't quite ended.

Arden Wills wasn't dressed to seduce. Her dark green pullover swam on her, just hinting at the curves beneath. Her old jeans were frayed and there was a patch on one knee. Her face was free of make-up. Yet her hair rippled around her like a halo on a Pre-Raphaelite model, beguiling and exotic. She made him want to forget duty, forget necessity, and tug her to him so she fitted between his thighs, cradling him with her hips.

'So, what is it you want?'

'Pardon?' Idris shoved his hands deep into his trouser pockets as he realised the direction his thoughts wandered. To whether she wore a bra beneath that bulky pullover and whether her pale skin was as petal-soft as he recalled.

'Why did you come here, if not to see your cousin?' She paused, her lips tightening. 'Surely not to catch up on old times.' Her breathing altered, drew short and jerky, as if she, too, remembered how it had been between them all those years ago.

'Why not?' Idris lifted his shoulders in a show of insouciance he was far from feeling. 'I was…curious about you. It's been, what? Four years?' As if he didn't know precisely how long it had been. His reign as Sheikh of

Zahrat dated from that week. 'There have been changes in both our lives.'

Her face stilled, her eyes darting to the side almost furtively, as if tempted to look behind her but thinking better of it.

Instantly Idris was on alert.

He couldn't read that look but instinct warned him something was afoot. Something she hid from him. His gaze lifted to the gleaming paint of the door behind her. What could she possibly feel the need to hide? She wasn't living in squalor, not here. Something sordid? A lover?

Adrenalin surged, coiling his tension tighter. He took another half step forward, only stopping when a small palm flattened against his chest. He felt the imprint of it through the fine wool of his suit. His skin tingled where she touched as if abraded. As if she'd scraped sharp nails over his bare flesh.

Idris sucked in oxygen and forced himself not to react.

'I don't want you here.' Those eyes were so huge in her face he felt he could dive into them.

His hand covered hers and fire danced across his skin before burrowing deep inside. A judder of potent sexual hunger tightened his groin.

'You need to say that as if you mean it.'

The scent of her was so vivid he could almost taste her on his tongue. Sweet with a telltale hint of warm musk. No woman before or since had smelled like Arden Wills. How had he forgotten that?

'I do mean it.' Yet her voice had a soft, wondering quality that reminded him of the night they'd shared their bodies that first time. Her eyes had shone with something like awe. She'd looked at him as if he were a glorious deity opening the secrets of the heavens, until her eyes clouded in ecstasy and she'd shattered in a climax so powerful it had hauled him over the edge.

His thumb stroked the back of her hand and she quivered. Her hand was small but strong. He recalled how, as her confidence grew, she'd been as demanding as he, exploring, stroking, driving him to the brink with her generous passion.

She'd driven him to flout his self-imposed rules and invite her to France on holiday with him, because a week together hadn't been enough.

Idris hauled himself back to the present. To the slant of sunlight burnishing her hair and the distant sound of a car. London. His betrothal. The peace treaty between his nation and Ghizlan's.

He shouldn't be here. His life was about duty, control and careful, deliberate decision-making. There was no room for spur-of-the-moment distractions.

In another second he'd step away.

But first he needed her to acknowledge what was between them. Even after all this time. Idris couldn't countenance the idea that he alone burned. Pride demanded proof that she felt this undercurrent of hunger. This electricity simmering and snapping in the air. The charge of heat where they touched.

'You need to leave. Don't make me scream for help.' Her head tipped back against the door, as if to increase the distance between them, yet her touch betrayed her. Her hand had slipped under his jacket lapel, fingers clutching his shirt. Heat poured into him from her touch, spreading to fill his chest.

He forced his hand to his side, conquering the impulse to haul her close.

'I said, leave me alone.' Her breath was warm on his chin and his thoughts whirled as he imagined her sweet breath on other parts of his body. He needed a moment to curb his arousal.

Here, on a London street!

Anger flared. At this woman. At his unruly body that for the first time in memory didn't obey.

'It's obviously escaped your notice, but I'm not touching you. *You're* the one touching *me*.'

His voice, crisp with challenge, nevertheless held that once heard and never forgotten deep note that resonated right to her core.

Arden blinked, dragging her gaze from his mouth and solid, scrupulously shaved jaw to his chest.

Heat scorched her cheeks at the sight of her hand clutching him, as if she couldn't bear to let him go. As if, even now, his desertion couldn't kill the slavish passion she'd felt for him.

Though, if he told the truth, he hadn't deserted her.

It was too much to take in.

Too terrible to think that perhaps he hadn't betrayed her as she'd believed.

Words trembled on her tongue, the truth she hadn't been able to share with this man for four years. But caution held her back.

She needed time alone to sort out what it meant if he *hadn't* deserted her. Time away from his piercing dark gaze and hot body that reduced her hard won defences to ash.

Arden dragged her hand away, pressing it against the solid door behind her. That was what she needed. To remember where they were and how much was at stake. She couldn't risk revealing too much.

'You need to go. This isn't right.' A weight lodged on her chest, making her breathless so she could only manage short sentences.

Something that might have been anger flickered across his face. Yet still he didn't shift.

Desperation coiled tight in her belly. A desperation

fuelled by the urge to spill everything to him, here and now, as if by doing so all her burdens would be lifted.

But Arden had spent a lifetime learning self-reliance. The last years had reinforced that. She carried her burdens alone.

'We've both moved on, Shakil.' It was as if she evoked the past with that one single word. 'Idris,' she amended quickly.

'Moved on where? To Hamid?' His voice was a low growl that sent fear feathering her skin. His head lowered and she felt tension come off his big frame in waves. 'You're afraid your lover will see us together?'

'Don't be ridiculous.' It came out as a hiss of distress. It had been bad enough realising last night that Hamid now saw himself as far more than a friend.

'Ridiculous?' Idris's eyes narrowed to ebony slits. Those carved cheekbones loomed threateningly high as his face drew taut. 'You call me ridiculous?'

Fire branded her neck as hard fingers closed around her nape, moulding to skin turned feverish at his touch.

Arden swiped her suddenly arid mouth with her tongue, searching for words to stop the fury in that glittering gaze.

But his touch didn't feel like anger. That was the problem. She could have withstood it if it did.

Arden trembled as the hand at her neck shifted and long fingers speared her hair, spreading over her scalp, massaging. Shivers of delight rippled through her and her eyelids hovered, weighted, at half mast. Tendrils of fire cascaded from her scalp down her spine and around to her breasts where her nipples peaked.

She swallowed convulsively and forced herself to straighten away from the door, even though it meant brushing against him.

'I didn't mean—'

'Of course you did.' His mouth twisted. 'You're right.

It *is* ridiculous. Impossible and inconvenient…and inevitable.'

Then, while Arden was still absorbing his words, his head lowered.

His mouth on hers was just as she remembered. A huge, tearing fullness welled in her chest as his lips shaped hers, not hard and punishing as she'd expected from the glint in his eyes, but gentle, questing. As if seeking an answer to a question she hadn't heard.

Shakil. The taste of him burst on her, rich and delicious. It was the one sense memory she hadn't been able to recall in the years since he'd left her. Now it filled her, evocative, masculine and, she feared, potently addictive. For her head was lolling back, lips open to allow him access.

Somehow her hands had crept up to brace on his chest. The steady thrum of his heart was a reassuring counterpoint to her sense of disorientation.

His other hand slipped around her waist, pulling her against a body that was all hard power, making her feel soft and feminine in ways she'd almost forgotten.

And still that kiss. No longer quite as gentle. Arden heard a guttural sound of approval as her tongue met his in a foray into pure pleasure.

He shifted and delight filled her as her nipples grazed his torso. She moved closer, absorbed in heady, oh-so-familiar delight, till a long hard ridge pressed against her belly.

Arden's eyes snapped open and she saw his eyes had narrowed to slits of dark fire. Then, over his shoulder, high up at street level, came a burst of light, a glint of sunlight off something. It was enough, just, to bring her back to reality.

'No.' No one heard her protest since their lips were locked.

She had to shove with all her might for him to lift his

head, blinking as if unable to focus. That might have made her feel better but for the realisation that just five minutes in this man's company had obliterated every defence she'd spent years constructing.

'No,' she gasped. That full feeling behind her breastbone turned to pain. 'This is wrong. We can't…'

She didn't need to go on. Sheikh Idris of Zahrat agreed completely. It was there in the dawning horror sharpening his features and the unsteady hand that swiped his face. He shook his head as if wondering what he was doing.

Nor did Arden need to shove him again. One swift pace backwards on those long legs took him almost to the base of the area steps and left her feeling appallingly alone.

Chest pumping, Arden stared at the dark-gold face of the man she'd once adored. The man who now looked at her as if she were his personal nightmare.

Desperate, she put her palms to the door behind her, needing its support.

Despite it all, the anger, hurt and betrayal that had shaped her life for four years, she'd harboured a hope that if they met again he'd admit he'd made a terrible mistake in leaving. That he'd missed her, wanted her, as she'd missed and wanted him.

In her dreams he'd never looked at her with horror.

Pain lanced her chest and kept going right down through her womb.

With a choking gasp of distress she whirled around, hauled the door open and slipped into her sanctuary. Her hands shook so much it took for ever to bolt and latch the door. When it was done Arden put her back to it and slid down to sit on the floor, arms wrapped around her knees as silent sobs filled her.

CHAPTER THREE

'YOUR HIGHNESS, IF I may?'

Idris looked up from the papers on the ambassador's desk. His aide, Ashar, stood in the doorway, expression wooden. That, Idris had learned in the turbulent first few years of his rule, was a sure sign of trouble.

Please, not another delay with the combined peace and trade treaty. Ghizlan's father might be eager to cement a dynastic bond with Idris but he wasn't past trying to wheedle more concessions before the betrothal was announced.

Idris turned to the ambassador, who, ever the diplomat, was already standing. 'If you'll excuse me, Highness, I'll leave you to check for news on that US investment project.'

Idris nodded. 'That would be useful, thank you.'

When the ambassador had left, Ashar entered the room, closing the door behind him. Silently he passed a computer tablet across the desk. Bold black lettering filled the screen.

Off the Leash in London, Sheikh Tastes Local Delicacies.

Beneath the headline was a photo. A close-up of Idris locked in an embrace with Arden Wills, her hair a riot of curls against the black of her front door.

The air rushed from his lungs as an unseen punch slammed a sickening blow into his midsection.

Damn it. Hadn't he known it was a mistake, going to her house? Hadn't it defied logic? Yet when she'd told him to leave, what had he done? Had he behaved like the sane, prudent man he was and returned to his embassy? No, he'd reacted like…like…

Words failed.

Worse was the fact that, facing a nightmare public debacle, he had total recall of her sweet mouth and her soft body moulding to his.

'There's more.'

Of course there was. It was the way of the world that you slaved twenty hours a day for your country and the first time in four years you did something utterly selfish, utterly incomprehensible, the press was there to turn a molehill into a mountain.

He sighed and forked his hand through his hair. 'Let me guess. Princess Ghizlan.'

He scrolled to the next page and the next headline.

Two-Timing Sheikh Keeps Fiancée and Lover in Same City.

Idris swore long and low. There was a photo of him and Ghizlan at the embassy reception. Beside it was one of him with Arden. His hand wrapped around her neck, pulling her to him, and her eyes were closed, those plump lips open, as if eager for his kiss. As if she hadn't just told him to take a hike.

Fire shot from his belly to his groin. Even now, with all hell about to break loose, his body was in thrall to the Englishwoman he should have forgotten four years ago. Instead he remembered it all. She'd been ardent, so deliciously honest and real. Her desire had been for *him*, not his wealth or connections. Together they'd created a magic he'd craved more of, though brutal logic said it must eventually burn out. Passion always did. That was how it always was for the men in his family, how it was for him—lust and desire, never anything more permanent.

He shoved the tablet across the table and shot to his feet, stalking away from the desk.

Of all the impossible timing. This was the worst. For his country, and for Ghizlan's.

Ghizlan! He'd put her in an appalling situation.

'Get me the Princess on the phone.' He spun around. 'No. Contact her aide and ask for a meeting. I'll come to her hotel immediately.'

Ashar didn't move. 'There's more.'

'More? How could there be more? There *was* nothing else. That—' he gestured to the photo of him hauling Arden into his arms '—is the sum total of what happened.'

His jaw was so rigid it felt as if it might shatter. Self-contempt swamped him.

How often had he told himself he was better than his uncle, the old Sheikh, who'd frittered his time and energy on endless lovers instead of governing? Or Idris's father, whose philandering destroyed his family and any respect he might have garnered from the people?

Idris had taken pride in devoting himself to his people, putting duty before pleasure. His planned marriage to Ghizlan was for the good of both nations. He'd modelled himself on the one completely honourable man in his family, his grandfather. The old man had been the sole exception in six generations to the rule that men in his family couldn't love. Idris didn't expect a miracle—to love one woman all his life like his grandfather had. But he aimed at least to be loyal to his wife. A great start he'd made on that!

'There's something you should see before you talk to the Princess.'

Ashar's expression was as grave as on the day Idris had returned home to find his uncle on his deathbed.

Idris put out his hand for the tablet. 'Show me.'

Ashar scrolled to another page, then passed it to him, half turning away as he did so.

Idris frowned. It felt almost as if Ashar was trying to give him privacy. The notion was laughable. His aide knew as many diplomatic and royal secrets as he did. More probably.

Then Idris looked down and felt the floor buckle beneath his feet.

Royal Baby Secret. Which Cousin Did Arden Seduce?

This time there were three photos. One of his cousin Hamid entering college with a briefcase in his hand. One of Idris in traditional robes, taken at some public event.

And one of Arden Wills holding a toddler in her arms.

Idris felt his eyes bulge as he took in the details. Arden's attention was on the child throwing bread to some ducks. A child whose face was golden, in contrast with her ivory and rose features. A child with glossy black hair and dark eyes.

A child with a remarkable resemblance to Idris at that age.

Or his cousin.

Idris tried to read the words beneath the photos but they blurred into lines of swarming black ants. He blinked and ordered himself to focus, but his eyes were drawn to that telling photo. Arden smiling radiantly at a child who, Idris would bet his sword arm, belonged to the royal family of Zahrat.

Sensation bombarded him and he had to brace his feet so as not to collapse back into the leather chair.

How old was the child? He knew nothing of babies. Two? Three?

Could it be his?

Shock scattered his thoughts. He should be planning an appropriate public response, deliberating on the fallout and talking to his almost-fiancée.

Instead he stared at the photo with something like possessiveness.

He was marrying partly to secure an heir but becoming a father was a political necessity, not a heartfelt desire. His own father had been distant and Idris knew little about good father-child relationships. He'd assumed his wife would take the lead in child-rearing.

Yet, looking into the laughing face of a child that might be his, Idris was gripped by a surge of protectiveness he'd never before experienced. This could be his son or daughter. The idea slammed into him like a physical blow, stealing his breath and obliterating any illusion of disinterest.

'Boy or girl?'

'A boy. She named him Dawud.' Not an English name then. There was obvious significance in that.

'Dawud.' An unseen cord tugged at his heart, making it thud faster.

Why hadn't she contacted Idris? Why keep his existence a secret? Anger stirred amidst the glowing embers of softer emotion.

Unless he's not yours.

Remember Hamid last night, his 'someone special'. Arden was living under his roof.

Yet if Hamid was the father, why not claim the child as his own? Hamid might have inherited the family practice of sowing his wild oats, but he had a serious side. He wouldn't shirk responsibility, especially if he cared for Arden as he seemed to.

Idris stared at the photo, trying to read the truth in the curve of the child's chubby cheek and wide smile.

That was when he realised his hand was shaking. And the feeling snaking through his belly wasn't mere curiosity but something perilously close to jealousy. At the thought of Hamid and Arden.

Idris dropped the tablet onto the desk and scrubbed a hand over his face.

Did he *want* the scandal of an illegitimate child? A child whose first, vital years he'd missed?

He'd have to be crazy.

His phone was in his hand before he realised. He called Hamid's number and looked up, surprised, to see the sun still streaming through the high sash windows. It felt as if time had galloped since Ashar had entered the room.

No answer from Hamid, just the message bank. It took far too long for Idris to remember his cousin mentioning an early flight to an academic conference in Canada. He was probably in the air, absorbed in one of his beloved journal articles.

Idris swung around to Ashar. 'Anything else?'

Ashar's lips twitched in what might in another man have edged towards a smile. 'That's not enough?'

'More than enough.' Scandal in London and no doubt at home, as well as in Ghizlan's country. A betrothal contract about to be signed, a peace treaty on the table and a child who might be his.

And, simmering beneath it all, the taste he hadn't been able to banish from his memory. The sweet taste of Arden Wills, sabotaging his ability to concentrate.

'Get me the Princess's suite on the line. And send a security detail to my cousin's house.'

'To keep the press back? They'll already be there in droves.'

'To observe and report back. I want to know what's going on.'

Whether the child was his cousin's or his own, Idris had a responsibility to protect mother and child from the notoriously intrusive paparazzi. At least till he sorted out the truth.

'And find out what time my cousin's flight touches

down in Canada. I want to talk to him as soon as he lands. Get someone to meet the flight.'

Arden ignored the pounding on the front door, turning up the television so Dawud could hear the music of his favourite children's programme. He sat enthralled, bouncing while he clapped his hands in time with the music.

When the reporters had descended on the house he'd cried, awakened from his nap by the hubbub of voices and the constant noise of the phone and knocking at the front door. Arden felt wobbly with frustrated outrage because even now they hadn't left.

She'd been more than reasonable. She'd gone to the door and asked politely for some privacy. She'd given a 'no comment' response to their frenzy of questions and faced their clicking cameras, giving them the pictures they wanted.

But it hadn't been enough. They'd clamoured to see Dawud. They'd even known his name. That was when anger had turned ice-cold, freezing her from the inside out.

She wouldn't let those vultures near her precious boy. They'd mobbed her, trying to follow her into her basement flat. Terror had grabbed her as she slammed the door shut, her hands slick with sweat.

She'd turned to find Dawud watching, eyes huge and bottom lip trembling, as the noise echoed through their little home.

There had to be a way out of this. Somewhere to escape. But Hamid was overseas and her friends had no more resources than she did. Certainly not enough to spirit her and Dawud away.

A shudder racked her. She needed to find somewhere safe till this died down. How she was going to do that when she was due at work tomorrow she had no idea. Would the reporters hound her at the shop, or mob Dawud's nursery?

Probably both. Her stomach roiled and nausea stirred.

She'd known she shouldn't have gone to that embassy reception. Not because she'd suspected for a moment she'd see Shakil… Idris as he now was. But because it was pure weakness to give in to her curiosity about his country. Look where it had got her.

It's not your fault, it's his. He was the one who kissed you. He was the one who wouldn't leave.

Yet, if she were truthful, those moments in his arms had been magic, as if—

A sharp knock sounded on the front door. That was when Arden suddenly realised how quiet it had grown. As if the crowd of reporters had left.

She didn't believe it for an instant. It was a trick to lure her out, preferably with Dawud.

Arden smiled at her son as he looked up at her, singing the simple lyrics they often sang together. She hunkered down and cuddled him, joining in.

But the rapping on the door started again. Peremptory. Unavoidable.

Kissing Dawud's head, she got up and walked softly into the tiny entrance hall, closing the door behind her. The letter box flap opened. She hadn't thought of that. She was just wondering what she could use to stick it closed when she heard a man's voice. A deep, assured voice that had featured in her dreams far too often in the last four years.

'Arden. Open the door. I'm here to help.'

Her feet glued to the floor. She was torn between the offer of help and the knowledge that this was the man who'd brought disaster crashing down on them.

And the fact that, despite a sleepless night, she was no closer to knowing if she wanted him in Dawud's life.

As if you've got a choice now.

In the background she heard a rising murmur of voices, presumably from the paparazzi. Yet he didn't speak again. Perhaps because he was used to minions running to obey his every whim. Yet she understood how much courage it took to stand there alone, with a mob of press recording his every move.

And he'd come to help.

She reached out and unlatched the door, staying behind it as she swung it open just wide enough for him to enter.

Swiftly he bolted the door then turned.

Idris. He was definitely Sheikh Idris now. There was no hint of Shakil, the laughing, passionate lover she'd known in Santorini. This man's face was a symphony in sombre beauty, lines carving the corners of his mouth, ebony eyebrows straight and serious.

'You're all right? Both of you?'

Arden nodded. To her dismay her mouth crumpled. Until now she'd been buoyed by fury and indignation. But one hint of concern and she felt a great shudder pass through her. She hadn't realised before how her anger had masked terror.

'Arden.' He reached out as if to take her arm then stopped. His mouth flattened and he dropped his hand.

'We're okay.' Her voice was husky. She told herself she'd react this way to sympathy from anyone after facing the press onslaught. It had nothing to do with the concern in his dark eyes. Yet that look ignited a new warmth in her frozen body.

Finally her brain engaged and she frowned.

'You shouldn't have come. You've made it a hundred times worse. What were you thinking?'

His eyebrows rose in astonishment. Clearly he wasn't used to anyone questioning his actions.

'It can't get any worse. Not after the photos they've already got.' He folded his arms over his dark suit, for all the world like a corporate raider contemplating a run on his stocks, not a Middle Eastern potentate. Surely sheikhs wore long robes and headscarves?

'But now they've seen you here they'll think—'

'They already *know.*' His tone was so grim it made the tiny hairs at her nape stand up. 'In fact—' he paused, his voice dropping to a silky, dangerous note that made her think of an unexploded bomb '—some would say they know more than I do.'

Arden wanted to say the press didn't know anything. They assumed. But it was splitting hairs.

'Couldn't you have sent someone instead?' She crossed her arms tight across her chest, where her heart catapulted like a mad thing against her ribs. Grateful as she was for assistance, she refused to feel guilty about what had happened. This wasn't down to her. *He* was the one who'd attracted press attention. She was a nonentity.

'I did send someone. But they reported you were surrounded. Your phone is switched off and I assumed that if a stranger knocked on your door, claiming to represent me, you'd think it was a ruse to get you out to face the cameras.' Ebony eyes held hers, challenging.

Reluctantly Arden nodded. He was right. She'd never have opened the door to anyone she didn't know.

'I had to come. There was no other choice.'

How did he sound so calm when they were in this mess? Arden couldn't begin to imagine how she and Dawud could go back to their normal, anonymous lives. She wanted to rant, to point the finger of blame at him, but what would that achieve? She had to protect Dawud. There was no time for the luxury of hysteria.

Besides, despite her fine words, she hadn't been forced into that telltale kiss.

Shame filled her. She'd clung to his broad-shouldered frame, losing herself in his sensuality, in the pull of an attraction that was as powerful as it had always been.

Despite the way he'd abandoned her years ago.

Despite the fact he had a fiancée.

Arden hated herself for that. She should be immune to him now. Her stomach dropped and she stepped away, her back colliding with the wall. Determination filled her. She would *not* fall under his spell again.

'What?' His voice was sharp.

'Your fiancée.' The word rasped out, rough-edged.

'Not my fiancée.'

'But Hamid said—'

'Hamid doesn't know everything.' That twist of his mobile mouth looked cruel. As if the words he held back would flay someone alive.

Slivers of ice pricked her all over.

In that instant he morphed from saviour to threat.

She'd been almost relieved to see him but suddenly, as if scales fell from her eyes, she saw him not as the man she'd once loved, or as Hamid's cousin and a potential safe harbour in this press storm, but as an absolute monarch, accustomed to getting whatever he wanted.

Arden licked her lips. 'What do you want?'

Her gaze flicked to the closed sitting room door before she could stop herself. He noticed. Of course he noticed. How could he not hear the muffled children's ditty and guess who was in there?

The fact he hadn't even turned his head towards the other room only scared her more.

Thinking he'd washed his hands of her once their affair was over, even covering his tracks with a false name, she'd believed herself a sole parent in every sense. But Idris was here now, and she realised in dawning horror that she had no idea how he felt about a child. A male child. A child he might consider his heir. A child he might try to take.

Terror dug razored claws into her belly and her stomach cramped so hard she doubled up, gasping. Surely he didn't plan to steal her baby!

'Arden? What is it?' This time he did reach out, long

fingers branding her upper arm and sending flames licking through her.

'Don't *touch* me!' It was a hoarse whisper, the best she could do. But it was enough. He reared back as if scalded.

She straightened, forcing herself to stand tall, jutting her chin to lessen the distance between them.

'Tell me what you want.'

Had she just made the biggest mistake of her life, letting Dawud's father into her home? A father who had the power, physically and financially, to take her baby away?

'Tell me!' Heat glazed her eyes. If he thought he was taking Dawud from her, he understood nothing about a mother's love.

Something she couldn't decipher glowed in those narrowed eyes. 'I want to get you and your son to safety, where you won't be bothered by the press. Then, we need to talk.'

Her stomach did that roller coaster dip again. *Talk* didn't sound at all appealing.

But she was out of choices. She and Dawud couldn't stay holed up, hoping the press would leave. They had to go out some time. Idris was her only lifeline. No one else could get them away from the press. She *had* to trust him, for now at least.

'Pack what the pair of you will need for a couple of days. There's a car outside to take you away and one of my men will be posted nearby to make sure none of the paparazzi break in here to get more fodder for a story.'

Arden's jaw dropped. She hadn't thought of that. Of some stranger pawing through their belongings, sullying their home.

'Don't worry. It won't happen. I won't let it.'

Arden snapped her mouth closed, reeling at his absolute conviction. Never in her life had she been able to rely on anyone. Every time she'd begun to trust she'd been let down. Her parents, foster parents, even Hamid, pretending there was more to their friendship than existed.

There was something inherently appealing about Idris's assurance. Just as well she knew better than to depend on him. But, for the moment, she and Dawud needed help.

'Give me ten minutes.' She started down the hall then stopped, hesitating outside the sitting room door.

'Don't worry. I'll wait here.' It was as if he read her mind, her worry about Dawud.

She hesitated, unable to dismiss the thought of him simply striding in, picking up Dawud and carrying him out of the door.

'You are both safe with me.' That deep voice mesmerised—so grave, so measured. She badly wanted to trust him. He took a single step nearer. 'You have my word, Arden.'

She caught the velvet brown of his eyes that from a distance looked pure black. She read determination in his jaw, strength in his proud stance and honesty in his direct gaze. For a second longer she wavered. Then she spun on her heel and darted into the bedroom.

She'd hear if he tried to scoop up Dawud and take him. Dawud would yell and it would be impossible to exit quickly with that mob outside.

Yet relief hit when she emerged to find him still in the hall. He stood, head bent as if listening to Dawud's high voice carolling enthusiastically. Arden dropped the two bags, a bulky one full of Dawud's toys and clothes and a small one for her.

Idris's head jerked up. 'Ready?'

Arden nodded, trying and failing to read his expression. 'I'll need a child's car seat and—'

'No need. Arrangements have been made for a car seat. All you need is your bags and your son.'

Your son. Not Dawud. As if Idris was trying to distance himself. Pain turned like a twisting stiletto in her chest. Arden told herself she was pathetic. Seconds ago she'd worried Idris might try to kidnap Dawud. Now she was disappointed he wasn't more enthusiastic about him.

He hasn't even asked if he's the father.

Because this whole situation was a mighty inconvenience for him. More than an inconvenience. Coming just before his marriage to Princess Ghizlan it must be a headache of massive proportions.

She made herself nod and put down the bags. 'I'll get him.'

'You can introduce me.' When she hesitated Idris continued. 'It will make things easier. It will be scary enough for him facing the crowd outside, even with my security men keeping them back.'

Arden hadn't thought of that. It was odd, and unsettling, having someone else point out what her son needed before she did. She couldn't get her brain past the immediate. Right now that was overwhelming. Introducing Dawud to his father. The man she'd thought he'd never know.

The doorknob felt slippery in her clammy hand and she breathed deep, securing a smile for her son. This had to be done and it was up to her to ensure he felt none of the tension crawling up her spine and along her hunching shoulders. Deliberately she pushed back her shoulder blades and walked into the room.

'Mama!' He swung round as the song ended, a huge smile on his face.

Reaction hit her square in the chest as she met his laughing gaze. Eyes of dark brown velvet, so like his father's. When he'd been born they'd been a constant, difficult reminder of the man who'd duped and deserted her. But over the years they'd become simply Dawud's eyes.

Now, seeing the similarities, not just in his eyes but in his whole face, from his jet dark hair to his determined chin, a powerful tide of emotion rose. Arden wobbled to a halt.

'Mama?' Dawud scrambled to his feet and came towards her, arms outstretched. But before he reached her he halted, head turning, eyes growing.

Arden sensed rather than saw Idris beside her. It was as if he generated his own force field, one that made her flesh prickle and tighten whenever he got close.

Was he as nervous as she? As if this were an irrevocable step beyond which the future could never be the same?

She fell to her knees and held her arms out for Dawud. 'Hello, darling.' Dawud's eyes remained fixed on the man looming over the pair of them, his head craning high to take him in.

Arden was just about to scoop him up when she felt a brush of air beside her as, in a single movement, Idris sank to the floor, settling cross-legged. His knee touched hers but he didn't seem to notice. His attention was fixed on Dawud.

Idris leaned forward a fraction and said something in his own language. Something melodic yet strangely husky, and made a fluid, graceful movement with one powerful hand from his face to his chest.

For a second Dawud stood motionless, then a smile creased his features. 'That!' He pointed at Idris, first his head then his chest.

Idris made the gesture again, slower this time, a courtly gesture of greeting, she realised. Dawud clapped his hands and chuckled, then waved one hand in front of his face, trying to emulate the gesture.

Again that unseen cord tugged at her insides. To watch Dawud smiling at his father, trying to copy him…it was something she'd never expected to see. Not after the hell she'd gone through trying to locate Shakil and finally acknowledging defeat. She didn't even know if she *wanted* to see them together, yet the shining joy in her son's face was hard to resist.

Unwillingly, as if forced by an unseen hand, she turned her head for a better view. The forbidding majesty who wore hand-made clothes worth more than she earned in six months smiled at Dawud the way Shakil used to smile at her.

Her heart knocked her ribs and dislodged the last of the air in her lungs.

She was still reeling when he turned. Was it imagination or did his eyes glow brighter?

'It's time we left. I can carry Dawud if you like. But my men will keep the paparazzi back so they can't jostle you and Dawud might be happier in your arms than mine.'

Arden nodded. Again he was thinking ahead to the logistics of getting them out of here. Of keeping them safe. She suspected this big man would protect Dawud from all comers. More, he was thinking of Dawud's feelings and his reaction to the stress of change.

A squiggle of heat channelled through her belly and she looked away before he could see how his consideration affected her.

She leaned forward and scooped Dawud into her arms, relishing his scent and the way he snuggled into her. 'Come on, Dimples. We're going out.'

'Man come too.' His gaze was still fixed on Idris.

'Yes, darling. The man will come too.'

The man in question was already on his feet, holding his hand out to help her up. More proof of his thoughtfulness.

But Arden pretended not to notice, scrambling to her feet without assistance.

Touching him was just too unsettling.

Already she feared she was about to walk out of the frying pan and straight into the fire.

CHAPTER FOUR

'WHAT IS THIS PLACE?' Arden had spent most of the trip focused on Dawud, in the car seat between her and Idris. Now she looked around the underground garage with its security door to the street already closing.

'My embassy. You'll be safe here. We approached from the back entrance and weren't followed. My staff ran interference along the route so the press can't be sure exactly where we've gone.' He turned and unclipped Dawud's safety harness as easily as if he'd been doing it for years.

Perhaps he had. The Internet search she'd done on him after the reception didn't mention a wife or children but—

Her thoughts frayed as Dawud leaned forward, reaching for Idris instead of her.

He was a friendly, confident child, but at the moment, selfishly, she felt a pang at his fascination with the big man looking down at him so intently.

Then it struck her that though his attention was fixed on Dawud, Idris hadn't reached out to take him. Because he felt her qualms? Or because he didn't want to?

Arden lifted her son into her arms, reassured by his warm weight and clean little boy scent.

'I'd prefer a hotel.' She was indebted enough to Idris. More, she knew a foreign embassy was like foreign soil. While here she was in his territory, under his control. Her nerves prickled with foreboding. A spectre of doubt rose. Had she walked into a trap?

Dark eyebrows rose speculatively. 'You'd prefer to run the gauntlet of the press? To hope no hotel employee sells photos of you both to the media?'

Arden gathered Dawud closer, instinctively drawing into the corner of the wide back seat.

'I hadn't thought.' Shock hammered anew and to her horror she began to tremble. It had been a terrible day that got worse by the moment. The picture he painted was as disturbing as the pack of jackals who'd howled questions at them when they got into the car, then tried to follow them down the street.

'It's all right, Arden. There's private accommodation here. You won't be disturbed while we sort out a solution. I can guarantee the discretion of every member of staff.'

Because he was an absolute monarch and he'd have their heads if they betrayed him?

The proud jut of his jaw and the fierce light in his eyes spoke of certainty.

Looking up into a face as hard and beautiful as that of some carved ancient god, Arden felt the terrible imbalance of power between them. He had only to snap his fingers and his staff would obey.

Had she felt this vulnerable facing the paparazzi?

'I need your word first. I want a promise that when I want to leave, with my son, you won't stop us. That we're both free to go.'

For a heartbeat fire pulsed between them. Then his gaze dropped to Dawud. Reflexively her hands tightened and Dawud wriggled, protesting, till she eased her grip. She didn't take her eyes off Idris. Nothing in the world was more important than her son. She'd never let him go.

'You have my word. You're not a prisoner but a guest.' He lifted his gaze to mesh with hers and heat consumed her.

'Come. Let's get the boy settled somewhere more comfortable so we can talk.'

Still Arden hesitated. She was wary of entering his territory. But it was worse than that. Her fear was sparked as much by the way the scent of sandalwood and hot male flesh filled her nostrils, stirring a longing she'd believed herself immunised against. Her body betrayed her with its yearning for a man who'd never be right for her. Even if he'd cared for her, which he hadn't, he was a royal sheikh, a monarch, and she was a single mum from a less than impressive family tree. She didn't belong here.

Frantic thoughts raced. Of her escaping with Dawud in her arms. But to where? Idris and the press would find them.

Idris didn't speak, just sat, watching her as Dawud shifted impatiently and demanded to be put down.

They both knew she was out of options.

Finally, heart heavy, Arden turned towards the door.

Arden had thought the embassy magnificent the night of the reception, with its soaring double storey ceilings topped by intricately glazed domes, its radiant chandeliers and of course the dais with the gilded throne. But she'd assumed the rest of the building would be a little more ordinary.

She'd assumed wrong.

For a start it was even bigger than she'd expected, not one building but several, with a private garden at their centre. Somewhere, she guessed, were offices where staff went about diplomatic duties, but she found herself in a town house, several storeys high and furnished in the luxury she'd seen only in lifestyle magazines.

Yet it wasn't the expensive fittings or exclusive address that impressed; it was the blessed quiet. Peace after the ruckus she'd left behind on her street. Arden hadn't realised how high her anxiety had been till her heartbeat finally eased into something like a normal rhythm.

She settled Dawud into a bright bedroom, spreading out his favourite toys where he could see them. To her surprise Idris didn't insist on that talk to 'sort out a solution'. Instead he left them to relax and explore. Then a young woman with a gentle smile brought a meal for Dawud, explaining the ambassador employed her to care for his children and that she'd been asked to assist, if that was acceptable.

Again Arden was given no cause for complaint. Her consent was sought, though Idris or some super-efficient underling had thought of and provided everything before she even asked.

It was ungrateful to feel *managed.* It was just that she was used to making her own decisions. She was dependent on no one, a lesson learned in childhood. Arden told herself she should learn to accept assistance gratefully, for Dawud's sake. But it was tough.

They had been treated with courtesy and respect. Yet she remembered the fire in Idris's eyes when he spoke of the press knowing more than he about Dawud, and again when he spoke of his cousin, as if there was a rift between the pair. None of that anger had been directed at her.

So far.

No matter how plush the surroundings, she couldn't forget they were in Idris's domain. Were they prisoners despite his promise? Arden shivered, vowing to leave as soon as possible.

Misha, the nanny, offered to sit with Dawud while Arden met 'His Majesty'. Arden was trying to find a reason to put off that meeting when Dawud's drooping eyelids opened wide.

'Man! Hello, man!' He sat up in bed, dimpling as he grinned, and Arden felt a familiar trickle of awareness course from her nape all the way down her spine.

Her breath snagged and her nostrils widened. She told herself she couldn't possibly detect the tang of sandalwood on the air, but her nerves rioted anyway. She swallowed, trying to banish the memory of how Idris had tasted, hot and delicious on her tongue. Not an ancient memory this time but one that was raw and new and all too disturbing.

Reluctantly she turned. Idris leaned in the doorway, immaculate in a dark suit that emphasised his height and hinted at hard-packed strength beneath. His stance was relaxed but there was nothing casual about his expression.

Arden's chest squeezed. He hadn't even noticed her. His attention was fixed on Dawud as if utterly absorbed. The stark intensity of that scrutiny made her stomach churn, as if the squirrels in their local park had invaded her body, leaping and circling faster and faster till she felt nauseous.

He turned, spearing her with that dark gaze, catching her unprepared. Fire licked inside and she pressed her palm to her belly, only to let it fall, knowing she gave away too much when he followed the movement.

'Everything is satisfactory?'

His calm riled her. She'd been through hell today, and was still scared of what the future held for her son. Yet Idris took it in his stride.

'If you call being hounded by the press satisfactory.' Her lip curled. 'Being forced to hole up here instead of…'

Silence descended as Arden ran out of energy, the air rushing from tight lungs. 'I'm sorry. That's ungrateful.' Even if it *was* his fault, manhandling her like that, especially in public. 'The room is lovely. And Misha—' she turned to smile at the young woman putting away some toys '—has been such a help.'

'Good. Then you have no qualms about leaving Dawud here while we share a meal?'

Of course she had qualms! Arden wanted to go back to the way things had been, just her and her precious boy, safe and secure.

Except then he'd never have a chance to know his father. Despite feeling she teetered on the edge of a very high, very dangerous cliff, Arden knew how important it was for Dawud to grow up supported by both parents. Even the fiasco with the press was worth it if they found a way for him to have a constructive connection with his father.

Apart from anything else, it would be far safer—if anything happened to her, Dawud wouldn't be adrift in the world as she had been.

She recalled the night she'd given birth in a bare hospital room, terrified and alone but for a midwife. She had friends but none close enough to share the intimacy of birth. It had struck her how utterly dependent her baby was on her. She'd vowed to do everything she could to give him love and the sense of belonging she'd been denied as a kid.

'Arden?' Idris took a step closer, frowning.

She blinked. 'Thank you. Dinner would be good.'

'Man!' called an imperious voice. 'I want man.'

'Please,' Arden said automatically.

'Peeze.'

Was that a twitch of Idris's precisely sculpted lips? Before she had a chance to decide, he crossed the room and sat on the edge of Dawud's bed.

Seeing them together, dark heads inclined towards each other, surveying each other with grave interest, Arden's heart gave a silly little flutter. Once, years ago, she'd longed for this, had spent so many hours fruitlessly searching for the man who'd left her pregnant and alone, refusing to believe he'd callously misled her. Until there'd been no alternative.

A hiccupping sigh rose as her little boy brought his hand up to his forehead then swiped it down to his chest, all the while watching the big man before him.

When Idris repeated the gracious gesture of greeting he'd used earlier, Dawud beamed. He swiped his little hand back down from his head in mimicry, this time all the way to his tummy. 'More.'

'Please.' That deep voice was gentle and Arden blinked, feeling foolishly emotional. It had been a long, difficult day. That was all.

'Peeze.'

Idris's mouth hitched up at the corner in a smile Arden had never seen before. A smile that melted a layer of the brittle protection she'd placed around her heart. He repeated the gesture yet again, this time accompanying it with a lilting flow of words in his own language.

His words wove like an exotic, alluring current around the room, mesmerising her, and she wasn't surprised when Dawud leaned closer, obviously rapt.

How long Arden would have sat there, enthralled, she didn't know. But Misha got up, excusing herself to go and tidy up the bathroom after Dawud's enthusiastic splashes.

Suddenly, with her departure, the atmosphere changed. Idris didn't turn but his words this time were clipped.

'I spoke to Hamid. He says the child isn't his.'

Arden blinked and found herself sinking into a nearby armchair.

'Of course he's not Hamid's!' What a crazy idea.

'Is he mine?' Idris asked before she could continue. Again, he didn't face her, but kept his gaze on Dawud. Trying to read her son's parentage in his face?

The sight of Idris's broad back felt like an insult.

'Let me get this straight. You think I went from your bed to your cousin's? What sort of woman do you think I am?'

This time Idris did turn. Unreadable sable eyes pinioned her to her seat. 'I don't know. That's why I ask.'

Arden sagged against the upholstery. Well, that summed up their situation. At twenty she'd spent a week with a man called Shakil and believed she'd met her soulmate, her one true love, and that she knew everything she needed to trust him utterly.

That week had changed her life. Would have changed

it even if it hadn't left her pregnant with her precious son. For the first time in years she'd dared to hope, dared to put her trust in someone.

But that life-altering week had clearly been something far...*less* for him. All those passionate words, the promise in his eyes and his touch, his desire to have her with him after Santorini...they'd meant nothing. Nothing except they were physically attracted.

Arden kept her head up as she met his gaze. 'Dawud is your son.'

She waited for some reaction but saw none. Did he feel so little? She'd have sworn she'd read at least a hint of deep emotion when he looked at their little boy. But maybe it was wishful thinking because she so wanted Dawud to be loved by both his parents.

And if he wasn't? She'd give her son so much love and support he'd never notice the lack from his father. Except she, of all people, knew it didn't work like that. Nothing made up for the absence of parents.

Her lip curled. 'I suppose you want a DNA test?'

'It would be sensible, since we're talking about the heir to a kingdom.'

Arden's fingers dug into the padded arms of her chair, biting hard. She told herself he was right. Of course he'd need unassailable proof Dawud was his. Yet it all boiled down to the fact he didn't trust her word.

It took a moment for the rest of his words to hit her. *The heir to a kingdom.* Did Idris intend to acknowledge his son publicly?

Arden was torn between relief that Dawud would have access to both his father and mother and burgeoning fear at what that acknowledgement might mean for their cosy life. Did Idris envisage sharing their son, half the time in the UK and half in Zahrat? The idea of being separated from her baby plunged a dagger through her heart. Until she told herself she was getting ahead of herself.

She looked across to see Idris again talking to Dawud in his own language, even teaching him to say something. Dawud's smile grew and grew as he parroted the simple sounds. Despite her fears, Arden knew that, however difficult this would be for her and Idris, for Dawud, having a family was immeasurably precious.

Misha returned and Idris stood.

'Nigh'-nigh', man.' Dawud opened and closed his hand in his three-year-old's version of a wave.

In response Idris said something first in Arabic, then followed it with, 'Goodnight.'

Arden crossed to the bed and kissed her boy, pushing back his silky dark hair. 'Night-night, sweetie.'

'Nigh'-nigh', Mama.' He pressed his hand to his mouth then flung out his arm in an exuberant kiss that made her smile despite the tension dragging at her belly.

She made herself turn away, reminded Misha to call her if Dawud had trouble settling and followed Idris from the room.

'What was that word you taught Dawud?' Arden asked him across the table laid for two in an intimate dining room.

She looked tired and tense but that didn't staunch the need dragging low through his body. She hadn't dressed up for dinner with him, wearing jeans and a T-shirt, not even any jewellery. Her only trace of make-up was a clear lip-gloss and something to darken her lashes. Yet Idris struggled against the need to touch her.

'*Baba?*' Idris passed her a platter of slow-roasted lamb before taking some.

'That's it. What does it mean?'

She wasn't looking at him as she helped herself to a

salad. She hadn't looked at him directly since she'd left the bedroom. As if the sight of him offended.

Was she blind to the fire of attraction crackling between them? Or pretending? Were her plain clothes an attempt to show she wasn't trying to impress? Or that she disdained him?

He didn't know what angered him more, her pretence or that she'd had his child in secret.

The soft lighting turned her hair to spun gold and the tantalising scent of orange blossom drifted to his nostrils. Idris felt his lower body jerk hard.

The fact Arden Wills got under his skin so easily made her dangerous. Idris had no intention of ceding power of any sort to anyone. Not after he'd spent years working day and night to cement his position as the youngest Sheikh in two hundred years. Too much effort had gone into stabilising his nation and building its future.

'*Baba* means Daddy.'

As expected, that got her attention. Her head shot up and once more he felt that jolt as their eyes met. Their kiss had been explosive. It made him wonder what a more intimate touch would be like.

'You don't even know he's yours. Not till you get your paternity test done.' Was that indignation? Certainly there was fire sparking in those extraordinary aquamarine eyes.

The jangling tension inside spread, his blood pumping faster.

Idris shrugged, adopting insouciance to hide his reaction. He wasn't ready to admit he didn't need a scientific test to know Dawud was his son. He couldn't explain his certainty because it defied logic. It wasn't wish fulfilment because, while he'd expected children with Ghizlan, he'd seen that simply as his duty.

Yet he'd looked at the boy and felt something he couldn't explain and had never expected. Certainty was part of it.

Happiness, a bright burst of pleasure and protectiveness was another. And relief. Because the idea he'd harboured since seeing the press reports, of Arden and Hamid as lovers, had made him feel wild, out of control.

Idris didn't do out of control. He did planned, logical, well-executed.

'You had no right.'

'Pardon?' He'd lost the thread of her conversation.

'You had no right to tell him you were his father.' Her small, lush mouth was set in a pout that would have been inviting, if not for her abrasive words.

He didn't bother to remind her he'd been speaking his own language, not English, and that the child hadn't understood. But he would soon. Idris would make sure of it.

'*No right?*' He planted his palms on the table and saw her lean back, away from him. 'I have every right. He's, what, three years old? All that time you kept him from me.'

That knowledge had battered him since the moment he'd walked into that basement sitting room and seen his son, a complete stranger yet still his son, sitting on the floor, clapping his hands. It was as if someone had scraped his heart bare, leaving it open and unprotected.

Even when some inner voice had taunted him with the idea the boy could be Hamid's.

'Not by choice. You lied to me about who you were.'

Idris shook his head. 'I told you—I didn't lie. I used an old nickname while I travelled to avoid publicity. I'd been under the microscope because of my family connections and wanted a break, to relax and be like everyone else. I had every intention of explaining who I was if you came with me to Paris.'

It still amazed him that he'd made that offer. But he hadn't been able to get enough of her. Arden's unstinting warmth and zest for life, the way she'd looked at him as if he made the sun shine and the moon rise, had been irresistible.

She didn't look at him that way now.

His jaw set. 'Everything else I told you was true.' Though he'd steered clear of his connection to royalty. 'There was no cause to deny me my son.' He stiffened as he fought the bubbling anger he'd repressed all day.

He flexed his fingers, resisting the urge to reach for her. To shake her into an apology? To kiss her till she stopped hissing at him as if *he* were at fault, not her?

'I didn't keep him from you!' Arden threw her napkin on the table and shoved her seat back.

Idris was on his feet before she was, ready to block the door, determined to have this out. He'd contained himself earlier, knowing the needs of the child had to come first. Patience was a hard won quality. One he'd mastered after assuming the throne, for implementing reform in Zahrat was a slow business. But his patience wore thin. This woman pressed all his buttons.

'Then why not tell me? What did I do on Santorini that convinced you it was better to raise our son alone? How can you justify keeping him from me?' Idris heard the harsh resonance in his voice and hauled in a deep breath. He hated revealing his feelings.

Arden planted her hands on her hips in a provocative stance. Her round chin angled up, her eyes sparked and through her white T-shirt he saw her nipples stand out as hard little points.

He flexed his hands again, resisting the need to reach out and touch. Abruptly he shoved his hands in his pockets.

'How was I supposed to contact you? Tell me that? You hid your tracks too well.'

'I did not—'

'No?' She stalked forward, her face tilted up to meet his. 'I never knew your family name.' She ticked off a finger. 'The one name you gave me was false.' Another finger ticked. 'When I found I was pregnant and contacted the hotel you said you'd booked on Santorini, they refused to confirm you'd been there, much less give me contact details.'

Idris scowled into her angry face. Those security arrangements were normal procedure to protect the privacy of the royal family. It had never occurred that they might have kept Arden from contacting him.

'I had no idea,' he said slowly.

'Sure you didn't.' Her lip curled and she rubbed her arms as if chilled.

About to bite out that hiding from women wasn't his way, Idris paused. If she *had* tried to contact him, how desperate must she have been when she couldn't locate him?

'When you didn't show at the rendezvous I assumed you were happy to walk away.' At the time, he'd had other things on his mind, like suddenly assuming the throne and responsibility for a nation.

'I told you, I did go. Just a little late. At the last minute I couldn't find my passport' Her chin hiked up and those aquamarine eyes held his. 'When the hotel refused to help me contact you I called the Zahrati embassy here in London.' Her mouth twisted and Idris felt a dart of discomfort.

'Do you have any idea how horrible it was, trying to locate you through official channels? All I could tell them was that your name was Shakil, you were twenty-six and spoke excellent English, that you'd studied in the US and you'd once broken your collarbone. I didn't even have photos of you since you were so camera shy.' Her mouth pursed, her nostrils thinning. 'Oh, they were very polite, very kind. I think they felt sorry for me because they guessed why I needed to find you so urgently.'

Heat washed her pale features but her gaze didn't waver.

Idris read hurt and defiance there and, if he wasn't mistaken, remembered embarrassment.

What had it been like to discover at twenty that she was pregnant to a stranger? To a man whose real name she didn't even know?

Guilt smote him. It reminded him of the blow he'd received at fourteen, learning traditional battle skills, when he'd been knocked, winded, from his horse and cracked a couple of bones.

Except that had been a clean blow in fair combat. This felt different, tainted with shame, though he hadn't intentionally misled her.

'I'm sorry.' He paused, knowing it wasn't enough. 'I apologise, Arden. What you went through—it must have been devastating. I really do regret that you felt deserted.' Idris stilled. She'd been so young. So bright and innocent. His lungs squeezed hard at the thought of her, scared and alone.

'I never meant to dupe you or hurt you. I only wanted a chance to enjoy myself without attracting public attention.' How selfish and irresponsible that sounded now. 'As for pregnancy, I assumed the precautions we took would be enough.' He felt his shoulders rise. 'I was thoughtless, not even considering repercussions, and for that I apologise again. But believe me, I wasn't trying to hide. Within a week of leaving Santorini I became Sheikh of Zahrat. It never occurred to me you couldn't find me if you needed to.'

Arden stared, her gaze raking as if sifting fact from the lies she'd imagined. 'I had other things on my mind than current affairs. Even if I'd read about it I wouldn't have made the connection between the Shakil I knew and a royal sheikh.'

Idris nodded. How could she have known? How could either of them? It was no one's fault, just an unfortunate series of circumstances.

Yet that edgy feeling of guilt still lined his gut. He remembered her telling him she had no family. Her parents had died years ago.

'You were okay? Through the pregnancy and birth?' It didn't matter what logic said. Honour dictated he should have been there to provide for her.

Her eyes rounded. 'As you can see, I'm fine.'

Which didn't answer his question. Instead it made him wonder what she hid. Had there been anyone by her side through that ordeal?

'You were well looked after?'

Her gaze hardened. 'I looked after myself. At least I had a steady job to go back to. That supported us both.'

Idris felt her stare like a slap, knowing it was what she didn't say that damned him. He knew next to nothing about childbirth but even he understood women needed support and rest, not just during delivery but after. How soon had she been forced back to work?

'I don't shirk my responsibilities,' Idris said slowly, watching the flash of fire in her eyes. 'If I'd known I would have helped, as I intend to help you now.'

The girl he'd known had been sweet, affectionate and easy-going whereas the woman before him was complicated, feisty and obstinate. Yet her passion and her determination to keep him at a distance only made his hunger for her more acute.

It was inexplicable.

'Good. I always wanted Dawud to know his father. It's important for a child to have a positive relationship with both parents.' She crossed her arms and surveyed him as if considering whether he measured up to her high standards.

Idris paced forward, closing the gap between them.. 'I agree. Which is why we'll marry as soon as possible.'

CHAPTER FIVE

Arden stared up into dark velvet eyes that glowed in a way she didn't like at all.

It made her think of how he'd hemmed her in against her front door and wrapped his big hand around the base of her skull, holding her captive as he kissed her senseless. And how she'd let him.

Of the heat that shimmered through her every time their eyes met, as if the smallest spark would ignite a conflagration she couldn't douse.

Of the way she'd melted at his touch, his kiss, even his voice.

She didn't want to melt. She wanted to cling to fury at his desertion, believing he'd deliberately dumped her. But, despite her anger and fear, Arden found herself believing the regret in his eyes, the honesty in his voice, the steadfastness in his body language. He hadn't intentionally left her high and dry. He'd sent someone to meet her and she hadn't been there.

An ache opened up in the pit of her belly. The fact it was random circumstance not deliberate intent that had kept them apart somehow seemed almost worse. And now this!

'Marry?' Her voice stretched and splintered.

'Of course. It's the logical solution.'

'Solution? I'm not a problem to be solved!' Easier to let anger hide her curious disappointment.

After all this time did she still pine for the fantasy she'd once harboured? Of him saying he loved her and wanted to spend his life with her?

Surely she was stronger than that.

Arden pushed by him to pace the room, passing the

exquisitely polished dining table with its crystal glasses, silverware and fine porcelain.

A table fit for a king. A king who'd planned to marry a princess. If anything was needed to highlight the differences between them that was it.

'What about your fiancée?' She swung to face him. Even from the far side of the room he was too close.

'I was never engaged. The betrothal wasn't finalised.'

Something in his voice told her he glossed over a difficult situation. Or maybe it was the hard line of his jaw. She could only guess at the diplomatic furore caused by those press reports.

'You don't just call off a royal marriage.'

'You expect me to wed Princess Ghizlan when I've discovered you're the mother of my son?' He grew before her eyes, his face taking on an implacable expression that made her think uneasily of his desert warrior heritage.

'I've been the mother of your son for years.' She folded her arms. 'We've survived quite well without you.'

It was the wrong thing to say. She knew it as soon as the words spilled out. The gleam in his eyes turned positively dangerous.

'I've been robbed of three years of my son's life.' He spoke quietly yet the lethal precision of those words sent her nerves into jangling alarm. 'I won't be robbed of more.'

'*I* didn't rob you of anything!' Her voice was overloud.

'Perhaps not.' She opened her mouth to speak again but the thoughtful, patient man who'd put Dawud's needs first all day had disappeared, replaced by a forbidding figure whose aggressive stance spoke of steely resolve. 'But the fact remains he's mine.'

'And mine!' Arden shot forward a step.

'Precisely. You said yourself it's best if a child has a positive relationship with both parents. Marriage will ensure that.'

'Marriage isn't required.' Arden stifled hollow laughter that she was rejecting him. Once the idea of marrying this man would have been a fantasy come true.

Because once she'd loved him with all the desperate, optimistic yearning of her young, innocent heart. She'd been drawn not just by his looks and charisma but by the way he *noticed* her. Shakil had made her feel special, as if she wasn't ordinary but remarkable. He'd shared new experiences with her, laughed with her, worked to please her with a generosity and charm that had seduced her completely. Now she realised she'd never really known him.

He tilted his head as if assessing her.

What did he see? An ordinary—too ordinary—young woman. Arden wasn't in the same league as Princess Ghizlan—beautiful, gracious and glamorous. Arden was a working class mum. She'd never owned a couture dress or mixed with the rich and famous.

Nor was she beautiful. Beneath the bright but untameable hair lurked an ordinary face, a short nose and mouth that, while well shaped, wasn't wide enough for current tastes. She juggled work and motherhood, was more at home singing nursery rhymes and cooking eggs with toast soldiers than dining in an elegant room like this.

'You're not thinking straight.' His jet eyebrows lifted and his eyes narrowed to gleaming slits, but Arden refused to be intimidated. 'This is a knee-jerk reaction. When you consider you'll realise the idea of us marrying is…'

'Logical? Long overdue? The best thing for Dawud?'

Arden shoved her hands on her hips, whipping up outrage. 'I was thinking more ludicrous, unnecessary and painful.'

'You think marriage to me would be painful?'

Arden couldn't tell if it was shock or fury tightening his face but he morphed from broodingly aggressive to fearsome in the blink of an eye. Idris looked like a marauder planning a raid on some unprotected outpost.

A shiver ripped through her but she stood her ground. 'You'd find it painful. I'm not cut out to be a royal wife.'

And it would be painful for her, living a parody of the life she'd once imagined with the man she'd loved.

A slashing gesture, like the downward slice of a sword, dismissed her argument. 'You can learn.'

'I'm not interested in learning.' Why couldn't he see they were mismatched?

He stepped forward, not stopping till she felt his warm breath on her upturned face. Arden swallowed as a frisson of fear skated down her backbone.

'It may have escaped your notice, Arden.' He lingered on her name and the frisson became something else. Something that made a mockery of her antipathy. 'But it doesn't matter what you're interested in. What you and I want no longer counts. What matters is what's best for Dawud.'

Stupidly, her breath caught. He'd touched a nerve. She'd do anything for her son, anything to ensure he had a bright, stable, happy future.

Except what Idris suggested was a recipe for disaster.

She folded her arms. 'Dawud doesn't need us to be married. It's far better if he has parents on friendly terms than ones making each other miserable because they married the wrong person.'

'Who do you want to marry?' It was out like a shot. 'My cousin?'

Arden backed a step and found her way blocked by a chair. 'No! Hamid is a friend, that's all.'

'Then who do you want to marry?' Idris stalked closer and Arden wondered how she'd ever considered him easy-going.

'No one. I was speaking in general terms. But that does raise the question of love.'

'Love?' He said it as if it was an alien concept.

'Of course.' Was he being deliberately difficult? 'If one of us fell in love with someone later…'

Idris shook his head. 'There's no danger of me falling in love with anyone else.'

For a split second the old Arden, the one she thought she'd left behind years ago, waited for him to declare he'd fallen for her all those years ago on Santorini.

It couldn't be true. That dream was ancient history. Yet her voice was husky. 'Why not?'

'I've never been in love and nor will I be. No one in my family marries for love.' He shrugged. 'We're renowned for being impervious to romance. Call it an inherited failing.'

'I see.' Stupid to feel disappointment. She'd known she'd only been a holiday fling. She'd long ago acknowledged her feelings for him were the product of girlish romanticism in the face of her first real crush.

'Unless you're afraid *you'll* fall in love?'

Arden's laugh was short and cynical. 'Definitely not.' The reality of becoming a single mother a week before her twenty-first birthday had shredded her romantic fantasies, even if seeing Idris again evoked shadowy memories of what she'd called love. She was too tired just getting through each day to think about romance.

'Good. Then that's not a problem.'

Arden shook her head. 'But there are plenty more.'

'Such as?'

Was he serious? The whole idea was laughable.

'Your people won't accept me as Queen.'

'My people will accept any woman I marry.' It was said with a conviction that told her it was the absolute truth.

'I couldn't accept the restrictions of being a woman in your country. Your traditions are different to mine.'

That pulled him up short. Arden watched his brow crinkle.

'It's true our traditions aren't the same,' he said slowly, 'but change is happening. My country is very different to the way it was four years ago. Besides, as my wife, you'd be able to model change for other women, to lead the way.'

'Princess Ghizlan would do that far better.'

He shook his head, his lips flattening. 'How many times do I have to tell you she's out of the picture? I can't ask her to marry me in the face of this scandal. The only decent thing I can do, for everyone, is marry you.'

That put her in her place. She was nothing but an albatross around his neck.

She heaved in a deep breath. 'I'm sorry for the trouble the news has caused. To *all* of us. My life's not going to be easy either, at least for a while. But it's not my fault. Nor do I think jumping into marriage is a solution. All I want is what's best for Dawud.'

'At last we agree on something.'

His words gave her hope. Maybe he could be persuaded. She hadn't exactly been tactful in rejecting his proposal. If you could call his statement that they'd marry a proposal!

Arden lifted her lips in a small, conciliatory smile. 'You're right. That's a starting point, isn't it?'

He gave no answering smile and Arden wondered how often people argued with the Sheikh of Zahrat. Was he so used to having his own way he couldn't concede there were other options?

'Look. Why don't we sit down and discuss some possibilities?'

To her relief he stepped back, allowing her to slip into her vacated seat. Just in time. Stress and weariness had taken their toll. Her legs shook as if she'd run all the way to the top of St Paul's Cathedral.

Idris settled beside her. 'You were saying?'

'Well…' She slid a fork across the tablecloth, watching

grooves appear then disappear in the fine linen. 'Perhaps he could spend part of the year with you.'

Just saying it stabbed pain through her chest. She couldn't imagine a day without Dawud. Her breath snared in an audible hiss.

But she had to be realistic. Dawud should have a chance to know his father.

'As a part-time prince, you mean? Living sometimes in my palace and sometimes in your basement flat?'

Arden's head jerked up. His voice was cool, almost detached, but surely that was anger she heard?

'It makes more sense than pretending the three of us can be the perfect family.'

'I'm not asking for perfection, Arden.'

She bit down her retort that he hadn't *asked* anything. But bickering would get them nowhere. She had to put aside resentment and fear and think of what was best for Dawud. Even if being with Idris made her feel trapped. 'Sharing him is a workable compromise.'

'You really think Dawud can go back to the life he used to lead now I know he's mine?'

Arden stiffened. The heavy silver fork thudded to the table. She worked hard to provide for her boy. 'Why not? A dose of working class reality to compare with palace life might be a good thing.'

Idris shook his head. 'You misunderstand. The damage is done now the world knows Dawud is my son. It's my duty, as well as my wish, to have him live with me. If I don't I'd be remiss and I'd be thought weak by my people. It would be an insult to you too, if I didn't marry you. And an insult to Ghizlan if I rejected her then didn't marry the mother of my son.'

Arden gritted her teeth. 'I'm a person in my own right.' She didn't care what his people or his Princess thought. All she cared about was Dawud.

'You would let your personal preferences stand in the way of Dawud's happiness and safety?'

'You're exaggerating. I've cared for him perfectly well up till now.'

'That was before.' A large hand covered hers, clamping it to the table. She was surprised how reassuring that touch felt. 'You've only had one day's taste of what the press can do. Do you want to put Dawud through that again and again?'

A chill invaded her bones. 'Surely once the novelty wears off…'

'Arden, this won't go away. Ever. Whenever there's an item of news about my country, or a slow media day, or a significant event for you or Dawud—a birthday, his first day at school, even weekend sports—the press will be there, snapping candid photos. They'll rehash the story—the difference between my life in the palace and his in London. Every step he takes will be pored over, particularly since he's so photogenic. Every decision you make as a mother will be scrutinised and judged.'

She was almost grateful for the warmth of his hand as her skin crawled at the picture he painted.

'Dawud won't have anywhere to hide. He'll be hounded, a freak for the press to exploit.'

Arden ripped her hand away and pressed it to her pounding chest. 'Dawud isn't a freak!'

'Of course not. He's a perfectly normal little boy.' Idris's voice curled comfortingly around her. 'I want him to stay that way.'

'By making him live in a palace!'

Idris's chuckle was rich and far too appealing. It reminded her of Shakil, the man who could make her heart turn over with just a smile. 'You make it sound like a prison. Believe me, Dawud can live a more normal life there than in London. In Zahrat I can protect you both.'

Arden swallowed a clot of apprehension. It was too extreme to contemplate. Yet in her heart of hearts she knew Idris was right. She and Dawud couldn't go back.

A great shudder racked her.

'I suppose we could try living in Zahrat, if you helped find us a house.' Could she work there? Did they even have florists? She put her hand to her temple, where a dull thudding headache had taken root.

'You would live in the palace. As my wife. It's the only sensible option. Together we can give him a stable home, no end-of-week handovers and complicated custody.' Idris didn't look aggressive now, just coolly composed. As if he knew he held all the aces.

Arden slumped in her seat. She felt cornered, her mind whirling fruitlessly as she sought alternatives to the one Idris presented.

'This is about Dawud,' he murmured. 'About what's best for our boy.'

Our boy. Not his son, or her son. *Our boy.*

That one small phrase bridged the gaping chasm between them. It made her feel less alone.

That shouldn't matter. She was used to shouldering responsibility. Yet there was a disarming allure to the idea of sharing this load.

'I need to think.' She slid her hand out from beneath his. 'I need time.'

'Of course. I'll come for your decision at nine tomorrow morning.'

At four the next afternoon, and after a night of soul-searching, Arden became betrothed to Idris, Sheikh of Zahrat in front of a throng of witnesses.

She'd planned to reject him. The idea of tying herself to the man who, accidentally or not, had left her floundering four years before, rankled. She wanted to walk away, defiant, independent and dismissive.

But she, more than most, understood what it was to be utterly alone and unprotected. If anything happened to her… No, Dawud had the right to grow up secure and loved, free from press intrusion, free to accept his birthright if he wished. And from all she'd been able to discover from the Internet, Idris would work as hard at being a good father as he did every other responsibility. He had a reputation for honest dealing and care for his subjects.

Yet her signature on the contract was shaky, like a child's just learning to write, because she trembled all over, her stomach twisting in knots. Beside her on his throne Idris signed with a slashing flourish that reflected complete ease.

No doubt he was used to signing important papers. But as she stared at the massive parchment with its gilt edging and beautiful decorative calligraphy border, Arden felt she'd signed her life away. Hers and her son's.

A chill clamped her neck and shoulders and her heart pounded so hard she was surprised no one heard it. She'd had no real choice, yet still she worried—

'Let me be the first to congratulate you.'

She looked up to see Princess Ghizlan. In an amber silk suit and a fortune in pearls around her throat, she looked every inch the glamorous, aristocratic princess. Everything Arden would never be, despite the costly outfit Idris had provided as an alternative to her ancient jeans.

Surprisingly the other woman's smile was warm and Arden felt grateful. She'd been alarmed when she'd spied the Princess amidst the serious men in the throne room. After all, she'd been all but jilted because of Arden.

'Thank you, Your—'

'Ghizlan, please.' She turned to Idris. 'Congratulations

on your betrothal, Your Highness. I hope you'll both be very happy.'

There was nothing in her face or his to indicate anything between them but calm goodwill. No tension, no fraught looks. Were they superb actors, Arden wondered, or was it true the match between them had been nothing but a formality? Arden's head spun. This royal world she'd entered was confusing and unnatural.

'Thank you.' His voice was deep and grave, a reminder that this ceremony was about securing his son's future, not anything as joyous or natural as a love match. He hadn't smiled once today.

Because this is about duty and respectability. Nothing more.

Arden's heart gave another heavy thump, rising up against her throat.

'I wondered if I might steal you away to take some refreshment.'

Arden was on her feet instantly then paused, wavering. Was she supposed to sit beside Idris to accept congratulations? But he was getting up and, frankly, she'd had enough formality.

'That sounds lovely.' As she followed the other woman to the lavish buffet her stomach growled. She'd been too nervous to eat.

'I'm the same,' said Ghizlan softly. 'I don't eat before official engagements then I regret it. They go on far too long.'

Arden cast a sideways look at the statuesque woman now filling a fine porcelain plate with delicacies.

'You really don't mind about…me?' she blurted out, then silently cursed her crassness. This wasn't the time or place. But she was curious about this poised, beautiful woman who'd so nearly married Idris.

The Princess cut her a swift look. 'Let's go somewhere

more comfortable.' She nodded to lounges in a corner Arden hadn't even seen.

All she'd noticed on entering the room was the crowd and Idris, tall and unsmiling. Her pulse had tumbled out of kilter as she drank in his spare, handsome features. It horrified her that just looking at him left her breathless.

'Arden? I may call you Arden?'

'Of course… Ghizlan. I'm sorry, I'm a little distracted.' She sank into a seat, carefully holding her plate of delicious-smelling food.

'I'm not surprised. If you're not used to these formal ceremonies they can be daunting.' The other woman leaned close. 'The trick is to have something else to think of during the boring bits. I do my best planning then.'

A smile tugged Arden's lips and some of that horrible, wound-too-tight feeling in her stomach settled. 'It's good of you to be so nice to me. I didn't expect—I mean, thank you. I didn't mean—'

Ghizlan's lustrous kohl-lined eyes widened, then she laughed, the sound rich and appealing. Male heads turned.

'You're absolutely welcome. I suspect I'm going to like you very much.'

Arden plonked her plate on a table and leaned closer. 'I didn't mean it to come out that way.'

Ghizlan waved away her words. 'It's good to hear someone so frank. You'll understand once you're hemmed in by diplomats and courtiers. And you're right.' She paused. 'This is tough for all of us.'

'I'm truly sorry about that.'

'It's not your fault. None of us had a choice once the news came out about your boy.'

Arden searched the beautiful face for signs of hurt but read nothing. 'It must be especially difficult for you.'

Ghizlan looked away. 'A diplomatic storm, that's for

sure. But it will pass. Our betrothal hadn't been formalised, and now, if you and I are seen together on friendly terms things will ease a little.'

Slowly Arden nodded. *That* was why Ghizlan was here. It wasn't simple goodwill behind this *tête-à-tête*. Disappointment stirred. 'I see. You think this—' her gesture encompassed the pair of them in the intimate cluster of seats '—will help stave off gossip?'

'Now *you're* offended. I'm sorry. I told Idris you mightn't want me here, but he assured me there was no sentimental attachment between you. Please forgive me.'

She made to rise but Arden's out-thrust hand stopped her. 'No, please.'

A roiling wave of emotion surged through her. Idris's words shouldn't hurt. They were true. Anything they'd once felt for each other was long dead. And what had Ghizlan done but try to ameliorate a disaster?

'I'm sorry.' Arden swallowed hard. 'I do appreciate you being here. It must have been difficult for you and it's nice to have another woman here.'

'I thought it might help. Plus it will take some of the fuel from the fire if it looks like I'm in London to support you instead of being on approval for Idris.'

'On approval?'

Ghizlan's face took on that smooth, unruffled expression that Arden now realised masked other feelings. 'Our marriage was to build a bridge between our two countries that have feuded for generations. It was tied to a peace treaty and a trade agreement but still, we needed a little time in each other's company to…test the waters.'

Arden blinked as something hot and jagged, something almost like jealousy, bit into her. But she jammed a stop on her imagination before she could wonder how far *testing the waters* went.

'There'll be hell to pay when I return home but meanwhile supporting you helps us both by deflecting the worst of the gossip.'

Arden looked into that beautiful face, so still and poised, and realised how much courage it took for the other woman to be here, smiling as if her hopes of marriage hadn't been dashed so scandalously. If she…*cared* for Idris…

To her amazement, fellow feeling rose. She'd loved and lost him once and it had soured her on the idea of love ever since. But she'd never forgotten the pain. It still sideswiped her when she least expected it.

'I like your thinking, Ghizlan.' Arden hesitated then plunged on. 'Maybe you could advise me a little about what to expect? I know nothing about protocol and ceremony, or even what I should wear.'

She looked down at the pretty pale blue dress that shimmered under the brilliant lights. It had appeared in her room this morning and she'd accepted it gratefully rather than face this ceremony in old denims.

If she let herself dwell on how unprepared she was, she'd hide away and never come out. Or work herself into a fury at how she was being railroaded. But it was too late for second thoughts.

'You like the dress?'

'It's gorgeous. But I have no experience in buying expensive clothes and I have no idea what's required for…' Arden's words faded as she saw the smile on the other woman's face. '*You* picked this?'

Ghizlan shrugged. 'Just gave a couple of suggestions. I thought, given how quickly this all happened you mightn't have anything suitable for today.'

Arden blinked as gratitude welled. 'You really are a nice woman, aren't you?'

Before she could feel self-conscious about blurting out her thoughts again, Ghizlan gave a delighted laugh.

* * *

Idris followed the muted sound of laughter to see both women with their heads together. One dark, one golden, both beautiful, his rejected bride and his affianced bride.

His belly tightened at the thought of the frantic work he had still to do to salvage something from the debacle caused by Arden and Dawud. Relations with Ghizlan's royal father were in tatters, as were the treaties they'd negotiated. Conservative elements in his own country were up in arms about his illegitimate son and his plans to marry an Englishwoman. Yet what alternative did he have?

Any other course would be ruinous.

Any other course would deprive him of his son and make Dawud an object of ridicule and gossip.

Any other course would deprive him of Arden.

He watched her lean in to talk with Ghizlan. The movement tugged her silk dress tight, outlining that slim, delicious figure he'd fantasised about all night.

With half an ear he listened to the conversation around him, the first steps in building a new rapport with representatives of Ghizlan's father. Yet his attention was fixed on Arden. The woman he would marry.

For the first time since he'd agreed to consider taking a bride, he felt a sharp tug of eagerness.

Arden might be trouble on two beautiful, sexy legs. She had no pedigree, no dowry or influence in his region. Worse, she had no training for a royal role, no knowledge of diplomacy or the arcane ceremonies and rituals which still persisted at court.

Yet she was the mother of his son and for that alone would be accorded respect.

Except that wasn't the only reason he would marry her, was it? Last night he'd confronted the uncomfortable truth that he couldn't in all honesty marry Ghizlan when it was Arden he wanted in his bed.

Want was such a weak word for the hunger simmering within him. It might be just sex, but it felt alarmingly like a compulsion. Like the weakness all the men of his family shared, a weakness he'd thought he'd put aside when he took on the sheikhdom.

He must learn to conquer this weakness or master it. He intended to approach this marriage like any other contract. With a cool head and in total control.

CHAPTER SIX

'An air-conditioned limousine will drive you and your son to the palace, Ms Wills.' Ashar, the Sheikh's aide, smiled reassuringly from the seat beside her on the plane. 'It's a short drive and it won't be long before you're settling into your rooms to rest.'

'Thank you.' A rest sounded wonderful. Even here in the comfort of Idris's private jet Arden hadn't been able to relax.

Perhaps because she wasn't used to people waiting on her. Misha, their temporary nanny, had taken Dawud to another cabin in the luxurious aircraft so Arden didn't have the distraction of a toddler who'd crush her new designer suit. Yet instead of revelling in the luxury of some quiet time Arden felt deprived. Of course she could have gone to him, but deep down she realised her stress wasn't about Dawud, it was about her fears for the future.

What had she done, agreeing to leave London and marry Idris? Could she marry him and trust him to do what was best for Dawud?

Logic reminded her Idris wasn't the carefree, careless young man who'd left her bereft and struggling. She'd seen the change in him. Yet she couldn't stifle unease.

Everything had happened so fast, the betrothal ceremony, the blur of new faces as Idris's personal staff were introduced. The shopping trip with Ghizlan to a famous couturier who'd opened his doors just for them while stony-faced security men kept the press at a distance.

Resigning from her job by phone had been a surreal experience. Her boss had read about her 'adventure' and had been agog for news. Arden was left with the unsettling suspicion she'd be more valuable to the business now she was an almost-VIP and potential drawcard than ever before. As for closing up the flat—it had been done for her. Idris had spoken to Hamid before she could, explaining she wouldn't be returning.

Of everything that had happened in the last few days, that was the worst. It felt as if her life had been ripped away. She'd poured in hours of work and what little cash she had, turning it into a warm, bright home, full of treasured memories.

It didn't matter that everything was done efficiently and with exquisite politeness by the royal staff. Beneath every courteous query about her preferences lay a stark, terrifying truth.

She had no choice in anything that mattered now. She'd agreed to marry Dawud's father and their lives would be dominated by that from now on.

'I'm sorry.' She blinked and focused on the royal aide. 'You were saying?'

'I asked if you'd like some water or anything else. You look pale and we're about to land. If you're ill…?'

Arden shook her head. 'I'm okay, thanks. Just tired.'

'Then I'll leave you alone for now.' Ashar nodded and melted away.

Arden's lips twisted. Wasn't that the perfect indicator of what this royal marriage would be like? It wasn't her soon-to-be husband asking about her well-being. Idris had excused himself as soon as they boarded and headed into a study off the main cabin. She'd barely seen him since she'd agreed to marry him. It was left to his ever-watchful staff to be concerned for her.

Arden straightened her shoulders. She didn't need their concern. She could do this. She *had* to do this.

No matter how tough, no matter how challenging her

new life, she'd face it like she'd faced everything else life threw at her.

After a lifetime solo, one important thing had changed. She was no longer alone. She had Dawud. He was more precious to her than anything, even phantom memories of first love and heartbreak.

She did this for her son.

Arden turned to look out of the window, staring at the misty blue mountains that rose in the distance, jagged and forbidding. Below her a broad, tawny plain sprawled to the coast where white sand edged a turquoise sea.

Zahrat. Legendary for its fiercely independent people and its arid vastness of desert and rugged mountains.

Despite her determination to be strong, Arden couldn't repress a fervent wish that she and Dawud were safely back in London, leading their familiar, ordinary lives.

From astride his horse Idris surveyed the people lining the streets that wound through the capital. Every man, woman and child, it seemed, had come out to see their Sheikh make his traditional entry to the city.

And to see his son, and the Englishwoman who'd soon be their Sheikha.

As decreed by custom, there was no applause, no shouting, merely bowed heads as he passed. Yet that didn't stop the crowd craning for a view of the vehicle following him, the car carrying Arden and Dawud.

He'd wondered how the news of his ready-made family would be taken. Not that anything would deter him from his duty to marry.

His people were proud and traditional. No doubt the older, more conservative ones would frown about a foreign bride. Yet he noticed a few silken banners, a customary sign of rejoicing, flying in the street. Turquoise for the sea that bordered Zahrat and scarlet for the desert at sunset, or, as popular belief had it, for the blood of their enemies, shed whenever the Zahrati defended their land.

Idris was musing on this sign of welcome when the Captain of the Royal Guard rode close.

'Highness. The car. It's stopped.'

Instantly alert, Idris whipped around, pulling his horse to a halt.

There was no sign of a problem yet his heartbeat quickened, his body tense, ready for action as he scanned the street for signs of an ambush. Security was a necessity these days, yet in his homeland Idris had always felt his bodyguard was more to satisfy tradition than because of any threat.

But if anyone were to threaten Dawud and Arden—

The rear door of the limousine opened and she emerged, the afternoon sun turning her hair to spun rose gold. The quiet crowd seemed to still completely. The silence grew complete so the thud of his horse's hooves as it pranced towards the car filled the void. That and the rough pulse of blood in his ears.

What was she doing? No stop had been scheduled. Was she ill? Was his son ill?

Idris vaulted from his horse, thrusting the reins into the hand of a nearby guard, then slammed to a halt.

That was why the cavalcade had stopped?

Arden crossed to the side of the street where the onlookers crowded in the shade of an ancient shop awning. Near the front of the packed group one single person had ignored tradition. A girl, no more than six or seven by the look of her skinny frame. She sat in a wheelchair, gripping a straggly bouquet of flowers, her eyes huge as Arden approached.

In her slim-fitting straw-coloured suit that gleamed subtly under the fierce sun, Arden probably looked like a creature from another world to the girl.

The sight of Arden, cool and sophisticated with her high

heels and her hair up, had stolen his breath when he'd seen her earlier. The air had punched from his lungs as desire surged, as fresh and strong as it had been years ago. Desire and admiration and something else, some emotion that was tangled up in the fact she'd borne his child. *His responsibility to protect. His.*

His visceral reaction had been possessiveness. The desire to claim her, and with far more than words, had sent him into retreat. He'd taken a separate vehicle to the airport and on the plane had immersed himself in work. Keeping his distance meant keeping control.

Arden stopped before the girl and crouched down, saying something he couldn't make out. He strode across, his steps decisive on the ancient cobbles.

The girl whispered something, shyly smiling, and held out the flowers which, he saw now, were no more than a collection of wildflowers such as grew in the rare fertile areas near the city. One of them, yellow as the sun, looked like a dandelion.

But Arden held them carefully, as if they were the most precious bouquet.

'*Shukran jazīlan,* Leila.'

The little girl's face lit up and from the clustering crowd murmurs rose.

Idris stopped, stunned. Arden spoke his language? He listened, amazed, as she went on, haltingly but competently, to ask where the girl lived.

The conversation was short, for soon the child noticed him and grew too shy to speak.

Idris repressed a frown. The girl's reaction wasn't surprising. People didn't address the royal Sheikh unless invited, yet he couldn't help but feel like a big, black thundercloud, blotting out the sun and marring their rapport. Especially when Arden looked over her shoulder, her mouth compressing when she saw him.

He didn't want her to look at him like that. He wanted her to look at him with the dazed longing he'd seen too briefly the day he'd kissed her at her front door. Or, better yet, with that expression of awe and bliss he remembered from years ago, when she'd been eager for him, especially in bed.

His thoughts horrified. Here, on the main street of his capital, under the gaze of thousands of his subjects, he was fretting over a woman. He was caught in a morass of political and diplomatic difficulties because of the current scandal—every waking moment he was busy negotiating a minefield of trouble and trying to salvage the peace treaty—and he let himself be distracted.

Arden stood and turned, her expression this time blank. Which, absurdly, made Idris clamp his jaw tighter as he took her arm and escorted her to the car.

She felt surprisingly fragile beneath the fine fabric of her new clothes, making him even more aware of the imbalance of power between them. He told himself they were both victims of circumstance. He did only what he must for the sake of his child and his country. But he disliked the reminder of Arden's fragility, the fact she'd given up everything she knew to come here, an unwilling bride.

He paused, breathing deep, searching for the sense of calm and control that had eluded him since Arden had burst back into his life.

With careful courtesy he helped her into the car, gave a few instructions to waiting staff, then stalked around the car and got in.

Arden's eyes widened as Idris took the far corner of the back seat. Even with Dawud's child seat between them Idris dominated the rear of the huge limo.

He'd looked larger than life astride his gleaming horse and to her dismay her heart had done crazy flip flops as she watched him through the windscreen. She'd never seen him in traditional dress and was amazed how the horseman's outfit with loose trousers tucked into long boots, a white headdress and light cloak had turned the most attractive man she'd ever seen into the stuff of pure fantasy.

The fantasy had died when she'd turned to find him looming over her like a disgruntled bear. He couldn't have made it clearer that she'd broken some taboo by getting out of the car and talking to little Leila.

Arden refused to apologise. Her heart had caught at the sight of the little girl and that one tiny token of welcome after kilometres of staring, silent, obviously disapproving people.

'Are you going to tell me off now or wait till we get to the palace?' She glanced at the closed window shutting them off from the driver and bodyguard in the front.

'Tell you off?' His words were abrupt, as if jerked from him.

Arden rolled her eyes and turned. He looked as forbidding as he had out on the street but stupidly some weak, utterly female part of her found him compellingly handsome. Her gaze dropped to his sculpted lips, now in a flat line, and she had the crazy impulse to lean over and kiss him till his pent-up fury disappeared.

That was one impulse she would *not* give in to!

She opened her mouth to speak but a sound stopped her. She whipped her head around to stare at the people crowding the street. The noise, a high-pitched, rhythmic trill, swelled, surrounding them, making the hairs on her arms prickle upright.

'What's that?' Reflexively one arm shot protectively across the front of the seat where Dawud slept.

'It's all right. It's nothing to worry about.' Idris's deep voice reassured. 'Quite the opposite. It's a sign of approval.'

'Approval?' Her head jerked around as the car slid forward.

Idris's lips quirked at one corner. Not quite a smile but the closest she'd seen to one in days, and even that had been directed at Dawud, not her.

'Don't look so worried. Approval of you.'

'Me?' She turned back to look out of the window, watching the faces slide by. 'Why? Because I spoke to that little girl? Surely it's not such a big deal.' In the UK it wasn't unusual for VIPs to talk with people who'd waited patiently to see them. Besides, Arden was a long way from being a VIP. She felt like an imposter in this procession.

'It *is* a big deal in Zahrat. Where the royal family is concerned tradition is slow to change. And tradition has it that when the Sheikh enters the city his people will greet him in silence, bowing to show their loyalty.'

Arden's heart sank. She hadn't even arrived at the palace and already she'd broken some important rule.

'So I shouldn't have stopped and got out?' She frowned. 'Leila won't get into trouble, will she? I spoke to her before she spoke to me, you know.'

He shook his head, that elusive hint of a smile rippling further along his mouth. She felt an answering pang deep inside. Once his smile had made her glow all over, when she'd believed he loved her.

'Far from it. She'll be the centre of attention. She'll probably dine out on the story when she's old and grey.'

'So it's just me who's broken the unwritten law.'

'More a guideline than a law.' Lustrous dark eyes held hers and Arden felt her heart thump against her ribcage. 'And I told you, that's approval you hear. You'll hear it again the day we celebrate our wedding.'

She'd got this far by not thinking about their marriage. It was a travesty of all she held dear. To marry not for love but for show went against all the hopes she'd once cherished.

'They were impressed too that you spoke our language.' He paused. '*I* was impressed. Why didn't you tell me?'

'Why should I? Clearly it made no difference to my suitability as your wife.' Was it imagination or did she truly taste bitterness on the word *wife*? 'Besides, I don't really speak it. I started learning but didn't get far. I was too busy with Dawud and work.' She thought grimly how those words glossed over her constant exhaustion as she'd struggled to provide for her son. Lucky she was good at her job so her boss had been understanding. 'I only know some very basic phrases but Hamid helped me practice the pronunciation.'

Idris's eyebrows slanted down in what could only be described as a scowl. What was his problem? That she only knew a few phrases after all? Or was it something to do with Hamid? Surely he wasn't still convinced she and Hamid were lovers? He'd spoken to his cousin. He must know now that wasn't true, even if Hamid had begun to see their relationship leading further than she wanted it to go.

'Nevertheless, it's a valuable bonus that you know as much as you do, and that you've demonstrated it to my people. That's one more thing in your favour when it comes to them accepting this marriage.'

'In addition to my son, you mean?'

Idris had made it clear their relationship, if you could call it that, was a necessary evil.

'*Our* son, Arden.'

For long seconds he held her gaze, till she felt heat rise in her cheeks and turned away. It was fantasy to imagine she read something intimate in those black velvet eyes.

The road was rising and above the rooftops a citadel rose, amber in the sunlight, on sheer cliffs. A massive palace grew there, apparently out of the very rock. Its roof glittered, dazzling her eyes even from this distance.

Idris must have followed her gaze.

'The Palace of Gold,' he murmured. 'Your new home.'

CHAPTER SEVEN

ARDEN HAD BEEN dumbfounded by the palace when she'd seen it from the limousine. But the interior was even more stunning. The older parts of the building featured walls studded with semi-precious jewels, while the modernised sections were unlike anything she'd ever seen.

She knew Idris was a man with a deeply sensual side but she was shocked at the luxury of his home. Until Ashar, her guide when Idris excused himself and disappeared down another corridor, mentioned it had been Idris's uncle, the previous Sheikh, who'd lavishly updated the royal accommodation.

Arden's suite was vast, comprising a bedroom for Dawud with a bathroom and playroom that linked to accommodation for the nanny. For Arden there was a sitting room, study and bedroom. The bedroom had three walls of pale sea-green silk which on one side hid a walk-in wardrobe and a bathroom almost as big as her old flat.

Scallop-edged arched windows gave an unrivalled view of the city and the coast beyond. Her bed, the biggest she'd ever seen, sat on a raised platform with ornamental drapes of silver tissue pulled back from the head. Exquisite raised plasterwork on the wall behind it gave the impression of a vast silvery tree with delicate curling shoots and leaves inlaid with mother-of-pearl.

She couldn't begin to imagine how many hours of craftsmanship had gone into decorating the room, much less the cost.

As for sleeping here…

Arden shook her head. She'd feel like an imposter,

curled up in that vast luxurious bed. The room was a breathtaking fantasy, designed for a princess.

She looked down at the silver-embroidered bedspread, noticing intricately stitched figures of horsemen in procession, banners streaming, riding across the spread. Horsemen with the proud warrior demeanour of Idris as he'd sat astride his stallion today. Until she'd stopped the cavalcade to talk with Leila.

Arden stared at her hand on the fine embroidery. Pale skin instead of the lovely golden colour of the locals and of Princess Ghizlan. Short, sensible nails. Hands that were nimble and strong after years working as a florist, wiring bouquets, lifting heavy buckets of water, snipping and arranging and making deliveries. *Not* the delicate, pampered hands of a princess, despite her recent manicure.

What on earth was she doing here?

Arden's knees gave way and she collapsed onto the edge of the mattress, chest tight and breath unsteady.

Just as well she'd left Dawud in his playroom under Misha's watchful eye while she explored the suite. Arden didn't want him to see her anything but calm. She couldn't afford to let her doubts and fears mar his acceptance of their new surroundings. Not if they were to stay here.

Anxiety gnawed at her belly.

She firmed her lips. She'd already faced this doubt and decided she was doing the right thing for Dawud. Yet that didn't stop the horrible sensation of being trapped. Losing control of her future scared her, as much as the unwanted emotions Idris stirred. The longing for what could never be. What she needed now was something familiar, something normal. Someone on her side.

Hamid. She hadn't spoken to him since the night of the embassy reception. The night her life went off the rails.

Arden reached for her phone, then hesitated. She'd

wanted to talk with Hamid about the change in him—from friend to would-be lover. But so much had happened that she hadn't picked up the phone. Now, thanks to Idris, Hamid knew she was betrothed to his cousin.

She drew in a slow breath. This wouldn't be easy. But no matter what false hopes Hamid had begun to harbour, he'd been a good friend when she needed him and she owed him an explanation. She'd never told him who Dawud's father was, because by then she'd given up trying to find him, believing Shakil had unceremoniously duped and dumped her. Hamid must be reeling too.

She punched in his number and lifted the phone.

Idris found her in the bedroom. She still wore the pale gold suit that emphasised her slenderness, but she'd kicked off her shoes. The sight of her bare feet on the intricate mosaic floor conjured images of the rest of her naked. Naked and willing in his bed. Once her fresh enthusiasm, sweet honesty and sexy body had made her more alluring than any woman he'd known. It seemed that hadn't changed.

His heart gave a now familiar thump—a symptom of the weakness he hadn't been able to eradicate. Even now when, because of her, he faced a diplomatic nightmare in his homeland and more especially with their regional neighbours.

Relations with Ghizlan's country had been tinder-dry for generations and the prospect of a dynastic marriage to seal their new-found peace was a huge win for his people's well-being. Now that was in tatters.

He should be dealing with the fallout, ensuring peace and prosperity, especially now he had a family to care for as well as a nation. Instead he'd taken a break from crisis talks that would go on all night to check on Arden. Idris raised a hand to knock but let it fall as she spoke.

'I understand, Hamid.' She leaned against the window

frame, her posture defeated—head bowed and shoulders slumped. 'Of course.' She swiped at her cheek. 'Goodbye, then.'

The sight of her dejection hit Idris a hammer blow. There was a crammed full feeling in his chest, the suspicion of an ache there at odds with the fire of anger in his belly. Was she really so cut up about leaving Hamid? Had she been in love with him?

Idris considered himself a civilised man, far removed from the tyrants who'd ruled this country long ago. Yet at the moment he'd happily have slammed his fist into his cousin before throwing him into a dungeon.

He stepped into the room, the riding boots he still wore loud on the fine tiles.

Arden's head whipped up and he had a swift impression of tear-glazed eyes and burning cheeks before she pivoted away to place her phone on a bedside table.

When she turned back her colour was high but she was completely composed.

'I'd prefer you to knock before coming into my room.' She folded her arms. Did she know how provocative she looked? Her hair was coming down in sensual waves around her shoulders and her touch-me-not air was an incitement to tip her back onto the bed and put an end to the pretence she didn't want him as he wanted her.

Except she'd been crying over his cousin. The thought was an icy douche to desire.

'You'll need to get used to my presence in the suite.' When she opened her mouth he continued. 'I intend to see my son regularly and establish a relationship with him. I've got three years to catch up on, remember?'

Slowly Arden nodded. 'Of course.' Her voice was croaky. 'But not in my bedroom.'

Idris was tempted to inform her this was the royal bedroom, to be shared by the Sheikh and Sheikha. But she looked so damnably vulnerable with her stiff spine and sad eyes. It made him feel, yet again, that *he* were in the wrong. When he was the one putting things right!

Besides, he'd promised himself he'd keep out of Arden's bed. There was enough scandal already. He would honour tradition and his bride-to-be by keeping his distance temporarily.

'Then come into the sitting room. We need to talk.'

Arden watched him disappear with a swish of his long cloak from spectacular shoulders and fought the squiggle of feminine heat swirling through her.

Would it always be this way? Would she always go weak at the knees around Idris?

She flattened her lips and told herself it was just memory—the fact he'd been her first and only lover. In time she'd look at him and feel nothing.

The enormity of that lie almost undid her. If anything, her yearning for the warmth they'd once shared, the crazy but potent sense of belonging, was stronger than in all the years since they'd parted.

She didn't want to face him. But she had no choice.

He stood near the window, feet wide, hands on hips, face set in stern lines. He looked as if he ruled everything he surveyed.

Arden bit down rueful laughter, realising it was true. He *did* rule it all.

'You wanted to talk?' She sank onto a chair, repressing a flutter of foreboding. His mouth looked stern, as if something displeased him.

That would be her. Already defying protocol on her first day as well as upsetting his plans for a grand marriage.

The idea of becoming Sheikha was as appealing as walking a tightrope. She hated the certainty she'd fail ignominiously.

'I do. We need to set some ground rules.'

'Ground rules?' Her brow puckered.

His wide shoulders lifted. 'We've had no discussion about our expectations of each other.'

Arden sank back. 'You mean like not coming into my room uninvited?'

His lips flattened but he nodded. 'That sort of thing.'

Arden racked her tired brain. This wasn't the best time to talk, when she was exhausted and stressed. But she owed it to herself and Dawud to take the opportunity.

'I want an equal say in all decisions affecting Dawud, his education and how he lives.'

Idris's black eyebrows slanted down. 'There are traditions around how a crown prince is raised.'

'And I'll try to respect as many of those as I can. But I insist on the right to decide, with you.' It was an enormous concession. She'd always made every decision for her son. Learning to share would be tough—relinquishing any control over him scared her. But she'd agreed living here was best for Dawud. Now, reluctantly, she had to make that work, no matter the personal sacrifices, like pretending to be something she wasn't and consulting Idris on important issues.

'If I don't like the traditional ways, I expect full consultation. I expect us to negotiate an agreed solution. And I need that agreement in writing.' Arden laced her fingers tightly. Idris had the weight of royal authority but she refused to budge. She couldn't gamble on Dawud's well-being. 'If you can't agree to that the deal is off.'

Those expressive eyebrows rose. 'You'd try to back out of the marriage?'

Arden lifted her chin. 'Not *try*. I *would*. I'm accepting your terms by coming to live here, and by agreeing to marry. But I won't give up the right to decide what's best for my son.'

For long seconds Idris surveyed her silently, then abruptly he nodded. 'That's fair. I agree.'

Arden sank back, her heart racing. She'd been prepared for a fight.

'What else?'

What else mattered as much as her son?

'I'll try not to flout too many traditions in Zahrat, but I'd prefer to wear my own clothes, western clothes, most of the time. I wouldn't be comfortable wearing a veil.'

His sculpted lips lifted at the corners. 'You may not have noticed, but veils are optional. A lot of women, at least in the cities, opt for western dress. Zahrat is traditional in many ways but very few would expect a European woman to dress in Zahrati costume.' He paused. 'Anything more?'

There were probably lots of things but that was all she could think of at the moment. Except for one thing.

'Even though this isn't an ordinary marriage, I'd prefer it if you kept any…liaisons private. I don't want to know about them and I don't want Dawud to hear about them when he's older.' It would be enough trying to make this marriage of convenience work without Idris flaunting his lovers. The idea of those faceless, but no doubt gorgeous, women made her feel nauseous.

'My liaisons?' The hint of a smile vanished from his face.

'Your lovers.' She dragged in a tight breath. 'I'd appreciate you being discreet.'

His nostrils flared as if he repressed annoyance, but he gave a curt nod. 'Agreed.'

Arden tried to feel relieved but instead felt absurdly wobbly. Her husband-to-be had just promised to keep his lovers out of sight. It wasn't as if this were a love match. It was a paper marriage for purely practical reasons, but it seemed plain wrong to go into it making arrangements for other women to share her husband's bed.

Especially when, to her dismay, he still made her crave intimacies she'd never shared with anyone but him. Not just sex but the warm feeling of being appreciated, being special.

'Arden?'

'Sorry?'

'I asked if there was anything else.'

She shook her head. 'That's all I can think of at the moment. Now, if you'll excuse me…' She made to get up from her seat.

'Not so fast. You haven't heard my expectations.' Gleaming eyes held hers and suddenly Arden found herself breathless.

'It's not enough that I move here and agree to marry you? I'm the one making all the concessions.' Her voice was strident, masking nerves.

'Believe it or not, we're both making compromises, Arden.' He said no more but she knew he was thinking of Princess Ghizlan, beautiful, charming, no doubt with a pedigree a mile long and an innate knowledge of diplomacy and protocol and royal ceremony and all those things Arden was totally lacking.

'Okay.' She knotted her fingers in her lap. 'What else?'

'Since you raise it, no lovers. Not even in secret. Once you marry me I expect complete loyalty.' His face had that stark look again, nostrils flared and jaw taut.

Arden stared. What difference could that make when this wasn't a real marriage? Then she realised she was about to protest just for the sake of it. She'd had no interest in men since Shakil/Idris, especially since Dawud's birth and her almost constant state of exhaustion. As for the frisson of erotic energy she felt when she was with Idris, she knew it was only a hangover from the past. She couldn't imagine herself ever having the time or inclination to fancy herself in love with anyone else.

'Okay.'

His eyebrows slanted up as if he'd expected an argument. 'And I'd rather you kept contact with my cousin to a minimum. Friendships between men and women aren't the norm in Zahrat and your friendship would be misinterpreted.'

'You don't ask much, do you?'

Idris said nothing, just waited for her response.

Once more she felt like refusing him, because surely what he asked was unreasonable. Except she'd already just said goodbye to one of her closest friends. Hamid had told her it didn't feel right to maintain their friendship once she married his cousin. Reading between the lines Arden knew he was hurt she'd chosen Idris. Whichever way she looked at it, her friendship with Hamid was in the past.

'Very well,' she muttered, 'I'll avoid contact with Hamid.' She paused, waiting for more. Except suddenly she couldn't take any more. Arden shot to her feet. 'If that's all, I'd like to be alone now. I'm tired from the trip.'

She was already heading for the door when his words pulled her up short.

'That's not quite all.'

'Yes?' She tried to guess what other condition he'd put on their arrangement. Limiting contact with her other friends perhaps? Or her freedom of movement? Wearily Arden pushed her shoulders back and turned, ready to fight for her rights.

'The wedding.'

'Yes?' *The wedding.* Not *our* wedding. The formal ceremony that would seal her fate and Dawud's. A tremor shot from her nape to the soles of her feet.

'It will be held in ten days.' His tone was even and unemotional. Everything Arden didn't feel at the prospect of marriage.

'So soon?' She pressed a palm to her chest where her heart nosedived.

He shrugged. 'There's no point waiting. The sooner this situation is settled the better.'

Situation being code for *scandal*. For an unwanted wife and an illegitimate son.

'Don't worry, all the arrangements will be taken care of.'

In other words she'd have no say in her own wedding.

Arden told herself that suited her perfectly. 'And if I want to invite anyone?'

'Let Ashar know and he'll organise the invitations.'

'I will.' She paused. 'That's all now?'

A tiny frown settled on Idris's brow. Why? Had he expected her to make demands about the size of the cake or the colour scheme? As far as Arden was concerned it was far better someone else organised the nuptial extravaganza. She didn't have the stomach for it.

'No, that's all.'

'Good. Then I'll see you later.'

She needn't have worried about Idris coming to her room. For ten days she never saw him alone.

So much for the rogue idea he might want her in his bed.

At least he was serious about building a relationship with his son. He'd breakfast with them then stop by after Dawud's bath to play a game or read a story in his own language. The gleam in Idris's eyes when he was with Dawud, the rich, enveloping sound of his laughter, tugged her back to those halcyon days on Santorini. Except, unlike *their* affair, this would last. For, to her surprise, she saw something like love in Idris's expression when he looked at their son, not duty. Their connection was real and growing. It brought a lump to her throat, seeing them together. She'd done the right thing—Dawud needed his dad too.

Inevitably though, Ashar waited in the wings, reminding Idris of his next meeting, making her wonder when he ever stopped.

Arden told herself she was grateful. She didn't *want* to see Idris alone. She had enough to do.

There were the language classes, classes on Zahrati customs and history, plus an increasing number of appointments and requests. Would she wear a gift of exquisite ivory silk from the silk weavers' guild at her wedding? Would she permit a women's embroidery group the honour of decorating the cloth with traditional bridal designs? Would she visit the school Leila, the girl she'd met during the procession, attended?

Her days were crammed and she lived on tenterhooks, knowing and hating the fact she'd inevitably make mistakes. It seemed impossible she'd ever succeed in this new role Idris expected of her. But if she failed would Dawud be accepted? That worry kept her trying, despite her reservations. Despite her exhaustion, she was too wired to sleep. Instead, each night she'd watch the shadows wheel across the vaulted ceiling above her bed.

Tonight, though, she'd sleep. Wedding preparations had begun at dawn and there would be not one but two ceremonies, one English and one Zahrati, followed by feasting and celebrations.

Butterflies, or perhaps a huge Zahrati eagle, emblem of the royal house, swooped and swirled in Arden's stomach as her attendants led her through the palace. As they approached the state rooms the exquisite furnishings became even more lavish, the scale of the interior growing till the cluster of twenty women were dwarfed.

With each step Arden felt the swish of fine fabric around her legs, the weight of heavy antique pearl necklaces so fabulous she hadn't believed they could be real. That was until her golden wedding coronet was placed on her head. Delicately made, it had flowers of ruby and sapphire, each with lustrous pearl petals.

Arden's neck was tight, her shoulders stiff and achy. She told herself it was fear that if she bent her head the coronet would slip off, despite the pins securing it.

But deep down she knew it was the thought of marriage to Idris knotting tension within her. Her heart raced as she halted before vast gilded doors.

Was she doing the right thing?

She was doing the only thing that seemed right for her son.

Still she was more nervous even than when she'd gone into labour.

Her retinue fussed and fiddled, tweaking her long skirts, adjusting her necklaces and bracelets. One elegant lady took Arden's hand in both of hers and said something earnestly in a lilting voice. The other women murmured the same words, smiling, and she guessed it was a blessing.

She was about to ask what they'd said when the doors swung open and sound assaulted her. Laughter, music, voices. Her eyes widened. She'd seen the Hall of a Thousand Pillars before. It was one of the most spectacular rooms in the palace, but never had she seen it filled to capacity. It looked and sounded as if the whole city had crowded in.

Arden stood, dazed. She swallowed hard and told herself she would not flee.

Abruptly all sound ceased as if someone had switched off a soundtrack. Every head turned towards her. She breathed deep, telling herself to enter, but her feet stuck to the floor.

She heard a noise—the steady pace of the man approaching her, tall and magnificent in traditional robes, dazzling in white and gold.

Arden's heart stuttered as he filled her vision, so imposing, so attractive. She reminded herself this was a sham marriage, perpetrated to protect their son. But as Idris smiled and took her hand, heat poured through her. Her pulse leapt and she leaned towards him, as naturally as years ago when she'd loved him with all her youthful heart.

'You are beautiful, Arden. Breathtaking.' The words were for her alone as his lips brushed her temple.

That was when she realised how dangerous this was. How easy it would be to believe the fantasy that she and Idris shared something more than the need to protect their boy.

It was as if she *wanted* to believe Idris desired her, respected her, loved her.

Arden closed her eyes, summoning the courage she'd built over the years when she needed to face down the odds and be strong for Dawud.

When she opened them Idris was still there, still looking like the answer to every woman's prayer.

But he was her partner in a contract, not her lover. Together they would protect Dawud and give him the future he deserved.

'Thank you for the compliment.' It was only encouragement to see her through a difficult day. 'And you look spectacular too.' She let him lead her into the vast room, head up, spine straight and a smile fixed on her lips.

Arden swayed with tiredness as her attendants stripped the exquisite ivory and gold wedding gown away and led her to the bathroom. Steam curled invitingly from the bath in the centre of the room and blush-pink rose petals covered the surface of the water.

A bath fit for a royal bride.

Suddenly all the pomp, glamour and luxury of the day mocked her.

She needed to be alone.

She'd done her best to play her part, smiling through the endless speeches and ceremonies. Not flinching when Idris took her hand and led her to a fabulous gilded throne. Nor when he fed her delicacies from his plate, his eyes shining with a look anyone who didn't know the truth would interpret as desire. Only Arden knew it was satisfaction that they'd got through the day without a hitch.

But enough was enough.

'Thanks very much, but no.' She shook her head as a servant approached, ready to attend her in the bath. 'I prefer to bathe alone.'

Still it took a few moments to convince them she was serious. When they'd gone she stripped off her lace underwear, pinned her hair and sank into the bath.

A sigh escaped. Or was it a groan? The warm water did marvellous things to muscles twisted with tension. For the first time in hours she began to relax in the bliss of the fragrant bath.

She was dozing, her head lolling against the cushioned headrest when she heard the door open.

'I'm fine,' she murmured drowsily. 'I don't need any help.'

'Not even to scrub your back?' The voice, deep and soft like a ribbon of plush velvet, stroked her bare skin.

CHAPTER EIGHT

WATER SPLASHED AS she sat up, twisting towards the door.

'Idris!' It was the barest wisp of sound. Her voice disintegrated as she took him in.

Gone were the white robes he'd worn for their wedding. Now there were only loose trousers of fine cotton, slung low across his hips. His torso was bare, a muscled, glorious expanse of dark gold with a smattering of ebony hair across his pectorals, resolving into a thin, dark line bisecting his abdomen. Arden remembered being fascinated by that line, and where it led, in the week they'd once spent together.

She swallowed hard.

As she watched, muscles rippled across his chest and abdomen, as if stirred by her stare.

Instantly she dragged her gaze up. It collided with a bright, intense look that reminded her she was naked.

Arden drew her knees up to her breasts, looping an arm tight around her legs.

'What are you doing here?'

His mouth curled in a smile that drove a sexy groove down one cheek and made her aware of a sudden ache of emptiness high between her legs.

It was the first genuine smile he'd given her in four years and it made her feel like the lovestruck innocent she'd been on Santorini, all breathless anticipation and hammering heart.

She hated that he had such power over her.

'Why are you here, Idris?' Her voice was sharp.

'I thought that was obvious.' He walked closer and

crouched down so his breath feathered her face. 'I'm here to help my wife bathe.'

'Wife in name only. And I'm perfectly able to take a bath alone.'

'But why should you when you have a husband willing and able to assist?'

'Husband in name only.' Arden gritted her teeth, annoyed at the way her body reacted to the rich, clean scent of sandalwood and man. As if four years hadn't passed. As if she were still besotted with him.

'On the contrary, our marriage is as real as two wedding ceremonies can make it.'

She shook her head, not in the mood for semantics. 'You agreed not to come into my room without permission.' It was a struggle to keep her voice even. All those years he'd visited her in her dreams, taunting her with the knowledge that, despite being an exhausted single mum, she was also a woman with needs. Now here he was in the too tempting flesh.

He braced his forearm on the edge of the bath, inches from her bare shoulder, and she shivered as if he'd touched her. 'Ah. That's where you're wrong. You mentioned that, but if you think back you'll remember it was one condition I never agreed to.'

He lifted his other hand and trailed the tips of his fingers in the water near her knees. He didn't touch her but the ripples he made were like tiny caresses teasing her flesh.

'Stop that!' He stilled and Arden dragged in a shuddery breath. 'Stop playing word games. You're not welcome here and you know it.'

Yet as she spoke Arden felt excitement rip through her at his heavy-lidded look. It stirred her body to tingling anticipation for his touch and, despite everything, for the unique sense of belonging and well-being she'd known in his arms. She reminded herself that was illusory but still her body trembled, igniting anger.

'We married for pragmatic reasons. Don't try to pretend this is about love.' She wasn't foolish enough to fall for that.

Idris shook his head, his expression too close to smug for her liking. 'That doesn't mean we need to keep our distance. Why should we when we want each other?'

'I don't—' Her voice cut out when his hand swirled through the water to caress her knee. Instantly a powerful judder of response racked her.

From a touch to her knee! That should be impossible. But so too should the avid look on Idris's face, as if he wanted to lean in and gobble her up, or maybe taste her slowly. Another quiver coursed through her and she pulled sideways, away from his touch, wrapping her arms tighter round her folded legs.

'Why don't you amuse yourself with one of your lovers and leave me alone?'

'One of my…?' For the first time Idris seemed lost for words.

'I don't want you in my suite.' Even though her body cried out for him. It was a shocking realisation but she'd get over it, just as she'd got over so much in the past.

'First—' he leaned in, all trace of a smile gone '—this is *our* suite. My bathroom and dressing room are on the other side of the bedroom.' Behind what she'd thought were blank walls? 'Rather than have you and Dawud settle into guest rooms then move after the wedding, I thought it would be less disruptive for Dawud in particular not to have to move twice. I've been sleeping elsewhere till the wedding.'

Dimly, part of her applauded his concern for their son. But mainly she was stunned by the revelation he'd expected her to share his bed all this time.

'Second, I don't have lovers waiting in the wings. I haven't had a lover in…' he shook his head '…a long time. I've been busy with other things.' He drew in a deep breath that expanded his chest mightily, reminding her of his sheer physical strength and beauty.

'Do you really think I'd go to another woman on my wedding night?' He looked angry, as if she'd insulted him.

'Why not? Unless you think because I'm conveniently close I'm available. If so, you're completely wrong.' Old bitterness welled. She understood now that Idris hadn't deliberately avoided her all those years ago but it was hard to erase the pain of rejection. 'You can't ignore me for weeks then swan in here, expecting intimacy.'

'Ignore you! I've seen you every day.' His face drew tight in that dangerous expression she'd privately dubbed his bronzed warrior look. 'I've spent every waking hour trying to smooth the way so that our marriage is viewed positively instead of as a hole-and-corner affair. So you and Dawud are accepted and welcomed. So we can live in peace and safety if I manage to salvage this treaty.'

Idris looked proud and forbidding. Yet Arden's heart leapt. There was something incredibly invigorating about being at the epicentre of all that furious energy.

But it wasn't enough.

'I'm not some *duty*.' She tipped back her head and glared. 'I'm a *person*. You can't treat me like a stranger then expect me to have sex with you.'

The harsh words jarred. Once she'd thought of it as making love. Glorious, heaven-touching love. But she'd learned a lot since those days of innocence. Idris had never loved her, though she'd been besotted enough to throw in her job and follow him to Paris.

His nostrils flared as he bent closer.

There was something incredibly intimate about the fact he was inhaling the scent of her skin and the exotic cinnamon and pomegranate wash they'd used on her hair this morning. He was drawing her in and, despite her anger, her body was eager for him to devour her.

'You think I treated you as a stranger?' His voice dropped to a deep note that wove its way into every sense receptor in her body. 'You think I ignored you?'

Idris tilted his head from side to side in a slow, emphatic negative. His hand closed around her knee in a deliberate, possessive hold that stilled her breath.

She'd never been attuned to any man as she was to Idris. Even wanting to break free, she couldn't deny the connection between them.

'For ten days I've worked myself into a stupor rather than come to your bed.' His voice grated, harsh and low. 'For ten days I've done the right thing, honouring you as a bride should be honoured. For ten days I've tortured myself with the sight and sound and scent of you.' He paused, inhaling again, and another of those erotic quivers coursed through her. 'But I didn't touch because I respected you. And I wanted everyone to know that.'

Idris leaned in, so close his dark eyes and golden skin filled her vision.

Arden was drowning in a sea of sensation. His touch on her bare skin, the intoxicating promise of sensual pleasure in his velvety eyes, the scent of him, potent male with a hint of sandalwood, even the sound of his breathing, steady and strong, dragged her down into a well of desire.

'And because you want me I'm supposed to welcome you with open arms?' Fear spiked. She suspected surrendering herself physically to Idris would be more complete, more irrevocable even than marrying him. A piece of paper, however important, was nothing compared with the intimacy of sharing herself.

'No, *habibti*. You'll welcome me because you want me

too. That hasn't changed, has it? The desire is as strong as ever.'

Arden opened her mouth to deny it when she realised he'd taken his hand from her knee. She felt it now underwater. Deep underwater.

Unerringly his big hand stroked between her legs, insinuating itself between her thighs and finding the spot where the heavy, sensual pulse of arousal struck hard and fast at the core of her.

Arden gasped and stiffened, clamping her thighs tight. It was too late. He was already there, stroking that most secret place with a sure yet delicate touch that sent whorls of excitement spiralling through her.

'Stop that!' She made a grab for his forearm underwater but couldn't shift him. Instead she felt the fine movement of tendons as his fingers flexed and stroked.

The sensation was too unsettling, as if she contributed to her own weakness, and she ripped her hand away, clutching the side of the tub instead, gasping.

She made herself stare up into his gleaming eyes. 'I don't want this.' But it wasn't true. Torn pride demanded she reject him. But the lonely, needy woman who'd once found magic with this man stirred to life.

'If I believed that for a second I'd walk out the door.' Abruptly the stroking fingers stopped, ending the addictive pressure on that sensitive nub, and to her dismay Arden realised her hips were tilting, lifting up towards his touch, pressing herself against him.

The tiny movement was utterly telling.

She stifled a sob of distress, of shame laced with despair. *She wanted him again...still.* As if those four lonely years had never been.

Yet instead of gloating over it, Idris said gently, 'Let me do this for you. You've been wound so tight all day I thought you'd break.'

Arden prised open tight lips, though what she'd have said she never discovered because he touched her again. This time he delved while his thumb circled, and sensation shot through her, making her jump and her breath snatch.

Instinctively she grabbed for support, one hand on the rim of the bath, the other on a hot, bony shoulder, padded with muscle.

'That's it,' he whispered, his voice at the same time soothing and incredibly sensual. 'Hold on tight.'

Eyes like the midnight sky held hers. This close she saw soft dark brown against black pupils. If it weren't for the fierce intensity of that stare she'd call it tender. Tender enough to soothe her lacerated, confused soul.

Then there was no time for thought as, with one deft stroke, Idris toppled her over the edge. Delight exploded, razing her defences and her self-protecting lies.

Dark eyes held hers as she rode wave after wave of pleasure till, at the end, she had no place left to hide. And no energy to maintain the fiction that she didn't want him every bit as much as she had four years ago.

Triumph warred with tenderness as Arden came apart at his touch. He felt each juddering spasm, heard each snatched gasp, her sweet breath was warm on his face, her hand clawing at his shoulder so hard she probably scored his flesh. And through it all those remarkable aquamarine eyes locked with his, drawing him into ecstasy till he feared he might explode, just watching her come.

It felt as if he'd waited a lifetime to possess her, not a mere couple of weeks. It was a miracle he hadn't simply stripped off and taken her where she lay in the water.

Except, even now on their wedding day, Arden didn't make anything easy. Accusing him of having a lover tonight of all nights! What sort of man did she think he was?

It infuriated him and slashed at his pride that she'd believe such a thing. He'd done nothing but treat her with courtesy and respect and still she…

She blinked and to his amazement moisture welled, drowning her lovely eyes. The sight jabbed something sharp and hard through his gut, skewering him. Her mouth twisted as if in anguish and she swung her head away so all he saw were damp wisps of rose gold hair clinging to her pinkened shoulder and throat.

She regretted this?

Idris slowly drew his hand back, feeling a final, needy clench of her muscles. Despite the bliss he'd given her, he hadn't broken down Arden's resistance. He knew he'd hurt her terribly, that she'd suffered because of his unintentional desertion. But he'd been sure she was ready to start afresh. Sure she wanted him as he craved her.

Had he really expected this to be so easy?

Somewhere Fate laughed at him and his foolish ego.

He looked at her ripe mouth, caught at one corner by white teeth as if even now she fought the bliss he'd bestowed. Her body might be ready for him, but emotionally Arden wasn't.

Memory slammed into him, of her bent head and defeated voice as she spoke to his cousin on the phone. She'd said he wasn't her lover, but clearly there was something between them, or had been, till Idris entered her life again.

He got to his feet, towering above her. In the sunken bath her milky pale body, flushed here and there with the rose blush of sexual satiation, was too much like the erotic fantasies he endured night after night.

Breathing quickly, trying to ignore the fragrance of sweet woman, he pivoted away, wrenching his mind from the need to possess her.

'Idris?' Her voice, husky and soft, tantalised. 'Where are you going?'

His shoulders set like granite.

'I won't force myself on an unwilling woman.' The knowledge she didn't want him scalded his pride and something else, something unnamed that hurt far more than he'd believed possible.

Idris heard the rush of sluicing water and felt warm drops splash the backs of his legs, sticking thin cotton trousers to steamy hot skin.

'*Unwilling* would be an exaggeration.' She was breathless. 'I was so sure I didn't want this. Now I don't know what to think.' The pain in her voice tore at him.

He closed his eyes, seeking strength. His groin was rock-hard, throbbing with the need, not just for release, but for *Arden*. He wanted to be inside her, feeling her come again, grabbing him tight with the undulating waves of her next climax. He wanted her complete surrender. He wanted her screaming his name—*his* name and no one else's.

He didn't think he had the stamina for any more celibate nights with her under his roof.

Hands clenched, he spun round.

Everything, his thoughts, his determination, even his pride, melted. Only his body grew impossibly harder at the sight of her, standing up to her thighs in water. Her hair glowed, framing her flushed face. Her beautiful Cupid's bow lips parted as if eager to taste him. Her eyes shone brighter than any gems in the royal treasury and her body was a symphony of delicate femininity. Between her thighs was that V of rose gold, hiding the gate to Paradise.

His gaze swept back up, pausing, fascinated by the delicate, shimmery striations just visible on her belly—marks where her satin-soft skin had stretched to carry his child.

A bolt of lightning struck down, welding his feet to the floor.

He'd never seen a more desirable woman, never felt such primitive possessiveness.

'Don't toy with me, Arden.' His voice was strangled.

She took a slow breath that lifted her tip-tilted breasts towards him. 'I'm not.' She swallowed and he watched the convulsive movement of her throat. 'I thought I could keep my distance. Keep separate. But I can't.' Her mouth crumpled at the edges and his chest squeezed. 'I was wrong. I want you, *still*.'

She didn't sound happy about it. He recognised the same conflicting emotions he felt—tension, need and something akin to fear at the force of what was between them. From the first he'd felt *more* with Arden. Every need, every emotion had been more intense, more real.

Arden held out her arms, slick and shining with water. 'Take me.' Her eyes held his and power jolted through him.

He needed no second urging. In one swift movement he scooped her up, one arm at her back and the other beneath her knees. Her wet, glorious body against his was a form of perfect torture as he marched across the marble floor and into the next room.

The cover of the vast bed had been pulled back, the sheets scattered with delicate petals.

There was nothing delicate about Idris's movements. Four huge strides took him to the bed. An instant later Arden landed on the mattress, her breath expelling in a soft *oof* of air as he followed her down, pressing against her slick body, revelling in the slide of smooth flesh against his.

A groan sounded in his ears. His? Hers? It didn't matter, for now she was touching him, her hands skidding over his shoulders and down his back, so low they slipped beneath thin cotton to cup his buttocks.

Instinctively he thrust forward, hard and high, revelling in the slide of flesh against flesh, heat against silken coolness. Her fingers curled tight, grabbing, as her thighs lifted, cradling around him in a damp caress.

Idris had a momentary impression of sultry, half-lidded

eyes, the eyes of a temptress inviting a lover, then Arden's hands slipped up his back, cupping the back of his neck to pull his head down.

Their lips fused and this time it was Arden setting the pace, Arden angling her mouth against his, a delectable hum of need vibrating from her throat and filling his mouth. Her tongue seduced his, eager and sensual, and he felt the power of that erotic connection right through him. His erection pressed heavily against her belly, his hips shifting with the unbearable tension.

Dimly Idris registered his complete loss of command over his body. It was moving of its own volition, incited by this sensual woman to abandon any hope of control or expertise. Instinct and hunger drove him. Already he was fumbling at the drawstring of his trousers, shoving the material down, scrabbling to be free.

He was just lowering himself back to Arden's delicious body when ingrained habit halted him.

'What's wrong?' Her words were the faintest, muffled sound in his mouth.

'Condom.' He paused, dragging air into tight lungs. Even as he said it he knew he wanted nothing more than to be inside her, no barriers between them. The thought was so arousing he scowled, drawing on every ounce of control not to shatter prematurely.

Idris wrenched away, lunging for the bedside table. Since they hadn't had that vital conversation about future pregnancies, he'd taken the precaution of bringing a box of protection. A large box.

'You were so sure of me?' Her voice held an edge.

Idris rolled on the condom, gritting his teeth at his sensitivity, then turned to her. Deliberately he slid his knee over hers, dragging it towards him, opening her thighs. His palm settled on her soft belly.

'Sure of *us*.' His voice was gruff. Speaking grew harder

each second. 'This is mutual, Arden. You must know that. I've been burning for you since I saw you again in London.'

Veiled eyes held his, as if she sifted the truth of his words. Then he lifted his hand to capture her breast and her breath hissed in.

She was so soft, so delicate, so perfectly made for him. How could he have gone all these years without finding her again and inviting her into his bed?

Idris lowered his head to capture her nipple between his teeth, grazing it gently, and she almost catapulted from the bed. He leaned over her, covering her, enjoying the slide of his body against her slick flesh.

This time he flicked her nipple with his tongue, cupping her satiny breast, overwhelmed by the familiarity of her. Beneath the fruit and flower aromas of Zahrat from the bath, it was the scent of Arden that befuddled his brain. The feel of her—familiar as if they'd shared a bed just days, not years, before, the tiny growl of arousal at the back of her throat that made his erection pulse eagerly against her thigh.

His hand tightened around her breast, his teeth nipped harder. Delicacy was beyond him. What he felt was too primal, too urgent to be contained.

Yet she welcomed him, grabbing his shoulders and urging him higher. He caught a flash of aquamarine between slitted eyelids, felt her restless bucking, heard those urgent mews of pleasure and knew she couldn't wait either.

Idris shifted to lie within her cradling hips, the bulk of his weight on his arms. His eyes rolled closed when she tilted her pelvis, grinding herself against him.

Then there was nothing but instinct and pleasure, pure pleasure, as he nudged her entrance and thrust home with one sure stroke.

She cried out, a husky sound of welcome that he tasted

as he took her lips, possessing her mouth in mimicry of the way he took her body.

Arden wrapped her arms behind his back, pulling him in. He slid further still when she lifted her legs and locked them around his buttocks.

The feel of her surrounding him everywhere was too much. He withdrew a fraction then surged high and hard and the ripples of pleasure began.

Fire caught his throat and chest, flames flickered in his blood at the tightness, the slick heat, the absolute perfection of her taking him in.

Another thrust and the ripples became shudders racking them both, making them jerk and shake together, turning fire into an explosion of white-hot ecstasy. Idris swallowed her shout of elation as he pulsed within her then disintegrated into tiny splinters of being. His world shattered in the exquisite pleasure-pain of sensation stronger than anything he could remember.

CHAPTER NINE

Arden was out for the count, limp with satiation, yet Idris couldn't keep his hands off her. She'd slept at least an hour and he was only human. He'd already fumbled on the bedside table for another condom and sheathed himself, yet still she hadn't stirred.

Idris ran his palm over the sinuous curve from her shoulder down her ribcage to her narrow waist then up to her hip. Lying on her side, that intoxicating female outline was even more pronounced.

His hand drifted from her hip to her belly, feathering the soft down between her legs, and she sighed in her sleep, shifting and stretching. He smiled, closing the gap between them. Immediately he felt her buttocks press back, cushioning his erection.

His breath stalled. His heart pounded so hard she must feel it hammering against her back.

'Shakil?' Her voice was a drowsy mumble that made him smile, though he registered chagrin that she'd used his boyish nickname.

Even half-awake she knew it was him. He'd hated the thought of the other men who'd no doubt been in her life. It was unreasonable, but he wanted to be the only man she'd ever had.

He remembered his soaring elation, the unexpected humility of learning he was her first lover. That had to explain this deeply proprietorial response he hadn't been able to conquer since London.

That and the fact she's your wife.

Your life has changed for ever.

Yet the dread voice of reason couldn't dim the sheer excitement of having her in his bed.

His.

Idris slid his fingers down, following that downy arrow to her sensitive nub. Her breath caught on a sigh and her pelvis tilted into his touch. She might be barely awake but she wanted him. He pressed his mouth to her neck, tasting the rich sweetness that was hers alone. Then her earlobe, scraping it gently with his teeth, and she shivered delicately, her back bowing again, arching that lush bottom into his groin.

But it wasn't enough. 'Tell me what you want.' He needed to hear it again.

'You. I want you.' Her voice was husky with desire and it aroused him as much as her sexy body. More. Her admission was potently exciting, even though he'd observed, as long ago as London, the attraction she tried to deny.

She wriggled, pressing herself against his groin, creating a firestorm of wanting.

In one swift movement he rose to his knees, grabbing her hips and lifting her so she knelt on the bed before him, his hands planted hard on her hips, caging her to him. Idris waited, breath bated, partly to give himself time to regain some control and partly to see Arden's reaction.

She bunched the sheet in her outstretched hands and shimmied her hips back and up into his pelvis.

Idris swallowed a groan of pain. It was exquisite torture, bliss and unbearable longing, kneeling here, with her so inviting before him. Impossible not to look down, to see her peach of a backside pushing at his erection.

Once again the firestorm hit—a blast of longing, of desperate arousal stronger than anything he could recall.

Had it always been like this? He'd thought his memories of their affair were coloured by the crises that followed, turning it into a glorious, perfect interlude because of the grimness immediately afterwards. He'd thought he'd imagined the perfection of their passion and that sense of being in the one place in the world he needed to be. But as he guided himself inside her, one hand welded to her hip, his rapt gaze on the erotic sight of their joining, he knew memory hadn't exaggerated.

Arden gave another shimmy of her hips so he lodged deeper in her welcoming warmth, and Idris knew once more the panicked delight of impending climax.

Where was his patience? His sensual prowess? His ability to savour sex and please his partner?

Gone the second Arden welcomed him into her body.

Desperately he bowed over her, one hand seeking her pouting breast, cupping it and rolling her nipple between thumb and forefinger so she jerked against him, her breath a hiss of air. His other hand arrowed down between her thighs, straight to her moist centre, pressing down on that sensitive nub as he withdrew then hammered home again, right to her core.

Her hands on the sheets were white-knuckled, her movements as she pushed back rough and urgent. He clamped his hand harder around her breast and she gasped, rolling her head back. Instantly he was there, leaning in, biting her earlobe, in time with the thrust of his body and the hard circling of his fingers.

'Yes!' Her triumphant shout filled the night. 'Yes, yes, yes. Shakil!' She grabbed his hand on her breast, pressing it to her as her body began to quiver around him. The quivers became shudders, caressing him, milking him with a sweet ferocity he couldn't resist.

With a groan of rapture he grabbed her hips and spilled himself, hard and fast into her slickness.

His last thought before he collapsed on her and rolled them both onto their sides, still joined, was that next time, surely, he'd be able to take it slow.

* * *

Arden squinted against the light. Surely it wasn't time to get up. Had they managed to sleep at all?

Heat bit her skin from her scalp to her toes and everywhere in between as she remembered the urgency with which they'd made love. With such desperation it made her think of stories she'd heard about people who'd survived some terrible life or death event and were driven by instinct to procreate.

Once she'd believed love was the reason she and Shakil had made the earth tremble on its axis. Now she realised sex and love needn't intersect. There was something about the man she'd married, something she responded to every time, that made the sex earth-shatteringly wonderful.

Sex, she reminded herself. Not lovemaking.

Disappointment eddied. With herself for not completely banishing that old yearning for love. A touch was all it had taken for Idris to smash through her caution. She'd acted as if the last four years had never been!

She opened her eyes wider, taking in the rumpled bed, the sun streaming in the arched windows and the complete absence of her husband.

There might have been rose petals strewn on the bed but this wasn't a hearts and flowers marriage. It was a cold-hearted convenience for the sake of their son and her husband's reputation.

'You look pensive this morning.'

Idris strode towards the bed, damp hair slicked back, buttoning his shirt.

Instantly Arden's heart fluttered and her stomach gave that little quiver of anticipation she despised. No matter how often she told herself she felt nothing for Idris, her body betrayed her.

She needed to conquer or at least control her response.

If she didn't she feared it would make her completely vulnerable.

'I need more sleep.'

Except one glance at him and it wasn't sleep on her mind. A pulse twitched between her legs and she shifted beneath the sheets, drawing his gaze. When his eyes met hers they gleamed hot and hungry and Arden found herself wondering at his stamina. How he found the energy even to walk she didn't know.

'Then sleep. I need to farewell those guests who stayed overnight.'

Reluctantly Arden dragged herself up against the pillows, drawing the cotton sheet around her, ignoring his raised eyebrow that reminded her he was intimately acquainted with every bare inch of her.

'If you wait fifteen minutes I'll come too.' Arden felt imprisoned in this new world that had been foisted on her, and by last night's proof of weakness. She didn't want to stay here, brooding, with the bedroom walls closing in. Besides, she had to start as she meant to go on. For Dawud's sake she'd fulfil her new royal role, as far as she could.

'No need.' His mouth widened into a smile that could only be described as smug. 'No one expects to see you today.'

Arden frowned. 'Yet they expect to see you?'

He grabbed his watch from the small table covered in condom wrappers, smiling at her as he strapped it on. The sight was ordinary yet intimate, reminding her they really were tied in marriage, husband and wife, come what may.

'As a vigorous man in the prime of life I'm supposed to take a wedding night in my stride.' His eyes flickered and Arden wondered what he was thinking.

'And the bride isn't?'

He shrugged and there was no mistaking the satisfaction in his tone. 'A new bride might be a little…tender, and need rest.'

'After a *vigorous* night with her new husband?' By a miracle Arden didn't blush. She was more than a little tender. She felt exhausted but also dangerously exhilarated, which disturbed even more.

'Precisely.' His high wattage smile rocked her back against the pillows. 'There'd be dismay if you appeared. People would think I hadn't done my husbandly duty.'

His words pummelled her. It had been husbandly *duty,* nothing more. Except, she guessed, surveying his lazy satisfaction, pride and the masculine ability to take pleasure wherever it was offered.

And she'd offered. She'd been as eager for Idris as he was for her. The difference was that to him she was just an available body. For her there still lingered shreds of the sentiment she'd once felt for him.

She had to change that fast, before she fell for that old romantic daydream.

'You never told me about that day in Santorini. What message you passed on.' The words blurted out before she realised she'd formed them. Suddenly it was vital she knew the whole truth.

'Sorry?' Idris was halfway to the door but turned at her words. 'What message?'

'You said you'd arranged for someone to meet me four years ago. At the rendezvous that last day when you couldn't meet me.'

'That's right.' Slowly he nodded.

'But you never told me what you'd instructed him to say.'

Dark eyes bored into hers. 'It hardly matters now. What matters is our future.'

Oh, it matters. From his sudden stillness, she guessed it mattered very much.

'Humour me. Was he going to take me to meet you in Paris or…?'

Idris breathed deep, his chest expanding as he took his time answering.

'I didn't go to Paris. My uncle was dangerously ill so I returned here.' He swung towards the door. But Arden wasn't letting him off. She'd spent years wondering about that day.

'So what was your message for me?'

He paused. For the first time Arden felt Idris was at a loss. Yet this was the man who took international scandals in his stride, even the discovery of a son and a forced wedding.

His gaze settled at a point beyond her head. 'To give my regrets and say we couldn't be together after all.'

Arden told herself she wasn't surprised, despite the chill clinging to her bones. 'To say goodbye.'

He nodded, his eyes briefly meeting hers. Then he exited the room.

It was what she'd expected—that, despite her girlish dreams, he'd planned to reject her that day. She, in her innocence, had fallen in love with the handsome stranger who'd swept her off her feet. But to him she'd been a mere holiday amusement. There'd never been any question of him taking her to his home. Her grand romance had been a fantasy.

Arden watched him leave and told herself she was grateful she'd finally unearthed the truth. What better time than now when, in the afterglow of Idris's lovemaking, she was in danger of reading too much into their intimacy?

He'd never wanted her as she'd wanted him. Never needed her.

Something inside her chest crumpled but she breathed through the pain.

It reinforced the lessons life had taught her. Those she

cared about always ended up leaving her to fend for herself. First her parents. Then the foster parents who'd changed their mind about adopting her when they discovered they were expecting a child of their own.

Then Shakil.

Just as well she wasn't in love with him any more. She'd moved on, even if Idris could still make her feel more than she should.

The only person she loved, who loved her back, was her son. That, she reminded herself as she shoved the sheet aside and headed for the bathroom, was all she needed.

At least Idris was honest about his feelings, or lack of them. She was grateful for that. He made it clear their marriage was solely to scotch scandal and provide a solid future for Dawud.

In the bathroom she wrenched on the taps in the shower, spurning the idea of a languorous soak in the tub. The decadence of that sunken tub, and what had happened there last night, was too dangerous. She needed to ground herself. A shower, fresh clothes and time with Dawud. Then she'd apply herself to the long, daunting process of learning what was expected of a royal sheikha.

It didn't matter that she felt doomed to fail and completely overwhelmed. She bit back a silent scream of hurt and helplessness, refusing to let tears well. She had to find strength. She *had* to make this work. Dawud's future depended on it.

Idris found her, not in bed but playing with their son in a private courtyard.

He forced down disappointment. He'd returned as soon as he could, the image of her waiting for him in bed, her hair a golden cloud around bare milk-white breasts, had distracted him through the protracted farewells, leaving him aroused and edgy. Never had the tedium of official duties weighed so heavily. He'd all but thrust the last guests through the palace portals.

He squashed annoyance that she hadn't waited for him, naked. He should be grateful she was a caring mother. Right? Wasn't that what this marriage was all about?

But as he stepped from the shadows of the portico it wasn't their necessary marriage consuming his thoughts. It was sex, hot and urgent, with the woman who diverted him from all thoughts of duty.

'Baba!' He heard the cry as Dawud's beaming smile caught him full-on. There was a curious thud in the region of his chest, as if his heart had missed a beat then pounded out of rhythm. Then he was crouching, arms open, as his son hurried over, his dark hair tousled into the beginnings of curls—just like Idris's own hair if he let it grow.

'Watch out, he's wet!'

But Idris didn't mind. He closed his son in his embrace, ignoring the way the little wet body saturated his clothes.

His son.

Idris had been surprised from the first at the feelings the boy evoked. They grew every day. And they made everything, the hassle of organising a royal wedding in record time, the frowning disapproval of the old guard, even the strained relations with Ghizlan's father, fade to nothing. He was more determined than ever to secure peace, now it meant protecting his son.

'Baba.' Dawud lifted a hand to Idris's face, tiny fingers patting at his cheek and nose.

Idris laughed and caught Arden's surprise. It made him realise how rarely he laughed. Until Arden and Dawud arrived he'd spent all his time working. Yet he'd enjoyed the last weeks with them, despite the enormous strain of dealing with crises.

He greeted Dawud in Arabic and was amazed when

Dawud answered in kind, lisping a little on the unfamiliar words.

'He remembered what I taught him!'

'He's a quick learner.'

Idris nodded, taken aback by the swell of pride at his boy's cleverness. Did all fathers feel this way? His father had never doted on him, caught up instead in his schemes for personal pleasure. Idris had been closer to his tutors, including the hard men who'd taught him the ancient arts of warfare.

'He likes to please you too.'

Arden's voice made him look up. She stood, hands clasped tight as if to stop from reaching out to grab their son. The twist of her lips told him it wasn't simple pride she felt. Didn't she trust him with Dawud?

Idris had worried he'd get this fathering thing wrong with no role model to guide him. So far he seemed to be doing okay but would instinct be enough as Dawud grew?

Yet even as the familiar doubt surfaced he noticed the way Arden's wet blouse had turned transparent, giving him a tantalising view of luscious breasts in a lacy half cup bra. She took his breath away every time.

Idris stood, lifting Dawud into his arms, but the boy wriggled to be let go. That was when Idris noticed the plastic toy boats floating in the shallow pools inlaid with tiny tiles of lapis lazuli, marble and gold.

His lips quirked as he put Dawud down and watched him plump with a splash into the couple of inches of water, immediately absorbed in his game with the boats.

'You don't mind him playing here?' Arden's expression was guarded. 'There's no playground but I thought he couldn't hurt anything here, if he's supervised.'

Idris thought of the painstaking, delicate work that had gone into creating the ornamental pools with their exquisite sixteenth century mosaics. They were national treasures, one of the reasons for the palace's heritage status.

'I think it's a perfect place to play with toy boats. I wish I'd thought of it when I was young.' When he was a kid there was no way any of his royal uncle's entourage would dream of letting a small boy enjoy such freedoms. 'We must see about a proper playground. Perhaps with a sandpit and a climbing frame?'

He watched with pleasure as some of the tension bled from Arden's stiff frame. 'That would be perfect. Thank you.'

That confirmed what he'd known from the first—the way to Arden's good graces was through their son. Even after a night spent in Idris's arms, she'd looked anything but relaxed until he started talking about plans for Dawud.

Regret stabbed. Was that really their only connection? Their boy? It should please him that Dawud was so important to her, yet pride demanded she acknowledge his own place in her life.

Then he saw the tension in her twined hands. Of course she wanted him. He couldn't have asked for a more willing, generous lover. But they were strangers still. He needed to give her time to adjust to her new life.

Idris settled himself on the warm flagstones behind their son, reaching forward to propel a tiny sailboat forward. Dawud crowed with delight, splashing his appreciation and chattering. Idris joined in, enjoying the game, heedless of the water drenching his formal robes. Dawud's excitement, the laughter, the spray of water in the sunlight, created a sense of well-being, as if for once there weren't a million tasks clamouring for Idris's attention. As if this simple joy was all that mattered.

Arden dragged a chair into the shade of an ornamental tree and sat on the other side of the pool, watching. It struck Idris that, no matter what the law said about his rights as a father, she was working hard to allow him access to his son. Not every woman would make it so easy.

'It must be hard, sharing Dawud after all this time.'

Her eyes widened, their pale depths glittering in surprise. 'I…' She shrugged. 'It takes a little getting used to. In the past I was the only one he'd run to. Me and his nursery teacher.'

'Not Hamid?'

The question was a mistake. Arden tensed and the easy atmosphere fractured.

'Hamid was always kind to Dawud but he never got down on the ground to play with him.'

Her words pleased Idris. It was petty to compare the relationship he'd begun to build with his son against his cousin's. Yet he couldn't fully excise that sliver of jealousy over the time Hamid had spent with Arden and Dawud in London.

'Hamid was a friend. He never acted like Dawud's father—'

'And he wasn't your lover?' Snaking distrust wound through him.

'I've said it before and won't say it again. You'll have to take my word for it.' Her chin lifted and her eyes flashed and Idris had never wanted her more.

Her stare might spit fire but, aware of their son playing between them, she kept her voice low. It struck him that his hunger for her wasn't purely physical. There was something about the way she protected Dawud that got to him at a level every bit as primal as sex.

The mother of his son. A woman who'd do anything for their boy, even marry a stranger in a strange land.

Pride throbbed through Idris. Pride and admiration. And, as ever, that undertow of desire.

'I apologise, Arden. I should have taken your word from the first.' Despite the remnants of jealousy, he believed her. What did she have to gain by lying? Even Hamid had made it clear they hadn't been lovers. Idris had to conquer this dog-in-the-manger jealousy. It was completely out of character.

Arden provoked emotions that were unique—both positive and negative. He wanted to understand why. Understand her.

'Why did you call him Dawud? A name from my country, not yours?' She'd believed he'd abandoned her, so it was odd she'd given their son a name that linked him to Idris's homeland.

She lifted her shoulders, her gaze veering away. 'I went to an exhibition of beautiful antique artefacts from Zahrat and discovered one of your rulers had been King Dawud. I liked the name and wanted our boy to have some connection to your country. To own a link to his father's heritage as well as mine.'

'That's very generous, given what you thought of me.' Idris frowned. 'It surprised me.' And it was one of the reasons he'd thought Hamid her lover.

'Wouldn't you have accepted him with an English name?'

Idris stared her down till her cheeks flushed pink. Surely she couldn't believe he'd ever deny his son? 'I would have accepted him no matter what. But it makes it easier for our people when he has a name they recognise.'

Again that little shrug. 'It's close enough to the English name David if he wanted to change it later. But I thought he'd appreciate some link to his father's culture.'

'That's why you began learning Arabic? To teach our boy?' Idris should have made the connection. Now it struck him how significant her actions had been. Even believing herself deserted, Arden had tried to build a bridge between their son and a cultural inheritance to which she was an outsider. Idris leaned closer, fascinated by such generosity of spirit.

'I wanted Dawud to feel he belonged, to feel a sense of connection, even if he never knew his father. I believe it's vital for a child.'

The way she spoke, the determined glint in her eyes, suggested this wasn't just about Dawud. Idris raked his memory for what he knew of Arden's history. All he knew was that she had no family. But maybe that explained her fierce purpose in giving Dawud links to his paternal as well as maternal cultures.

He was about to ask when Dawud set up a grizzling cry. Instantly Arden was on her feet.

'It's past nap time. I'd better dry him off and let him rest.'

'I'll carry him.' Idris scooped up Dawud and tucked him close. Despite the wetness and the jarring kick of one small heel against his ribs, he enjoyed holding his boy.

They walked together into Dawud's room where Idris reluctantly handed him over. The interlude of intimate communication was over. He should return to his office. It might be their honeymoon but securing peace took precedence, especially now he had a family as well as a nation to protect.

Yet Idris paused, watching mother and son. Again that hard thud resonated through his chest as if his heart beat out of sync.

'Thank you, Arden.'

Her head shot up, her brows furrowing in puzzlement.

'King Dawud was my grandfather. A great leader and revered among my people.' It was a shame his son, Idris's uncle, hadn't ruled in the same mould. 'I'm honoured you named our boy after him, and pleased that you thought to give Dawud such a gift. You could as easily have severed any connection with my country. I appreciate what you've done for him.'

Her eyes rounded, her mouth opening a little before she snapped it shut. 'It seemed only right.'

Idris knew that for many women doing what Arden had would have been a step too far. He admired her for that.

He was discovering Arden was far more than a sexy bed mate and the mother of his son. She might even have the strength and generosity to prove the naysayers wrong and become the Sheikha his kingdom needed. The wife he hadn't realised he wanted till now.

Perhaps marriage wouldn't be nearly the trial he'd imagined.

CHAPTER TEN

ARDEN SMOOTHED THE skirt of her full-length dress. The silvery material was soft as gossamer, the cut amazing. Only the best for the Sheikh's wife.

She stared at the intricately inscribed wedding band on her left hand, proof she really was the Sheikha.

Her mouth quirked. Her life was full of such proofs. She hadn't slept alone since the wedding and had grown used to curling up against Idris's hot, muscled body through the night. She'd almost become accustomed to the hum of arousal that filled her when he looked at her with that particular gleam in his dark eyes.

She'd stopped fretting over the fact she enjoyed the sex, enjoyed being with him. Surely it made sense to accept the perks in this marriage of convenience. Especially when increasingly she caught glimpses of the charming, engaging man she'd known before duty took over Idris's world. That man made her smile even when her day had been exhausting.

A pity she found it far more difficult being royal.

The sight of people bowing before her made her feel a fraud. Even on her visits to schools where the children seemed fascinated by their ruler's foreign wife, Arden felt like an interloper. She enjoyed being with the kids, sharing their smiles and enthusiasm, but all the time she knew they believed her to be someone special when really she was utterly ordinary.

Except for the fact she'd married Idris.

Daily she struggled with the simplest of royal protocols. As for understanding who was who in the complicated hierarchy of regional politics… Arden had given up trying to follow the complex behind-the-scenes machinations and treated everyone with the same courtesy she would have in London. She'd seen raised eyebrows at several gaffes but it was the best she could do. She wasn't bred to this role like Princess Ghizlan.

The thought of Ghizlan made her eyes dart to her dressing room's full length mirror. Arden didn't have Ghizlan's panache but she had to admit that tonight she looked different. With her hair up and wearing a stunning silver couture dress, she looked a far cry from the frazzled single mum who'd attended the royal reception in London in a borrowed dress.

Different enough that Idris would notice?

Of course he'll notice. He doesn't miss anything.

What you mean is, will he appreciate you as he would someone like Princess Ghizlan?

The snide voice made her stiffen. Was she really that pathetic? Idris noticed her. And he was attracted. Their passionate lovemaking proved that.

But Idris made the best of circumstances, as she did. He hadn't chosen her because he loved her, or because she met the qualifications of a well-bred princess. He hadn't really chosen her. She'd been foisted on him by circumstance and scandal.

And still she craved—not his approval—but his admiration. She wanted to be more than an encumbrance or a convenient partner.

Arden stared into the shadowed eyes in the mirror and knew that was bad. She shouldn't need any man's admiration to feel good about herself. This…craving was a weakness. A sign she felt far more than she should for the man she'd married.

Or perhaps, she thought with relief, it was just that things were so different here. She was out of her depth so surely it was natural to crave a sense of belonging, of being appreciated.

A glance out of the window at Zahrat's capital city, a mix of ultra-modern and traditional architecture, reminded her how far she was from home. Everything here, though fascinating and often surprisingly modern and easy, was foreign. Her experience of the world beyond the UK was limited to the single week in Santorini when she'd met and fallen for Idris.

She had so much to learn. No wonder she was floundering, despite the intensive lessons. She hated feeling so out of her depth. It ate at her self-respect.

'Sorry I'm late.' The deep voice made her spin round.

Idris stood in the doorway, in his tailored tuxedo looking scrumptious enough to eat.

Heat radiated across Arden's throat and cheeks as she remembered the way she'd nibbled her way along his body this morning. She'd paused to savour the taste of him till he'd growled impatiently and flung her onto the mattress, imprisoning her with his bulk and driving them both to completion with a series of quick, perfect lunges that reminded her again how very good he was at sex, how experienced, especially compared with her.

'Are you okay?' His brow knitted and he stepped closer. 'I'll be by your side all evening. There's nothing to worry about.'

Arden forced her mind away from the delights of his naked body. 'Of course there isn't. Who'd get nervous about a royal reception for several hundred VIPs?'

Idris smiled and her heart gave that little shivery beat. The man had too much charisma, especially with that hint of a laugh in his eyes. 'Most of them will be more nervous than you. Besides, all you need to do is smile and be yourself. They'll be charmed.'

Sure. As if the local glitterati were interested in the

ramblings of a London florist whose passions, apart from her son and her sexy husband, were gardening, tennis and curling up with a good book.

'I've brought you this. I thought you might like to wear it tonight.' He held up a box of royal-blue leather, stamped with ornate gilt work. Arden recognised it. The diamond and pearl necklaces she'd worn at their wedding had been lifted reverentially from similar boxes.

'That treasury of yours must be enormous,' she murmured, forcing a smile to cover her nerves. The value of the pieces she'd worn at the wedding had only added to her tension. What if she'd damaged them?

'It's big enough. Remind me to take you to look. You could pick out some pieces you like.'

Arden couldn't imagine it. She wasn't the sort to wear pigeon's egg rubies to show off her newly manicured hands.

'Aren't you going to open it?'

Her eyes snapped to his. She thought she read excitement there. But she must have imagined it—a second later and the impression was gone as he glanced at his watch. It was time they made their appearance.

Taking a deep breath, Arden lifted the tiny gold latch then raised the lid. Whatever she'd been about to say disintegrated as she gasped, barely able to take in what she saw.

'You like it?'

Arden shook her head. Surely it couldn't be real.

'Of course it's real.' Had she spoken aloud?

A large, square hand plucked the exquisite choker necklace from its nest of oyster satin and lifted it, dazzling her.

The piece was about two inches wide, diamonds and platinum creating a delicate tracery of leaves that sparkled outrageously. Above and below it was edged with what looked like ribbon but was actually square cut green stones she guessed were emeralds. The necklace secured at the back and at the front it dipped gracefully towards a single huge faceted emerald drop.

'I've never seen anything like it,' she croaked. It should belong to an empress.

'Here, let me.' Idris stepped behind her and she felt the cool weight of it around her throat, the pendant heavy against her skin while his fingers deftly closed the clasp at her nape. 'Take a look. It goes perfectly with what you're wearing.'

Arden was still in shock and it affected her hearing. To her ears Idris's voice sounded strangely hoarse. And the grip of his hands as he turned her towards the mirror seemed to dig in too hard.

She lifted her head and stared.

'Well?' Idris cleared his throat over unfamiliar tightness. 'Do you like it?'

'I don't know what to say.' In the mirror Arden's eyes were huge, but she didn't smile.

Why didn't she react? In the past generous gifts to lovers had been received with enthusiasm.

But this was different. *She* was different. He'd never had a lover so unconcerned with his prestige and wealth. Arden tried hard to fit in with life at court but he suspected she wasn't impressed by its pomp.

Which made him wonder how she felt about *him*. It niggled that, except when they were naked, he found it hard to read her thoughts.

He'd commissioned this personally with her in mind. He'd seen some preliminary work by a renowned jeweller and immediately imagined it gracing Arden's slender throat. He'd never before had something made specifically for any woman. Was that why he was eager for her reaction?

It looked superb. Regal but feminine. Elegant but incredibly sexy. So sexy he wanted to see her wear it and nothing else. He wanted to ignore the guests waiting in the Hall of a Thousand Pillars and make urgent love to her.

Then make slow, thorough love to her all over again.

He was on fire and not just because she looked spectacular in silk and emeralds. He always burned for her. Even when she wore old clothes to finger paint with Dawud. Especially when she wore those tight jeans…

Idris forced his hands from her bare arms, looking over her shoulder at her reflection in the glass.

His wife. His queen.

She was beautiful.

'Say you like it.' The words jerked out, appallingly needy, as if he craved approval. It was an unfamiliar feeling, one that disturbed him.

'I like it.' Their eyes met in the mirror and his doubts fled. What he read in her face, the softening warmth and wonder, were everything he could want.

It reminded him of her ardent passion. Every time they had sex she made him feel more than the man he'd been before. He was rapidly becoming addicted to that radiant pleasure.

This was the first time Arden had regarded him with that glowing wonder when they weren't having sex. Idris wrapped an arm around her waist, tugging her back against him, revelling in the way she fitted so perfectly.

'Though I'm not sure it's really me,' she whispered. 'I'm more a noodle sort of girl.' Her mouth twisted wryly in that self-effacing way and Idris recognised the reference to the bangle she and Dawud had made one day out of dry pasta.

'Believe me, it's you.' She mightn't be the most classically beautiful woman in the world, but Arden had a vibrant loveliness all her own. 'You look spectacular.'

Soft colour washed her cheeks. 'Not as spectacular as you.'

'Even without diamonds?' He pretended to preen and was delighted when she giggled.

Two months of marriage and he'd discovered her smiles could change his mood in an instant. Each one felt like a gift to be savoured. More and more he found himself responding, teasing and laughing, living in the moment instead of always focused on work.

Why was Arden's warmth and enthusiasm so potent? He put it down to the fact it was easier to live with a woman who was upbeat and practical, ready to meet him halfway. He'd discovered marriage far less difficult than expected, if he didn't count the continuing fallout over his choice of bride. Though even that was fading as diplomacy, frantic hard work and his bride's refreshing ways worked their magic.

'Diamonds would be overkill with that dinner jacket.' Her smooth brow furrowed. Her fingers went tentatively to the emerald resting just below her collarbone. 'You're sure about this? I can't help feeling nervous wearing something so expensive and beautiful.'

Idris had never heard any woman express such a sentiment. Arden continued to surprise him.

'I'm sure. You can pretend it's made of pasta if that makes it easier.'

She grinned and a shaft of warmth shot straight through him. 'I might just do that.'

'Come on, Princess.' He turned and held out his arm.

He couldn't describe the feeling inside when she smiled up at him and slipped her arm through his. Satisfaction, triumph, pride. None quite captured the unfamiliar blast of delight he experienced as he swept out of the room with Arden on his arm.

Arden was flagging after the initial round of introductions but gamely kept her chin up. How Idris managed so many handshakes, so many bows and introductions from people all eager to make an impression, she didn't know. Her muscles ached from fatigue, even though she'd taken Ghizlan's advice and worn beautiful shoes that were still comfortable and not skyscraper tall.

She wished Ghizlan was here. It would have been comforting to have a friend on her side. People were generally pleasant, except for those few older men who always regarded her stonily as if her presence was a catastrophe. Arden drew in a slow breath, reminding herself acceptance would take time.

Nevertheless it was tough keeping up the image of royal correctness. Formality didn't come naturally to Arden.

Ghizlan had understood her total inexperience. There'd been no need to pretend with her and that had been liberating. Against the odds they'd bonded over the fiasco in London. Ghizlan had texted answers to questions about dress codes and etiquette, along with scurrilously funny anecdotes about ceremonial disasters, for months now. But in the last few days there'd been nothing. Not since her initial response to Arden's sympathy on her father's unexpected death.

Ghizlan had returned home and it was no surprise she had no time for messages. Idris said there was some question over who would succeed Ghizlan's father as Sheikh. Ghizlan would be busy with that and—

'Excuse me, Sire. I must talk with you.'

Arden blinked, stirred from distraction by the voice of the palace steward. The line of people being presented had petered out so she and Idris stood a little apart from the throng, on the royal dais. Two thrones inlaid with gold and precious stones dominated the area and she'd deliberately turned her back on them. Silly to be overawed by some furniture but they, like the eye-watering perfection of the necklace she felt every time she swallowed, reminded her she was an imposter here.

'Can't it wait?' Idris matched his voice to the steward's low tone.

'I'm afraid not, Your Highness. I would have done something about it before but you asked me to leave tonight's arrangements to my staff—'

'Because I entrusted you with the celebrations to open the new city hall and convention centre next week. I value your expertise to bring it off in style.'

'I pride myself it will be a success, sir. But in my absence there's been a…regrettable error of judgement. A problem with the banqueting hall I've just discovered.'

'A problem? It was in perfect condition yesterday. Has it been damaged?'

A tingling began between Arden's shoulder blades. A tingling that skittered down her spine and wound into her belly, unsettling her already nervous stomach. She swung around to meet the palace steward's eyes just before he dragged his gaze back to Idris.

The tingling became a wash of foreboding, stirring nausea. Had she erred again? And tonight of all nights, when she'd been at such pains to complete her royal duties with grace and decorum?

'Not damage as such, Your Highness. If I'd been here it would have been rectified immediately. Unfortunately my second in charge, though competent, isn't as familiar with the way things must be done.'

The old man's eyes flickered but didn't meet hers. Yet Arden knew instantly he was remembering the times they'd clashed. The day when, thin-lipped, he'd warned her that using an ancient mosaic-floored corridor for games with Dawud was inadvisable. And that allowing a group of visiting schoolchildren into one of the palace courtyards might not only damage national treasures but show disrespect for royal tradition.

His manner intimated that disregard for the riches surrounding them was only what he'd expect of an outsider who had no concept of Zahrati custom and sensibilities.

'I'm afraid it's probably my fault,' Arden said, her voice defensively brusque. She was tired of being on the back foot, continually reminded of the many ways she didn't measure up as a royal spouse. Not that Idris ever said a word. But others, like the steward, were always sure to tell her.

'Your fault?' Idris smiled and heat danced through her, reminding her of the strange intimacy between them when he'd given her the necklace. Of the sense, for a second or two, that maybe she was wrong and there was more to their marriage than convenience and necessity.

The steward shuffled his feet and the idea shattered.

'I suspect the problem relates to today's visitors. Am I right?'

She met the steward's guarded stare with outward confidence. She mightn't like the man, might even believe he was deliberately difficult, but she had no intention of showing her horror that once more she was in the wrong. First there'd been the contretemps when an elderly lady had curtsied to her and Arden had impulsively helped her rise when it seemed her knees had locked. How was she to know that touching a stranger at court without invitation was a shocking misdemeanour?

Since then there'd been several *faux pas*. The night she'd used a fruit spoon instead of the purpose-designed sorbet spoon from the vast array of gold cutlery was the least of her dining mistakes. The reception where palace staff, eager in the knowledge their new Sheikha had a reputation for liking flowers, had installed numerous floral arrangements complete with trailing jasmine. Sadly Arden hadn't thought to warn them she was allergic to the scent and she'd spent the evening sneezing through every speech.

'I met with some school groups today.' She turned to Idris, her smile perfunctory. 'You said it was all right to have them here.'

Since her visit to Leila, the girl who'd offered her a bouquet in the street, Arden had been invited to several schools. Seeing the enthusiasm of both children and adults, Arden had sought Idris's approval to invite some school groups to the palace. Today goggle-eyed children had taken in the grandeur of the reception rooms while teachers expounded on the palace's historic treasures.

Another reason the steward disapproved of her. Previously only VIPs saw the palace interior. In Zahrat there was traditionally little direct contact between the royal family and their subjects.

'I'm sorry,' Idris murmured. 'I didn't ask you how the visits went.'

'Excellent. I thought it a success, and so did the teachers. The children were excited but very well behaved.' Arden glimpsed the steward's impatience and felt her heart sink. Obviously something had gone wrong. She hoped some priceless ornament hadn't been damaged.

'So what's the problem?' Idris turned to the steward.

'It's the banqueting hall, Sire. I just returned to the palace and saw the room had been *decorated* in a way that made it unfit for tonight's formal dinner.' He almost groaned his horror. 'I told the staff to fix it immediately but was informed the Sheikha had said the...decorations were to remain until she directed otherwise.' His glare said what he thought of that.

Over the steward's shoulder she saw staff opening the doors into the adjoining banqueting room. Arden's pulse fluttered as she remembered how that room had looked today when the children visited. Laughter bubbled inside but it died as she watched the first of the exquisitely dressed VIPs pass through the open doors. They all looked so suave and important.

'I'm sorry.' She swung around to Idris. 'It's my fault. The younger children brought gifts as a thank you for their visit and I said we should display them. Some of the staff seemed eager to remove the decorations as soon as possible but I didn't want to disappoint the kids by taking them down while they were in the building. I told the staff to leave them till I instructed they be removed.' Except later she'd forgotten.

'That's the problem?' Idris frowned. 'Gifts from children in the banqueting hall?'

The steward stepped closer. 'No fault attaches to the children or teachers. The gifts were a sign of appreciation. But sadly they are inappropriate in such a majestic setting. Especially given tonight's formal diplomatic dinner.'

The man didn't look at Arden, but something inside her shrank. Clearly if fault lay anywhere it was with her.

Once she'd have thought the old man overreacted, but she knew Idris had faced a firestorm because of their marriage. He'd worked tirelessly to rectify damage from the scandal. Tonight was a major part of his campaign to have his nobody of a foreign wife accepted. The place was filled with diplomats and VIPs.

Had she sabotaged it? Arden felt sick at the thought.

'Thank you, Selim, for the warning. We'll manage from here. I'm sure it will be all right.' Idris took her arm, holding it high as he led her off the dais and towards the crowd disappearing into the banqueting room.

Arden's stomach felt like lead but she had no choice but to tilt her head up, fix on a smile and follow his lead.

Idris paused in the doorway to the vast banqueting room and tightened his lips to repress a broad grin. Elegant guests milled around tables laid for a seven course banquet. Surrounding them were pillared walls of shell-pink marble carved by master craftsmen generations ago. And blooming on the priceless marble was a lopsided, improbable field of bright blossom.

Huge paper flowers in purple, orange, sunburst-yellow and even sky-blue crowded the surfaces in ragged, enthusiastic abandon. He spied names written in crayon on the leaves.

Idris paced further into the room, Arden with him, her hand cold in his. Was she so nervous of the official reception? She'd done marvellously through the lengthy introductions, greeting people with a charm and warmth that came naturally to her. She was a people person and a welcome breath of fresh air.

'It's fine,' he said under his breath, pressing her hand reassuringly. 'Nothing to worry about.'

Her fingers twitched in his hold and she nodded, but her smile looked fixed. Damn Selim for bustling in, making a fuss and upsetting Arden.

That was why Idris had put the steward in charge of the city hall opening. It was an excuse to get him out of the palace. Idris knew he took any chance to show her up.

He led Arden towards a cluster of lopsided sunflowers. 'I've never seen the place so festive.'

She looked up, eyes wide. 'Not even at our wedding banquet?' she murmured.

Idris remembered the cloth of gold swags at each entrance, the garlands of exotic lilies intertwined with crystal and pearls on each table. 'These are simple but they're gifts from the heart.' He preferred them to the formal opulence of the wedding.

He turned, smiling and raising his voice so the guests could hear. 'I hope you enjoy the decorations for our meal tonight. You all know my wife's interest in our children and her visits to local schools. These are gifts brought by students from those schools. I think you'll agree they show great enthusiasm and creativity.'

There was a murmur of voices and a few nods though some of the guests still looked bemused.

Idris caught the eye of the Minister of Education, one of the government leaders who'd actually been eager for the modernisation Idris had been leading.

The Minister inclined his head. 'Encouraging our children in art as well as the sciences is traditional in Zahrat. It's good to see that continuing with the personal support of our new Sheikha.' He smiled and Idris heard Arden's snatched breath. She hadn't expected the compliment.

The realisation angered Idris.

He'd been so frantic dealing with the fallout from his sudden marriage and its impact on both the peace treaty and his own position. Becoming a husband and father had distracted him too. He'd known Arden faced difficulties but hadn't realised she felt so vulnerable. Guilt hit.

He pulled her close, abandoning any pretence of royal dignity as he wrapped his arm around her waist, ignoring the way she stiffened.

'Come,' he ordered, his voice rough with barely concealed annoyance at himself. He should have done more, he saw now, to ease her into her new responsibilities. He should never have left it to his staff. 'Tell me about these flowers. Particularly this one.' He injected a light-hearted note. 'It seems, intriguingly, to resemble a camel.'

Tense she might be, but Arden was quick. 'That's because it's a camel, despite the petals. The little boy…'

'Ali?' Idris tilted his head to read the name written on one knobbly camel's leg.

'That's it.' Her smile looked almost natural now. 'Ali confessed he didn't like flowers. He likes camels so that's the shape he cut out. But when he heard the class had been asked to make flowers for me because I liked them, he compromised by putting petals on his camel. That's why the hump droops.'

Idris chuckled, imagining the scene, and there was a ripple of laughter as guests moved to inspect the work.

By the time they sat down to dinner, Arden, sitting opposite him with an ambassador on one side and the Minister for Education on the other, looked almost relaxed. Her smile wasn't radiant, but as the meal progressed the horrible tension he'd felt in her dissipated and she charmed her companions with her ability to listen and her direct questions.

Idris had been right. Arden would make an excellent sheikha. Just as she was a superb mother. And as a wife—

She lifted her head abruptly, catching him staring. Pink stained her cheeks as their eyes met. By the time she looked away Idris found himself impatiently counting the time till they could be alone together.

CHAPTER ELEVEN

IT WAS WELL past midnight when they reached their private apartment. Arden was exhausted. Every muscle groaned from being held taut so long. Her jaw ached from smiling and a stress headache throbbed in time with the beat of her pulse.

Idris had handled the situation suavely, turning what could have been embarrassing into an opportunity to promote his agenda for improved education.

Yet the fact remained he'd had to cover for her slip up. Again.

Everyone made mistakes. It was just that hers were always in a glaring spotlight of public disapproval. And after months of marriage she was making as many as ever.

Arden had known she wasn't suited for the role of royal wife. How long before her shortcomings created a rift between Idris and those who supported him?

She knew he was popular—he'd gathered support through sheer hard work and the positive results of every hard-won reform. But she also knew there were traditionalists in high places horrified at the scandal surrounding his marriage. And her unsuitability as his wife. People who could make trouble, not just for her but for Idris and all he was trying to do.

She'd been on tenterhooks tonight, trying to remember the correct forms of address and so many other minutiae of Zahrati custom. She'd been congratulating herself on getting through the first part of her trial by etiquette when the steward brought his news.

Nor had she missed her husband's set expression when he'd entered the banqueting hall and discovered its elegance marred by wonky paper flowers. Idris hadn't been impressed.

'I'm really sorry about tonight.' She crossed to the dressing table, pulling out hairpins, stifling a sigh as the tight, elegant coiffure disintegrated into waves around her shoulders.

'Sorry?'

Arden put the hairpins down, hating that her fingers shook. Keeping up the appearance of ease all evening, while her stomach roiled with nerves, had taken its toll.

Abruptly she turned, only to find Idris right behind her. He grabbed her shoulders before she could walk into him, his dark eyes peering straight into her soul.

Arden's heart kicked. Even weary and despondent, desire shivered through her. Her need for him was constant, unrelenting. He didn't love her and her love for Idris had died in the years she'd believed he'd abandoned her, yet her yearning for him only seemed to grow.

If she wasn't careful he'd take over her life even more than he had already. She'd lost her home, her job, her independence. She couldn't afford to lose any more. She needed to be able to stand up for herself and her son.

Arden sidestepped, dragging in a quick, relieved breath when he dropped his hands.

'I'm sorry about the banqueting hall. That was my fault. I should have had the artwork taken down hours ago.'

She just hadn't thought of it. Straight after the school visits she'd met a delegation of women who'd travelled two days to present their new Sheikha with gifts they'd prepared themselves: delicious attar of rose scent and exquisitely woven stoles. Then there'd been an afternoon crammed with language lessons and appointments, including one with a stylist who'd clearly been challenged by Arden's riotous hair. There had been barely enough time to see Dawud before his bed time.

'Don't fret, Arden. It's not a problem.' Idris's soothing voice only stirred her guilt. She knew tonight could have been a disaster. 'Our guests loved the decorations.'

He stepped into her line of vision but didn't touch her. Arden was glad. She wanted distance, didn't she?

Except, stupidly, she also wanted to lean her tired head on her husband's broad shoulder.

'Only because you turned it into something they could relate to. If not for that…' She shook her head, remembering the initially stunned looks from their guests and the palace steward's outrage.

'You're worrying too much. You saw the reaction Ali's camel got.' Idris's chuckle wrapped around her like balm on a wound and the gleam in his eyes tugged at her. 'Maybe we should add Dawud's finger painting to the display. What do you say? I think the boy's got real talent.'

Despite herself Arden grinned, thinking of Dawud's latest picture of the three of them, all heads and spindly legs. And how Idris had joined in the painting, teasingly threatening to daub her nose with red paint when she dared to critique his efforts.

'Our guests were delighted by the art. It's exactly the down-to-earth touch I want. The palace has been cut off from the people too long. Maybe we should expand those school visits into a regular programme.'

'Your steward will love that,' she murmured, trying and failing to picture the old man smiling as children invaded the Hall of a Thousand Pillars.

Instantly Idris sobered. 'He won't be here. Tomorrow he'll be relieved of his duties.'

Arden gazed, stunned at Idris's stern expression. It gave the lie to his assurance that tonight had been a storm in a teacup.

'I told you—' she stepped near, inhaling the scent of

sandalwood and spicy male '—that was down to me. It wasn't his fault.'

Idris shook his head. 'I'm not worried about the banqueting hall. What concerns me is that Selim made a ridiculous fuss about it in front of you. I know he's a stickler for the old ways and he makes you nervous with his fussing. That's why he's been working outside the palace.'

Arden's jaw dropped. 'Because of *me*?' She was torn between dismay that her discomfort had led to such drastic action and glowing warmth because Idris had tried to make things easy for her.

His mouth tightened, his expression austere. 'You are my wife and his queen. If he makes you uneasy he goes. Permanently.'

Arden blinked. Before her eyes her husband had morphed into the proud autocrat she remembered from London. It struck her that she hadn't glimpsed that man lately.

Idris might get distracted by politics but she enjoyed being with him. He was patient and gentle with Dawud, passionate with her. Good company, she realised, sometimes teasing but never dismissing her concerns. Never aloof.

The autocratic warrior King hadn't made an appearance in ages. To her surprise she wasn't fazed by him any more. Now she understood that expression was Idris determined to do what he believed was right, even if difficult. He'd moved on from the carefree, thoughtless man she'd once known. She discovered she actually liked this man better—the complex mix of strength and honesty, of decency as well as passion and humour.

'You can't dismiss him.'

'I won't have him making you nervous. He undermines your confidence.'

Arden stared, flummoxed that Idris had noticed what

she'd taken care to hide. 'How do you know? Most of the time you're not around when I'm with him.'

One sleek jet-black brow tilted high. 'I notice everything about you, Arden.' She had the strangest sensation of his words echoing endlessly within her. His stare was intense, as if he read her deepest secrets. He lifted a hand, stroking her cheek in a butterfly touch that resonated right to her core.

Arden felt the weight of something powerful between them, something she couldn't name. Then he spoke and the instant shattered.

'He unsettles you. He'll leave tomorrow.'

She caught Idris's wrist. 'No. Don't do it.'

'I won't have you undermined.'

Arden's lips curved in a tight smile as she recognised that her husband's support bolstered her flagging determination. It was *she* who'd made a mountain out of a molehill tonight. She'd let herself be led by Selim, fretting over something that, now she considered properly, was a minor glitch.

'He works hard and he's good at what he does. He doesn't deserve to lose his job.' Still Idris looked unconvinced. 'I can cope. I *prefer* to.'

'There's no need. Let me do this for you.' The look in his eyes made her chest tighten as she forgot to breathe. She dropped her hand from his. She wasn't used to being looked after. It was nice but scary too…unfamiliar.

'I know you're trying to help but it would be wrong. He *does* fuss and make me feel like an uneducated barbarian—' Idris's breath hissed. 'But he's retiring soon.'

'In thirteen months.' Idris must have checked. For some reason that lightened her mood. He really had given this thought, and not just tonight.

'That will give him time to train his replacement. Besides, I can learn a lot from him.'

Still Idris frowned.

'Did I ever tell you about my first boss, when I began as a florist?'

He shook his head.

'She must have liked something about me since she hired me but to begin with I never did anything right, even sweeping the cuttings off the floor.'

'She sounds like a tartar.'

'She was. But she was also passionate about what she did and expected the best. She insisted everything I did was the best it could be.' Arden shook her head. 'I remember rewiring the first bridal bouquet I did for her until I got it just right. But in the end I was glad she was so picky because I acquired the skills and confidence to cope, no matter how demanding the work.'

Something like a smile danced in Idris's eyes. 'That's why you'd rather keep our palace perfectionist?'

Arden lifted her hands, palm up. 'He's here and has an encyclopaedic knowledge of royal ritual and custom. I might as well make the most of him, even if he does make me want to gnash my teeth sometimes.'

Idris's laugh curled round her like tendrils of silk, caressing tight muscles. Even the dull headache diminished a fraction.

'On one condition.' The laughter faded. 'If you change your mind, or if I catch a hint of disapproval from him, he's out.'

'Agreed.' Yet still Idris didn't look totally sold.

'I'll be fine, really.' Surprisingly, after the doubts that had dogged her so long, she actually believed it. Something had changed tonight and it made her more than ever determined to make a go of this official side of their marriage.

The private part was already working well.

Well? She'd never imagined anything so good. Dawud was thriving. Idris was a caring, involved father and as a husband…she couldn't ask for more. He was considerate, passionate and respectful of her needs.

It would be too easy to believe their union was real, a marriage of hearts as well as minds. Alarms sounded in Arden's head. This was no match made in heaven.

She shifted back a fraction, making her point. 'I appreciate you supporting me. But it's important that I stand on my own two feet. It's the only way I know.'

Freshly showered, Idris flicked off all the lights except a bedside lamp and slipped naked between the sheets. Arden was in her bathroom and he'd been tempted to seduce her there. Except he remembered how she'd trembled with tiredness as they talked. He'd seen her tension and guessed her head ached. She'd slitted her eyes against the light and more than once lifted her hand to her forehead, massaging absently.

When her bathroom door opened, predictably his body tightened with desire. Her hair was a frothing, rich gleam around pale shoulders and her lacy nightgown clung to that delicious body the way his hands itched to.

Day after day, night after night, he couldn't get enough of Arden. A heavy schedule, the burden of renegotiating a new agreement with neighbouring kingdoms, all the concerns of a ruler for his country, couldn't distract from this hunger. It puzzled him how passion kept growing, intensifying rather than diminishing with familiarity.

She slipped into bed and he saw the shadows beneath her eyes, the furrow of pain on her brow. Regret rose. He could convince her into sex. She'd enjoy it—he'd make sure of it. But Arden had had enough for one night.

'Here, move closer.' He lifted the sheet, encouraging her to his side of the bed.

'I'm tired, Idris.' Even so, he saw the way her gaze dipped down his bare body.

'I know, *habibti*. You can just sleep.'

He'd never been fond of sleeping tangled up against anyone. The exception had always been Arden. When they'd first met he'd put it down to exhaustion, after wearing themselves to the point of oblivion with sex. These past months, though, Idris had discovered he *liked* holding her as they rested. It felt…satisfying.

'It doesn't look like it's sleep you have in mind.'

His erection throbbed in response to her stare and Idris hauled her close. Instantly his body hardened still further, eager for intimacy. The wriggle of her hip then her buttocks against his arousal as she turned to spoon against him, tore the air from his lungs.

'Stop twitching,' he growled.

Was that a tiny, breathless laugh? He slid his arm around her and cupped her breast, his thumb moving in a deliberate, slow caress of her peaking nipple.

'Idris!' The sibilant was soft and drawn out, just the way he liked her saying his name. A grim smile tightened his features as he tried to ignore the pleas of his body.

He distracted himself with the fact she'd called him Idris. In the first weeks of marriage Shakil had been the name on her lips when she urged him on in the throes of passion, or when she cried out in climax. It had felt oddly as if she betrayed him with another man. Shakil might only have been his younger self but Idris had wanted Arden in the present, making love to *him*, not a memory.

He hadn't heard the name Shakil for more than a month. That pleased him, satisfying a proprietorial side to his nature he'd never before recognised.

'Shh. Relax.'

'How can I relax when you do that?'

Sighing, Idris released her breast, sliding his hand down lace and silk to splay over her belly.

He focused on controlling his breathing and found his thoughts turning to the idea of Arden carrying his baby. He'd missed so much—her pregnancy and Dawud's early years. The idea of sharing such experiences appealed, the idea of her pregnant again stirring impulses he was trying to stifle.

'You're twitching,' she murmured.

'You're distracting me.' He only had to catch her light orange blossom scent and he was distracted. 'You said you were used to looking after yourself. Why is that?' Talking would take his mind off his body's torture. Besides, he wanted to know.

'I'm used to being alone.'

Idris found that hard to believe. But then he'd been stunned all those years ago in Greece to discover Arden was a virgin. 'Are all the men in England blind?'

She huffed out a laugh and the movement made him grit his teeth. He was sensitive—too sensitive.

'You're such a smooth talker.'

'Only stating the truth. Surely in all these years there was someone…with you.' Idris chose his words carefully.

'I *told* you; your cousin was just a friend. A good friend and, after a time, my landlord. But that's all.'

'No need to get het up. I believe you. But in four years there must have been someone.'

'Must there?' She paused and Idris realised he had second thoughts. He didn't want to know about her love life after all. 'Well, you're wrong. There was no one.'

'No one?' It barely seemed possible. Yet elation rose in a soaring wave. It shouldn't matter. She'd been a free agent, like him. Yet the idea of Arden with other men—

'Don't sound so surprised. I was pregnant to start with and later…' Later, what? Surely he didn't expect her to say she'd pined for him. Not when she'd thought he'd dumped her. 'Later there were barely enough hours in the day for everything that had to be done, looking after Dawud, working, scrimping to make ends meet.'

Guilt tightened his gut. His splayed hand pressed her close. 'You don't have to worry about being alone ever again.' He'd take care of them both. They were his responsibility. More, he *wanted* to look after Arden and Dawud.

Instead of easing in his embrace, Arden stiffened as if she might pull free of his hold.

'What is it?' Sixth sense told him he'd hit a nerve.

'Nothing. I'd like to sleep now.' But she held herself rigid, her breathing short. She was hiding something or, he amended, protecting herself. From him? The idea was like biting down on a crisp apple, only to taste the sourness of decay.

'I mean it, Arden. You have me now, as well as Dawud.' Surely she didn't think he'd abandon them? Not after he'd gone to such lengths to marry her?

'Yes.' Yet her voice didn't convince.

'Why did you make such a point earlier about the fact you were used to standing up for yourself?' She'd made similar comments in London.

'I told you; it's what I've always done.'

Silence. Not the companionable silence of a few minutes ago, but an edgy wariness. He'd bet her eyes were wide open. He felt tension hum through her.

'Me too,' he said slowly, deciding against another direct query. 'I was an only child. That makes a difference, don't you think?'

She shrugged. 'I suppose so.'

'I wasn't close to my parents. Well,' he amended, 'to my mother when I was very young. But she died when I was just a kid.'

'Really? How old were you?'

'Four.'

'I'm sorry.'

'It was a long time ago. I had my father and aunts and uncles, plus my cousin, Hamid.'

'Your father brought you up?'

Idris felt his lips tighten. 'My father wasn't a hands-on dad. He had other interests.' Like seducing other men's wives. His father's relentless pursuit of pleasure and string of conquests hadn't made him warm or contented.

Idris had started out the same. Not seducing other men's wives, but sowing plenty of wild oats.

'I was brought up by tutors and members of my uncle's court. There was a focus on honour and duty.' Probably to counteract the wayward tendencies of the males in his family. 'How about you?'

'Sorry?'

'Who brought you up? I know your parents died but I have no idea when.'

Seconds stretched before she answered. 'They died when I was six.'

'Both?' His voice was sharp with surprise.

'It was a car accident. They died at the scene of the crash.'

Something about her tone made his nape prickle. 'You were there?'

'In the back seat.'

'Oh, Arden.' He wrapped himself tighter around her, tugging her back against him. 'I'm so sorry.'

'Like in your case, it was a long time ago.'

'But still tragic.' And difficult for her even now. It was there in her too flat voice and the way she held herself. 'It's young to lose your family.'

'Yes,' she said dully. 'I was losing them anyway but death is so final.' She drew a deep breath, her ribs expanding against his chest. 'They used to argue a lot. That night in the car, they thought I was asleep and they were at it again. Dad said he was getting a divorce and they were fighting over who'd have me. Dad didn't want to take me and Mum was upset, saying she couldn't manage alone. In the end they didn't have to worry.'

What could he say to that? Idris didn't try. He pressed his lips to her hair, gently reminding her of his presence.

'Did you have any family at all? Aunts and uncles?' He, at least, had had extended family when he'd lost his mother.

Arden shook her head. 'I went into foster care.'

'I'm sorry.' Idris couldn't believe he'd never thought to learn her history. Surely it had shaped Arden. Shame was a hot blade in his belly. He'd been too busy with other things to try understanding the woman he'd married.

'Don't be. It was okay most of the time.'

'And the rest of the time?' He'd heard appalling stories about defenceless, vulnerable children.

'Truly, it was okay. I was with one family for years. They treated me like their own little girl and I was happy. They were very kind.' Yet sadness lingered in her voice.

'But you left them?' he guessed.

'They planned to adopt me. They couldn't have children and wanted to keep me as theirs. But right at the end, before everything could be finalised, a miracle happened.' Her voice was matter-of-fact, as if she recited words supplied by someone else. It made his chest clench. 'They discovered they were expecting, not just one baby but twins.'

Arden drew a deep breath. 'They were nice people and upset they'd led me on only to disappoint me. They just couldn't afford three children or find space for that many. It wasn't anything personal.'

'Of course not.' Yet he wanted to find them and screw their necks for the pain they'd caused her.

Now he had some inkling of why Arden was so adamant about standing up for herself. Had there ever been anyone she could rely on long term?

She'd witnessed her parents squabbling about who'd

have to take her as they tore their family apart. Then she'd lost them both in horrific circumstances. Years later she'd lost the second secure home she'd known in a way guaranteed to break any child's heart.

And don't forget your part in her life. You seduced her and walked away without a backward glance. She thought you'd deliberately dumped her, abandoned her without a thought that she might be pregnant.

It hadn't been deliberate but he hadn't considered possible consequences. He hadn't made sure she was okay. He'd been too wrapped up in Zahrat and his own concerns.

He tightened his arms about her but now there was nothing sexual about his embrace. 'I'm here and I'm not leaving,' he whispered against her hair, shutting his eyes as her sweet fragrance filled his senses. 'I'm not walking away from this marriage. You and Dawud are safe with me.'

He'd make her happy. Make sure she never regretted marrying him.

CHAPTER TWELVE

A SHARP RAP on his open office door made Idris look up from his computer. Ashar, his aide, was already crossing the room, his expression shadowed. Foreboding streaked through Idris at that look.

'What is it?' Some new disaster. The treaty?

'Everything's under control; they're both safe.' Which meant it was Arden and Dawud.

Idris surged to his feet. 'Define *under control*. What's happened now?' It wasn't that Arden attracted trouble. It was more that her limited knowledge of Zahrat and her enthusiasm sometimes led her into unexpected situations.

Not just her. The palace was awash with children's artwork: flowers, animals, even a few dragons and a sea monster. Since news of the decorated banqueting hall got out, schools across the country had sent contributions for display. The Ministry of Education had quickly brought forward reforms to encourage creativity and innovation in schools to take advantage of public interest. A display of the art was planned for the new city hall, along with awards for teaching innovation—all part of the agenda to increase school attendance.

'You're sure they're both safe?' Idris leaned forward on fisted hands.

'They're fine. Their bodyguard is following them.'

The steely grip of tension in Idris's shoulders and spine didn't ease. 'Following? That implies they don't know where they're going.'

'That's why I came to see you. To check if you know of the Sheikha's plans for the afternoon.'

Idris shook his head. 'A visit to a community playgroup

with Dawud then back here.' Idris had thought long and hard about letting his son accompany Arden on the visit, but she'd been so eager and so persuasive. He'd wondered if Arden was lonely for the company of women her own age, young mothers with children. Her life was so different here from what it had been in London.

'They went to the playgroup, then they walked to the covered market where they bought food.'

Food? When they had a galley of chefs busy in the palace? It didn't make sense. There'd been no mention of a trip to the market this morning. 'Where are they now?'

'Driving the inland highway. The Sheikha is driving herself.'

Idris frowned. It was usual for Arden to have a driver as well as bodyguards. Mainly as a symbol of her status, since the threat level in Zahrat was virtually non-existent. But there was still the possibility of danger.

A new thought struck. That highway led to Zahrat's interior mountain range and to the airport. Arden wouldn't head to the mountains so late in the day. But the airport?

He rounded his desk, heading for the door. 'Get me the chopper *now*, and a line to the head of security.'

The *whoomp, whoomp, whoomp* of a helicopter split the late-afternoon quiet. Arden looked up, wondering where it was heading, but the endless blue sky was clear and the sound ceased. It must have landed nearby. She recalled Idris saying they used helicopters for mercy hospital flights. Perhaps someone had been injured on the highway.

'Mama. Look at fiss.' Dawud dragged her attention back to the pond where ornamental fish darted, glinting in the sunlight.

'Yes, darling. Lovely fish.' She grinned at her son's fascination with water—an unexpected trait in the son of a desert sheikh. Back at the palace he loved nothing better than paddling in the reflection pools. It was time she taught him to swim. She'd feel better when she knew he could keep himself afloat.

'Come on, our picnic's ready.' She patted the soft grass beside her in the dappled shade.

'Bye-bye, fiss.' He waved solemnly to the fish then trotted over to plop down beside her.

In the same instant swift movement in her peripheral vision made her twist around.

'Idris!' He strode across the garden courtyard, his expression harsh. Behind him she saw two men in black, her security detail, melting back behind the golden stone arches of this ancient palace. 'What are you doing here?'

'I could ask you the same thing.' He sounded different, his accent pronounced, his tone terse.

He looked different too.

Almost, she realised in shock, like the arrogant man she remembered from London. The autocratic warrior prince who expected instant obedience. His expression was stern, almost harsh.

'Baba!' Dawud was on his feet in a moment, hurrying towards his father, arms upstretched. Idris scooped him up in one easy movement, swinging him so high he giggled.

Arden watched the carved lines of Idris's face ease, his face creasing into a smile as Dawud wrapped his arms around his neck, burrowing close. Her heart leapt hard against her breastbone, seeing her son's unquestioning love for the big man who'd been a stranger till a few months ago, and such tenderness in Idris's expression. She'd done the right thing for Dawud, marrying Idris.

His gaze caught hers again and something hot and potent shivered through her.

'What are you doing here?'

'Having a picnic.' She waved to the packets she was unwrapping—dates and apricots, flat bread, soft goat's cheese, nuts and her favourite tiny pastries filled with pistachios and drenched in sweet syrup. 'Would you like to join us? I wasn't expecting to see you till tonight. Did your plans change?'

'You could say that.' He moved closer, Dawud tucked in his arms.

'You look tense. Is something wrong?' She frowned. The way he looked at her began to make her nervous.

'A slight crisis, caused by the fact neither your security detail nor the palace staff had any idea where you were going this afternoon. You gave your bodyguards the slip.'

'I did no such thing! I told them I wanted time alone with Dawud. I didn't see them after that.'

Idris shook his head. 'You thought they'd return to the palace without you? That's more than their jobs are worth, or their honour. They withdrew to give you space but they couldn't let you walk off alone. You gave them the fright of their lives when they lost you in the covered bazaar.'

Arden scrambled to her feet, shock hitting.

'You told me Dawud and I were safe in Zahrat. Everyone was friendly in the markets, and you said yourself it would be a good thing for us to get about more with the people, rather than being surrounded by courtiers.'

Idris shut his eyes for a second and Arden knew he was gathering his patience. She hated this feeling that, again, she'd inadvertently done the wrong thing. Nor was she used to explaining her every move.

'Is it so wrong to want to spend time doing something normal?'

'Normal?' He looked as if he'd never heard the word.

Arden gestured wide. Even her choice of picnic spot was dictated by the fact royals didn't simply set themselves down to eat in public parks. Weeks ago Idris had shown her this little palace on its own rocky outcrop just beyond the city. It had been the dower residence of his grandmother and Arden loved its tranquillity and beauty. Today she hadn't been ready to return to the palace and, after just over three months in Zahrat, this was the only other private place she knew.

'Yes, normal. Doing a little shopping. Passing the time of day. Spending time with other mothers and children.'

It wasn't till she'd visited the playgroup that she'd realised how much she missed those small freedoms. She'd been invited in her role as Sheikha, but in reality it had been plain Arden, mother of an inquisitive, busy toddler, who'd chattered with the other mums. 'I need some freedom, Idris. You must understand that.'

With a sigh, Idris lowered Dawud to the ground then wrapped his palm around the back of his neck as if easing an ache. It made her want to massage his knotted muscles, and wish she'd never even thought of a picnic.

Dawud plonked down at their feet and reached for some dried apricots.

'Idris?'

'I understand. You weren't born to this world. It takes a lot of adjustment. But next time let the staff know what you intend. You caused a security scare going off grid like that.' The corners of his mouth tucked down and he rolled his shoulders.

Seeing his tension, Arden felt a familiar wriggle of guilt in her belly. She got it every time she said the wrong thing at a royal event or broke some unwritten tradition.

'How much of a security scare?' Her eyes rounded. 'That helicopter?' At his nod she squeezed her eyes shut. Had they mobilised the army too? She felt about an inch tall. 'I'm so sorry. I didn't realise.'

Idris was right. She didn't understand all the rules. His life would have been easier if he'd married a real princess who knew how to behave and didn't disrupt the smooth workings of the royal machine.

Arden shook her head. She refused to go there again. She was doing her best.

'Hey.' An arm wrapped around her, tugging her against him. She opened her eyes to find herself fixed by his dark, velvety gaze. 'It's all right. There's no harm done.'

Her mouth crumpled in a travesty of a smile. 'I'm sure it's not but thanks for pretending. Just tell me, my bodyguards won't get into trouble, will they?'

He shook his head. 'Chastened but fine. Think of it as keeping them on their toes.' A sudden grin lit his face. 'You're good for them. They have no chance to get complacent.'

This time her smile felt real, but still distress lurked. She'd so enjoyed this afternoon. Hadn't dreamed it could hurt.

'What are you thinking?' His breath warmed her forehead as his arm slipped around her waist.

'That next time I want to go on a picnic I'll probably have three chefs and a dozen attendants with me. After filling out a security form detailing my intended movements down to the minute.'

'It's not that bad.' When she raised her eyebrows his lips twisted. 'Not *quite* that bad. And I'll see what I can do about making things easier. Starting right now.'

'Now?' Surely her little escape had ended.

'Now.' His voice deepened and a slow smile lightened his features. 'You've got me away from the office and I intend to make the most of it. I vote we play hooky together.'

Abruptly he sank to the ground, pulling her with him so she fell across his lap. She had an impression of midnight eyes and gleaming golden skin then his lips were on hers, not softly but with a pent-up hunger she recognised. Arden grabbed his shoulders, fire igniting instantly at her feminine core.

She was just going under for the third time when a strident voice piped up. 'Mama.' A little, warm body pushed against her, one sticky hand touching her cheek. 'Dawud kiss too.'

She heard Idris's chuckle, felt him shift to tug Dawud close and for one exquisite moment let herself believe in the perfection of the three of them together, like a real family.

Idris made the most of his unscheduled escape from royal duties, turning the afternoon into an idyllic family adventure exploring the tiny but lovely old palace. Tiny by Zahrati standards. It was still a mansion, filled with gorgeous furnishings and with an unrivalled view to the coast, the city and the mountains beyond.

With Dawud they investigated, admiring splendid mosaics, bedrooms and grand salons. The palace was furnished with beautiful antiques but somehow felt more like a sprawling home than a royal estate.

Evening came and with it a grander picnic than anything Arden had imagined. White coated servants from the Palace of Gold spread turquoise and scarlet rugs on the grass. Braziers were lit around the garden, glowing and scented. The array of delicious food was a feast for the senses.

Later the servants disappeared and Dawud's nanny carried him, sleeping, to the car for the drive back to the citadel.

Finally alone, Idris insisted on feeding Arden dessert with his own hands. Ripe peaches, bursting with rich juice, dark red grapes still with the bloom of the vine on them and sweet oranges.

Then he licked up the spills where juice had dripped. She laughed, buoyed by the delight of this special time alone, by the hungry look in her husband's eyes and the eager yet tender touch of his hands as he stripped her clothes away. It was no surprise when Idris carried her inside to find that one of the beds had been made up with fine linen sheets scented with cinnamon and rose petals. Candles glowed around the room, turning it into a romantic bower.

'The honeymoon we never had,' Idris said when she exclaimed at the beauty of the scene. Then he laid her on the bed and she stopped thinking about her surroundings.

Arden gasped for air, her lungs tight. Her blood pounded as bliss shuddered through her in aftershocks so intense she thought they'd never end.

She didn't want them to end. Not when Idris was there, above her, inside her, surrounding her with his big body and powerful shoulders, quaking like her as his climax slowly faded. She felt the throb of his life force, the sensation that together they touched heaven, and she didn't want to let go.

She loved him coming apart in her arms, his weight hemming her in, his breath jagged in her ear, his formidable control shattered. In this they were equals and she revelled in it.

He groaned against her shoulder, sending fresh waves of pleasure juddering through her. Then Idris rolled onto his back, pulling her with him to sprawl naked across his steaming body.

Arden squinted one eye open, seeing the pink flush of dawn streaming in the open window. Soon Idris would get up to begin work.

But she didn't want to leave the Dower Palace. The spell of the place enveloped her. She wanted to hold Idris here, make him stay so she could enjoy the luxury of being alone with him, away from royal responsibilities. Here she'd felt not only happy but cherished.

Was she reading too much into last night's bliss? Into

their sexual compatibility? Was she mistaking the after-glow of orgasm for a tenderness centred on mutual feeling?

'I was thinking,' he murmured, his lips moving against her hair, one arm wrapped around her waist.

'Hmm?'

'About another baby.'

Arden stilled, her finger poised where it had been stroking light circles across his ribs.

'A baby?'

'A brother or sister for Dawud. What do you think?' Did she imagine a thread of excitement in his voice? No. She'd been wrong. Idris sounded as calm as ever.

'You want another child?'

'Don't you?'

Yes. The answer slammed into her. She didn't need to think about it. Something deep down, something intrinsic to the woman she was, knew the answer as if she'd pondered it long and hard.

Arden blinked, stunned by the excitement she felt bubbling up. She'd got pregnant so young she hadn't really had time to think about having kids and since having Dawud she'd been too busy even to consider a relationship and another child.

'Arden?' Idris crooked a finger under her chin, lifting her face. He was propped up a little, his arm folded behind his head. The way he lay emphasised the impressive muscles of his arm and shoulder. Instantly heat drilled through her tight chest to her pelvis. Exhausted from sex and still she craved this man!

'Yes? I…' She refocused on his question. 'I don't know,' she prevaricated, for reasons she didn't understand. 'Why do you want another?'

Those jet eyebrows crunched together as if he didn't like her question. Had he expected her to jump at the idea? That was intriguing.

'Don't you think a sibling would be good for Dawud?'

'Possibly.' Actually, she thought it would be wonderful but she reminded herself she owed it to her son and herself to do more than act impulsively. She'd done that when she fell for Idris years ago and it had turned her life on its head.

'Neither of us had siblings. We know how lonely that can be, especially when tragedy strikes.'

Grimly Arden nodded, her stomach cramping, not at the memory of those lonely childhood years bereft of family but at the idea of anything happening to Idris.

Horror filled her. A deep-down chill like the one she'd felt six months ago when for a few heart-numbing minutes she'd lost Dawud in a crowded shop.

She laid her palm flat on Idris's chest, feeling the steady thump of his heart, telling herself it was stupid to hypothesise about tragedy striking down Idris.

'Besides,' he went on, unaware of her fear, 'it sounds old-fashioned but it's a good way to ensure the security of the throne, and the nation, for the future. That's an important consideration too.'

'In case anything happens to Dawud?' Her voice was harsh.

Idris cupped a soothing palm around her bare shoulder. 'Nothing is going to happen to Dawud. But you never know—' he smiled in the way he knew made her melt '—our firstborn may want to go off and become an academic like my cousin, or a rock star. Having a brother to take the throne—'

'Or a sister,' she bit out, anger rising. As the law currently stood, only a male could inherit the throne. Unfair as she thought it, it wasn't that fuelling her temper. It was the notion she should have Idris's child to keep the throne safe and avoid political turmoil. They were talking about children! Children who deserved to be loved for themselves. Not pieces in some dynastic game!

'Or a sister.' Idris raised one eyebrow. 'Which would lead us to a discussion on exactly how many children we'd like to have.'

She recognised that lazy smile. It spoke of sexual promise. She had no complaints about making love with Idris. He made her feel not only satisfied but treasured. Which showed how skilled Idris was. To him having a child meant sex, which he clearly enjoyed. Enjoyed it enough to appear almost insatiable for her, a woman foisted on him by circumstance rather than personal preference.

But having a baby was about a lot more than that, as she knew too well.

'I'll think about it.' She pulled back, putting a little distance between them and watching his complacent smile slip. 'It's a lot to ask.'

His stare raked her. Clearly he hadn't expected that response. 'Of course.' Yet a frown rippled his broad brow and his grip on her shoulder tightened. 'There's plenty of time to think it over. Neither of us is going anywhere.'

Because he'd given his word.

Because he'd married her in front of thousands of witnesses.

Because he had no other choice but to stick with her.

Suddenly exhaustion filled her.

She hadn't married for love, other than the love of a mother for her child. She'd actually been enjoying her marriage to Idris, discovering as the months passed that their marriage suited her. *He* suited her. Even her life in Zahrat, though still challenging, brought satisfaction and a tentative sense of accomplishment. So why did the reminder that this was a purely practical union bring a bitter taint to her tongue?

Because your husband sees all this—you, your marriage, even your children—through the lens of practicality. Whereas for you...your heart is engaged.

Idris hauled her close, cupping the back of her head and drawing her against his chest. Automatically Arden fitted herself to him, one knee across his thigh, an arm round his waist.

But her mind raced, horrified by the stark truth of her discovery. That sudden, unbearable flash of insight had exploded her convenient belief that she could accept a loveless marriage.

Furtively she blinked back the haze of moisture misting her view of the dawn.

How had she deluded herself so long? It seemed impossible she'd never seen the truth before.

You didn't want the truth. You were wilfully blind because you knew the implications and didn't want to face them.

Arden bit her lip and tried not to panic, but it was almost impossible.

She'd congratulated herself on being reasonable and civilised, giving Dawud's father shared access. Accepting a sensible, convenient marriage though it meant living with a man she barely knew and embracing a whole new culture, giving up her safe, familiar world.

She'd even applauded the fact she could embark on a sexual relationship with the man she'd once loved and it wouldn't matter.

Of course it mattered.

Some sly part of herself must have realised the truth from the first. That it hadn't been so much of a sacrifice to marry him.

Because she was in love with Idris.

She had been all along. Only pride and pain had made her pretend she wasn't.

He was the only lover she'd ever had and, she realised with a hollow fear that threatened to engulf her, the only man she'd ever want.

* * *

Back at the Palace of Gold, Arden paced her sitting room, arms folded tight around her middle as if that could prevent the deep-seated ache inside.

Idris had left her with a bold kiss and a gleam in his eyes as soon as they returned from the Dower Palace. She'd clung to him, desperate to be held, though her brain said she needed to break free and decide what to do. For that she needed space and solitude.

First she'd cancelled her appointments for the day, surprising an understanding smile on one of the secretaries. Arden supposed all the palace staff knew she and Idris had spent an unscheduled belated honeymoon night.

Then she'd gone to Dawud, eager for the familiarity of his sturdy little frame and bright smile. She joined him in a game involving toy cars and a road map floor mat and lots of noise. But even as she smiled and crawled along, there was a terrifying blankness inside her where she fiercely shut out the hurt that would flood in if she let it.

Finally, when she felt calm enough to face what she must, she'd left Dawud with Misha and come here to her room. Stopping by the window she stared out beyond the city to the small Dower Palace.

She longed to recapture the magic of last evening. The thrill of being with Idris, not as a bride forced upon him by circumstance but as his lover. The woman who loved him and for a few thoughtless hours had lived as carefree and content as if he loved her too.

The wall damming the dark pain cracked and despair poured out, making her clutch at the window frame with the force of that hurt.

Desperate, she told herself nothing had changed. Idris had never pretended to love her. He was decent and caring, dependable, honourable and, yes, charming. She loved his wry humour and he was great with Dawud. The pair were building a fantastic rapport.

It was she who'd changed. Or, if her suspicions were correct, not changed, but finally realised she'd been fooling herself. Because she loved Idris with all her being. Just as she'd loved Shakil all those years ago. Loved and lost.

Arden clawed the window frame and sank, a bundle of brittle bones, onto the window seat.

Loving and losing was a constant theme in her life.

First her parents. Then her foster parents. Then Shakil.

Now Idris.

No, she wouldn't lose him, not that way. He'd promised to stay with her, support her and do the right thing by Dawud. He'd do it, she knew he would. She knew him now, better than she had all that time ago. He saw this marriage as his duty and he'd stick at it no matter what.

There'd be no divorce. But Arden wasn't a naïve girl now. She knew a man like Idris would have sexual needs long after he lost interest in her. This honeymoon period, prompted she guessed by novelty and his desire for more children, would end soon enough.

What then? Arden had told him she didn't want to find out about his lovers. He hadn't demurred, simply agreed and moved on. At the time she'd been devastated at the idea of marrying a man already planning to be with other women.

That was before she realised she loved him.

How could she cope when he turned away and discreetly found with other women what he no longer wanted from her?

A tearing sound rent the air and she realised it was a groan of pain.

Idris would turn his back and she'd be left high and dry. Again.

Once more she'd got her hopes up. She hadn't consciously thought that one day her husband might come to love her but it had been there, a hidden nugget of hope, all this time.

She'd always craved love, stability, someone to value her as the most important person in their life. Every time hope had been snatched away.

Was that her fate? To seek love and always be disappointed?

She couldn't live like this, as merely a necessary wife. Idris cared about her but not enough. Loving him when he felt only mild affection, seeing him turn to other women, would destroy her. She wouldn't let that happen. She would be strong, for herself and for Dawud. It was the way life had made her.

Arden got to her feet, grimacing at her creaky movements, as if the hoary fingers of age already claimed her. Slowly she straightened, her eyes fixed on the beautiful little palace beyond the city.

She had to find a way to survive this deal they'd made, do the best for Dawud, and for Idris, but keep her self-respect. And she had an inkling how she could do it.

This time she wouldn't be the one left behind.

CHAPTER THIRTEEN

A QUICK RAP on his study door made Idris look up, his brain still grappling with the new draft of the treaty.

Ashar stood in the doorway, his features so carefully blank that unease instantly ripped up Idris's backbone. It reminded him of yesterday when his aide had come to report that Arden was driving out of town, destination unknown.

This was worse. He sensed it.

'Tell me.'

Not Arden. Not Dawud.

The ferocity of his fear for them paralysed him.

'They're both fine. Both well.' Ashar stepped over the threshold, closing the door behind him, and Idris sagged in his swivel chair, his fingers grabbing the edge of the desk too tight. His heart catapulted against his ribs, its rhythm sharp.

'But?' Idris tried to tell himself it was another small misunderstanding. It couldn't be anything major. Despite her doubts, Arden was increasingly adept at dealing with courtiers and the public. As for visiting VIPs, she charmed them with an ease that made him want to laugh. This was the woman his advisers had doubted could hold her own in public and she was proving his best asset with her unconventional, direct ways.

He wished he'd had her at his side when he'd first taken the role of Sheikh. The burdens would have been much lighter, and his life so much better.

'Tell me, Ashar.' His aide's silence was unnerving.

Idris watched him take a chair on the other side of the desk. 'The Sheikha and the little Prince are both at the Dower Palace.'

Idris let his pent-up breath surge out. For a moment he'd feared something terrible.

'Another picnic?' A smile curved his mouth. He'd toyed with the idea of shirking all his appointments today and spending time with his family. Amazing how much the idea appealed. He'd had to force himself out of Arden's arms and their bed in the little palace, telling himself this new treaty, and the meeting on improving infrastructure for remote provinces, were too vital to delay.

But he'd vowed to take Arden back there soon. Last night had felt like the honeymoon they'd never had. More, as if they'd found a new level of understanding. Their necessary marriage had blossomed in a way he'd never expected. She made him *happy*, he realised. Happy and proud. It was a revelation.

Ashar shook his head. He opened his mouth but didn't speak. Instead he cleared his throat.

Foreboding dimmed Idris's smile. 'Out with it, quickly.'

Ashar looked down at his hands. 'The Sheikha has co-opted several palace staff to help her refurbish the Dower Palace.'

'Refurbish?' Idris didn't know if he was more perplexed by the idea of it needing refurbishment or the fact Arden had directed staff to do anything. She was notoriously unwilling to issue orders, unused to having paid servants.

Ashar shrugged. 'Perhaps not refurbish. But open up the rooms ready to be lived in.' He paused, his gaze lifting to Idris. 'She gave the impression the order came from you.'

Ashar met his wary eyes. They both knew Idris had given no such order.

'Anything else?'

His secretary's expression flickered with something that might have been sympathy. 'I understand your wife and son's belongings have been packed up and moved out of the Palace of Gold.'

* * *

Idris slammed the door of his four-wheel drive and signalled his staff to remain here in the courtyard of the Dower Palace. Anger took him across the cobbled yard to the arch where ancient wooden doors, said to be as old as his family's rule on the throne of Zahrat, sat open.

A couple of strides took him to another, smaller courtyard and a maid, her arms full of bed linen. Her eyes rounded when she saw him and she stopped, curtseying.

'You're to leave here now and return to your usual duties.' His voice rasped out, harsh and unrecognisable. Like the fury he only just held in check. Fury that Arden would play such a game, trying to make a fool of him. 'Tell the other staff to stop what they're doing and get out immediately. Close the front doors behind you.'

She bobbed her head and scurried away, clasping the linen to her chest.

Idris stalked forward, through more doors, across the courtyard where just last night Arden had lain in his arms while he fed her sweet treats and seduced her into boneless compliance.

Of all the emotions that had rushed through him at Ashar's news, the strongest was hurt. Hurt that after all he and Arden had shared, after the sense of wordless understanding he'd woken to this morning, she should play such a trick. He couldn't believe she'd deliberately make him a laughing stock. Or that she was attempting some sort of blackmail, moving out to secure a better deal for herself.

When had he not given her what she desired?

When had he withheld his support? His riches?

When had he been anything but the best husband he could be? And in return he knew she'd strived to meet the demands of her new role.

So what was she playing at?

If she was unhappy she just had to say and he'd deal with the problem.

But this wasn't something she wanted him to fix. That was clear from the fact she'd moved out and taken Dawud.

This was a pre-emptive strike.

He'd trusted her! Let her become part of his life in ways he'd never imagined letting any woman, and she'd betrayed him.

He couldn't believe it. Or the excruciating ache in his heart.

Room after room passed. Some untouched, some bearing traces of recent change. Dustcovers removed. Mirrors sparkling. Mosaic floors glistening from scrubbing. He passed the room where they'd spent the night but it was deserted. Another room and there was a familiar white bed, tucked in a corner by the window. The mat he'd bought Dawud, a carpet road map for him to play on, lay beside it. Idris recognised the books and toys on top of a new dresser, and in the bed a tousled dark head, a small hand still grasping a teddy as Dawud slept.

Idris stopped, his heart skidding against his sternum as relief battered him. *Dawud was safe.*

He drew in a deep breath, then another, trying to ease the hammering of his pulse as his gaze ate up the sight of his boy.

Something, some infinitesimal sound made him turn. Seconds later he was in the doorway of another bedroom. A white sheet snapped in the air as it was flung across a bed. A bed much smaller than the one he and Arden shared. Yet it was Arden smoothing the crisp cotton down the mattress. Arden, not in her finery but wearing a simple white sleeveless dress. Arden with her hair gleaming in the sunset glow coming from the window.

Idris stepped into the room, securing the door behind

him. The snick of the lock made her look up, then her hand was at her throat, her face pale as chalk.

'Idris! You scared me!'

He folded his arms across his chest, not bothering now to keep a lid on the ire that had burned and bubbled since his aide's visit. Was Idris the last in the royal compound to hear that his wife had moved out, sneaking their son with her?

Arden's hand fell to her side and she backed a step as if the sight of him frightened her. *Good!*

'I didn't expect to see you yet.'

Yet? That implied she *had* intended to see him. He felt a trickle of relief. Till he wondered where she'd planned to meet him. In the office of a divorce lawyer? No lawyer in the country would take her on. He'd see to that.

'I suppose you're wondering what I'm doing?' Her hands twisted together till she saw him notice and hauled them behind her back like a naughty schoolgirl. But this was no teenage prank.

'Why don't you say something?' Her voice was thin, as if stretched taut by emotion. Which was all wrong. She'd planned this deliberately, with cold calculation. *He* was the one feeling.

'I'm waiting for an explanation.'

'I…' Her hand climbed her throat again, fingers splaying nervously, till she blinked and dropped her arm. Her chin tilted. 'I'm moving out.'

Idris stared, watching her lips circle the words, hearing them resonate in his ears, and yet the sound didn't seem real. It was as if she spoke from a long distance, the words muffled by the skip of his pulse and the throbbing tension wrapping him so tight he felt his skin would split and bleed.

'Explain!'

'Dawud and I—' She gestured: a quick circular motion

encompassing the room and, presumably, the one next door. 'We'll live here. It will work out better this way. I was going to tell you—'

'Really? And when were you going to impart this news?' His voice was barely above a growl, low, guttural and cold as her frigid English heart. 'Before or after the whole city heard about it?'

Her eyes widened and her mouth sagged. 'No, I—'

'No, you weren't going to tell me after all? You were going to let me find out for myself? Just as, in fact, I did?'

Fury rose to towering levels. He paced the room, planting himself between Arden and the door. She'd betrayed him, made a fool of him, stolen his son. He'd woken this morning to a sense of peace and promise unlike any he'd ever known. He'd looked forward to building a family with her and all the time she'd planned to leave.

He'd never known such pain as that tearing at his vitals. Only years of warrior training kept him upright.

If she thought he'd permit her to get away with this she was incredibly naïve.

Arden looked up into hard, fathomless eyes. She didn't recognise them. Didn't recognise the man before her. This wasn't the bronzed warrior prince she'd come to love. This was a stranger. As he uncrossed his arms and flexed his fingers she shivered.

She told herself to buck up. She'd known this wouldn't be easy. But if she was to preserve her sanity and her self-respect it had to be done.

'Why don't we go somewhere more comfortable and sit down to discuss this?' She felt trapped by his forceful presence, literally cornered.

'Stop delaying.' He widened his stance and re-crossed his arms over his powerful chest, reinforcing that potent male power battering her shredded nerves.

How was she supposed to fight him when part of her wanted to nestle against that broad shoulder and accept what he offered her, even though it wasn't enough?

Arden swallowed a tangle of emotion and forced herself to meet his glare.

'This marriage isn't working for me. I had my doubts from the start, you know that, and…' She gestured vaguely. 'Well, it turns out I was right.'

'In what way isn't it working?' His face was so flinty, his expression so fixed, his lips barely moved.

'I don't feel…' *loved.* She couldn't admit that. 'You must understand.' Another quick wave of her hand. 'Zahrat, living in a palace, marriage to a sheikh; it's all a far cry from what I'm used to. And what I'm comfortable with.'

Was it possible that his thinned lips tightened even further?

'I don't feel able to continue like I have been, so I've come up with a compromise.'

'This doesn't look like compromise to me,' he snarled. 'This looks like desertion.'

Arden jammed her hands onto her hips, summoning anger to block out the pain in her heart. 'Desertion would be me taking Dawud on the next flight out of here and filing for divorce.' Her breath came so fast she couldn't keep going.

She heaved in more air and dredged up some words before he interrupted. 'Instead I propose to live here with Dawud. Close enough that you can still see him daily. He can go to the Palace of Gold to visit you or you could come here.' She paused. Having Idris here in what would be her sanctuary would just prolong her heartache. But what alternative could she offer?

Idris opened his mouth and she raised a hand to stop him. 'Just hear me out.' She snagged another quick breath. 'This way you have the marriage you needed and the heir but without the encumbrance of…me. You know I'm not good at the whole royal thing. Everyone will understand the split. I told the staff it was your order that I move here. People will think *you've* set me aside, and they won't be surprised because everyone knows I'm an embarrassment.' Heat crept up her cheeks at the memory of so many public blunders.

But in the scale of things those mistakes meant nothing. Not compared to walking away from the man she loved. Dully she wondered how long it would be before the hurt started to ease. Or if it ever would.

'I won't embarrass you if I'm living here, out of the public eye. And you'll be free to take lovers without worrying about me being on the premises.' Something within her collapsed, crumpling at the thought, but she kept her chin up. 'It's the best solution.'

Except she didn't believe it for a moment. Living in Zahrat, so close to Idris, would be torment. Yet for Dawud's sake she'd endure it.

Idris's gaze bored into hers. 'This is the second time you've mentioned my lovers. You seem inordinately interested in them.' Something flickered in that enigmatic dark stare. 'Why is that? Are you intending to vet them yourself to see they're not a negative influence on our son when they meet?'

'You wouldn't do that! You promised to be discreet and not flaunt them in front of Dawud.' Fury rose, a fiery column, scorching her from the inside. She actually took a step closer till she read the predatory stillness in Idris's big frame, the intensity of his haughty glare, and realised he was deliberately taunting her.

That casual cruelty punctured her indignation, leaving her empty and fragile. She swayed, praying for the strength to see this through.

'It's time to admit it's not working and accept a sensible compromise. You've done everything that could be expected of you, Idris. You've married me and legitimised Dawud. You've upheld your honour.'

Idris stared at her. A nervous, defiant woman who looked like the beautiful wife he'd taken to bed last night but couldn't be. His wife had spent the evening sighing her pleasure while setting out to please him more successfully than any other woman ever had.

Then, as usual, she'd curled confidingly close. He'd grown used to her snuggling against him as if, even in sleep, she needed physical intimacy to settle.

He'd grown used to greeting the dawn making love to her. More often than not sharing a bath or shower with her. He'd even become accustomed to chatting with her after formal events, sharing observations and insights, always fascinated by the different perspective she provided. And breakfasting with her and Dawud, enjoying a growing understanding and shared purpose in caring for their boy. He'd been proud of her progress in dealing with state occasions, and her surprising aptitude at his language. He'd laughed with her over things he'd never been able to share with others and found increasing pleasure in relaxing with her.

Over the past months she'd become more than a convenient bride. She'd become his *wife*.

How had it all gone wrong?

Why had she done this?

Idris stepped closer, watching with mingled satisfaction and pain as she shrank against the wall.

'Honour! You talk to me of honour? As if that's all this marriage is about?' He was so incensed he had to work to keep his voice low enough that it didn't disturb Dawud in the next room. Fire ran in his veins, a white-hot incendiary burn that ate him up from the inside, devouring him. Or perhaps that was the anguish he was trying not to think about.

'What about *us*, Arden? You and me? And Dawud?' He leaned over her and her head tilted back against the wall. But she didn't look scared any more. She looked tired, and that tore at him.

After what she'd done, and the way she'd insulted him, he felt *concerned* for her?

'As you say,' she said softly, 'this marriage is about you and me and our son. I think it best for Dawud not to grow up watching our marriage disintegrate. Better to make an amicable break now and come to a compromise that allows him to grow up with both of us.'

Compromise. There was that word again. Idris had never hated it so much.

'You're lying. Whatever is behind your actions, this isn't about Dawud. This—' a sharp gesture encompassed the half-made bed and his errant wife '—is about you and me.'

Instinct drove that observation and he saw it confirmed when her eyelids fluttered and her gaze skated sideways, as if she were scared he'd read the truth in her expression.

What *was* the truth? She'd hurt him as surely as if she'd taken his grandfather's ceremonial sword and sliced Idris right through the chest. He'd never experienced anything like this pain he was helpless to understand or control. It made him even more determined.

Another step took him into her space. Her chin tipped high to keep him in her sights. He sensed her fight or flight response in her sharp, tremulous breaths and her air of expectation.

Just let her try to flee. He'd enjoy stopping her.

'What could it be, I wonder?' He thought over her explanation.

'All that about being an embarrassment to me is whitewash. You don't embarrass me and you never have. You know that. I'm *proud* of the way you've adapted. You've got a gift for putting people at their ease, a gift for making them feel welcome. You like people, you're interested in them and that shows.'

Her eyes grew wide. 'But I—'

'No buts. You know it's true. Don't I tell you time and again how wonderful you are? How quickly you've mastered your royal duties? You've already won the hearts of half the schoolchildren in the country and their parents. That only leaves fifty per cent to go.'

Where he found levity from Idris didn't know, but the idea of Arden hiding like some shameful secret was totally absurd.

Her reasons for moving out didn't make sense.

'Then there's the question of my lovers.' She flinched then schooled her expression into immobility. His hunter's instinct sharpened.

She cared about him having women?

Of course she cared. He'd be outraged if she didn't.

The idea of Arden and his cousin as lovers had unearthed previously unknown violent instincts in Idris, till she'd convinced him there'd been no man in her life for four years.

No man in her life but himself.

His thoughts slowed to a familiar, all-consuming satisfaction. Idris was her only lover and he intended it to stay that way. He couldn't countenance the idea of Arden with any other man. Ever.

Sudden heat bloomed in his chest as realisation smacked him.

He rocked back on his feet, actually taking a half step away as knowledge smote him.

'My lovers,' he repeated slowly, his brain, *finally*, catching up with instinct. 'You don't want to meet my lovers.'

The voice wasn't his. It was hoarse, thick and dull, stunned by what he'd blithely never considered before.

Had he really been so blind?

His heart hammered against his ribs and his breath came in sharp snatches, dragged into lungs that felt too small to cope with the enormity of the knowledge battering him.

'You promised. You agreed not to flaunt them so Dawud or I would see them.' She glared, hands on her hips, her bottom lip jutting belligerently. In her white silk dress, with her hair in gilded waves around her shoulders and her aquamarine eyes dazzling like gems, she was stunning.

How could he want another woman when he had Arden?

He shook his head, blinking at the patent absurdity of it.

She stepped forward, prodding his chest. 'A man of *honour* wouldn't go back on his word.'

Idris clapped his hand over hers, pressing it against his racing heart. He saw her still, her eyes widen from slits of anger to pools of shimmering surprise.

'Feel that?' His voice was a raw rasp. 'You do that to me, Arden.' As he said it Idris felt the power of it fill him like a shaft of sunshine streaming all the way to the bottom of an abandoned, empty well.

Except he didn't feel empty now. He felt filled to the brim with fierce, choking, glorious feeling.

She tugged at her hand, her mouth turning down, her brow knotted. 'You're angry at the inconvenience I'm causing. That's all.'

'Not angry. Furious. I was furious. But I'm not now.'

Yet his heart rate didn't ease. His temper might have dried up but what he felt now was simultaneously the most amazing, frightening thing he'd ever experienced.

He swallowed hard, his Adam's apple bobbing painfully.

'I don't care, Idris. I just want you to let me go.' Arden's voice rose in a wailing sob that cut him to the bone. Her pain was his, tenfold.

He lifted his other hand and stroked the hair from her cheek, marvelling again at the softness of her skin. He closed his eyes, trying to save this moment of absolute awareness, inhaling her light orange blossom fragrance.

'There will be no other women.'

Finally she stopped trying to free herself. 'Pardon?'

'There won't be any other women for me. I never intended to take another lover.'

'But you agreed—'

His eyes snapped open and he looked down into her stunned face. 'I agreed never to flaunt a lover. I never said there would actually *be* any lovers.' He paused, amazed at how slow-witted he'd been. He'd never questioned why that was. 'I knew even then that I'd want no one else. I haven't since I met you again.'

Her mouth tightened. 'You're saying that because you think it will make me change my mind. But it won't. It's nothing to me if you have a whole harem of lovers.'

'Isn't it?' He cupped her cheek. 'You may not care but I would. I just couldn't do it.'

He stared into her grumpy, set features and told himself he owed her the truth, even if by some ill-omened fate he was wrong about Arden's feelings for him. His pulse sprinted like a mad thing and fear tightened his belly.

'Aren't you going to ask me why I couldn't take a lover?'

She blinked then looked away. He felt her tremble and her pain made his chest seize. 'Don't do this, Idris. I don't think I—'

'I couldn't take another woman into my bed because there's only one woman I'll ever want, in my bed and in my life. That's you, Arden. I love you, *habibti*. I have from the start, though I was too slow to see it. I felt it. I hated believing there'd been other men in your life. I hated feeling that you didn't need me or want me. That's one of the reasons I acted so quickly to secure you, before you could run off again.'

'I never ran anywhere.' Her eyes were round as saucers and her tremor intensified till she shook all over.

'It felt like it.' Now, in retrospect, he realised that was exactly how it had been. 'I deserted you because I had to face my responsibilities, my *duty*.' His mouth twisted. 'But it seemed like you'd run away with my heart. I never felt for any woman what I felt for you. Not in all the years we were apart.' He shook his head. 'Why do you think I made a beeline for your house the morning after the reception? I *had* to see you again, had to be with you, even though it was total insanity if I really planned to marry someone else.'

'Idris?' Arden's voice was a tremulous whisper, her mouth working. 'Please. Are you just saying this because—?'

'I'm saying it because it's true, Arden. I love you. You make me feel whole.' He fell to his knees before her, ignoring generations of royal pride, knowing only that he *had* to make her believe. He gathered her hands in his.

'I didn't think it possible. The men in my family never lose their hearts. All except King Dawud, my grandfather, who adored my grandmother till his dying day.' Idris pressed her hands, willing her to believe. 'That's my excuse for not realising how I felt about you. It didn't even occur to me that the jealousy and lust, the pride and admiration, the liking, were all part of love.'

He lifted first one of her hands, then the other, pressing kisses to each. 'I love you, Arden, with all my heart. With all that I am. On my honour, on the honour of my family and the memory of my grandfather, it's true.' He paused, emotions surging so high speech was difficult.

'But if you don't believe me yet, don't worry, you will. I intend to convince you every day for the rest of our lives.'

If she let him.

Tears glistened in her eyes and his heart cramped. Dismay filled him and dread that perhaps he'd been wrong to imagine she cared for him.

But before he could conjure a protest she'd sunk to her knees before him, her hands gripping his strongly.

Heart in mouth, he watched her raise his hand, then press her delicate lips to it. A ripple ran up his arm, across his shoulder to splinter to spread through his body. Slowly she kissed his other hand and his heart sang.

'I love you, Idris.' Those stunning eyes, washed, he realised, with tears of happiness, were the most beautiful in the whole world. 'I loved you in Santorini. I even loved you in the years we were apart though I told myself it wasn't so.' Her mouth curved in a secretive smile that melted his soul. 'I'll always love you.'

A huge sigh escaped him, shuddering out the pent-up breath he'd held too long. His whole being felt renewed, stronger, better. 'Then we're perfectly matched. For I will love you till the last breath in my body, and beyond.'

He watched the stars shine in her eyes, the sun rise in her smile and knew he'd come home.

'I have a suggestion.'

Her gaze slid to the bed beside them and he laughed, the sound of pure joy ringing around them. 'Soon, Arden.' Already he was strung taut and eager for her. 'But I wanted to suggest we move in here together, you, me and Dawud.'

'Really? But you need to be at the Palace of Gold. All your official responsibilities…'

'*Our* official responsibilities,' he amended. 'I propose that during the week we stay there, and do what's expected of a royal sheikh and sheikha. And on weekends we live here, out of the limelight, just being a family.'

'You could do that? Really?'

'*We* can do it. With some planning I don't see why not. In fact, I insist.'

Her smile said everything he could have wanted as he pulled her to him.

'It sounds just perfect.' Whatever else she intended to say was lost against his lips as he bestowed the first kiss of the rest of their lives. A kiss of love, offered and received. A kiss of promise.

* * * * *

EXCLUSIVE EXTRACT

Hotel magnate Nate Brunswick's faith in marriage has been destroyed by his father – but searching for his beloved grandfather's lost ring leads the illegitimate Di Sione to an inconvenient engagement! Mina Mastrantino can only pass the ring on once she's married. A divorce should be easy... but their exquisite wedding night gives them both far more than they planned!

Read on for a sneak preview of
A DEAL FOR THE DI SIONE RING
by Jennifer Hayward

"You're an honorable man, Nate Brunswick. *Grazie.*"

"Not so honorable, Mina." A dark glitter entered his eyes. "You called me improper not so long ago. I can be that and more. I am a hard, ruthless businessman who does what it takes to make money. I will turn a hotel over in the flash of an eye if I don't see the flesh on the bones I envisioned when I bought it. I will enjoy a woman one night and send her packing the next when I get bored of her company. Know what you're getting into with me if you accept this. You will learn the dog-eat-dog approach to life, *not* the civilized one."

Why did something that was intended to be a warning send a curious shudder through her? Mina drew the wrap closer around her shoulders, her gaze tangling with Nate's. The glitter in his eyes stoked to a hot, velvet shimmer as he took a step forward and ran a finger along the line of her jaw. "Rule number one of this new arrangement, should you so choose to accept it, is to not look at me like that, *wife*. If we do this, we keep things strictly business so both of us walk away after the year with exactly what we want."

Her gaze fell away from his, her blood hot and thick in her veins. "You're misinterpreting me."

"No, I'm not." He brought his mouth to her ear, his warm breath caressing her cheek. "I have a hell of a lot more experience than you do, Mina. I can recognize the signs. They were loud and clear in my hotel room that day and they're loud and clear now."

She took a deep, shuddering breath. To protest further would be futile when her skin felt like it was on fire, her knees like jelly. He watched her like a cat played with a mouse, all powerful and utterly sure of himself. "The only thing that would be more of a disaster than this day's already been," he drawled finally, apparently ready to have mercy on her, "would be for us to end up in bed together. So a partnership it is, Mina." He lifted his glass. "What do you say?"